LESSONS IN LOVE

"I thought we were friends, Addie."

Will wasn't being fair. He knew it, but he didn't care. Something was happening between them. Something he didn't understand. Something he'd never felt before. He wanted to be with this woman. He wanted to hold her, kiss her, make love to her.

"We *are* friends," she replied, not looking up.

He tipped her chin with his index finger, forcing her to lift her gaze to meet his. She had the most amazing eyes. Right from the first he'd felt mesmerized by them.

"Then you'll come back to the ranch?" he asked. "You'll continue the lessons?"

Addie stepped back from him, stopping when she was pressed against the table. "I...I'm behind on my lesson planning. I'll come out to your ranch on Monday after school." There was a pleading look in her eyes. "I promise."

He could understand why she looked half-frightened. He was half-frightened himself. He'd never felt anything like this before in his life.

Other *Leisure* books by Robin Lee Hatcher:
DEVLIN'S PROMISE
THE MAGIC
MIDNIGHT ROSE
PROMISE ME SPRING
PROMISED SUNRISE
DREAMTIDE
PIRATE'S LADY
PASSION'S GAMBLE

The Americana Series:
REMEMBER WHEN
FOREVER, ROSE

Where The Heart Is

ROBIN LEE HATCHER

LEISURE BOOKS  NEW YORK CITY

FIC
HAT

A LEISURE BOOK®

December 1997

Published by

Dorchester Publishing Co., Inc.
276 Fifth Avenue
New York, NY 10001

ISBN 0-8439-4334-3

Printed in the United States of America.

To Jerry,
For giving my heart a home.

Where The Heart Is

Prologue

Connecticut, June 1880

"I really cannot see that you have any other option, Miss Sherwood."

Addie glanced up, her gaze meeting the attorney's. She knew Mr. Bainbridge had spoken to her. She even understood what he'd said. Still, it seemed unreal.

Mr. Bainbridge, who had been her father's lawyer for the past twenty years, rose from his chair and rounded the desk to stand in front of Addie. "Miss Sherwood, you must be practical. The house is not yours. You have very little money, nowhere to live, no family to take you in." He offered her a patient smile. "If you marry me, you won't find yourself in need of charity."

She shook her head slowly, trying to clear the strange buzzing in her ears. This couldn't be happening. It couldn't be.

Mr. Bainbridge's mouth thinned. He ran the fingers of one hand over his graying hair, then abruptly returned to his leather-upholstered chair behind the desk. Once he was settled onto it, he leaned forward, his meticulously manicured hands folded on top of her father's will. "I have made you an honorable offer, Miss Sherwood. My children are badly in need of a mother, and you are badly in need of a home."

Addie stared at him blankly. She knew she must look obtuse, but she couldn't seem to help herself.

"If I may be blunt, Miss Sherwood"—His tone implied he thought he was addressing a half-wit. "—the truth is that you are no longer in the first blush of youth, and by no means could you be called a beauty." He leaned back in his chair, crossing his arms over his chest. "What else are you to do if you don't marry me?"

Addie felt starved for air. Her chest hurt, and she was finding it difficult to think. She rose quickly to her feet. "I must go," she said softly as she turned away.

"Miss Sherwood . . ."

She glanced back. "I appreciate your offer of marriage, Mr. Bainbridge, but I'm unable to give you an answer. I am . . . it is . . ." She swallowed the hot lump in her throat. "I must think on it," she whispered, then fled from the lawyer's office, her head lowered, her gaze downcast.

She hurried along the bustling streets of Kingsbury, hoping to get home before she fell apart at the seams.

And she *was* going to fall apart. She was going to shatter into a thousand pieces. The buzzing in her ears wouldn't go away. Her skin felt too tight for her body. She couldn't make her thoughts focus.

It couldn't be true. Surely Papa hadn't sold their home. And what of Mr. Bainbridge? Offering to marry her so she could watch after his seven children! Not even pretending to care for her. He didn't want a wife. He wanted a slave.

Someone should tell him slavery was abolished years ago, she thought angrily.

On the heels of her anger came the threat of tears, burning the backs of her eyes. She quickened her steps.

It was a long walk to the edge of town, but the way was familiar. Adelaide Sherwood had lived in the same house for twenty-seven years. She'd been born in her parents' bedroom. Years before, after Robert had broken their engagement and later eloped with Eliza Dearborn, Addie had come to accept that she would live out her life in her parents' house—the only home she'd ever known. She'd been certain she would die in the same bed in which she'd been born, the bed in which first her mother and then her father had died.

Turning the corner, Addie stopped and lifted her gaze to the small house at the end of Bayview Lane. There was nothing remarkable about the house. It was narrow and two-storied, with whitewashed siding and green shutters framing the windows. Tulips bloomed beside the walk leading to the front door. Addie had planted the bulbs ten years ago. She'd thought she would see them in bloom for many years to come.

The house is not yours.

How could she leave it? Where would she go?

I have made you an honorable offer, Miss Sherwood.

Marry Mr. Bainbridge? He was nearly as old as her father.

My children are badly in need of a mother, and you are badly in need of a home.

Addie felt the tears welling up in her eyes again. She blinked them back, swallowing hard against the lump in her throat. Once again, she dipped her head forward, her gaze turned upon the walk before her, and headed toward the house at the end of the street.

I really cannot see that you have any other option, Miss Sherwood.

What was she to do? she wondered desperately as she opened the door and entered the house. What on earth was she to do?

Addie paused in the tiny foyer and started to remove her black bonnet. As she did so, she caught sight of her reflection in the mirror above the table. Her hands froze in midair as she stared at her image.

A smattering of freckles danced across a nose that was too long and too narrow. Wisps of her flaming red hair, curly and unruly, had already pulled free from the severe bun at her nape. She had an indisputably stubborn chin, a mouth that was much too full, and green eyes that sloped up at the outer corners. Cat-green, the other children had called them when she was in school, and then they'd dubbed her Catty Addie.

Mr. Bainbridge was quite right. She wasn't a beauty. She never had been. Once Robert had told her she was "striking," and she'd believed him—before he'd eloped with Eliza, shattering Addie's illusions once and for all.

If you marry me, you won't find yourself in need of charity.

"Why, Papa?" she whispered as she finished removing her bonnet, then turned away from the mirror. "I don't understand why."

Matthew Sherwood hadn't been a wealthy man, but he'd provided for his wife and daughter as best he could on a teacher's meager earnings. Addie had never known want, not even after her father's ill health had forced him to retire from teaching. Addie had thought her future, though lonely, was at least secure.

But nothing was secure. Her father had sold their home—*her* home—without telling her. The agreement had been that the house would become the property of the buyer two months after Matthew's death. That was only six weeks away.

And Addie had no place to go.

Chapter One

Idaho Territory, August 1880

Will Rider stared at the little girl who was standing in front of the stage office, a slip of white paper pinned to the bodice of her plain brown dress, a dress that was clearly two sizes too big. The brim of her calico bonnet shaded her face from view, but Will didn't have any doubt she was his niece. There weren't any other seven-year-old girls arriving in Homestead this morning.

He felt an odd tightening in his chest as he watched her. She was clutching a rag doll as if her life depended on it. It was easy to see she was frightened. Truth was, he felt just as scared as she looked.

Well, it wasn't doing either one of them any

good to leave her standing there. Drawing a steadying breath, Will stepped onto the boardwalk and strode toward the child.

At the sound of his footsteps, she turned, tilting her head and looking up at him. The rest of her features went unnoticed once he saw the pair of luminous brown eyes glittering with tears.

"Are you Lark Whitetail?" he asked.

She nodded.

"I'm your uncle Will."

She nodded again, then dropped her gaze back to the dusty toes of her worn shoes.

Lord help him. He didn't know anything about children. Especially not about little girls.

"That letter for me?" he asked, even though he could read his name written on the paper in large letters.

Without answering, Lark freed the pin and handed him the note. She kept her eyes averted.

Will opened the slip of paper and pretended to read it. He could make out a word here and there but not enough to know what it really said. When Mrs. Jones's first letter had arrived a week ago, telling him his niece was being sent to live with him—and why—he'd pulled an old and useful trick. He'd handed the letter to Griff Simpson, his ranch foreman, and said, "Does this say what I think it does?" Then, before Griff had a chance to reply, he'd added, "Just read it aloud. I want to see if I *really* understood it."

He didn't want to use that ploy again with

Griff. His foreman probably already knew Will couldn't read—lots of folks couldn't, but it was a source of shame for Will. It hadn't mattered back when he was just riding the range, but now that he was part of a community—and most folks hereabouts were educated—it seemed to matter more all the time.

He looked at the page of jumbled letters, finally deciding there couldn't be much of importance in it. It was very brief. The fact was, his niece was here now and she was his responsibility. Anything else the note might say was inconsequential.

"Well . . ." He refolded the note and shoved it into his pocket. "So you're Lark."

She glanced up at him. "Are you really my uncle?"

His chest tightened. She looked so forlorn, so lost. "Yep."

"My mama's brother?"

"Yep."

"I don't have any brothers."

"So they told me."

"My mama was pretty," she whispered, her lip quivering.

He thought for a moment before saying, "You look like her a bit." He hoped that was true. He hadn't seen Patricia in eighteen years. She'd been about Lark's age when he'd left Chicago, but time had faded his memory of his little sister.

More tears pooled in Lark's eyes, but she didn't let them fall. "My pa's mother was an

Indian." She paused for a heartbeat. "That makes me a breed. Folks don't like breeds."

"Who told you that?" Will snapped, angered that anyone would say such a thing to a child.

"Mrs. Jones."

"The old biddy," Will muttered as he took hold of Lark's hand. "Come with me. I'd guess we need to get you a few things before we head out to the ranch." With his other hand, he picked up her carpetbag, then drew the child toward Barber's Mercantile at the west end of Homestead's main—and only—street.

Emma Barber loved to rearrange the stock items on the shelves, but it drove Stanley, her husband of twenty-two years, crazy. Perhaps that was one of the reasons she enjoyed it so much.

"Consarn it, Emma," he would say. "What'd you go and move those bolts of cloth for anyway? Don't you think folks like to know where to find things when they come into the store?" His face would get all red and he would start marching around the shop, waving his arms and ordering her to put things back where they belonged.

Stanley was so blasted entertaining when he was in one of his royal fusses.

When the bell over the shop door rang, she turned away from the fabric bolts, half-hoping to find Stanley standing there with his adorable glower in place. Instead, she saw the owner of the Rocking R Ranch.

Tall and whipcord strong, Will Rider was a handsome man with tawny hair and striking blue eyes. It amazed Emma that no woman had been smart enough to catch him for a husband. If she'd been younger and single, she might have given him a run for his money herself.

"For goodness sake," she said in a tone of mild surprise. "Will Rider, as I live and breathe. We haven't seen you in town in a coon's age."

She waited for him to comment, but Will only touched his hat brim in reply, so Emma shifted her gaze to the girl he had in tow. She was a cute little thing with large eyes and golden-brown skin.

"And who's this you've got with you?"

"My niece. Lark's come to live with me."

"Lark . . . What an unusual name." Emma stepped toward the twosome, stopping in front of the girl. She reached down and placed her index finger under the child's chin, forcing Lark to look up at her. It wasn't difficult to read the girl's sadness and fear in her dark brown eyes. "Welcome to Homestead, Lark. How old are you?"

"Seven, ma'am."

"My Leslie's six. She'll be glad to have a new friend." Emma smiled encouragingly, then glanced up at the lanky rancher. "What can I do for you, Will?"

"Lark's going to need some things." He held up a tattered carpetbag. "This is all they sent with her."

Emma was dying to ask who *they* were and

why they'd sent Lark to live with her bachelor uncle, but she didn't. Stanley was forever reminding her that folks had a right to their privacy. He didn't seem to understand that Emma only wanted to help.

And it was plain enough Will Rider was going to need some help. He looked like a cowpoke whose horse had just run off and left him stranded in the middle of the desert.

"Let me have a look," Emma said, taking the bag from him. She carried it over to the counter and opened it. "Land sakes, there's nothing but a worn-out rag in here."

"That's my daily dress, ma'am," Lark offered in a voice just above a whisper. "The sisters at the orphanage said I'm not supposed to wear my good one except for the trip here and on Sundays, if you've got a church."

An orphan, huh? That explained a lot.

"We've got us a church." Emma glanced at the oversized dress the child was wearing. "Is *that* your good dress?"

Lark nodded.

"Thought as much." She returned her gaze to Will. "You don't worry 'bout a thing, Will. We'll get her fixed up. After six of my own, I know just what she'll need."

"Appreciate it."

She waved away his thanks. "It's what I'm here for." Taking hold of Lark's hand, she turned toward the selection of children's readymade clothing on a table near the store window. "Did Stanley tell you we've found us a schoolteacher? Looks like we're going to need that old cabin of yours after all." She held a dress against Lark to check for size. "We were beginning to doubt if we could find someone willing to come to Homestead."

Lark tugged on Emma's sleeve. "Ma'am?"

She turned her attention to the little girl. "What is it, child?"

"Would *that* fit me?" Lark pointed toward a yellow dress embroidered with sunflowers. Her eyes were as round as saucers and filled with hope.

Emma was pretty fair with a needle and thread—a woman had to be to raise six young'ns—and this particular dress would have had to be three sizes too small for Emma to deny Lark her wish. "I guess we can make it fit," she said, reaching for the yellow dress. "You come on back with me and we'll try it on you." She glanced toward Will. "You go on about your business, Will. Come back for Lark in an hour, and I'll have her all ready to go."

Will nodded. His gaze shifted to the girl beside Emma. "You do as Mrs. Barber says. I'll be back for you soon."

The door opened to the tinkling sound of the bell. Will stepped outside, then closed the door behind him.

Lark's hand slipped into Emma's larger one, causing the woman to look down at the girl.

"Will he come back?" she whispered uncertainly.

Emma's chest tightened. "I've never known Will Rider not to keep his word. He'll be back. Don't you worry."

Lark's shy smile was worth many hours of sewing on a bright yellow dress.

Standing outside on the boardwalk, Will stared down Main Street, feeling awash with helplessness.

Just what was he going to do with Lark?

Will was a loner, a wanderer. He'd spent most of the past eighteen years riding herd and mining for gold and traveling all over the great West. He hadn't given any thought to settling down until he'd hitched up with old Rick Charles on a cattle drive six years back. It was Rick who'd brought Will to Long Bow Valley. It was Rick who'd chosen the site of their first cabin beside Pony Creek, brought in a small herd of shorthorns, and said he wasn't budging until somebody put him six feet under.

That's just how it had happened, too. Will had buried the stubborn old coot over a year ago, but by that time, he'd grown used to the idea of staying on at the Rocking R Ranch and making a success of it.

Will started walking, a frown drawing his brows together as the question returned. What was he going to do with Lark? He didn't know anything about raising a kid. And a girl at that.

A girl. Just what he needed in his house. Will

didn't have much truck with women. His mother had cured him of ever giving any thought to shackling himself to a female. Martha Rider had done nothing but spread misery as far back as Will could remember. He wasn't about to chance falling into the same trap as his father. He preferred to give women a wide berth—especially women with marriage on their minds.

Then he thought about Justine and admitted to himself that all women didn't want marriage. Justine had never pretended to be searching for a ring and a Mrs. added to her name. Justine had wanted little more than a good time, pretty things, and a warm body to lie next to at night. Will had understood that about her. But he'd figured she was *his* girl and owed him a little bit of loyalty.

He'd been wrong about that, too. He'd found it out when he got back early from a cattle drive and found her in bed with a deputy sheriff.

No, Will didn't have much truck with women, and his opinion of the fair sex wasn't ever going to change as far as he could tell. Without a doubt, matrimony was not something in Will Rider's future. He'd have sworn to it on a stack of bibles.

He shook his head, ridding himself of the unpleasant memories of his mother and Justine. After all, he reminded himself, Lark wasn't the same as a marriage-hungry female. She was just a little girl. A lonely, scared, orphaned little girl. But just what was he supposed to do with her?

"You're lookin' mighty low there, Will."

He stopped and turned toward the familiar voice. "Afternoon, Sheriff."

Hank McLeod, a barrel-chested man with steel-gray hair and eyes to match, tipped up his Stetson. "Care to tell me what's troublin' you?"

"Nothin' the law can help me with."

With a patience born of a lifetime of experience, Hank waited in silence.

Will shrugged. "My niece arrived on this morning's stage. My sister and her husband died last year, and the girl's come to live with me." He didn't bother to tell the sheriff that his mother had refused to give her own mixed-race granddaughter a home, and it had taken the people at Sisters of Charity almost six months to locate her uncle.

"Sorry to hear that. 'Bout your sister, I mean."

Will gave another shrug of his shoulders. "Truth is, I don't know anything about raising a girl. What am I supposed to do with her out on that ranch of mine?"

"I reckon you'll do just fine. There's not much to raisin' kids. I managed it with my own two."

"You make it sound easy." Will wasn't fooled. He knew it wasn't simple. His own childhood had been less than wonderful. What if he made Lark as miserable as he'd been as a boy?

"Nothin's ever easy," Hank answered. "A man just does the best he can. You'll do all right."

Slowly, Will shook his head. "I don't know. . . . Besides, you had a wife to help raise yours."

"True enough." The sheriff grinned. "Guess there's a woman somewhere in the territory who wouldn't mind marryin' you and helpin' to raise your niece. We could start lookin'."

"No, thanks." He shook his head again, more emphatically this time.

Hank's smile disappeared. "You could always think about lettin' other folks adopt her if you just don't want her."

Don't want her? Will pictured Lark's round, sad eyes and the frightened expression on her pretty face. He hadn't said he didn't want her. She'd already had enough people telling her that. He wasn't going to be one more doing the same.

"I guess we'll manage," he said a bit gruffly.

Hank grinned again. "I guess you'll do just that."

Chapter Two

Addie braced herself against the bone-jarring motions of the stagecoach. Silently, she prayed she would make it to Homestead in one piece, but she wasn't certain even the Almighty could keep the driver from killing himself—and Addie, too—before they arrived at their destination.

The stage lurched suddenly as it careened around the side of the mountain. Addie squealed as she was tossed to the floor. Her hat fell forward, covering her eyes and knocking several hairpins loose.

"The man is insane," she muttered. "Stark raving mad."

She pulled herself onto the seat, then tried to straighten her hat and hair. But it was useless. She would never manage to get her unruly hair back into a neat bun, not until she was standing on solid ground and could use a comb and water to tame her wild curls.

Heaven help her! What was she doing in this godforsaken wilderness?

I really cannot see that you have any other option, Miss Sherwood.

The coach pitched in the opposite direction. She grabbed hold of the door to keep from sliding off the seat a second time and contemplated a few choice words for the despicable man in the driver's box once they reached Homestead—*if* they didn't end up in the river instead!

You cannot be serious, Miss Sherwood. You cannot mean to refuse my offer.

Mr. Bainbridge had been wrong about her not having any other options, and he'd been wrong about her not refusing his offer of marriage. She'd told him so in no uncertain terms. And then she'd answered the advertisement for a schoolteacher in a small western community called Homestead. Several weeks later, she'd packed everything she owned into two trunks and boarded a westbound train. Those same two trunks were now strapped to the top of this dreadful stagecoach which was trying to rattle her joints until they came unhinged.

Addie leaned back against her seat and closed her eyes. She was grateful to be nearing the end of her journey. It seemed like years since she'd boarded the train in Kingsbury. She'd passed through all manner of strange country and been bumped and jostled by all manner of rude people. She longed for a bath and a night in a real bed.

The memory of her home on Bayview Lane came swirling into her mind. She would have sworn she could smell the salty winds and hear the pounding surf of the sea.

She felt a stab of homesickness, followed by an even stronger pang of fear. It wasn't an unfamiliar feeling. Fear had been taunting her ever since she'd left Mr. Bainbridge's office after refusing his offer of marriage.

What if she failed? What if she couldn't do this? What if she were a miserable teacher?

You can do this, Adelaide. You have the gift to teach.

"I hope so, Papa," she whispered, as if he were there with her, as if she'd really heard him speaking those words of encouragement.

Matthew Sherwood had been a devoted father and a wonderful teacher. He'd known how to make his students eager to learn. He'd done that with his own daughter. Her favorite memories were of the hours she'd spent with him in his cramped study at the back of the Bayview house, the two of them poring over musty-smelling books and then discussing the things they'd read. Sometimes, their lively debates had become quite heated, father and daughter both determined to prove their opposite points of view, and she'd loved every minute of it. She'd never felt inadequate when she was debating with her father.

I can do this, she thought to herself. *I'll be a good teacher.*

The coach slowed slightly and the road seemed to even out. Addie opened her eyes and grasped hold of the door with one hand, then leaned toward the window for a better look.

They had left the winding mountain road behind. Spread before them was a long, crescent-shaped valley. Tall grasses waved in a hot summer's breeze. Majestic mountains—their rugged sides thick with pines, their granite peaks barren—jutted toward a wide expanse of blue sky. Dark purple wildflowers colored the land like a royal cloak. It was a beautiful sight. Quite the prettiest sight she'd seen in many days. She wondered if she was getting close to her destination.

As if she'd asked the question aloud, the driver shouted, "We're comin' up on Homestead, miss."

Homestead, she thought, and immediately forgot the majestic mountains, the blue sky, the purple wildflowers.

She brushed futilely at her dust-laden skirt. She knew her face must be likewise smudged. She could only hope her bonnet concealed most of her untidy hair. She wished she could have arrived looking her best, but there was nothing to be done about it now.

She closed her eyes and whispered a quick prayer that the townsfolk of Homestead would approve of her.

* * *

"More coffee, dear?"

Hank lifted his cup in answer to his wife's question, and Doris filled it to the rim with the dark brew. "Stage ought to be in before long," he said before blowing on the hot liquid.

"If it's on time." Doris set another plate on the table, then filled a second cup with coffee. Finally, she pulled out the chair opposite him and sat down. "What do you suppose he'll be like?"

"Who?"

"You know who," she answered with a mock scowl. "The teacher. Mr. Sherwood."

"Oh. *That* he. Don't know. Reckon we'll have to wait and find out, just like everyone else."

"Hank McLeod, you're an infuriating man. Have I ever told you so before?"

He grinned into his cup. "Time or two, Dorie." He sipped more coffee. "Just a time or two."

Companionable silence settled over the kitchen as Doris ate her lunch and Hank drank his coffee, his gaze turned out the window onto the main street of Homestead.

Hank liked being the sheriff here. One day was pretty much the same as the next. Truth was, about the most excitement folks in Long Bow Valley had was the arrival of the weekly stage up from Boise City, and it only stopped long enough to toss down the mail pouch. It wasn't often the stage brought a warm-blooded passenger along with the post. Folks were still talking about the arrival last week of Will's niece.

As if she'd read his mind, his wife asked, "Have you heard how Will Rider's getting along? Emma said he was like a fish out of water with that niece of his."

"He was nervous all right, but I imagine he'll make out."

"Emma says the little girl's pretty as a picture, but so sad it near to broke her heart."

"Guess she's got cause to be sad. Wouldn't be easy, losing your folks and having to leave everything familiar."

"Poor little thing. Left all alone in the world. I can't help thinking about our Sarah. What if something were to happen to Tom and Maria? What would happen to Sarah then?"

Hank set his coffee cup on the table and rose from his chair. "We raised our own two. I guess we could raise our granddaughter." He thought of the little toddler with her golden hair and blue eyes. Lord, she did know how to wrap her grandpa around her little finger. "But there's not much point in frettin' over something that's not about to happen."

Doris reached forward and took hold of his hand as he moved around the table, drawing him close to her chair. She pressed her cheek against the back of his fingers. "Every so often, I remember how lucky I am," she said softly.

He stroked her hair with his free hand. "I'm the lucky one, Dorie."

A few minutes later, Hank stepped through his front doorway, pausing as he settled his wide-brimmed Stetson onto his head. Slowly, he let his gaze move along Main Street.

He'd meant what he'd said, about him being the lucky one. A man couldn't ask for a better wife than Doris. They'd seen their share of ups and downs, good times and bad in the thirty-three years they'd been married, but she'd stuck by his side through it all. She hadn't ever complained, not even when he was a young lawman, dragging her and Tom and Anita around the country from job to job. Now they had a nice little house in quiet little Homestead, the children were grown and married with children of their own, and Hank had his job as sheriff in a town where nothing much ever happened.

No, he didn't figure a man could ask for a better lot in life than the one he had.

Emma was so excited she could hardly stand it.

Stanley must be feeling it, too, she thought as his arm tightened around her shoulders. She glanced up at the man beside her.

He smiled and winked. "You did it, Emma," he whispered.

She grinned in reply.

Yes, she'd done it, and it hadn't been easy. She'd had to fight plenty hard to convince the other members of the town council that it was time to hire a schoolteacher. There'd been plenty of resistance. Some folks didn't think book learning had much merit. Others thought children could learn well enough at home, taught by their own parents in the evening after the day's chores were done. But Emma had persisted until she either changed their minds or just plain wore them down. Stanley'd told her he never doubted for a moment that she would win in the end.

Her thoughts returned abruptly to the present, and her pulse quickened as she spied the spiral of dust just east of town.

"It's coming!" she cried, causing her husband and the others waiting with them to fall silent as they waited expectantly.

Beyond the rooftop of Barber Mercantile, the spiral became a dirty brown cloud against the cerulean sky. Unless there was a herd of wild mustangs coming to town, it was a sure bet the stage was about to arrive.

An excited murmur arose. In a few minutes, they would all get a glimpse of A. L. Sherwood, Homestead's first teacher.

As the stage rolled to a halt, Addie looked out the window, but she couldn't see anything for the swirl of dust that filled the air. It took a moment for the dirt cloud to blow on down the street.

Addie swallowed hard, trying to subdue the anxiety that was threatening to consume her. She would be a good teacher, she reminded herself. Her father had trained her well. She'd been at the top of her class in normal school.

She had her teaching certificate. She liked children. She could do this. She could.

Just before the dust cleared, she heard the chattering voices and knew there were people waiting beyond the door. Were they there because of her? Had others come with Mrs. Barber to meet the stage? What would they think of her? Oh, how she wished she'd had time to wash and change before anyone saw her.

Addie drew in a deep breath and let it out slowly. She tried again, in vain, to tidy her hair. She couldn't help wishing she was petite and blonde and beautiful instead of tall and red-haired and plain.

"Afternoon, folks," she heard the driver say as he jumped down from his perch atop the coach. Then the door opened.

Please . . . don't let me fail, she prayed before sliding forward on her seat, grasping hold of the door, and stepping down to the ground. *Please let them want me to stay.*

As she glanced up, she found about a half-dozen people looking at her. Then, in perfect timing, their gazes shifted back to the door of the stagecoach. No one spoke.

After a moment, it occurred to Addie that these people were expecting someone else. Mrs. Barber apparently hadn't received her wire about Addie's arrival on today's stage. Straightening her back and lifting her chin, she said, "Can anyone here tell me where I might find Mrs. Barber?"

The gazes all returned to her, but no one answered her question.

"Mrs. Emma Barber?" Addie said again. "I believe she runs the mercantile. If you could just give me directions . . ."

A short woman with a round face and graying brown hair stepped forward. "I'm Mrs. Barber."

Addie felt a rush of relief. "Thank goodness. I'm Adelaide Sherwood. I was afraid you didn't receive my . . ." Something about the surrounding silence made her stop speaking. She moved her eyes from one person to the next.

"A. L. Sherwood?" Emma asked, her voice sounding strained.

"Yes." She glanced back at the woman. "You were expecting me, weren't you?"

Emma looked up at the tall, very thin man beside her, then back at Addie. "No, Miss Sherwood. I'm afraid we weren't expecting *you*."

Chapter Three

"But I sent a telegram," Addie said.

Emma wore an odd expression. "I got the telegram all right, but we still weren't expecting *you.*"

"I'm afraid I don't understand. You were all . . . Weren't you here to meet me? I . . ." Panic caused her throat to tighten. Had she come all this way for naught? Had she misunderstood? Had they not wanted her for the job? Would she be forced to return to Kingsbury?

The man standing behind Emma stepped forward. "I'm Stanley Barber. What my wife's trying to tell you is that we thought A. L. Sherwood was a man."

Addie felt a terrible chill shoot up her spine, despite the sweltering August sun. "A man. But I'm not . . . why would you . . ."

Stanley thrust out his hand and took hold of hers, pumping it enthusiastically. "We can see we were wrong, Miss Sherwood. Welcome to Homestead."

"Thank you, Mr. Barber," she responded automatically, not really believing him, certain she was anything but welcome. They'd expected a man. They'd *wanted* a man.

"For pity sake. What's the matter with me?" Emma said. "Let me introduce you to folks, and then we'll get you out of this sun. You've met my husband, Stanley." She took hold of Addie's arm and drew her up onto the boardwalk. "This here is Doris McLeod. She's our postmistress."

"Welcome to Homestead, Miss Sherwood." Doris wore a friendly smile set in a well-worn face. Gray curls peeked from beneath a pale blue bonnet that matched the woman's eyes.

"Thank you."

"And this here's her husband, Hank McLeod," Emma continued. "He's our sheriff."

"Pleased to meet you, Miss Sherwood." The sheriff tipped his hat.

"Thank you, sir," Addie replied softly, staring up at the large older man. She imagined his sheer size would keep trouble at bay and suspected he made a fine sheriff.

Emma turned her toward a pretty woman about Addie's own age, who was holding a squirming child in her arms. "This is the McLeods' daughter-in-law, Maria, and their granddaughter, Sarah."

"Welcome to Homestead," Maria said. "We're so glad you've come."

Addie relaxed slightly as she returned the woman's smile. "So am I."

"And this here . . ." Emma tugged on her arm. " . . . is our pastor, Reverend Pendroy."

A short, stocky gentleman, wearing a clerical collar beneath his double chin, stepped forward. "How do you do, Miss Sherwood? We're very pleased you'll be joining our community."

"Thank you, Reverend. It was good of you to meet the stage." She let her glance move over the others standing nearby. "It was good of all of you to come."

"Stanley," Emma said in her take-charge voice, "you see to Miss Sherwood's things. I'll take her back to the house and get her something to eat." To Addie, she said, "You'll have plenty of time to talk to everyone later. For now, I'd bet you'd like a moment to freshen up and relax. It's no easy trip up from Boise City. Maybe someday they'll bring the train out this way, and a body won't have to put up with that wretched stagecoach anymore."

Before Addie scarcely knew what was happening, she was being led away from the stage office, her arm still firmly held within the crook of Emma Barber's elbow.

"I'm sorry about the mix-up, Miss Sherwood. About you being a man, I mean. I guess, if I'd thought about it, I would've known you weren't, just by the look of your handwriting. I just got it in my head that a woman wouldn't take it upon herself to come all the way out here alone and never gave it another thought."

"Mrs. Barber, if you have some objection to me, I'll . . ."

"Nonsense. We're glad to have you."

Addie wished she were convinced of that.

"You're going to like it here. Most folks are real friendly. We've got us a nice church and a Ladies' Literary Society." Emma pointed to a large wooden building some distance away. "That's the Richmond Sawmill. Old Mr. Richmond built it on Pony Creek just over four years ago. Tom McLeod runs it now. Stanley and I built our house and the mercantile a few months later, and it wasn't long before a town was springing up around us. The folks all come together last year to build us a church. Glass windows and a steeple and a fine bell. It's back behind us, at the west end of town. That's where you'll be holdin' school for now, but we'll have the new schoolhouse up come spring. We've already got in the desks and a blackboard." She nodded to her right. "That there is the jail, and across the street is Doc Varney's office. Doc's a bachelor. He lives above his office."

Addie's gaze moved from one building to the next. They were all made of wood, most of them whitewashed. There was plenty of space left between buildings. Some of them were placed close to the street, others were set far back from the road in a haphazard fashion. It was nothing like the neat, close-set style with which she was familiar. The false front of the jail was lettered with the word *Sheriff*. A shingle hung beneath the porch of the two-story building across the street, bearing the words *Kevin Varney, M.D.* Next door to the doctor's was an L-shaped building shaded by several poplars and some tall pine trees. It seemed to be their destination.

"That's Barber Mercantile," Emma said as she guided Addie across the street toward the store. "Our home is in the back. You come on inside, and I'll make you a hot cup of tea while you freshen up."

Moments later, Addie was ushered into a bedroom with lacy white curtains at the windows and a matching comforter on the bed.

"There's water in the pitcher there," Emma said, motioning toward a porcelain basin and pitcher. She pulled a towel from beneath the dressing table and placed it in front of the mirror. "You take your time, and when you're ready, come on into the kitchen. I'll have your tea and a bite to eat waitin' for you."

"Thank you."

The door closed behind Emma before Addie could say anything else.

Left alone, Addie sat before the dressing table and stared at her reflection in the mirror, confirming her worst suspicions. She looked positively dreadful.

She felt like crying.

They'd expected a man. They'd *wanted* a man.

She supposed she should have given her name as Adelaide Louise when she'd answered the advertisement for a teacher instead of using her initials, but she'd always signed her correspondence as A.L. Sherwood, just as her father had always signed as M.A. Sherwood. It hadn't occurred to her that she should have done otherwise.

She drew in a shaky breath, then let it out. She wouldn't allow herself to give in to tears. She hadn't cried since the day Mr. Bainbridge had made his charitable offer of marriage. She wouldn't start now. She had come to Homestead to teach, and that was exactly what she was going to do.

Quickly, she removed her hat and set about straightening her hair. With a firm hand on the comb and plenty of water, she managed to tame her curly tresses, recapturing the fiery-colored hair in a bun at the nape. Once that was done, she washed her face and hands, then set her hat back in place and rose from the low stool. Drawing another deep breath, she left the bedroom and headed toward the kitchen.

Emma glanced up as Addie entered the room. "There you are. And your tea is all ready for you." She motioned to the large table in the center of the kitchen. "Sit down, Miss Sherwood. Do you mind if I call you Adelaide?"

"My friends call me Addie."

"Addie. I like that. And you call me Emma." She brought a steaming cup of tea and set it before Addie, then sat down in a nearby chair. "Just take a moment to relax. The house is quiet for a change. The children are all down at the swimming hole, but they'll be back soon enough."

"How many children do you have, Mrs. Barber?"

"Emma, remember? And the answer is six."

"Six? Good heavens!"

Emma revealed a pleased, maternal smile. "Six. Albert's the oldest at sixteen. Annalee's fifteen. Ryan's twelve. Rachel's eleven. Loring's eight. The baby is Leslie. She's six. They're bright, every one of them, and I've done my best to teach them, but they need schoolin' as much as any child in Long Bow Valley. Albert thinks he's a bit old, but he'll be there, same as the others."

"I'm looking forward to meeting them."

"Well, they're going to be mighty surprised when they meet you. They've been expectin' *Mr.* Sherwood, just like the rest of us." Emma's brows drew together in a frown. "I suppose we'll need to find a family to put you up," she said, more to herself than to Addie. "I'd be more'n happy to do it, but our bedrooms are all full as it is."

Addie stiffened in her chair. "Put me up? But I thought I was to have a house of my own."

"Well, you were, Addie, but I don't think Mr. Rider's place is suitable for a woman. It's just a one-room log cabin. Hasn't been lived in for . . ."

"It will suit me fine."

"But it's out a ways from town. Not a bad walk, but still . . . You'd be livin' alone. It just don't seem right somehow. I'm sure we could find a family willing to give you a room."

"I assure you, I'd much prefer to live alone. And I don't mind a walk. I'm used to walking." Addie leaned forward in her chair. "Emma, I value my privacy. One of the reasons I answered your advertisement was because it mentioned that a house was provided for the teacher. That shouldn't change simply because I'm female."

Emma shook her head thoughtfully. "I suppose it'll be up to Mr. Rider. It's his place."

"Then I should go speak to this Mr. Rider at once."

The older woman watched Addie for a moment before saying, "I'll have Stanley drive us out to the Rocking R."

Addie contained an audible sigh of relief. "Thank you," she said softly.

Will wiped the sweat from his brow with his shirtsleeve as he walked across the corral, then pulled his hat brim low on his forehead to shade his eyes. He couldn't remember an August this hot since he and Rick Charles first came to this valley.

Tossing the coil of rope over a fence post, he opened the gate and left the corral. Long strides carried him toward the house. His sharp gaze caught a flicker of movement at one of the windows, and he knew Lark was watching his approach. He also knew that if he lifted his head so she could see his eyes she would back quickly away, hiding herself from view.

He suppressed a frustrated sigh. Their first week together had been anything but a sterling success. Lark was as skittish as a colt around him. When he spoke to her, she jumped as if he'd threatened her. When he asked her to do something, she obeyed quickly, as if she were afraid of the consequences if she didn't. She never uttered a word unless he asked her a direct question. In fact, she was so quiet, it would have been easy to forget she was there at all.

It was apparent that his worst fears had been fully justified. He didn't know how to take care of a little girl. He was making her miserable, just as he'd been as a child. Despite his bumbling efforts at playing the devoted uncle, she was still afraid of him.

He cursed softly. He couldn't blame Lark. What did he know about making a kid feel loved and cared for? It wasn't as if he'd ever felt that way himself. His childhood memories were grim. He couldn't remember a single time of any real happiness.

He thought of some of the families he knew in Homestead, families like the McLeods and the Barbers. Sometimes he saw the way those people looked at each other and he wondered, *Is it real?* He found it hard to think so. No one in his family had ever even pretended to love each other. Except maybe Patricia. Sometimes he'd thought his little sister loved him. But saying the words *I love you* wasn't something any of the Riders had ever done.

Will was just reaching for the knob on the front door when he heard the rattle of harness. He turned around.

Even from a distance, he recognized Stanley Barber's pencil-thin frame in the driver's seat of the fringe-topped surrey. His wife sat beside him. Someone else was in the second seat behind them, but he couldn't make out who.

Will took a couple of steps forward and waited for the surrey to arrive.

"Afternoon, Will," Stanley called as they drew closer.

"Afternoon," he replied, tipping the brim of his hat slightly back. "What brings you out this way in the heat of the day?"

The merchant drew the horse to a halt and glanced behind him at the woman bathed in shadows. "This is Miss Adelaide Sherwood, from Connecticut."

"Howdy," Will responded.

"Miss Sherwood's our new schoolteacher. We thought we'd better let you know before we moved her into that cabin of yours."

"But I thought . . ."

Stanley nodded. "So did we."

"Mr. Rider." Her back toward him, the woman stepped down from the surrey.

Will's first impression was of height. Miss Adelaide Sherwood was as tall as most of the men in this valley and taller than some. The top of her head was nearly at eye level with Will. She was slender, with soft curves breaking the straight line of her brown traveling dress.

The hair that peeked from beneath her straw hat was the color of burningbush in autumn, and the wisps around her nape coiled in tight curls.

All this he noticed before she turned to face him.

When she did turn, Will found himself staring into the most unusual green eyes he'd ever seen. Almond-shaped, they were the shade of unripened apples. The oval pupils were obsidian black. He scarcely noted the rest of her face that, at best, seemed merely ordinary.

"Mr. Rider, I was told everyone expected a *Mr.* Sherwood. I'm sorry for the misunderstanding, but I've assured Mrs. Barber that my qualifications are still the same."

Her voice was soft, cultured, and feminine. For some reason, he'd expected something deep and no-nonsense, something more befitting her overall appearance.

"Apparently," she continued, "there is some question of whether or not I should have the use of your cabin?"

Will glanced at Stanley. Stanley jerked his head toward Emma.

"I thought Addie might want to board with a family rather than stay all alone," Emma stated. "That cabin of yours is a bit rustic and secluded. I said we'd need to check with you."

"Mr. Rider?" Addie's voice drew his gaze. "The Barbers took me by your old place on the way here. I assure you, it will suit me quite adequately."

Just what he needed—a woman living on Rocking R land. Right now, she was saying it would suit her just fine, but before long, she'd be asking him to help her with this and to please do that. She'd think he was responsible for her well-being. Give her a few weeks, and she'd be complaining about there not being a pump indoors or that the cabin was too drafty.

Will shook his head. "Mrs. Barber's right. That cabin's no fit place for a woman. You'd be better off in town."

"Mr. Rider, am I or am I not correct that you agreed to let A. L. Sherwood live in your cabin should the teaching job be accepted?" Addie reached into her leather traveling bag and pulled out an envelope. She removed the enclosed letter, and after unfolding it, held it toward him. "It says in here that housing will be provided by Mr. Rider if I should accept the position."

"We thought A. L. Sherwood was a man," he replied, fighting to keep his voice calm.

"My gender has nothing to do with my ability to teach the children of Homestead, and it has nothing to do with my desire to live in my own house."

He looked at the stubborn set of her chin, noticed the indignant flash of her eyes. He didn't doubt for a moment that she meant what she said. Still, a woman on the Rocking R could only spell trouble. "You'd be better off in town," he said again.

"Are you going to honor your word, Mr. Rider?" She raised the letter and waved it in front of him.

Annoyance shot through him at her challenge. He felt trapped, and it wasn't a feeling of which he was particularly fond. "If that's what you want, Miss Sherwood, then I suppose I've got no call to keep you from it. Just don't go thinking I'll be making any improvements to the place, just 'cause you're a woman."

Addie managed not to let out an audible sigh of relief. She'd been so afraid he wouldn't change his mind. "Thank you, Mr. Rider," she said softly, her anger fading. "I assure you, I shall ask no special favors of you."

He shrugged, but she guessed he was still irritated.

It wasn't a very good way to start, challenging the man who would be her landlord, questioning his integrity. But what else was she to do? Having found herself with no home and on the receiving end of offers of charity, Addie valued her independence a great deal. And it hadn't been fair of him to want to renege just because she was female. She'd come all this way to teach school. She'd kept her part of the bargain. It wasn't so much to expect him—and the rest of the town—to do the same.

"How's that niece of yours, Will?" Emma asked, abruptly changing the subject.

"Fine."

His reply seemed so abrupt that Addie immediately wondered if he spoke the truth.

Once again, Emma's voice intruded. "Why don't you bring her out here and introduce her to Miss Sherwood? I'm sure she'd like to meet the new teacher."

Will shrugged, then turned and walked toward the house. He opened the front door and called, "Lark, come out here."

A moment later, a young girl of about six or seven stepped through the open doorway. Her eyes were downcast, her hands clenched together in front of her calico frock. An aura of loneliness and sadness surrounded her.

Empathy sparked in Addie's heart. She saw herself as a child, heard the other school children teasing her, felt anew their spurning of Catty Addie. Intuition told her that this child had suffered the same sort of rejection that Addie had once felt, and she immediately wanted to help ease the hurt.

She leaned forward and held out her hand. "Lark, I'm Miss Sherwood. I'm going to be your teacher when school begins."

The girl looked up. Addie didn't think she'd ever seen a child so beautiful before. She had a heart-shaped face, golden-brown skin, and doe-like eyes. Her long hair was straight and black as coal.

Addie waited patiently for Lark to take hold of her hand. Finally, she did so. Addie smiled as she closed her larger hand around Lark's smaller one. "I'm new to Homestead. Perhaps you can help me get to know everyone?" She squeezed the hand she held.

Lark shook her head as she looked down at the ground once again. "I don't know anyone either," she whispered.

Addie straightened; her gaze darted to Will.

"Lark just came to live with me a week ago," he said in explanation.

A strange tingling started up in her stomach as she took her first really good look at her new landlord. He was, without question, the singularly most handsome man she'd ever seen. He had a distinctly masculine face, each feature chiseled with perfection; tawny hair, dark gold with pale yellow highlights, the color of a wheat field at harvest; eyes like a morning sky; and shoulders broad enough to carry any burden. And tall. So very wonderfully tall. How could she have stood there, arguing with him over where she would live, and not really looked at him?

"Addie?" For the third time, Emma's voice interrupted her thoughts.

Feeling like a child caught sneaking a peppermint stick from the mercantile jar, she turned, her throat suddenly dry, preventing her from speaking.

"We'd best be on our way. You'll want to settle in 'fore dark."

"Yes," she managed to say, the word sounding more like a croak. "Yes, I'm ready." She glanced back down at the child. "Good-bye, Lark. I'll see you again soon. I think we're going to be good friends, you and I."

This time, Lark almost returned her smile.

Addie stepped quickly toward the surrey. As she reached to take hold of the seat, she felt a hand cup her elbow. She glanced to the side, meeting Will's gaze, and felt another tingle in her stomach.

Wordlessly, he assisted her as she stepped up into the surrey.

Emma leaned forward to look around Stanley. "We're going to have us a picnic after church on Sunday. Folks will want to meet and welcome Addie to Homestead. Everyone's curious about our schoolteacher. You and Lark be sure to come. I'll make extra food."

"Wouldn't want to put you out."

"No bother at all," Emma said with a wave of her hand. "Might as well cook for ten as for eight."

"Be obliged," Will responded with a tap to the brim of his hat. He stepped back from the surrey. His eyes moved briefly to Addie, then he glanced down at his niece as Stanley drove away.

Chapter Four

Addie awakened just as the sun was cresting the mountain range in the east. Golden light spilled through the lone square of window near the door, illuminating dust motes in the air.

Pushing herself up against the pillow at her back, she stared around the log cabin. There was a large stone fireplace which took up most of one wall. A cast-iron stove for cooking stood on the opposite side of the room. Nearby was a box, stacked high with split wood. Kettles and pans hung on nails in the wall above the stove. A shelf held a few tin plates and some chipped crockery. A narrow cupboard contained what foodstuffs Emma had put in before Addie's arrival. A small table stood in the middle of the room, two slat-backed chairs slid up tight against it. A commode with two drawers was placed next to her bed, and beside it was a small stand holding a pitcher and bowl for washing.

Before leaving her in her new home yesterday, Emma had spent a great deal of time apologizing for the meager furnishings and had promised to provide more necessities before the week was out.

Addie couldn't argue with Emma's assessment. The cabin did lack more than a few amenities. It was, indeed, rustic and sparse. Still, she felt a strange sense of satisfaction as she looked about her. It wasn't that her homesickness for Connecticut and the sea had gone away. She knew home to her would always be the house on Bayview Lane.

Yet Addie couldn't deny that there seemed to be a rightness about her being here. With a certainty that was strange to her, she knew this was where she was supposed to be. For the first time in many weeks, she felt a lessening of the fear that had been her constant companion since the death of her father.

Tossing aside the blankets on her bed, she sat up and lowered her feet to the cool, hard-packed dirt floor. She wrinkled her nose. A dirt floor was one thing she would *never* look upon with favor.

Quickly, she reached for her slippers and put them on, then drew her robe from the foot of the bed. Pulling on the light wrap, she rose and walked to the door.

Outside, the air was crisp and scented with pine. A soft breeze ruffled the long grasses that grew knee-high, reminding her of the rolling seascape of home. The gurgling sounds of the nearby creek mingled with the whisper of the trees and the sweet chirping of birds. The sun on her face promised to be scorching by noon, but for now, its golden touch was gently warm.

Leaning against the log wall of the cabin, Addie crossed her arms in front of her chest, closed her eyes, and breathed deeply. She was filled with a wondrous sense of adventure, as if life had just opened up for her as never before. The sameness, the routine, that had been her life had been turned over, like an upset apple cart. It was gone forever. Everything was new and unexpected now.

Perhaps things happened for the best. Perhaps this was why Papa hadn't told her of their precarious finances. Perhaps this was why he hadn't told her he'd been forced to sell the house. Maybe he'd known she needed to see something beyond Kingsbury and her home on Bayview Lane.

And she *had* needed to leave, she realized with surprising clarity. Ever since Robert had jilted her all those many years before, she'd made that house her sanctuary from the world. She'd been trained to be a teacher and yet she had never taught, choosing instead to remain close to her father. Hiding out was what she'd been doing. Hiding from life and its disappointments.

Well, she wasn't going to hide any longer. She had no unreasonable expectations of what life would bring. She knew she wasn't destined to marry—unless she was willing to settle for an offer like the one Mr. Bainbridge had made. But she could make a difference as a teacher. She could touch the lives of children. That was important. How many times had her father told her so?

"I'm going to be all right, Papa," she whispered, and then she smiled.

Will poured himself another cup of coffee from the blue-speckled pot on the stove, then returned to his chair at the table. He had a full day ahead of him. He needed to check the herd grazing at the northwest end of the valley, and there was that buyer coming to look at some horses for the U.S. Cavalry tomorrow. He needed to have several of his best geldings picked out for him.

But instead of concentrating on those matters, his thoughts kept going to the schoolmarm staying in the old cabin on Pony Creek. He'd been meaning for weeks to check the roof on the place, but he'd never gotten around to it. It hadn't seemed all that important when he thought the teacher was a man. But now . . .

He remembered the stubborn tilt of Addie Sherwood's chin and the determined, half-wary look in her unusual green eyes. She probably didn't need his help. A more independent-looking woman he didn't think he'd ever met. No doubt she was also stubborn, obstinate, bull-headed, mulish, and difficult. He'd known it the moment he laid eyes on her. Damn-fool female, choosing to live in that old cabin instead of rooming with one of the families in town. Just proved he was right about her. Stubborn. Just plain stubborn.

Then he remembered the way she'd leaned low and talked to Lark, the way she'd brought the hint of a smile to the child's face. It was the first time he'd seen Lark look remotely happy since she'd climbed down from the stagecoach. *He* sure hadn't managed to coax a smile out of her in the week since she'd come to live with him.

Hell! He supposed he'd better see to that blasted roof before the weather decided to turn. It wouldn't do to have Miss Sherwood drown in her bed. Not when the entire valley was counting on her being there to teach school.

He'd known letting her have use of the cabin wasn't a good idea. He'd known having a woman living there would be a lot of bother. She hadn't even been there twenty-four hours, and already she was fouling things up, making things difficult for him.

Setting his cup on the table, Will looked across the table at Lark. Her eyes averted as usual, she was methodically cleaning her plate of every bite of her breakfast.

"Lark."

She glanced up, looking ready to bolt.

"I'm going down to the cabin where Miss Sherwood is staying to check on the roof. I'll only be an hour or so." He slid his chair back and stood up, then carried his dishes to the sink. He frowned thoughtfully for a moment before turning and asking, "Would you like to come with me?"

For a moment, he thought she might agree to his offer. Then she lowered her gaze and shook her head.

He quelled the irritation he felt at her rejection. She was just a little girl, he reminded himself. He had to give her time. She'd been bounced around pretty hard. She was used to the likes of that old biddy at the orphanage. He needed to have a bit more patience. Once Lark knew him better, she wouldn't act this way.

"Well . . ." He started toward the door. "Guess I'll be on my way then." He reached for his hat, then glanced over his shoulder. "You sure you don't want to come with me?"

"No," she whispered. "Thank you, Uncle Will."

It wasn't as if he hadn't tried, he told himself as he walked toward the corral. Maybe if he felt more comfortable around children it would be different. But he just wasn't used to them. He didn't know how to act with Lark, how to talk to her. Unlike Miss Sherwood, he couldn't make her smile either.

He had a bad feeling that he wasn't ever going to make much of an uncle, and the thought depressed him more than he cared to admit.

* * *

Hank sat at the back of the church, his legs stretched out before him, one ankle crossed over the other. He folded his arms over his chest as he listened.

"I don't mind that she's a woman," Doc Varney said. "Lots of women teach school until they marry or after they're widowed. But I don't think it's proper for her to be staying out there on the Rocking R Ranch."

"Why ever not?" Emma asked.

"Well, Will Rider's a bachelor, for one thing. So are all his cowhands. It just doesn't look right, her living out there completely unsupervised and without proper protection. She ought to be here in town."

Stanley shook his head. "That old cabin of Will's is nearly a half mile from his ranch house. It's not like she's staying in the same place with him and his men. As for protection, old Mrs. Keiser hasn't seemed to need any since her husband died last fall. We haven't had any trouble in these parts from Indians in years. No reason to think we will now." He ran the palm of his hand over his head. "Besides, Miss Sherwood'll be cookin' and cleanin' for herself. It'll save someone a lot of work, not boardin' her in."

Ellen Pendroy, the reverend's sister, spoke up. "I'm still concerned about what sort of example she might be setting for the children. A woman living alone without proper guidance." She touched her handkerchief to her forehead, as if the mere thought had caused her to feel faint. "There could be a problem with gentlemen callers. If she were living with her father or brother or an upstanding family here in town, it might not be a worry, but . . ."

"We don't need no schoolteacher anyway." Glen Townsend glowered at those sitting nearby. "Man or woman. Waste of time and money. Children oughta be helpin' their parents run their farms and businesses. My boy's old enough to be havin' a job of his own 'stead of sittin' in school. Book learnin's not gonna make no difference to Mark. If it were up to me, I'd send that lady schoolteacher packin'."

Hank tried to check his dislike of Glen Townsend. If there was anyone he'd like to see sent packing, it was him. Glen was a drunkard, and a mean one at that. Hank had already broken up two fights this month that Glen had started. He was afraid that one of these days he was going to arrive too late, and he'd find someone dead on account of the man.

"I believe it's our duty to give Miss Sherwood a chance to prove herself," Reverend Pendroy interjected. He ignored the disappointed look his sister gave him. "She seemed like a very fine woman to me when I met her at the stage, and she *has* come a long way at our invitation."

"What about the older boys?" James Potter asked. "Miss Sherwood's not going to have any trouble with my girls, but we all know the boys like to create a bit of mischief now and then. Sometimes it takes a man to make 'em toe the line like they should." He scratched his head with the middle finger of his right hand while staring at the floor. "And how's she gonna manage, gettin' back and forth to school, if we get an early winter?"

Doris's hand touched Hank's leg. He glanced at his wife, then spoke up. "I guess she'll manage just like your wife does, Mr. Potter. Same way we all manage. As for the problem with the boys . . ." He paused, his gaze sweeping over the room. A wry grin curved his mouth. "I reckon there's more than one mother here who can give Miss Sherwood a hint on how to handle them, if she doesn't already know."

Good-natured chuckles were heard around the room, and a few women whispered their accord.

"What about her salary?" Glen demanded loudly. "We offered a man's wage. We ain't gonna pay her the same, are we?" He glared at Emma. "Ain't it true we could get a woman teacher for nearly half what we offered this Sherwood woman?"

"It's possible, but is it fair? Miss Sherwood traveled out here all the way from Connecticut on our promise of two hundred and twenty-five dollars a year. It wouldn't be honorable for us to reduce it now."

Roger Morris, a farmer who worked a small parcel of land not far from town, rose from the wooden pew. "I guess I might be considered a newcomer myself, bein' here only since spring, so maybe I don't have a right to speak, but Miss Sherwood did mislead us. When the school board considered her application, they thought she was a man. Perhaps that was her intention when she used her initials instead of her name. It's possible she's been less than honest and honorable with us."

Glen mumbled his agreement.

"Of all the nonsense I've ever heard," Emma sputtered as she jumped to her feet. She swept the room with an indignant gaze. "Listen to yourselves. Miss Sherwood's come here to teach our children, and we oughta be glad about that. It wasn't like we had a whole lot of applicants to choose from, now was it? Now we've got us a qualified teacher, and we're sittin' here wonderin' if we ought to send her away and worryin' about where she ought to be livin' if she does stay and talkin' about payin' her less than we promised. The reverend's right. We have a duty to let her prove herself. And if she wants to live in that old cabin of Mr. Rider's, then it's none of our concern. You only have to meet her to know Miss Sherwood is a lady of unquestionable morals and good breeding."

"I still say a teacher's an expense this town don't need," Glen grumbled.

Emma tossed him a cutting glance. "We decided against you and those of similar thought months ago, Mr. Townsend. This meeting is about Miss Sherwood and where she should live. If you have nothing constructive to say, then you needn't feel you're required to speak."

Glen's hands tightened into fists. Hank immediately straightened in his chair, prepared to step in if there was trouble. He couldn't be sure whether or not Glen noticed him, but a moment later, Glen got to his feet and left the church without another word.

Emma drew in a deep breath. "Oh my, I am sorry," she said, looking contrite. "I didn't mean to lose my temper. But we *are* being unfair. Miss Sherwood has a right to live alone if that's what she chooses. We did say the person hired would have a private house when we advertised for a teacher. I know most schoolteachers are boarded out, but that wasn't the case here. We promised a place of their own. We didn't say it'd only be that way if the teacher was a man."

Thoughtful silence filled the room.

"My comment about Mr. Rider and the Rocking R was no doubt inappropriate," the doctor said at last. "I suggest we meet again next month to assess the situation. We'll know better by then how things are working out."

The others agreed, and before long, everyone had filed out of the church.

As Hank descended the steps, he pictured Miss Sherwood in his mind. He had a strong feeling she'd get on all right if folks would just give her a chance. Everybody deserved a chance.

Addie poured the pitcher of water over her head, gritting her teeth against the cold as she rinsed the last of the soapsuds from her hair. Her eyes squeezed shut, she felt around the grass for the towel she'd brought with her from the house. When she found it, she wrapped it turban-style around her head, then sat up straight.

A sigh of pure pleasure escaped her lips. It was amazing how much better she felt now that she'd bathed and washed her hair.

After a few moments, she rose from the ground, gathered the pitcher, basin, and soap, and carried them back inside the cabin. She set the articles on the table, then picked up her comb and returned outdoors. Not far from the cabin was a large, moss-covered rock, bathed in morning sunlight. It was there that she sat and started to comb out her waist-length hair.

She closed her eyes and lowered her head toward her right shoulder as she worked out snarls in her damp tresses. Mentally, she began to tick off items she needed to purchase at the mercantile.

She wanted a curtain for the window and some rugs to cover the dirt floor and a bathtub—most definitely a bathtub. She would also like another oil lamp and perhaps a comfortable chair to sit in before the fire after a long day of teaching. She would need a more suitable pair of walking shoes, too. It was nearly a mile to the church, and Emma had said winters could bring heavy snow to this valley. And then there were some additional food supplies to set in.

When her hair was dry, she decided, she would put on one of her good dresses and walk to town. She would give her shopping list to Emma Barber. Then she would ask to see the church, since that was where she would be holding classes until the town built a separate school. It wasn't long now before classes were to begin, and there was so much to do to get ready before then.

"Mornin', Miss Sherwood."

With a gasp, Addie jumped to her feet and whirled about.

Will Rider sat astride an enormous buckskin, his forearm braced upon the saddle horn, his eyes shaded by the wide brim of his hat.

Addie clutched at the front of her wrapper and tried to hide her bare feet beneath her nightgown. She pushed her wet hair back over her shoulders, knowing it would make little difference in her bedraggled appearance. She felt the rush of blood into her cheeks, burning her skin. No one but her father had seen her in such a state of undress before. Certainly no stranger ever had.

"Sorry to come by so early. I'm here to have a look at your roof."

"My roof?" She glanced toward the cabin.

"It's been a while since anyone lived here. I thought I'd best make sure the roof won't leak next time it rains."

"I see." She wished she could disappear. To think of this man seeing her this way. It was most embarrassing.

"You just go on about drying your hair. This won't take me long."

She watched him step down from the saddle and walk toward the cabin. She liked the way he walked, with an easy, strolling sort of gait. She liked the way he looked in his worn denim britches, the way they hugged his legs and . . .

The blush in her cheeks deepened as she quickly turned away and sat down on the rock once more. What on earth was she thinking? She had never had such unladylike thoughts in her life—not even when she was young and so in love with Robert. To find herself staring at a man, a perfect stranger, like that. . . . What if he'd seen her? She pressed her fingertips against her cheeks and willed her pulse to slow to a more normal pace.

After a moment, she resumed combing her hair, determined not to think about the man any further. The last thing she wanted was for her new landlord to think Addie Sherwood was looking for a husband.

Will could feel her discomfiture all the way up on the roof. He hadn't missed the blush in her cheeks or the way she'd clutched at her robe. It was kind of funny actually. He could have told her she wasn't the only woman he'd ever seen in a wrapper with her hair down, but somehow he didn't think Addie Sherwood would find that information very comforting. Especially since the women he'd seen like that hadn't been unmarried schoolmarms from back East.

Squatting on the roof peak, he glanced down at Addie. She was pulling the comb through her damp hair again. He'd never seen hair that color before. He'd always been partial to brunettes himself, but then, he'd never known anyone with red hair quite like hers.

And those green eyes. He couldn't forget those green eyes. . . .

He reined in his thoughts abruptly. Letting his imagination run wild could get a man in plenty of trouble. Miss Sherwood was not the kind of woman who provided a man with an afternoon's entertainment. And that was the *only* kind of woman Will had any interest in.

Quickly, he returned his attention to the roof. He meant to finish his inspection and then get the heck out of there. The last thing he wanted was for the new schoolmarm to think Will Rider was looking for a wife.

Chapter Five

On Sunday morning, Emma walked along Main Street with her arm laced through Stanley's, the children all following behind them as they made their way toward the Homestead Community Church. The morning sky was clear from one end of the valley to the next, and it was a relief to feel a crisp nip in the air that hadn't been there for weeks. Perhaps the hot spell was about to break.

Emma glanced over her shoulder to make certain she had no stragglers. The three boys were especially prone to hanging back, waiting for a chance to sneak away, perhaps go fishing or swimming. For some inexplicable reason, they seemed to think their mother wouldn't notice they were missing when the family took its place in the pews. They apparently also believed fishing and swimming were worth the scolding they would receive later, along with the extra chores they would have to perform for the following week.

This morning, however, no one seemed inclined toward such shenanigans. Perhaps it was because they were all eager to get a look at the new schoolteacher. Today would be Miss Sherwood's official introduction to the good folks of Homestead and Long Bow Valley, and the Barber children were just as curious as everyone else.

Glancing ahead to the church, set against a grove of quaking aspens and pine trees at the west end of town, Emma decided it was going to be a red-letter day for Reverend Grant Pendroy. The church was already surrounded with wagons and buggies and saddle horses. She certainly hoped their pastor had prepared an appropriate sermon for such an occasion. The people of this valley were a God-fearing lot, but Reverend Pendroy didn't often have a congregation this large willing to listen to him at one time.

Emma's gaze shifted from the church to the site of Homestead's school. A church *and* a school.

Her chest felt just a bit puffed up with pride. She knew pride came before a fall—it had to be especially shameful to feel such a thing on the Sabbath Day—but she hoped the Good Lord might forgive her the indulgence this once. After all, Homestead had come a long way in just four short years. It wasn't every town of this size that could boast of having a church with their very own minister, a schoolmarm to bring education to the children and a touch of culture to the community, and before long, a schoolhouse.

As they approached Townsends' Rooming House, the front door of the two-story house opened, and Virginia Townsend and her two children stepped onto the porch. The poor woman looked frazzled as usual.

"Good morning," Emma called.

Virginia jumped as if Emma had hurled a stone rather than offering a greeting. Her hand fluttering at her throat, her smile forced, she called back, "Good morning, Emma, Stanley. It's a beautiful day, isn't it?"

Just then, Glen Townsend—his face unshaven, his shirt untucked and slovenly—came out of the house. He spoke to his wife in a low voice that caused her to nod quickly, then scurry back inside. Glen's gaze darted toward the street and momentarily met Emma's. His nose and lip wrinkled in an expression that could only be called a sneer. Then he, too, stepped back through the doorway.

"That man calls the devil his personal friend," Emma muttered beneath her breath.

"Now, Emma. Don't be judging others," Stanley admonished gently.

"It's not judgin' when you're callin' things as they are, Stanley Barber," she retorted with conviction. "That man has a streak of sheer meanness in him, and he uses it plenty on his wife and children. And that boy of his is cut from the same piece of cloth as his father. He's a bad one, that Mark Townsend. A bully, plain and simple. When I think of what Virginia and little Rose have to put up with, it likes to break my heart."

"Maybe having his children in school will help."

Emma glanced up at her husband. He was smiling at her tenderly, and before long, she returned the smile. Except for those times when she moved stock around in the store, Stanley was an amazingly patient and tolerant man. He'd had to be to put up with her all these years, she thought as she squeezed his arm in silent communication.

They were lucky, and she knew it. They had six healthy, happy children, and their home had been filled with love throughout the twenty-two years of their marriage. It wasn't very many people who could say the same.

The rattle of harness and the clip-clop of horses' hooves drew her attention back to the church as another wagon rolled to a stop nearby. She waved at the Potter family and bade them good morning, but Stanley didn't give her the opportunity to stop and chat. His firm hand guided her toward the steps leading up to the church door, where Reverend Pendroy stood greeting his parishioners.

"Good morning, Emma, Stanley," he said to them as they climbed the steps. "Good morning, children."

Stanley returned the reverend's greeting, then said, "Looks like you're going to have a full house."

"Indeed."

"Has Miss Sherwood arrived yet?" Emma asked.

The reverend shook his head. "Not yet."

"Oh dear." She glanced toward the road. "I hope something hasn't gone wrong."

Why, of all mornings, did this have to be the one when she didn't awaken before sunrise?

Addie walked as swiftly as her long legs would carry her, but she was afraid it wouldn't be swiftly enough. She just knew she was going to be late for services.

Why, oh why, did it have to be *this* morning?

She hoped she was presentable. Her pale green dress had always been one of her favorites; she thought it flattering to her odd coloring. Still, she felt as if she'd thrown herself together in haste and feared she looked it, too.

If only she hadn't overslept. . . .

She heard the approach of a wagon behind her and glanced over her shoulder as she stepped closer to the edge of the road. She felt her pulse speed up when she recognized Will Rider, his niece sitting beside him.

She turned her head forward again, her gaze set on the road before her, and quickened her pace even more. She hadn't seen the rancher—much to her relief—since the day he'd come to inspect the roof, and she wasn't happy to see him now. She didn't like the way he made her feel. She reminded herself that he'd been less than gracious about her using his cabin. He didn't want an old maid schoolmarm living there, that was plain enough. He probably didn't even want her for the teacher.

And he wasn't the only one who didn't approve, she was sure. When she'd gone into town to purchase more supplies, she'd seen the glances, caught the whispers. She didn't have to be a genius to understand what was going on. The town had thought A. L. Sherwood was a man. Because she'd disappointed them, she would be expected to prove Adelaide Louise Sherwood was as good a teacher as any man could be. No, more than likely she would be expected to prove she was *better* than any man could be. It wasn't fair, but that's how things were.

The wagon drew up alongside her.

"Mornin', Miss Sherwood."

"Hello, Mr. Rider," she returned with a quick glance, never slowing down for an instant.

"Looks like we're both runnin' late for Sunday service. You'd best ride the rest of the way with us."

"I wouldn't want to impose," she replied stiffly.

"No imposition. We're all going to the same place." He pulled the horses to a halt.

Reluctantly, Addie stopped, too.

Will hopped down from the seat and held out his hand. "Here. Let me help you up."

She felt ridiculously lightheaded as her hand touched his. "Thank you."

A moment later, they were both on the wagon seat, Lark between them, the horses once more trotting toward town. It took Addie a little longer to quiet the tingling sensations that had started up in her midsection.

She didn't know why this man had such a strange effect on her. It wasn't as if she was totally without experience with men. She'd been engaged when she was eighteen. Robert had even kissed her a few times. She recalled that she'd felt just a trifle naughty—and at the same time, eager for more. That was a little like what she felt now.

She stifled a groan. How could she let herself think such things? It had to be the strain of coming to a new town and now being late to church. That had to be the explanation. She most certainly was not going to allow herself to go on acting so foolishly.

When she finally felt in control again, she turned her head to the side. Will's feet were braced against the front of the wagon. He was leaning forward, his forearms resting on his thighs, the reins laced through his long fingers. Strong, callused hands, the skin bronzed by the sun. She wondered what it would feel like to have those fingertips run along her bare arm.

She felt the heat returning to her cheeks. What on earth had come over her? she wondered. What if he could tell what she was thinking?

It wasn't likely, she realized as her gaze darted to his profile. He didn't seem to be aware that she was sitting so close to him. Certainly he hadn't made any attempt at conversation since helping her into the wagon.

And why would he? He'd merely done the neighborly thing by offering her a ride to town. He certainly hadn't done it because he found her attractive. A handsome man like Will Rider could have his pick of women. *Beautiful* women. He wouldn't be interested in a plain-faced old maid from Connecticut.

If I may be blunt, Miss Sherwood, the truth is you are no longer in the first blush of youth, and by no means could you be called a beauty. What else are you to do if you don't marry me?

Addie swallowed the lump that rose in her throat as she recalled Mr. Bainbridge's brutal but honest assessment of her appearance. Then she sat up straighter on the wagon seat, mentally chasing the memory away. She couldn't care less what Mr. Bainbridge thought—or what Mr. Rider thought, for that matter. If she'd wanted marriage, she could have had it. She'd come west because she hadn't been willing to settle for such an arrangement. She might not be in her first blush of youth and she might not be a beauty, but she *could* be a good teacher. That was all that mattered.

She could begin proving it right here and now, she realized. Determinedly, she turned her eyes upon Lark. The child was staring down at her hands in her lap. As she had the first time they'd met, Addie sensed it wasn't mere shyness causing Lark to act this way. There was a deep-down kind of hurt inside her. Addie hoped she could help, whatever the problem.

"It's a beautiful day, isn't it, Lark?" she said cheerfully. "I love mornings. Here you can smell the pines. Back home, I could always smell the sea."

The girl didn't look up or reply.

"It's a bit frightening, meeting new people. I lived in the same town, in the same house, all my life before coming here. Would you mind terribly if I held your hand when we go into the church? I think it would give me a bit more courage if I already had a friend."

Lark lifted her chin and raised her gaze to meet Addie's. For a moment, they simply looked at each other. Then Lark slid one hand over to Addie's lap. With a smile of gratitude, Addie took it within hers.

Will would sure as heck have liked to know what it was about Miss Adelaide Sherwood that made Lark react to her the way she did. When he tried to befriend his niece, she just withdrew. But with Addie it was different. She came along and asked to hold Lark's hand and there it was.

Friends, just as simple as that.

He frowned and tried not to give in to the exasperation he felt.

Hell, he'd known he wasn't cut out for raising a girl. Why was he so all-fired upset about how things were working out? It wasn't as if it had come to him as some sort of surprise.

He slowed the horses to a walk as they rounded a bend in the road and the church came into view. Although he couldn't claim to be the most faithful of churchgoers, he knew he'd never seen so many wagons, buggies, and buckboards around the church since the town had first joined together to build it.

"Looks like everyone in Long Bow Valley has turned out to meet you, Miss Sherwood."

Glancing her way, he saw the blood drain from her already pale cheeks. He wondered if she were going to do something foolish like faint. But she didn't. She simply sat a little straighter, a little taller, her chin punctuating the air and her mouth set with resolve.

She has courage, I'll give her that.

He stopped the horses in the first bit of shade he could find, then looped the reins around the brake handle and jumped to the ground. He reached first for Lark, lifting her from the seat. Next, he offered his hand to Addie.

"Thank you, Mr. Rider," she said softly as he helped her down.

As soon as she dropped his hand and stepped forward, Lark slid in beside her and they joined hands. Addie smiled down at the girl with a look of conspiracy, as if the two shared a great secret.

The two of them look right together.

Will was strangely disturbed by the thought.

Chapter Six

Meeting everyone hadn't been so bad after all, Addie thought as the Potters and their three daughters walked away from where she was sitting with the Barbers. There were those who objected to a woman teacher, and it had been simple enough to tell who some of them were. There were also many who had welcomed her with warmth.

It wasn't going to be easy, but she meant to prove herself, not just to those who wanted her to leave but also to those who hoped she would stay. Most of all, she supposed she wanted to prove something to herself. But now wasn't the time for such grim thoughts. Today was a day for enjoying herself.

She looked around at the picnicking families who had spread their colorful blankets across the churchyard. Children's laughter punctuated the air as they ran and jumped and played games. The lunch Emma had packed for them had been truly delicious, and Addie felt drowsy and contented after eating more than she should have. It would be lovely, she thought, to remove her hat, lay back on the quilt, and take a nap.

Her gaze lighted on Lark as she stood waiting her turn with the jump rope. The corners of Addie's mouth curved slightly as she watched the child, remembering how Lark had held her hand throughout the church service. She had stayed close beside Addie until Addie insisted she go play with Leslie Barber and the others. Although Lark had been reluctant and shy at first, before long she'd been joining in the games and laughter.

Just then, Lark glanced toward the Barbers' picnic site, directly at the place where her uncle had sat to eat his meal. It was empty now, and Lark's sudden alarm was evident. Frantically, her gaze darted around the crowd until she found Will with Stanley and a group of farmers and ranchers. Addie watched the panic slowly drain from Lark's face.

"Makes your heart ache, watchin' her, don't it?" Emma said in a low voice.

Addie turned toward the other woman. "Yes, but I don't understand. She rarely talks to him, doesn't hold his hand as she does mine. But when he's not close to her, she seems terrified."

She let her voice trail away, silently asking her questions with her eyes.

"I'm afraid I don't know much of the story myself. She just came to live here the week before you. She was stayin' at an orphanage somewhere. I think she's afraid she'll have to go back to it. She's afraid Will's going to leave her, too. Leastwise, that's how I figure it."

Addie nodded. That explained a great deal about Lark's behavior. She understood what it was like to be left alone with no place to call home.

Emma covered the few remaining pieces of fried chicken with a towel and set the plate in a basket. "So tell me how it feels, Addie, now that you've met everyone. Do you think you're going to like it in Homestead?"

"Yes, I'm going to like it here." Addie smiled gently. "Of course, I'll miss the sea . . . and my home." She pictured them both in her mind as her smile faded. "I'll miss walking on the beach and watching the ships pass by in a morning mist. And there's that special tang of the sea air." She breathed in through her nose. For a moment, she could almost smell the sea.

"So why did you leave?"

Addie was silent a long time before answering Emma's question. "My mother died almost ten years ago. My father died this year. He was forced to sell our home just before he died. There was nothing keeping me there after that." She paused, waiting for the painful tightening in her chest to ease. When it did, she sighed, then held her head high and said, "I had my teacher's certificate, and it was time I used it. When I saw your advertisement, I made up my mind to see more of this great country. I'd heard so much about the untamed West, it seemed a good place to start."

"There was no one special, no young man in your life who objected to your leaving?"

Addie shook her head as she thought of Mr. Bainbridge. "No." Then she thought of Robert, a memory of long ago. She thought of the devastation she'd felt when he'd broken their engagement. She'd known then, with painful clarity, that she wasn't destined to marry and have a family. "No," she added softly, "there was no one who objected to my leaving."

"Stay away from my sister, *breed*."

Addie's thoughts were yanked back to the present by the angry voice. Silence spread around the yard as all eyes turned upon Mark Townsend. The burly fourteen-year-old had grabbed his little sister by the collar of her dress and was holding her, stiff-armed, off to one side and behind him as he glared down at Lark.

"You hear me? You stay away from Rose. My pa don't want her learnin' no filthy injun habits."

"Let me go!" Rose shouted, her fists flailing but not quite reaching her brother's back. "You let me go!"

Mark ignored her. He simply turned and headed toward the rooming house near the center of town, dragging his younger sister along with him. Quickly, their mother gathered up her blanket and picnic basket and hurried after them.

Without hesitation, Addie rose from the ground and started toward Lark. The other children had all backed away during the commotion. Uncertainty kept them from drawing near again. Lark's eyes had filled with tears, but she courageously kept them from falling.

Will was tempted to catch the Townsend boy and whip his behind with the nearest branch he could find. Whip him until he couldn't sit down for a solid week.

He stepped away from the other men just as Addie reached Lark. He stopped and watched. He saw her lean over and say something to the girl. The tenderness reflected in her expression made her appear almost pretty.

After a minute or two, she spoke softly to the other children nearby. The youngest Barber girl was the first to move closer. Others soon followed suit. A minute or two later, the long jump rope was being turned again, and this time Addie Sherwood was in the center with Lark, the two of them jumping over the rope as some of the girls chanted a sort of rhyme.

Will had never seen a grown woman skipping rope before. With one hand she held her skirts up just high enough to reveal the top of her walking boots and a glimpse of stockings. Her other hand rested on top of her hat to keep it from bouncing off as she jumped.

Emotions squeezed his heart as his gaze shifted to Lark. She was smiling again. He had Addie Sherwood to thank for that.

"Got herself a way with the children, don't she?" Stanley asked as he stepped up beside Will.

"Yep."

"Yessir, I think she's going to do right fine here in Homestead. Right fine." Stanley dropped a friendly hand onto Will's shoulder, then turned and walked back toward Emma.

Will returned his gaze to Addie. Her feet had become tangled in the rope, and she was laughing along with the children as she tried to free herself. There were bright pink spots in the apples of her cheeks, and wisps of fiery red hair had pulled free to curl around her nape.

She did have a way with children. She'd been able to do in minutes what Will had been unable to do in almost two weeks—make Lark smile. He wondered if Patricia had been anything like Addie. Had his sister been the sort of woman who would skip rope at a picnic? Had Lark's mother smiled and laughed the way Addie did?

Addie would make a fine mother. If I married her, Lark would have the mother she deserves.

The idea caught him totally unawares. When he realized what he was thinking, he felt a shock run clean through him.

Marriage? It was insane. Marriage was the last thing he wanted. It was a trap he'd always sworn to avoid. He hadn't even considered it with Justine, though he'd been right fond of her—until he found her in his bed with the deputy. And even if he had considered marriage some time in his past, Justine had cured him of ever considering it again.

He turned and strode off in the direction of Pony Creek. He raked the fingers of one hand through his shaggy hair, trying to clear his thoughts. But once the idea had taken hold, it wouldn't shake loose.

Would a marriage of convenience be such a bad thing?

It wasn't as if Addie was a vain, self-centered beauty, like his mother, who was determined to nab herself a rich husband. She sure as hell wasn't a fun-loving, hard-drinking gal like Justine who hated to spend even one night alone.

No, Addie was a good-hearted, upright, motherly sort. He needed only to see her with Lark to acknowledge that. Marriages were made for lesser reasons than the happiness of a child. He had that big house with plenty of rooms. Surely he and Addie could work out some sort of living arrangement that would suit them both.

Stopping on the bank of the creek, Will stared down into the crystal-clear water. A rainbow trout swam upstream, its belly close to the smooth stones at the bottom of the creek.

Marriage to Addie Sherwood? It was crazy! Or was it? It wouldn't *really* be a marriage, after all. It would be more of a business arrangement. She would agree to raise Lark, to give her the kind of upbringing the child should have, the kind he didn't know how to provide. In return, Will would give Addie a home. She wouldn't have to stay in that spartan cabin. She wouldn't even have to teach school if she decided she didn't want to.

He turned his back on the stream and gazed toward the picnic area behind the church. He saw families beginning to pick up their things and head for their wagons. It took him a moment to find the tall redhead in her green dress. Lark was right beside her, their hands joined together as they had been much of the day.

How many chances did a man have to do the right thing in life? Lark needed a mother—even if he didn't need a wife—and he was pretty sure Addie would fit the bill. Of course, Will didn't know much about Addie, but he knew the important things. Lark liked her. Lark trusted her. And Addie was good to Lark. He guessed that was all that mattered.

He would do it, he decided. He would ask Addie to marry him and be Lark's mother. Soon. He would do it soon.

Rose didn't care if it was a sin. She hated her pa.

"What do you mean, lettin' our girl play with some breed!" Glen Townsend backhanded his wife.

Virginia staggered backward with a whimper, her arm raised to ward off the usual counterswing.

"Leave her be," Rose shouted as she threw herself between her parents. "Don't you hit Ma again."

Her pa's gaze focused on her. Her legs went mushy, and her stomach sank. She knew better than to call attention to herself when her father was in one of his drunken rages.

"See what I mean? See what happens? Listen to how she's talkin' to me."

Before Rose could run, her father's arm shot out and he caught her by the hair, jerking her toward him. "I'll not have you sassing me, miss." He shook her hard. "Do you hear what I say?"

"I hear, Pa," she answered, her teeth rattling as her head bounced forward and back. "I hear."

"Glen, please . . ." Virginia beseeched.

Her pa shoved Rose toward the doorway. "You git up to your room and stay there 'til I tell you to come out."

Biting back tears of pain and anger, she ran up the stairs and into her bedroom. She leaned against the door and sank to the floor, covering her ears with her hands. She didn't want to hear when Pa hit Ma again. She didn't want to hear the crash of broken furniture. And she didn't want to think about the bruises that would keep Ma inside the house for the next week or so.

No, she didn't care if it was a sin to hate her own pa. She hated him . . . and her brother, too.

Addie was sorry to see the day end. All her worries about meeting the people of Homestead had been for naught. The majority had made her feel like an important part of the community already. Those whose welcome had been less than warm would see that they were wrong, in time.

"Miss Sherwood?"

She turned at the sound of Will's voice. "Yes?"

"We'd be happy to give you a ride back to your place. It's on our way."

She glanced toward the wagon. Lark was already waiting on the seat, her expression hopeful. She supposed she could hardly refuse. After all, it was on their way, just as Will had said.

"Thank you, Mr. Rider. I'd be most grateful."

By the time they reached the cabin, Addie had reason to question how grateful she was. Will hadn't said a word the entire time. Worse yet, she'd felt a growing tension throughout the trip. She had a dreadful suspicion that the silence and tension had something to do with her.

After Will helped her down from the wagon, he released her arm, then took a step back from her. "Miss Sherwood, I'd like to come by tomorrow and speak to you about a matter of some importance."

She felt the nervous beating of her heart. Whatever could he wish to speak to her about? Had he decided to evict her from the cabin? Had he joined forces with those who wished her to leave?

She stiffened her back and lifted her chin. "If you'd like, you may speak to me now."

"No." He glanced toward the wagon. "I'd just as soon do this when Lark isn't with me, if you don't mind."

Her pulse quieted somewhat. She was overreacting. She was jumping to conclusions. Surely, if he meant to evict her, he would simply tell her and get it over with. Perhaps the matter concerned Lark. Yes, that must be it. He wanted to discuss his niece.

"Tomorrow will be fine, Mr. Rider. Would afternoon be convenient?"

"I'll be here." He touched his hat brim. "Goodbye, Miss Sherwood."

She watched him climb onto the wagon seat, take up the reins, and drive away.

And somewhere in the back of her mind, the thought echoed, *He's coming to call tomorrow. He's coming to see me.*

Chapter Seven

Addie awoke with a start. The dream lingered around the fringes of her consciousness, leaving her feeling vulnerable and exposed. It seemed so very real.

She tossed aside the blankets and rose from the bed. Pulling on her wrapper, she hurried over to the fireplace and stoked the fire. The days might very well be hot in this country, but the nights were surprisingly cold.

It wasn't long before firelight danced across the walls of the one-room cabin, making it seem more cheerful. Addie sat down on one of the straight-back chairs and stared at the yellow and orange flames. She tried not to think about the dream, but she failed.

She'd been in Mr. Bainbridge's office again. He'd told her she had to leave her home. She'd told him she had nowhere to go, and then he'd proposed marriage to her. And finally, he'd started to laugh. She'd backed toward the door, ready to leave, but her shoes had felt weighted. Then she'd heard the other laughter. She'd looked up, and there had stood her father and Robert. They'd been laughing, too. No one had said anything. They'd simply laughed and laughed and laughed—until she'd awakened.

"Why?" she whispered.

She wasn't sure what she meant. Why had her father sold their home without telling her? Why had nothing turned out the way she'd once thought it would? Why had she been forced to leave her home and the sea to live in this far-off place where nothing seemed familiar?

She hugged herself and swallowed the tears that burned her eyes and throat.

Dreams were silly things, she reminded herself. They meant nothing. Her father hadn't been a cruel man. He would never have laughed at her. And Robert? He might not have wanted to marry her, but he wouldn't have laughed at her either. Besides, she'd gotten over her heartache years before. She'd accepted that it was for the best their engagement had been broken. A marriage between them would have been a grave mistake. She never would have been happy, living in New York City. She'd been much better off staying in Kingsbury and taking care of her father.

She dabbed her eyes with her handkerchief, then blew her nose, telling herself once again that dreams were silly and baseless. They made no sense. A person could dream absolutely anything. They weren't the least bit grounded in reality.

She sniffed and blew her nose a second time. "Better now?" she asked aloud.

Taking a deep breath, she thought she did feel better. Maybe she'd just needed to have a good cry. Perhaps that was why she'd had such a ridiculous dream.

She used the poker to move the logs, causing the fire to burn brighter. Then she rose from the chair and returned to her bed. Drawing the covers up beneath her chin, she closed her eyes and willed herself to go back to sleep.

Miss Sherwood, I'd like to come by tomorrow and speak to you about a matter of some importance.

With a groan, she rolled onto her side and pulled her pillow over her head.

Not now, Mr. Rider, she thought in response.

But there he stood in her mind—tall and lean, a lazy smile on his handsome face, his Stetson pulled low on his forehead to shade his eyes. He was coming to discuss something of importance. What was it? Her thoughts raced as she tried to guess why he'd asked to speak with her.

Does it matter?

Her heart beat a staccato rhythm in answer to her unspoken question.

She would bake something. A cake, perhaps. The cabin would be filled with delicious odors, and she could offer him something to eat. She would have fresh coffee ready and . . .

She made another noise of protest as she turned onto her other side and resolved not to think about anything more. She was simply going to go back to sleep. She wasn't going to think about Kingsbury or Mr. Bainbridge or Papa or Robert or . . . or Will Rider.

Will had dressed in his Sunday-go-to-meetin' suit and his newest black felt Stetson. He'd even shined his boots for the occasion. It might be just a business proposition, but he supposed a man should look his best when he asked a woman for her hand in marriage.

He rode his buckskin up to the cabin at a few minutes after twelve o'clock. She'd said afternoon, and that's exactly what it was. He was anxious to get this over and done with.

As he drew Pal to a stop, the cabin door opened and a cloud of smoke billowed out. He heard a fit of coughing just before Addie appeared in the doorway, waving her apron as fast as she could. He vaulted from the saddle and raced toward the cabin.

"Don't fan the flames," he yelled. "You'll only make it worse." He grabbed her by the arm and roughly jerked her outside. "Stay put," he ordered. "I'll save what I can." He moved toward the well pump, his hand already reaching for the bucket placed close by.

"Wait! Mr. Rider, there's no danger!"

He ignored her as he filled the bucket and headed for the cabin.

"Mr. Rider!"

"Stay back!"

Eyes narrowed, he stepped inside. Through the smoke, he caught sight of a flicker of orange. He hurled the contents of the bucket. A loud hiss filled the room as steam and smoke barreled toward him. He backed out the doorway, his eyes smarting.

That was when he heard what sounded like laughter. He stopped and glanced over his shoulder.

There was a sooty smudge on her nose and evidence of watering eyes. Tight curls of red hair had pulled free from the usually smooth bun she wore at her nape. But instead of looking frightened, her eyes were twinkling with mirth.

She covered her mouth, trying to hide her smile. "There . . . there wasn't a fire, Mr. Rider," she managed to say.

"What do you mean?" He turned toward her. "I saw . . ."

"You've just doused the stove, that's all."

"But . . . but the smoke."

She fought off fresh giggles. "I'm afraid I burned the cake I was baking for your visit."

"A cake?" He turned his gaze toward the cabin. The smoke was already thinning.

"Yes."

He looked at her again. He didn't feel much like laughing himself. He felt like a fool. And if there was one thing Will hated, it was having a woman make him feel like a fool. "I take it you're not much of a cook, Miss Sherwood?"

She shrugged, unruffled by his insult. "My father never complained about my cooking."

He had the decency to feel of pang of shame. "I'm sorry. It's just . . . I thought . . ."

"You thought I was burning down your cabin," she finished for him. "At least you decided to pull me to safety instead of letting me burn with it." She rubbed her arm where he'd grabbed her moments before, her eyes still sparkling.

Was she mocking him? he wondered.

She glanced at the cabin. "I'm sure it must have seemed I was in danger. Thank you for saving me."

He stared at her, not sure how to respond.

Her smile broadened. "You wouldn't care for some cake, would you? It's just out of the oven. A bit darker than I usually make it, but it's quite moist, I believe." Her eyebrows arched expressively. "A bucket of water will moisten even *my* baking, Mr. Rider."

Finally, even he couldn't deny the humor of what had happened. "A bachelor never turns down an offer of dessert, Miss Sherwood. Not unless he's got a better cook than I've got." He bowed in her direction.

Her eyes met his, and slowly, her smile faded. He was sorry to see it go.

She stepped back from him. "Why don't we sit down over there?" She motioned toward a cluster of trees. "I doubt we'd want to go inside quite yet."

"Out here is fine." He was tempted to take hold of her arm, but she led the way before he could act on the impulse.

He watched her settle onto a log. She sat with her back ramrod straight, her shoulders as stiff as a soldier at attention. She took a moment to smooth her skirt with her hands; then she glanced up at him.

Suddenly, his throat felt tight and his thoughts were all jumbled up in his head. He wasn't quite sure how to go about proposing to a woman. Maybe it wasn't such a good idea. Maybe he should just forget it.

"You said there was a matter of importance we needed to discuss?" She sounded every inch a schoolteacher.

"Yes." He cleared his throat. "Yes, there is."

"Is it about Lark?"

He heard the gentleness in her voice as she spoke his niece's name. Some of the tension left him. He was right about her. She would be good to Lark.

"Yes," he replied. "In a way, it is about Lark." He stepped toward her, pulling his Stetson from his head as he did so.

Addie wasn't sure why her heart started racing uncontrollably at just that moment. Perhaps it was because she had to crane her neck to look up at him.

"Please sit down, Mr. Rider," she said in a soft voice. She pulled her skirt over on the log, making space for him.

"Thanks."

Her rapid pulse apparently had nothing to do with his standing and her sitting. Her heart didn't slow at all when he sat beside her. In truth, it seemed to quicken, making her feel lightheaded and breathless.

Rather than looking at her, Will stared at the crystal-clear creek.

He has a wonderful profile, she thought.

"I'm not sure I know how to say what I want to say." He cleared his throat.

Just looking at him made her feel like smiling again. The fluttering of her heart was actually quite a pleasant sensation. "The best way is to just say what's on your mind," she advised.

"Yes . . . well . . ." He cleared his throat again as he raked the fingers of one hand through his hair. "You see, Lark just arrived in Homestead a couple of weeks ago. Her parents both died from influenza—there was an epidemic on the reservation—and Lark was sent to stay at an orphanage until the authorities could find me."

"Emma told me."

He glanced at her quickly, then returned his gaze to the creek. "I'm not cut out to be an uncle, let alone a father. I don't know anything about kids, especially little girls. I was watching you with Lark yesterday. She takes to you, Miss Sherwood."

She subdued a desire to lay her hand over his and tell him that everything would work out all right. She thought any man who cared what kind of father he would be was destined to be a very good one. "I think it's because we're a little alike, Lark and I," she suggested.

"Whatever the reason, I got to thinking yesterday that Lark needs you." He spoke very quickly now, his words almost running together. "And this cabin isn't much of a place for you to live. I was thinking maybe you'd consider being Lark's mother."

Her eyes widened, and her heart seemed to skip a beat or two.

Will turned toward her then. His expression changed from uncertain to solemn. "What I'm proposing, Miss Sherwood, is that you marry me and move to the main house. This isn't much of a place, and you'd be more comfortable there than you are here. I know we're pretty much strangers, but I think we could get on well enough to live together. I'm not suggesting anything . . . well, intimate. What I mean is, you could have your own room. You could keep teaching school if you wanted and the school board didn't object. We'd go on as we are now, except you'd be there for Lark. She needs a mother, Miss Sherwood." Abruptly, he quit speaking and waited in silence for her to reply.

It was as if she were in two places at once. She heard Mr. Bainbridge's words as clearly as she had heard Will Rider's. They blended together until she had difficulty telling them apart.

I have made you an honorable offer, Miss Sherwood . . .

I'm not suggesting anything . . . well, intimate . . .

There was an odd ringing in her ears. She shook her head, trying to clear it.

My children are badly in need of a mother . . .

You'd be there for Lark. She needs a mother, Miss Sherwood . . .

Her chest felt hollow.

You are badly in need of a home . . .

This isn't much of a place, and you'd be more comfortable there than you are here . . .

Her entire body felt numb.

What else are you to do if you don't marry me?

She felt her throat tightening, felt the hot sting of tears behind her eyes. The last thing Addie wanted was to let Will see her cry, yet that's what she feared she was about to do.

Somehow, she found the strength to rise from the log and step away, keeping her back toward Will. "Your proposal has come as quite a surprise, Mr. Rider." She was amazed at how normal her voice sounded. "But I'm afraid I must decline."

"Perhaps if you thought about it, gave yourself a chance to get to know . . ."

She lifted her chin as she dragged in a sharp breath, then turned to face him. "I'm sorry, Mr. Rider. I have no wish to marry." She crossed her arms over her abdomen. "I believe it would be more advantageous if you spent some time getting to know your niece. It's important that the two of you become friends. I know what it means to be close to one's father. My father and I were inseparable. Those years with him have left me with memories I shall never forget. Your niece needs that same closeness with you."

He looked as if he might try to persuade her to change her mind.

"Thank you for coming," she said quickly. "I know you are only trying to do what is best for Lark." *Please go,* she added silently. *Please go now.*

He stared at her a moment longer before settling his hat over his tawny hair. "I guess it wasn't such a great idea. I hope you won't hold it against Lark."

"Of course not, Mr. Rider. I understand. Good day."

"Good day." He walked over to his horse, mounted up, nodded in her direction, and then rode away.

The moment he disappeared from view, she sank down, hot tears scalding her eyes as she pounded her fists against the ground.

Why? Why aren't I good enough for a man to love?

Chapter Eight

Addie took a deep breath, then reached for the bell rope and began tolling the opening of the first day of school. Children of all ages hurried toward the steps of the church.

"Mornin', Miss Sherwood."

"Good morning, Miss Sherwood."

"Mornin', ma'am."

They filed passed her, the girls with their hair tied back with ribbons, the boys with their hats in their hands. Most of them carried lunch pails. Some carried slates and tablets. A few had brought their own books from home.

Addie returned each of their greetings, trying all the while to look calm and composed, trying her best to look like a teacher. It was a little unsettling to find that two of her students were nearly as tall as she was, especially when one of them was Mark Townsend. From what she'd seen of him, her first Sunday in Homestead, she knew he was going to be a difficult student.

Mark gave her a look that told her exactly what he thought of school, then moved on inside.

There was no doubt about it. She was going to have trouble with that boy. She wondered how she was going to handle it. What if she wasn't able to maintain order inside the classroom because of him? What if he thwarted her authority at every turn? It would prove a woman couldn't handle this job. The school board would be forced to replace her. Then what would she do?

Before her panic took the bit in its mouth and ran away with her, she reined it in. She was *not* going to let Mark Townsend or anyone else intimidate her. She'd come to Homestead to teach school, and that was exactly what she was going to do.

She stood a little straighter and held her head high, prepared to enter the classroom. The sound of an approaching wagon caused her to glance back at the road.

Addie felt the blood rush to her cheeks when she recognized the driver. Mark Townsend she could handle, she thought. Will Rider was another matter.

She hadn't seen the rancher in the week since he'd proposed. He hadn't been in town the two times she'd walked into Homestead during the week, nor had he attended church services the day before. She'd been immeasurably relieved by his absence. However, she'd known she couldn't avoid him forever. Now she was going to have to look him in the eyes and pretend she hadn't been hurt by his indifferent offer of marriage.

She stood straight, her chin raised and her hands folded sedately in front of her. It didn't matter that his proposal had been indifferent, she reminded herself. She wouldn't have been interested in marriage even if Will Rider had tendered some affection for her. Finding a husband wasn't why she'd come west. She had no cause to feel flustered or embarrassed at the sight of him. None at all.

Will pulled his team to a halt, and Lark scrambled quickly down from the wagon seat. She hurried up the steps, pausing in front of Addie.

"Am I late?" she asked, her gaze anxious, her voice soft.

"No, Lark. You're right on time." She touched the child's dark hair, then folded her hands again. "Go on in and find yourself a seat."

Addie would have loved to follow right behind Lark without looking at Will, but she knew it would be rude not to acknowledge him. She squeezed her hands as she turned his way.

"Good morning, Mr. Rider," she said softly.

"Miss Sherwood." He touched his hat brim. "I'll be coming by for Lark after school. If you'd care for a lift back to your place . . ."

"No, thank you," she replied, alarmed at the thought of sitting next to him on the wagon seat. "I . . . I have errands to take care of in town."

"All right then." He tapped his hat again, seeming completely unaware of her discomfiture. "Good day."

"Good day, Mr. Rider."

She stood at the top of the steps and watched as he drove away, waiting until her pulse slowed to a more normal rhythm before she went inside to face her pupils for the first time.

Chad Turner looked up from the forge as Will walked into the smithy. "Be right with you, Will," he called as he placed the glowing iron onto the anvil and began molding it with a rounding hammer.

Will watched as Chad thick muscles bulging beneath his sweat-soaked shirt—pounded the horseshoe with a steady cadence, the sound ringing loudly in the low-roofed enclosure attached to the livery stable. Will had met a lot of blacksmiths during his lifetime—he'd pounded his share of iron himself—but he'd never known any better than Chad Turner.

When he was finished, Chad dropped the horseshoe into a bucket of water to the accompaniment of a long hiss and rising steam. He wiped his blackened hands on his heavy leather apron as he turned away from the anvil. Then, with a quick swipe of his fingers, he brushed his dark hair off his forehead.

"What brings you to town, Will?"

"School started today."

Chad raised an eyebrow. "School?"

"I'm surprised no one's told you the news. My niece is living with me now. She arrived about three weeks ago." Will pushed his hat back from his forehead. "How was San Francisco?"

"Big. Too many folks all in one place. I remembered in a hurry why I decided to put down roots in Homestead."

"And your sister?"

Chad grinned. "Prettiest bride I ever did see. Makes a man realize he wouldn't mind a wife and family of his own if he could just find a girl like Susan."

Will thought of Addie with her flaming hair and unusual green eyes. He wondered what it would have been like, having her for a wife. Then he pictured the look on her face just before she'd refused his proposal. It made him feel uncomfortable. He closed his mind against the memory.

"I've got a little gelding that's overreaching," he said, returning his attention to the business that had brought him to the smithy. "I was hoping Lark—my niece—could use him to ride into school. Thought if you've got the time, I'd bring him in later this week, see what you can do to correct the problem."

"Sure. I'd be glad to have a look at him. Why not bring him in on Friday? I'm behind on a few things right now, after being gone for so long, but I ought to be caught up by then."

"I'll do that." Will tugged his hat lower on his forehead. "See you Friday."

With a brief nod, Chad turned back to his forge. He pumped the billows a few times to stoke the hot coals, then reached for the tongs and another horseshoe. By the time Will reached his wagon, he could hear the steady ringing of the hammer once again.

During the drive back to the ranch, Will thought about Chad's comment about a man not minding having a wife and children if he could just find the right woman to marry. He supposed that might be true. There probably were men cut out for marriage. Reluctantly, he even admitted all women weren't like his mother or Justine.

There were the Barbers, for instance. Stanley and Emma seemed happy enough. Of course, he wouldn't care to live with Emma. She was too busy organizing everything and everyone, but her heart was in the right place. She wouldn't ever do anything to hurt anyone intentionally. She didn't have a mean or selfish bone in her body.

Then there were the McLeods. They'd been married over thirty years, and they seemed happy, too. There were times when Will had seen Hank looking at Doris in a special way that made Will feel just a bit envious. He wondered if there was a secret to that kind of happiness.

His own parents certainly hadn't known the secret if there was one. His mother had taken great pleasure from making those around her miserable. He remembered how beautiful she'd been, but there'd been no beauty in her heart. Her tongue had been sharp, always ready to belittle others. According to Martha Rider, her husband had never lived up to his potential, her son had been destined to be a ne'er-do-well, and her daughter had been far too plain to ever land a husband of good breeding and standing in society.

Will's memories of his father were mere shadows in comparison, perhaps because Phillip Rider had shut himself away from all members of his family rather than deal with his wife. At one time, so Will had been told, Phillip had been a popular man about town. Not wealthy, but full of the promise of success to come, he had wooed and won the former Martha Vanderhoff of Chicago, Illinois, and they had been married with a great deal of pomp and circumstance—the only way Martha did anything. Their wedding day had been the last truly happy day of Phillip's life.

Will remembered the bitter, cruel things his mother had said when her husband died, acting as if Phillip had left her a widow intentionally.

Perhaps, Will thought sadly, he had. Death had been one way to escape. Will had chosen another. Immediately after the funeral, he'd thrown a few things together and left his mother's house for good.

He shook his head, chasing the memories back to some forgotten corner of his mind. He didn't like thinking about his childhood or his parents, any more than he liked thinking about marriage.

Marriage . . . It had been a stupid notion, the idea of taking Addie Sherwood for a wife just to give Lark a mother. He thought of the stubborn tilt of Addie's chin and the way she'd challenged him to keep his word the first time they'd met. He also remembered the cool look in her eyes this morning. For all he knew, she could have a tongue sharper than Martha Rider ever dreamed of having. She was probably a real shrew.

Yep, he was lucky she'd turned him down.

Addie closed the book and glanced up at the faces of her students. "I believe that's enough for today. Class is dismissed."

A general commotion ensued as feet hit the floor, friends called to friends, and the children all dashed for freedom. Within moments, the room was empty.

Addie leaned forward, resting her forehead on the backs of her hands that were crossed atop the desk. She let out a lengthy sigh of relief. She'd done it. She had successfully completed her first day as a teacher. All the lessons she'd learned from her father and at the normal school so long ago hadn't been for naught.

Drawing in another deep breath, she straightened. She hadn't time to dawdle. There were still things to do before she returned to her little cabin on Pony Creek.

Quickly, she cleaned the blackboards, then made sure all else was in order. Finally, she picked up her books and her handbag, put on her bonnet, and headed for the door. She found Lark sitting alone on the steps. The rest of the children had all scattered for their homes.

"Your uncle isn't here yet?" Addie asked as she closed the door behind her and locked it.

"No." Lark glanced up, her pretty face pinched with worry. "Do you think something's happened to him? He said he'd be here. Maybe he's had an accident."

Addie settled onto the step beside Lark. "I'm sure nothing has happened to him. He's just running a bit late." She reached out, smoothing a dark lock of hair behind Lark's ear. "Did you enjoy the first day of school?"

The girl nodded.

"You read well for your age. Where did you go to school?"

"At the orphanage. But Miss Calhoun wasn't anything like you. She was old . . ." She dropped her gaze to her hands. Her voice lowered. "She was mean and ugly, too."

Addie supposed she should chide the child for speaking unkindly of another, but she didn't.

"It was Mama who taught me to read," Lark added in a whisper.

"Would you like to tell me about your mother?"

Lark glanced up, eyes swimming with tears. "Mama was pretty. She had golden hair, but her eyes were brown like mine. Pa always said

Mama looked like an angel." Two tears trailed down her cheeks. "Do you think she's an angel now, Miss Sherwood?"

Addie placed her arm around the girl and drew her close against her. "I'm sure she is, Lark. And your father, too."

"Mrs. Jones said . . ." She sniffed. "Mrs. Jones said God wouldn't let a woman who'd marry a . . . a heathen into heaven. She said all Indians are godless savages who will burn in . . . in hell."

Addie wished she could tell this Mrs. Jones what she thought of a woman who would say such a thing to a child. It was the most unchristian thing she'd ever heard. "Oh, Lark, that isn't true." She cupped Lark's chin with her hand, forcing her to look up. "God doesn't pay any heed to the color of a person's skin. It's what's in your heart that matters to Him. I'm sure your parents are together in heaven, and I'm certain they're glad you're living with your Uncle Will."

Lark sniffed again. "Really, Miss Sherwood?"

"Really."

A moment of silence followed, then Lark said, "I don't think Uncle Will is glad I'm living with him."

Addie's arm tightened as she offered an encouraging smile. "You're wrong, Lark. Your uncle wants very much to do right by you." A wave of sadness washed over her. "You'd be surprised to what lengths he'll go to make sure you're happy."

The rattle of harness interrupted any further conversation, and they both looked up to see Will driving his team of horses toward them.

Relief filled Lark's eyes as she hopped to her feet. "He came."

"I told you he would." Addie rose from the step, too. The sight of Will caused her heart to race.

What would it have been like to awaken in this man's arms? If she'd agreed to his proposal, might they have shared more, given time? Might he have grown to care for her?

She hoped he was too far away to see the flush her thoughts brought to her cheeks.

"Go on now," she said, her hand against Lark's back. "I'll see you tomorrow."

Lark took a step down, then spun around and threw her arms around Addie's hips. She gave a quick squeeze. "Thanks, Miss Sherwood." She turned and raced down the steps to the wagon.

Will leaned over and pulled her up onto the seat beside him. Lark gave him just the shadow of a smile, then waved at Addie. Will glanced her way, too, touched his hat with his index finger, and turned his team toward home.

Addie squelched the sudden loneliness that surrounded her. She had no call to feel lonely. She had a busy, full life, what with teaching and all. She was important to the children of this valley. She had much she could share with them.

Holding herself erect, she descended the church steps and headed east toward the center of town.

Chad lowered the horse's leg to the ground, then wiped the sweat from his brow with his forearm. "Just one more, girl, and we'll be finished," he said to the mare, giving her a friendly pat on the rump.

He walked behind her and bent over to lift a rear leg, cradling it with his thigh. He placed the shoe against the hoof, checking for size and shape. Almost perfect. He lowered the mare's leg again.

"Hello?" a feminine voice called from inside the livery. "Is anyone here?"

Chad straightened. "I'm out back," he called in response. "Be right with you." Setting aside the horseshoe, he strode toward the rear door of the barn.

The woman was standing at the front of the livery stable, sunlight pouring in behind her, casting her in a silhouette. Chad knew right away she was a stranger to him. He guessed she was the new schoolmarm. Emma Barber had told him the teacher was a tall woman.

"Mr. Turner?"

"That's me." He stopped not far from her, still squinting his eyes against the light at her back.

"I'm Addie Sherwood." She had a pleasant voice.

"I guessed you might be." He rubbed his hands against his leather apron. He started to offer his right hand, then pulled it back before she could take it and soil her gloves. "Sorry. Welcome to Homestead."

"Thank you."

Chad could make out her face now. He liked what he saw. It wasn't a beautiful face, but there was something very appealing about it. Warm, he thought. That was it. It was a warm face. The sort a man would enjoy looking at on a daily basis.

The thought made him want to smile. Single women were in short supply in these parts, and he hadn't been fooling when he'd told Will that his sister's wedding had set him thinking about taking a wife. He had a real hankering to find himself a woman to love. When he'd heard the schoolteacher had turned out to be female, he'd been curious. Now, he was downright pleased.

"You've probably heard I'm living in Mr. Rider's old cabin on Pony Creek. I'm going to want another means of transportation besides my feet to get me to and fro." She smiled. It was a nice smile. "Mrs. Barber told me you sometimes have horses for sale. I'm looking for a good, sound, well-behaved animal. And I'll need a buggy, too. Emma said you could build me a buggy for a better price than she could order one in."

He knew his face must be streaked with sweat and blackened by his work at the forge, just as his forearms, revealed by his rolled-up sleeves, were streaked and blackened. Most of the time, his appearance didn't bother him while he was working, but at the moment, he wished he'd had a chance to clean up.

"Are you able to help me, Mr. Turner? With the horse and buggy?"

He made himself quit staring at her. "The buggy's no problem, but I don't have a single horse for sale right now. Sold my last one just before I went down to San Francisco."

"Oh." Her mouth turned down in disappointment.

Damn! "To tell you the truth, the place to buy a horse is out at the Rocking R. Will Rider has the best stock in the territory. Just about anybody can tell you that."

"Mr. Rider . . . I see. Well, I suppose I should talk to him then. What about the buggy? Nothing fancy, mind you. Just whatever's necessary. I don't have unlimited funds." She named an amount, her expression hopeful.

He'd consider doing it for nothing if he thought it might make her look at him in a favorable light. "That's agreeable to me. I'll see to it right away. Should have it for you by the end of next week."

"Thank you, Mr. Turner."

"Glad to help, Miss Sherwood."

She turned to leave.

"Miss Sherwood?" He stepped forward.

She stopped and looked back at him. She had the prettiest green eyes he'd ever seen.

"If you'd care for some advice, I'd be glad to take you out to look over Will's stock, pick out a good buggy horse for you. I'm a pretty fair judge of horseflesh." Of course, so was Will Rider, but Chad didn't feel he had to tell her so.

"That's very kind of you, Mr. Turner."

"If you don't mind waiting, I could hook up the team and drive you out there now, if you'd like."

Her eyes widened slightly. "I wouldn't want to put you out."

"No bother. I just finished shoein' my last horse for the day," he lied. Luckily, Mr. Potter wouldn't be in for his mare until morning. "Besides, I promised Will I'd look at a horse of his that needs some corrective shoein'. I'd be going out there anyway."

"Well . . ." She pressed her lips together in thought, then said, "I *was* hoping to get a horse soon. I suppose if it's no bother . . ."

Chad grinned. "You wait here. I'll be ready in a jiffy."

Chapter Nine

Will stopped the horses by the barn but didn't move to get down. All the way home he'd been thinking about the way Lark had turned and hugged Addie Sherwood. It wasn't easy to admit, but he knew he would like it if the girl did the same to him.

"Lark . . ." He glanced to where she was sitting beside him.

She looked up but didn't reply.

He cleared his throat. "I was wondering . . . Are you unhappy living with me?"

Her eyes widened, and she shook her head.

"You're sure? It seems . . ."

"I'm sure, Uncle Will. Please! Don't send me back to the orphanage." The words seemed to tumble out of her. "I'll be good. I won't be any trouble. I promise. You don't need to buy me any more clothes. I got plenty. And I'll work hard. Really I will. Just don't send me back." Her eyes filled with tears, and she quickly looked away.

"Hey, wait a minute." He took hold of her chin, forcing her to meet his gaze. "I wouldn't ever think of sendin' you back to that orphanage. Is that what's been bothering you?"

Her quivering chin was her only reply.

She reminded him of Patricia when she'd found out he was going away after their father's funeral. She'd looked at him with the same wide eyes, trying—just like her daughter was now—to be brave but unable to hide how afraid and lonely she was. He'd ruffled her hair and told her he'd see her again one day. He never had.

Guilt-ridden, he pulled his sister's child onto his lap and hugged her against his chest. He realized—belatedly—that it was the first time he'd held her, probably the first time he'd shown her any real affection since the day she'd arrived. But then, he'd never been much one for showing his feelings. No one in the Rider family had been—except maybe Patricia.

Suddenly, a lot of things seemed clear to him that he hadn't understood before. "Listen, Lark. I'm not sending you away. We're together, you and me. Understand?"

"You could die, too," she whispered. "Like my mother and father."

"I guess any of us could die. That's just the way things are in this world. But we can't go around thinking about dyin' or losin' those we love. We can't go around bein' scared all the time." He felt an unfamiliar tightness in his heart. "We're family. We've got to stick together."

She pressed her face against his chest. "Tht wat mmm erddd set." Lark's voice was muffled by his shirt.

"What?"

She tipped her head back, a tremulous smile on her lips. "That's what Miss Sherwood said. She said you'd do a lot just to make sure I was happy."

He winced. He knew what Miss Sherwood had been referring to, and he preferred not to think about it.

"Miss Sherwood's just about the nicest person I've ever met," Lark said softly. "Don't you think so?"

He smoothed her dark hair back from her face. "Yeah. Sure I do." But talking about the teacher made him feel uncomfortable, and he quickly changed the subject. "Come on with me. I want to show you something."

Holding on to her arms, Will lowered Lark over the side of the wagon until her feet touched the ground, then he jumped down from the wagon seat, took hold of her hand, and led her toward the barn.

Inside, it smelled of hay and horses and manure. Light poured in through open doors at both ends of the spacious building, making dust particles floating in the air glimmer like miniature stars. Several horses thrust their heads over the gates of their stalls. Pal nickered as Will and Lark approached.

"Hey, fella," Will said as he stroked the buckskin's muzzle. Then he moved to the next stall over. "What do you think of this little guy, Lark?"

His niece looked through the slats of wood at the bay gelding. He was a small horse, just under fourteen hands, but he was well-muscled with good conformation.

"Oh, I like him," Lark whispered.

"Good. He's yours. Can you ride?"

"He's mine?" She looked up at him, then back at the horse. "He's really mine?"

"Yep." Will grinned as he watched Lark climb up the fence to look over the top railing.

Maybe raising a kid wasn't going to be so hard after all. She didn't really need a mother, and Will hadn't ever needed a wife. He and Lark were going to do just fine, the two of them alone.

"Can you ride?" he asked again.

"A little. Pa was teaching me how before he took sick." Her smile vanished, and he knew she was thinking again about her parents' deaths.

"Then there won't be much I have to tell you," he continued, hoping to distract her. "First, you've got to learn how to take care of him. The most important thing a man owns is his horse—next to his saddle, that is. So it's up to you to make sure he stays fed and watered. Do you think you can do that?"

"Yes."

"Good. Now, what are you going to call him?"

Her brows drew together thoughtfully. "I don't know."

He took hold of her waist and lifted her down from the stall fence. "Well, you think about it. Right now we need to get supper started. It's Frosty's night off," he added, referring to the Rocking R cook.

Side by side, they headed toward the barn door. Just before they reached it, Lark said, "Uncle Will? Thanks for not sending me back to the orphanage."

"Don't mention it." There was an odd lump in his throat.

Seconds after they had stepped outside, Lark pointed to the east. "Look! It's Miss Sherwood."

Will's gaze followed the direction of her finger. It was Addie, all right. No one else had hair that color. It was easy to spot, even with most of it hidden under a straw bonnet. He also recognized her straight posture and the way her hands were folded in her lap. She always sat like that, whether in a wagon or on a moss-covered rock or in a church pew.

His gaze shifted to the driver of the wagon. He felt a jolt of surprise when he recognized Chad. What was he doing with Addie?

"Afternoon, Will," Chad called as the wagon pulled into the yard.

So this was why she'd turned down his offer of a ride back from town.

"We need your help," the blacksmith said.

We? Will raised an eyebrow.

"Miss Sherwood's ordered a buggy made, and now she needs a reliable horse. I told her you had the best stock in the territory."

Will turned his eyes on Addie. "I think I've got a few that might suit your purpose." He reached to help her from the wagon.

She glanced at his proffered hand, then lifted her gaze to meet his. He felt a now-familiar twinge of guilt for the way he'd proposed to her. He would have to be a cold-hearted son of a gun not to realize his proposal had been a bit insensitive. Of course, he hadn't understood it at the time. He'd been too busy trying to buck up his courage to ask her to marry him when it was the last thing he'd really wanted himself. But later, when he'd thought about it, he'd known he'd gone about things all wrong. It was better for everyone that she'd had the good sense to turn him down, but he'd still like to mend a few fences, see if they couldn't at least be friends. After all, she was Lark's teacher. It wouldn't do for the two of them to be on the outs.

"Let me show you what I've got," he said, still holding out his hand.

Finally, she took hold of it and stepped down from the wagon. The instant her feet touched the ground, she pulled her fingers free of his. She stood stiffly before him, chin high, back straight. Only when Lark moved to stand beside her did she reveal any trace of a smile.

"We didn't know you were coming to look at horses, Miss Sherwood," the girl said.

"Neither did I." Addie glanced toward Chad. "Mr. Turner suggested it."

For some reason, Will felt like grinding his teeth. "I didn't know you two had met."

"We hadn't 'til this afternoon," Chad replied as he walked around the back of the wagon. "Miss Sherwood came in to buy a horse and buggy, and I offered to bring her out. Thought I could have a look at that gelding you said was overreaching while I'm here. Save you a trip into town Friday."

Will glared at the other man from beneath the brim of his hat, his eyes narrowed. "I thought you were behind on your work after your trip to Frisco."

The blacksmith wasn't about to be baited. He merely grinned. "I am." He motioned toward the barn. "Well, what have you got to show the lady? Do you have any good buggy horses or not?"

Still feeling unreasonably grumpy, Will replied, "Over here," then led the way.

Behind him, he heard Lark say, "Uncle Will just gave me my very own horse. Do you want to see him, Miss Sherwood?"

"I'd love to," Addie replied softly.

Addie wished she hadn't come. She was never going to feel comfortable around Will Rider again. Every time she was with him, she would relive the humiliation of his proposal. Foolish, foolish woman—to have allowed herself to think he might be attracted to her. She knew such things didn't happen to women like her.

She wished Chad hadn't suggested coming here. She wished she'd looked at buggy horses anywhere else. She wished they could leave now.

Addie stared over the top rail of the corral as Will brought out another horse from the barn, this one a flaxen-maned mare. She was a showy animal, neck arched, tail held high, hooves prancing. Her sorrel coat gleamed with reddish highlights, and her golden mane and tail were long and thick.

Addie immediately forgot about going elsewhere to buy a horse. She might not know much about the noble animals, but she knew she'd never seen a prettier horse than this. Common sense told her she couldn't afford the mare. This animal had to be more costly than the previous three Will had shown them put together.

Chad pushed off from the corral fence and walked over to the mare. He exchanged a few words with Will, then proceeded to pick up the horse's legs one at a time and check them over, just as he'd done with the others. When he was finished, he stepped back and watched as Will lunged the mare on the end of a rope.

"Isn't she pretty?" Lark asked, echoing Addie's thoughts.

"Yes," she answered breathlessly. "She's beautiful."

Her gaze shifted to the man at the opposite end of the rope. He was turning slowly in the center of the corral, guiding the horse with low voice commands. She could see the muscles flex in his forearms, the skin bronzed by the sun. She sensed the controlled strength in the breadth of his shoulders. His eyes were hidden in the shadow of his hat brim, but somehow she knew he watched the animal with a kind of pride.

He's beautiful, too.

"Whoa." Will's command brought the mare to an immediate halt.

Addie blushed, feeling like he'd been commanding her thoughts to stop.

"She's good and sound," Chad said as he walked toward her. "I doubt you'd find any better. Will says she's broke both to harness and the saddle."

Addie glanced again at the mare as Will led her over to the fence. She knew it was terribly foolish to want the horse so badly, but she couldn't help herself.

She lifted her chin and tried not to let her yearning show on her face. "How much do you want for her, Mr. Rider?"

He stared directly into her eyes for what seemed a very long time. It took all her willpower not to squirm beneath his gaze.

Finally, he bumped his hat with his knuckles, pushing it up on his forehead. "I'll sell her to you for fifty dollars."

"Fifty dollars?" It was far less than she'd expected but more than she'd meant to spend.

"Fifty?" Chad echoed. The expression on his face confirmed to Addie that the price was surprisingly low.

"Sorry. Can't take less. You think on it." Will turned away and led the mare back into the dark recesses of the barn.

Chad shot a quick glance in Addie's direction, then looked toward the barn again. "Well, I'll be . . ." he muttered.

Addie scarcely heard him. Fifty dollars. It was a lot of money. She probably could find another horse for twenty-five dollars, perhaps even less. Only she wanted this one.

Fifty dollars. She had enough money, but after she paid for the buggy, it would take nearly all of her remaining savings to pay for the mare. She knew she could live on her teacher's salary, as long as there weren't any unexpected expenses, but it was frightening not to have something to fall back on. There was still a chance the school board would decide to let her go.

If she was sensible, she would buy the gray mare Will had shown her first. The gray was much more appropriate for a spinster schoolmarm. Plain, solid, dependable, sensible—just the way she'd always been.

Will reappeared in the barn doorway and started toward her.

"I've made up my mind, Mr. Rider," she said impulsively, before common sense could reassert itself. "I'll take the mare."

Will knew he could have gotten four, maybe six times the amount for that mare. He didn't know what had possessed him to offer her to Addie Sherwood for a mere fifty dollars.

Maybe Addie's eyes had something to do with it, he thought as he looked down at her. He'd seen the longing in them when he'd led the mare out of the barn. He would have seen it if he'd been standing a hundred feet away.

He stuck his hand out toward her. "You've got yourself a deal, Miss Sherwood."

She hesitated a moment before taking hold of it and sealing the bargain with a firm shake.

"When do you want her?" he asked.

A small frown puckered her forehead. "I'll need to do some work on the pen behind the cabin. I hadn't thought to find a horse so quickly. I only decided to get one this morning. Would Saturday be all right?"

"I'll be glad to help you with any repairs," Chad offered quickly—before Will had a chance to do the same.

Will couldn't remember the last time a man had irritated him as much as Chad Turner had today. "Fine. I'll plan on bringing the mare over to your place Saturday afternoon."

Minutes later, as he watched Chad and Addie driving away, he wondered again about what had gotten into him. He'd always been a shrewd horse trader. He'd never made such a poor deal in his life as this one.

It just wasn't like him.

Chapter Ten

Rose closed the outhouse door and started toward the group of boys playing baseball in the field behind the church. They wouldn't let her join in. She knew it without asking. Baseball was for boys, they would say. Still, she thought she'd give it a try.

Then she saw Lark sitting all alone in the shade of the aspens and birch trees. Her brother didn't like Lark just because her pa was part Indian. Mark said Rose couldn't play with her on account of it. Rose didn't know what difference it should make. She thought Lark was nice.

She veered off her original path.

"Hi," she said as she sank down in the wild grass.

"Hello." Lark looked at her shyly.

"I'm sorry about what my brother said to you. At the church picnic, I mean."

Lark glanced down at the ground where she was slowly pulling strands of grass from the soil. "It's all right."

"You can't pay him no mind. He's mean to everybody." Just like their pa, she thought. "You like it here in Homestead?"

"Yes."

"I was born in Minnesota, but I don't remember ever livin' there. We come here when I was five. Where're you from?"

"Montana." Lark looked up again. "My father taught English on the reservation. He said education was the only way things would ever change for his people."

"He was a teacher?" Rose pictured a man standing up at the front of the classroom and shivered. She didn't think she would like that much. "I'm glad Miss Sherwood came to Homestead. She's real nice."

Lark smiled. "I know." Suddenly, her smile vanished and she shrank back toward the trees.

That was the only warning Rose had before she was yanked up from the ground by one braid.

"Thought I told you to stay away from the breed," Mark said, giving her hair another harsh jerk.

"Let go of me!" Rose shouted at him. "You let me go *now!*"

She slapped at his arm, but it was like butterfly wings beating against a glass jar. Her brother laughed as he held her at arm's length. She quieted, still glaring at him. He relaxed for just a moment.

A moment was all she needed.

Rose kicked out, connecting her shoe with his shin even harder than she'd expected.

"You little she-bitch!"

She put up her arms, but not in time. The back of his hand hit her jaw and sent her flying back against a tree. Her jaw hurt, her back hurt, even her toe hurt, but she didn't care. She came flying back, her head down, a cry of rage on her lips. She hit him in the belly with the top of her head and was satisfied to hear the *whoof* of air rush out of him.

The satisfaction didn't last long. For the second time, he grabbed her by the hair, holding her up on her tiptoes just long enough for him to slap her again.

Rose shrieked her fury, her arms flailing at him. It was pointless. She knew it was pointless. It was always like this. He wouldn't stop until he felt like it, and nothing she did could hurt him enough to make him stop.

He yanked on her hair, laughing now.

"Mark Townsend, you stop that this instant!"

Mark stilled, then turned his head. Rose followed the motion.

Miss Sherwood stood not more than ten feet away, her eyes sparking with anger, the rest of the children gathered behind her. "Let your sister go, I said." Her voice was soft now but still forceful.

Mark released Rose's hair, then dropped his hands to her shoulders. He glared into her eyes. "I'll finish with you later, brat." He gave her a little shove, making her stumble backward.

"Come inside with me, Mark," Miss Sherwood said sternly. "We're going to have a talk."

Her brother took a step toward the teacher, his fists clenched. Miss Sherwood didn't budge an inch. Fear welled up in Rose's chest. What if he hit her like Pa hit Ma? What if he hurt her so bad she decided to leave Homestead? Then they wouldn't have school anymore. Then she'd be home again all day. Then she wouldn't have a place to go to get away. Rose didn't want that to happen. She liked school. Miss Sherwood didn't shrink around like Ma, and it was fun to play with the other children for a change.

She couldn't let Mark hurt her. She couldn't let Miss Sherwood leave Homestead.

Rose hurried forward. "I . . . I'm okay, Miss Sherwood," she said quickly.

The teacher looked down at her a moment, her gaze softening. She cupped Rose's chin with her fingertips. "Are you certain?"

Rose nodded.

Miss Sherwood looked at Mark again. "Inside, young man."

"No."

Don't let him hit her. Oh, please God, don't let him hit her.

"I will not tolerate this sort of behavior, Mark Townsend. Now come inside with me."

"No."

"Then I shall be forced to discuss the matter with your parents."

Mark sneered at her. "My pa don't care what you've got to say."

She acted as if he hadn't spoken. "Please go home and tell them to expect me at the close of school." Her chin lifted and her gaze never wavered. "You are dismissed." She reached for Rose's hand, then turned her back on Mark. "Recess is over, children. Return to the classroom." She looked toward the grove of trees and held out her other hand. "Come along, Lark."

Rose knew she was going to pay for this later. Mark wasn't going to forget it. But for right now, she thought she'd just savor the way the teacher had stood up to him.

Two hours later, when Addie dismissed the children for the day, she was still quivering inside over the incident with Rose and her brother. She didn't know if she'd ever been as frightened as the moment he'd stepped forward, as if to strike her.

Her third day of school, and she'd already been defied by one of her students. It wasn't a very auspicious beginning. A *male* teacher would probably have handled it much differently. That's what her detractors would say.

She wondered what her father would have done.

Matthew Sherwood had been a gentle man, soft-spoken, thoughtful. He would have handled the Townsend boy with great wisdom, convinced him of the error of his ways, made him see that violence was never the answer. In no time at all, he would have made a fine scholar out of a coarse boy who used his fists instead of his brains.

"Oh, Papa, I wish I could ask you what to do."

She took a deep breath. She hadn't the time to sit here and wonder what her papa or any other man would or wouldn't have done in the same situation. *She* was the teacher, and *she* had done what she thought necessary. Now she would have to speak with the Townsends about their son.

Gathering up her things, she left the church, locking the door behind her as she went. With purposeful steps, she headed for the Townsend Rooming House.

Her knock on the front door was answered almost immediately by the mouse-like woman she knew to be Virginia Townsend. Virginia's chin was tucked in toward her chest, and she held her head at an odd angle.

"Miss Sherwood . . . I wasn't expectin' . . . that is, what can I do for you?"

Addie waited for the door to open wider so she could step inside, but it didn't happen. Finally, she said, "I'm sure you're in the middle of preparing your supper, but I need to speak to you about your son. Is your husband home by any chance?"

"Oh, no." Her eyes darted nervously from the floor to Addie and back again. "He's still at the mill. He won't be home for some time."

"Well, I suppose I can tell you, and you can inform Mr. Townsend."

"Mark's been causin' trouble, hasn't he?" Virginia's hands twisted before her.

"I'm afraid so. I was forced to send him home from school this afternoon. He was fighting with his sister." Addie inhaled. "Actually, he was beating her. I feared he would hurt her severely. When I demanded he stop and go inside, he refused to obey. I could not allow such defiance, Mrs. Townsend."

"Of course not." Virginia would not look Addie in the eyes. She glanced everywhere else but never directly at the teacher. "Mark is . . . he's a spirited boy . . . like his father. I'm sure he didn't mean to . . . I'm sure he wasn't trying to make trouble. It was probably Rose's fault. She . . . she probably provoked him."

"It was most certainly *not* Rose's fault." *He's just a bully,* Addie thought, but managed to keep her opinion to herself. "If Mark continues to be disorderly in school, Mrs. Townsend, I'll have no choice but to expel him. I must have his word he'll behave. Will you tell your husband that?"

"Yes . . . yes, I'll tell him." Virginia narrowed the opening in the door. "I'll tell him right after supper."

"Thank you."

The door closed.

Addie stood on the porch for a moment, contemplating the woman's odd behavior. It was almost as if she was afraid of Addie. She'd thought the woman a timid thing when they'd met at the church picnic, but the demeanor she'd just witnessed went beyond timid. Addie could almost taste the fear still lingering in the air.

She turned around—and gasped. She was standing almost nose to nose with Mark.

"You tryin' to cause me trouble, Miss Sherwood?"

She stepped back. "I beg your pardon."

"My pa don't need you comin' 'round here, sayin' bad things about me. If you don't want more trouble than you can handle, you keep away from my house."

She saw his fists clench and his biceps flex. She felt the force of his rage like a physical blow. Her mouth went dry, and her heart raced.

"You understand me, Miss Sherwood?"

A wagon clattered along the street, distracting him. Addie took that moment to step around the boy and walk swiftly away from the rooming house.

Instinctively, she headed toward the opposite end of town, knowing she wasn't ready to go home just yet. She didn't want to be alone. She felt badly in need of a friendly face, and Emma Barber had the friendliest face in all of Homestead, as far as Addie was concerned.

Her new friend was refilling a jar on the counter with peppermint sticks when Addie stepped inside the mercantile.

"Good gracious!" Emma exclaimed. "You're as white as a ghost. What on earth is the matter?" She hurried around the counter to take hold of Addie's arm.

"Nothing's wrong. I must have been walking a bit too fast. I'm just a little winded." She pulled her arm back, not wanting Emma to feel how it was shaking.

The older woman didn't look convinced. "Well, come on back to my kitchen and let me get you a cup of coffee. That'll brace you up."

Addie offered a weak smile. "Thank you. I'd like that." Her expression sobered quickly. "I shouldn't be taking you away from your work."

"Land sakes, don't apologize. I'm glad for an excuse to sit down for a minute or two."

While Addie sat in one of the chairs around the table, Emma took two cups from the cupboard and filled them with hot coffee before carrying them to the table. Then she opened the icebox and pulled out a small pitcher filled with cream.

"Help yourself," she said as she set the pitcher in front of Addie. She scooped a generous helping of sugar into her own cup and began to stir it with a spoon. "So tell me. How's your first week of school going?"

Addie's mouth tightened. She didn't want to lie, but she didn't feel like telling anyone about her encounter with Mark. She wanted to handle the matter herself as best she could. Besides, even though Emma wasn't one of them, Addie knew there were those who thought the school board should have sent her packing her first day in town. This sort of incident would be just what they needed to use against her.

"Anything I can help with?" Emma asked gently.

"No." She shook her head, staring all the while into her cup, as if searching for answers.

"Gettin' settled in a new place is never easy. I couldn't imagine what Stanley thought he was doing, movin' us all here before there was hardly a soul in the valley. I thought for sure he'd gone plum loco. I just knew we were going to lose every red cent we had." She sighed and took a long sip of coffee. "But I'm glad we stuck it out through the rough times. It's been worth it."

Addie glanced up. A whisper of a smile curved her mouth. "My father would have liked you, Emma. He always admired common sense."

Her comment obviously pleased Emma. The woman grinned. "Tell me about your father."

Tell her about Papa? How could Addie describe the most perfect man she'd ever known? Matthew Sherwood had been more than just her father. He'd been her teacher, her inspiration, her best friend.

"Papa was a professor at a private academy. He tutored his better students in our home as well." Addie's expression was wistful. She did so wish she was more like her father. "Papa always understood young people, and they respected him. He was such a gentle man, but very wise, and everyone—old and young—seemed to recognize that from the moment they first met him. I think sometimes I was jealous of how much time he gave to others."

"That's understandable."

"But Papa preferred to have just Mama and me with him in the evenings. He always said that was his favorite time of day, after his students left and he was alone with his girls." She shook her head, her smile completely gone now. "After Mama died, he didn't want to ever be alone. He wanted me always with him. His health was poor, and he couldn't teach any longer. I think he missed the inquisitive minds and the youthful ideas that had surrounded him for so many years."

"He sounds like a wonderful man."

"He was." Addie straightened in her chair and lifted her gaze to meet Emma's. "I wish he were here now. There are so many questions I'd like to ask him."

Emma leaned forward. "Maybe I could help."

Addie shook her head. "You know what I think he would tell me? I think he'd say I need to work things out for myself. And he'd be right, too." She laid her hand on top of Emma's. "But thanks for asking."

Emma placed her other hand atop Addie's. "Well, you just know you've got a friend if you ever need one."

Addie smiled, thoughts of Mark Townsend fading completely in the warmth of Emma Barber's kitchen.

* * *

"Something botherin' you, Lark?" Will asked, breaking the silence that had filled the room ever since he and his niece had sat down for supper.

She shook her head without looking up at him.

He felt like swearing. He'd thought they were over this. Things had been pretty good between them ever since they'd had that talk and he'd given her the little bay for her very own. She'd started opening up a bit to him. She'd even smiled now and then.

Okay, it had only been a couple of days, but he'd seen some important changes in those two days. He'd gained a lot of confidence in his ability to be a good uncle to Lark.

But tonight it seemed as though there'd been no change at all. They were right back where they'd started. Ever since she'd come home from school, she'd been silent and skittish.

Will set his fork on his plate. "I think you'd better tell me what's troublin' you." His tone brooked no argument.

This time, Lark looked up. Beneath the golden hue of her skin, she seemed oddly pale. "I . . . I'm worried about Rose."

"Rose?"

"She wants to be my friend."

He tried to think of who the little girl might be, but he had to admit he'd never paid much attention to the children of the valley. "What's got you worryin' about her?"

"Her brother. He was hitting her. He snuck up behind her at recess and pulled her up by her hair and started hitting her just because she was sitting with me. He told her to stay away from me because . . . because I'm a . . . breed."

Will's jaw tightened. Now he knew who she was talking about.

"Miss Sherwood made him stop." Her eyes widened, her voice dropped to a whisper. "And then I thought he was going to hit her."

He pictured the Townsend boy in his mind. Mark might still be young enough to attend school, but he was built like a full-grown man. Will remembered how Mark had dragged his little sister home from the church picnic.

The idea of that big lumphead threatening Addie was more disturbing than it should have been. From what he remembered of his own schooling, teachers didn't usually have trouble keeping order in a classroom. Not as long as they had a ruler or paddle handy.

"What did Miss Sherwood do?" he asked.

"She sent him home. She was real mad. I could tell."

Just as he'd thought. Addie knew how to handle the likes of Mark Townsend.

Lark dropped her gaze back to her untouched supper plate. "He scares me, Uncle Will."

Will forgot about the teacher as he stared at the top of his niece's head, but he didn't forget his anger at Mark. "Come here, Lark," he said gently.

She obeyed, skirting the table, her gaze still downcast. When she reached him, he pulled her onto his lap, then forced her chin up with an index finger.

"Look at me."

She did.

"There's plenty of ignorant people in this world. We're never going to be without them. The Townsend boy is one of them. Mark picks on those who are weaker than him, just so he can feel like a big man. Do you understand that?"

She nodded.

He drew in a deep breath, hoping he was saying the right things. "I never knew your father, and I never saw your mother after she was around your age. But I know if Patricia . . . if she . . ." The unfamiliar word seemed lodged in his throat, but he forced it out. "If she loved him, then he must have been a special sort of man. She had to . . . love him an awful lot to leave Chicago and go live with him on the reservation in Montana. She must have been a real strong woman, just like you're going to be."

Tears filled Lark's eyes, making them glimmer.

"And you've got no call to be ashamed because you've got Indian blood. It's no different than those who've got Irish blood or German blood or Swedish blood. It just makes your skin a different color is all. I'm not tellin' you you're not going to have trouble because of it. You are. There'll always be some, like the Townsend boy and that Mrs. Jones from the orphanage, who're going to look down their noses at you and try to make you feel inferior, but don't you let them do it. You hear me now?"

She sniffed and nodded.

"And don't you go being afraid of Mark, either. I won't let him hurt you."

"What about Rose?" she asked softly. "What if he hurts her? *Really* hurts her."

Will didn't know how to answer that question. He didn't have a right to interfere in another man's business. It was up to Glen Townsend to reprimand his son, and Will had a strong suspicion such a reprimand wouldn't be coming. He suspected Mark had learned his behavior from his own father. He doubted Glen would care if Mark slapped his sister around a little.

"I don't know," he answered honestly, "but I'll try to think of something. All right?"

Lark nodded. He could see the trust in her eyes, and it made him feel both proud and unsure. He wanted her to trust him, but what if he failed her? What if he couldn't do the things he'd promised to do?

No burden he'd carried before had ever seemed so heavy—or so worthwhile.

Chapter Eleven

Addie walked at a brisk pace on her way to school the next morning. Every so often, she caught a glimpse of the rooftops of the houses and businesses of Homestead, ribbons of smoke curling skyward, but between her cabin and town, there were no other farms or ranches. She never met anyone along the road at this time of day, and she'd found she enjoyed the solitude of her morning walks.

However, this morning her thoughts were somewhat less than pleasant. She'd been awake much of the night, trying to decide what to do about Mark. She still wasn't certain she'd done the right thing in sending him home, then attempting to speak with his parents. She knew the boy's father didn't approve of her as a teacher. She suspected that he didn't approve of schooling in general. Maybe all she'd accomplished yesterday was ending the boy's education—what there'd been of it. She'd already seen how he struggled with *McGuffey's Eclectic Third Reader.* He should have been far beyond that book. He should have been tackling much more difficult subjects. After all, he was fourteen years old already. There were many teachers in this country who were only two or three years older than Mark.

If Addie could just make him want to learn . . .

As she'd done so often since leaving Connecticut, she again questioned her qualifications as a teacher. What had ever possessed her to think she could do what her father had done? She was no match for Matthew Sherwood's brilliance as an educator. She couldn't even fill his shadow.

Before depression could get a solid grip on her mood, she thought about her other pupils, the ones who were eager to learn, the ones who came to class every day with wide eyes and thirsty minds. There weren't many of them, but there were enough. She would concentrate on them. She was going to follow Emma's advice and stick it out through the rough times.

By the time the church came into view, Addie had managed to bolster her self-confidence enough to make her look forward to greeting her students for the day. What she didn't expect was to find Mark waiting for her on the church steps.

He was lounging against the railing, his left foot resting one step above the right. He didn't straighten when he saw her nor indicate that he meant to move out of her way.

Addie stopped at the bottom of the stairs. "Good morning, Mark." She waited, her heart thumping in her chest, for him to say something.

He didn't try to disguise his dislike for her. She could see it in his dark eyes, the set of his mouth, and his insolent posture, not to mention his tone of voice. "My pa says as long as he's got to pay for Homestead to have a school, I've got to attend. So here I am."

"Does that mean you intend to obey the rules of this school? And me?" She kept her voice steady and didn't allow her gaze to waver from his. "I'll not tolerate fighting in the schoolyard."

He shrugged. "I guess that's what it means."

"Then you'll be welcome back in class." She started up the stairs toward the front door.

Mark straightened abruptly, blocking her way. She glanced up to meet his gaze and felt a shiver of fear streak through her. There was a look of mocking laughter in his eyes that made her think of the way a cat toyed with a mouse. She knew he was issuing a silent threat of some sort. She hated herself for feeling intimidated by it. She shouldn't feel this way. She was the adult here. At twenty-seven, she was practically old enough to be his mother.

"You're in my way, Mark," she said evenly, proud that her voice didn't reveal the uncertainty she felt.

"Oh . . . I guess I am, aren't I?" He stepped back and let her pass.

She could feel his eyes on her back as she placed the key in the lock and fumbled to open the door.

Chad whistled as he loaded cut lumber from the sawmill onto the bed of his wagon. He'd been waiting three days for the chance to go out to Addie Sherwood's place to work on the corral. Now that he'd caught up on his backlog of work, he could spare a few hours to do a neighbor a favor, just as he'd told her he would.

He grinned as he checked his supplies—hammer, saw, plenty of nails, shovel. He knew he wasn't simply helping out a neighbor. He was doing this because he wanted Addie to think of him as more than just Homestead's blacksmith. He was doing this so she'd see him as a possible suitor.

Of course, he wasn't the only man in the valley who'd taken notice of the new schoolmarm. Will Rider had noticed her, too, and he certainly had a lot more to offer a woman than Chad did. Will owned a big spread with plenty of cattle and horses grazing on it. He had that new two-story house with plenty of modern conveniences, like a water pump right in the kitchen and a big stove, brought all the way from back East. Those had been Rick Charles's ideas, according to Will, but they'd be nice incentives when a man went looking for a bride. Maybe that's what Rick had been thinking when he built the new ranch house. Maybe he'd planned on finding Will a wife, whether Will wanted one or not.

Well, Chad didn't intend to let Mr. Rider have a chance to convince Addie that he had more to offer than the town blacksmith. The livery and smithy might not be making a lot of money just yet—and maybe Chad wasn't ever going to be rich—but he was making enough to support a wife. Besides, he thought with another grin, Will wasn't nearly as friendly as he was. Anyone in town would say so.

He heard the sounds of children and turned to gaze down the street toward the church. School was just letting out. Perfect timing.

He stepped into his office located near the front of the livery. Opening a desk drawer, he pulled out a small, chipped mirror and checked his reflection. He rubbed his fingers over his cheeks, still mostly smooth from his morning shave. Then he ran a comb through his thick, mahogany-brown hair. Satisfied that he looked fair enough, he returned to his wagon, vaulted up onto the seat, and turned his team toward the west end of town.

A few children were still lingering near the church, but most had disappeared by this time. He passed Mark Townsend just as the boy reached the rooming house. Mark glanced up, and their gazes met briefly. Chad nodded a greeting but didn't bother to speak.

When Chad had first come to Homestead, he'd roomed with the Townsends. He'd stayed only until the livery was built.

Then he'd moved into the room that was now his office until he could build a house of his own upstream from the sawmill on the banks of Pony Creek. He hadn't wanted to stay under the same roof as Glen Townsend any longer than necessary. The man drank too much for Chad's liking, not to mention the cold-hearted way he treated his wife, ordering her about as if she were his servant, never sparing a kind word or a gentle touch.

It sure wasn't how Chad would treat a wife if he had one—*when* he had one.

Just as that thought played through his head, he saw Addie step out of the church and turn to lock the door. She was dressed simply in a white blouse and green skirt, and her hair was hidden beneath a matching green calico bonnet.

He slapped the reins against the broad backs of the horses, causing them to break into a trot. He managed to arrive at the church just as Addie reached the bottom of the steps.

"Whoa," he called as he reined in the team. He flashed Addie what he knew to be a charming smile. "Afternoon, Miss Sherwood."

She returned the greeting. "Good afternoon, Mr. Turner."

"I was just on my way out to your place."

"Really?"

He jerked his head toward the lumber in the back of the wagon. "Thought I'd better take care of that corral and lean-to, like I promised, before Will brings over that horse you bought. Wouldn't do to let a sharp little filly like her get loose." He hopped down from the wagon and motioned toward the seat. "You're welcome to ride with me, if you'd like."

Addie was no stranger to the way gossip worked. She'd already been seen riding with Will one Sunday, and just over a week later, she'd gone with Chad out to the Rocking R. If this kept up, before she knew it she would find herself with a reputation undesirable for a schoolteacher. She might even be suspected of being a *femme fatale,* a regular scarlet woman.

She couldn't help her wry smile. It was such a ludicrous thought. No one in their right mind could ever think such a thing about her. She wasn't the sort to have one beau, let alone two. Certainly no man would ever be swept away in a fit of passion for her, so there was no danger of her falling into temptation and risking her reputation in that regard.

"I take it that means you accept," Chad said as he held out his hand.

She realized she was still smiling. "I guess so," she replied and stepped toward the wagon.

Addie enjoyed the ride out to her place. As she'd discovered the first time they were together, Chad Turner was friendly and talkative. He chatted comfortably all the way out from town, offering information before she could ask for it, answering any question she did have a chance to pose. She envied the ease with which he talked about himself, envied his natural confidence. She wondered what it would be like to be so sure of oneself.

"My sister, she really likes the city, but I like small towns," Chad informed her. "People are friendlier in a place like Homestead, more willing to lend a hand when a neighbor needs help. It's a whole sight easier to make friends here than in the city, too. Look at you and me. Only known each other a few days, but already we're friends, I'd say. You sure wouldn't find nobody in Frisco goin' out of his way to . . ."

She looked at him as he talked. Chad was a good-looking man, about her own age. He had a square face with a high forehead, and his brown eyes, flecked with gold, were capped by thick eyebrows. He wore his dark brown hair combed back from his face. He was a big man with broad chest and shoulders and muscular arms and legs. He wasn't much above average height, but tall enough to keep her from feeling awkward and gangly.

Suddenly, she found herself comparing Chad to Will—and Chad came out wanting. Will was taller, leaner, and his facial features were close to perfect. Just looking at him could make Addie's heart race.

Addie swallowed and tried to chase Will's image from her mind, but he wouldn't go. She saw him seated on that big buckskin of his. She thought of the way he'd climbed up on her roof, the way he'd moved, the sureness of his walk. She remembered his hands, the way he looped the leather reins through his long fingers. She saw his golden hair, so shaggy around his shirt collar, badly in need of a trimming.

"I just added a second room and a loft to my place this summer. Even have a wood floor. The way folks keep moving into Homestead, I'd say my business can only keep growing, too. I guess some folks wouldn't think much of the work I do, but I like working with animals and with my hands. Gives me a sense of accomplishment. Why, just the other day . . ."

Will was quieter than the gregarious blacksmith, too, she thought as she watched Chad. Will let his eyes do more of the speaking for him. She remembered the way he'd struggled with the words when he'd proposed to her.

A cold knot formed in her stomach at the memory. She didn't like to think of that day. It was too painful, too embarrassing. She wished it had never happened. More than anything, she wished she hadn't been foolish enough to believe a man like Will Rider could feel for her on anything other than a purely impersonal level.

"Miss Sherwood?"

She blinked as she was dragged back to the present by the sound of Chad speaking her name.

"Is something wrong?"

She felt the blood rising in her cheeks. She shook her head, praying he wouldn't see her blush.

"If there is, I'd be more than happy to try to help any way I can. All you have to do is ask."

Addie shook her head again. "No, there's nothing wrong, Mr. Turner. I'm afraid you caught me with my mind wandering. I was . . ." She searched desperately for an excuse. "I was just thinking about one of my students."

She was saved from saying more as the wagon arrived at her cabin.

There was only about a half hour of daylight left when Addie came outside, carrying a cup of coffee for Chad. She saw him drive one last nail into the new corral fence, then step back to survey his work. She stopped and studied the transformation that had taken place behind the cabin. She could scarcely believe it was the same place.

"It's amazing," she said, meaning it, looking at the sturdy corral and the covered shelter that butted up against the cabin. "I can't believe what you've done in so little time. It's wonderful."

He shrugged off her words, but his smile told her he was pleased by what she'd said. He took the cup from her hands and took several quick sips of the hot brew.

"Whatever can I do to repay you for your work?"

"I didn't do it for payment, Miss Sherwood." He paused, and a frown knitted his eyebrows. "But come to think of it, there is one thing."

"What's that?"

"I'd take it kindly if you'd think about calling me Chad and allow me to call you Addie."

She hesitated only a moment before replying, "I suppose it would be all right."

"Good. Then I guess I'll be on my way, Addie." He passed the cup back to her. "You just let me know if there's any other help you need."

It was almost as if he were trying to court her, she thought as she watched him toss the tools he'd brought with him into the back of his wagon. But she knew that wasn't possible, and so she dismissed the thought as more foolishness.

Chapter Twelve

The following Saturday, Addie awoke before sunrise, as was her habit. But today she didn't have to leap out of bed and hurry with her morning chores before walking into town. Today she could allow herself the luxury of lying still beneath the warm quilts on her bed and just letting her thoughts wander.

She reflected on her first week as a teacher. With the exception of the incident with Mark, the past five days had gone smoothly. Many of her students had never attended school before, and they were curious about everything. Most of the children were eager to learn. She had the feeling she was going to have to work hard to keep one step ahead of them.

She mentally ticked off the things she'd learned about her students—who was slow and who was quick, who was quiet and who was loud, who was shy and who was stubborn.

Stubborn . . . That seemed an appropriate description of Rose Townsend. The child didn't back down from a fight, not even when the opponent was a big brute like her brother. She was obstinate and apparently fearless, yet Addie suspected there were deeper, more complicated feelings and personality traits hidden just beneath the surface. But about one thing there was no question—Rose's friendship with Lark. The girl was determined about that, no matter how much her brother objected.

Addie pulled the covers up tighter beneath her chin as her thoughts moved to Lark Whitetail. She thought she'd seen some positive signs this week. At least Lark seemed to smile more easily than when they'd first met. She didn't seem as fearful either. The girl was still too reticent and shy to suit Addie, even though she understood the reasons for such behavior. If it weren't for Rose's persistence, Lark might have spent the entire week of lunch hours and recesses sitting alone in the grove of aspens beside the church. But all in all, Lark was slowly becoming a part of the community of children, and Addie suspected things had improved at home, too.

Lark needs you. . . . I was thinking maybe you'd consider being Lark's mother.

Addie closed her eyes, hoping to shut out the sting in her heart, a pain caused not so much by the memory of Will's words, but because she wasn't someone's mother, would never be someone's mother. She would like to hold a child in her arms and pour out all the love inside her, but having a child of her own wasn't enough to make her marry a man she didn't love, a man who didn't love her in return. She wanted more from life than that. If she'd been willing to settle for a marriage of convenience, she could have had a home and children, possibly even a child of her own. But she didn't want to settle. She wanted more, so much more. She knew it was an impossible dream, but it didn't stop her from wanting.

She needs a mother, Miss Sherwood.

She let out a deep sigh. She supposed Lark did need a mother, but she wasn't the woman for the job. She would have to be satisfied to do her best to help the child in her role as teacher.

Addie turned onto her side, her thoughts shifting to Lark's uncle. It would certainly be easier to help the girl if Addie didn't feel so uncomfortable around her guardian. And she was convinced that Will was equally ill at ease whenever he was within sight of Addie. She supposed it was up to her to change the situation. She knew she became quite rigid and her tone brisk whenever Mr. Rider was nearby. Perhaps if she could relax around him and forget he'd ever proposed to her—and why—then they could become friends. It's what would be best for Lark, and after all, they both wanted to do what was best for the child.

She smiled, feeling some self-satisfaction at having reasoned things out so sensibly. Now all that was left was to put her plan into action.

She opened her eyes and stared across the cabin at the fireplace, willing it to produce more heat before she had to get out of bed. She wondered how cold the Idaho winters might be if it was already like this in September. Then she decided she'd better not think about it.

With a resigned groan, she tossed aside the warm blankets, grabbed her wrapper, slipped her feet into a pair of house shoes, and hurried across the room. Thankfully, there were still hot coals beneath the banked ashes. Addie shoved in several large pieces of wood along with some kindling, then watched anxiously until hungry orange fingers began curling around the fuel.

As soon as the fire was burning brightly, Addie turned her back on the hearth and looked around the one-room cabin. It hadn't been easy, but she'd made the place more livable since her arrival. Of course, it would never feel like home—home was over two thousand miles away—but she had managed to give her new abode a comfy, welcoming feeling.

Her mother's favorite jasper tableware was lined up on the shelf. Photographs of her parents had been lovingly placed on the mantel above the fireplace. Yellow gingham curtains framed the lone window. Two rugs now covered much of the cold earthen floor. There was even a bouquet of late fall wildflowers—the last of the season—in a jar on the table.

As the room warmed around her, Addie sighed again, this time with contentment. Then she reminded herself that it was time she got on with her day. There was much to be accomplished—laundry to wash, bread to bake, even wood to chop. And this afternoon, Will would deliver her horse.

She felt a thrill of excitement. It was only because she'd never dreamed of owning such a beautiful animal, she told herself. That was the only reason for the sense of anticipation churning in her midriff.

The cry of a magpie echoed above the babbling water of Pony Creek. A crisp morning breeze disturbed the branches of the poplars, causing the leaves to applaud the passing riders.

Will followed the trail that bordered the banks of the quick-flowing rivulet. He led the way on Pal, Addie's mare following behind, a long lead rope attached to her halter. Lark brought up the rear on her little bay.

When she saw her uncle glance back at her, Lark flashed him a grin. It was funny how good her smile could make him feel. He'd be embarrassed if anyone were to guess it meant as much to him as it did.

"You doin' okay?" he called back to her, though he could see she was.

At the same time that she bobbed her head in affirmation, she patted the gelding's neck. Dark Feather, she'd named the bay, because, she'd said, his forelock looked like a feather.

Will turned his eyes forward again. Here, along Pony Creek, he could see the first signs of autumn. The leaves on the cottonwoods and aspens were just beginning to turn. Soon the valley and surrounding hillsides would be ablaze with the colors of fall—reds, oranges, golds. And winter, with its blanket of white, wouldn't be far behind.

While they were still some distance away from his old cabin, he caught the scent of wood smoke in the air. It reminded him of the last time he'd come calling on Miss Sherwood—smoke and a bucket of water and an overcooked, waterlogged cake. Not that he liked remembering it. It still made him cringe to think he'd actually proposed marriage to a woman he hardly knew, just because he didn't know how to raise his niece.

He saw a silver-gray curl of smoke rising above the treetops and wondered if she might need another cake extinguished. Thinking back, he had to admit it had been an undeniably funny moment, though he hadn't thought so at the time. He remembered the way Addie's eyes had twinkled with mirth. She'd tried so hard—unsuccessfully, as he recalled—to keep from laughing at him.

Now, remembering, he smiled, too.

The cabin was almost within view when he heard the sounds of woodcutting. He immediately thought of Chad and wondered if the blacksmith had come to see the schoolmarm again.

Unconsciously, he nudged Pal with his heels, hurrying the buckskin forward.

Addie had only been chopping firewood for half an hour, and already her back hurt, two calluses had formed on her palms, and there were rings of sweat staining her blouse underneath her arms. She could scarcely believe she'd been chilled when she'd first awakened this morning.

She paused to look at the miserably small amount of wood she'd managed to split in the past thirty minutes. At this rate, she would never be finished before noon, and there was so much more she had to do today.

Well, nothing would get done if she just stood around thinking about it.

Pressing her lips together in determination, she bent to lift another length of wood, placing it onto the broad stump that was her chopping block. Then she flicked her hair back over her shoulder and picked up the ax again.

She stared hard at the wood, looking at precisely the spot she meant to strike with the sharp edge of the ax. Taking a deep breath, she swung with all her might. The blade skimmed along the side of the log, knocking it off the stump and sending it rolling toward the creek.

"Not again!" she cried in frustration as she turned to retrieve it.

And that was when Will Rider appeared out of the trees, leading her new mare behind him, followed by Lark.

"Oh no," she whispered. "Not now."

He stopped his horse and stared at her.

She knew she looked a sight. This morning, she'd tied her waist-length hair at the nape with a ribbon, but some time ago, the ribbon had pulled loose, leaving her curls in wild disarray. She was wearing her oldest blouse, a drab shade of brown, and she'd left off her petticoats so her skirt wouldn't get in the way while she was chopping wood. She couldn't imagine how she could possibly look worse than she did at this moment.

She straightened her shoulders and lifted her chin. "You're early, Mr. Rider. I didn't expect you until this afternoon." She heard the prim, reprimanding tone of her voice and was immediately sorry for it. She'd decided this morning that she wasn't going to react rudely to him.

"You shouldn't be doing that," was all he said as he dismounted. He tossed his horse's reins around the corral railing, then strode purposefully toward her and took the ax from her hand. "Here. Let me."

She saw his gaze flick to her hair, and she nervously reached to push it back from her face again.

Will had the unwelcome urge to touch her hair, see if it felt the way it looked—hot and fiery. He could almost imagine it would burn his fingers if he did.

She stepped back from him, her hand fluttering to her throat in a purely feminine gesture. Her cheeks were flushed with color.

"Why don't you let me do this for you?" he asked, more gently this time.

"Oh, I couldn't."

"I'd welcome a cup of coffee when I'm finished." He turned his head. "Lark, why don't you go inside with Miss Sherwood and help her with that coffee while I chop up some firewood?" He looked at Addie again. "Please. Let me do this."

"But I . . ."

"Please."

Her face seemed to soften. The blush faded until there were only two circles of color remaining in the apples of her cheeks. "All right, Mr. Rider." She turned toward Lark. "Would you like to come inside with me?"

The girl nodded as she slid from the saddle, her dress riding up to reveal her bloomers. The minute her feet touched the ground, she pushed the material of her skirt back into place, then tied her gelding next to her uncle's horse and hurried over to Addie. Together they walked into the cabin.

Will hadn't been wrong about the two of them looking right together, he thought as he grabbed a chunk of wood and set it on the tree stump. Addie had a way with Lark that Will would never match, not if he lived to be a hundred.

* * *

After preparing a fresh pot of coffee, Addie hurried to make herself presentable. She tamed her hair with water and comb, then twisted it into a proper bun. After washing herself with water from the basin, she donned a suit of dark yellow grosgrain, trimmed on the bottom with two gathered flounces. She knew the gown was far better suited for an eastern parlor than a one-room cabin in the remote West, but it had always succeeded in giving her a bit of confidence. She felt the need of it today.

Lark sat at the table, her eyes politely averted, until Addie was finished dressing.

"There," Addie said as she stepped toward the center of the room. "I feel ready for company now. Let's go see how your uncle is coming, shall we?" She motioned for Lark to join her.

Will was just stacking the last of the split firewood when the two of them stepped outside. He leaned the ax against the cabin, then rolled down his shirtsleeves as he looked up.

"That should keep you for a few weeks," he said.

"I can't thank you enough. It would have taken me all day, and I still wouldn't have finished it." Her gaze darted toward the three horses, standing beside the corral. "Would you like that coffee now? It should be ready."

"It can wait. I can see you'd rather have a look at your horse." One corner of his mouth turned upward.

She responded with an apologetic smile. "I'm afraid I would."

Now his grin was complete. "I understand." He glanced at his niece. "So does Lark. She got her own horse this week, too."

"I remember." Addie looked down at the girl standing beside her. "Are you caring for him all by yourself?"

"Ah hmm." Lark's face lit up. "I named him Dark Feather. What are you going to call yours?"

"Oh my. I hadn't given any thought to a name." She frowned. "Do you suppose you could help me with that?"

"Sure." Lark took hold of her hand and pulled her toward the corral and the waiting horses.

Addie glanced back over her shoulder at Will. When their eyes met, she felt an odd tingling in her stomach. She quickly returned her attention to Lark.

"Maybe you could go riding with us sometime," the child was saying.

"I'm afraid I don't know how to ride. My father and I always kept a buggy horse, but she was an old and temperamental beast. I never had a saddle horse."

"Uncle Will could teach you. He's a good teacher. Just like you, Miss Sherwood."

Addie had never seen the girl so animated. It was obvious that the gift of the horse had been a smart move on her uncle's part.

"Could you, Uncle Will?" Lark asked, looking behind her. "Could you teach Miss Sherwood to ride?"

Addie felt that confounded heat returning to her cheeks again. "I'm sure your uncle is far too busy for such things," she answered quickly. She waited half a heartbeat, then glanced up at Will.

He was wearing a thoughtful expression, almost a frown. It made her stomach sink.

Suddenly, he strode over to his niece. He picked her up by the waist and lifted her onto Dark Feather's back. "Why don't you show Miss Sherwood what you've learned?" He handed up the reins as he gave her a wink.

"Watch me, Miss Sherwood," Lark said as she guided the horse away from the house.

"I don't know if I'm as good a teacher as you," Will said, "but I'm a fair horseman. I think I could teach a lady to ride. You want to learn astride or sidesaddle?"

"Really, Mr. Rider." She felt the blush deepening. She kept her gaze glued to the child on the small bay gelding. "Don't feel you need to do this just because Lark . . ."

"That's not why I'm doing it. I thought maybe we could work out a trade."

She was taken completely by surprise. "A trade?" She turned her head to look at him once again.

He was watching her with a steady blue gaze, his expression dead serious.

"I'm afraid I don't know what . . ." she began, feeling a trifle breathless.

"I'd like you to teach me to read and write, Miss Sherwood."

"To read and . . ." She stopped, certain she was about to insult him with her incredulous tone. It wasn't that it was so unusual for a man to be unable to read, but she sensed it was a sore point with Will Rider. She realized that she would have done this for him, whether or not she needed or wanted riding lessons. But she also realized his pride was involved. "I think that would be a fair trade, Mr. Rider," she continued softly.

The tension seemed to leave him. His mouth relaxed, and there was a genuinely warm look in his gaze as he stared down at her.

She envisioned him sitting at the table inside her cabin, his head bent over a book, with her seated by his side. She could see the flicker of lamplight on his dark gold hair and almost hear the deep timbre of his voice as he read aloud. She felt aglow inside, just thinking about it.

"I'll bring a saddle over tomorrow," he said, breaking into her daydream. "If you want a lady's sidesaddle, you'll have to order one through the mercantile, but I'll tell you right now, most women out in these parts don't bother with such nonsense."

Her heart was beating much too rapidly. "Then I won't either."

"You're not watching, Miss Sherwood," Lark called just then.

Addie tore her eyes away from Will, reminding herself that it was a teacher he wanted. That was all.

Chapter Thirteen

Addie's second week of school began much like the first—the ringing of the bell, the students filing inside—but with two noticeable differences. First, she wasn't nearly as nervous as she'd been the week before, and second, Mark Townsend didn't give her his usual defiant look as he passed by. In fact, he actually smiled. She found his apparent good humor disturbing. Although she wanted to trust the boy and to believe he'd decided to cooperate, she was certain there were other reasons for his behavior.

It wasn't until midmorning that she discovered what was behind Mark's change of attitude.

Her students were all bending over their readers. Except for an occasional sniffle or the sound of a shoe scuffing against the floor, the schoolroom was silent. Unsuspecting, Addie opened her desk drawer—and her heart nearly stopped. Three field mice, their tiny heads crushed, lay in a neat row in the middle of the drawer.

Later she would be amazed at her ability to think or act calmly. Even at the time, it surprised her that she could sense several pairs of eyes turned upon her. She swallowed the scream—as well as the bitter taste of bile—that had risen in her throat. She forced herself to move slowly, purposefully, as she withdrew a sheet of paper from beneath the tiny corpses, then closed the drawer. She dipped her pen in the ink and began to write, but the words made no sense. It didn't matter. She was only waiting for her heart to stop its furious hammering, for the tremor in her hands to pass, and for the silent scream to fade from her ears.

Fifteen minutes later, she rose from her chair and turned to the blackboard, picked up a piece of chalk, and wrote the word *courage* in large letters. With back straight, shoulders level, and head held high, she turned to face the class.

"All right, children. Your reading time is over." She waited until all the books had been closed and all eyes were upon her before she continued. "Who can give me a definition of the word I've written on the blackboard?"

She waited for someone to raise a hand, but no one did. As she moved her gaze around the room, it was easy enough to figure out which students had known in advance of the prank. Older boys, all of them. Several had the decency to look ashamed. But not Mark. He wore a smirk as he leaned back against the desk behind him, his arms crossed in front of his chest.

Finally, Imogene Potter raised her hand.

"Yes, Imogene."

"It means you're not afraid of nothing."

"Not afraid of *anything,*" Addie corrected, "and, no, that's not quite right. Would anyone else like to try?"

She waited again, but no more hands went up. Once again her gaze moved about the room, touching briefly on each student.

"Many people think courage means not being afraid," she continued at last, "but that isn't true. Courage means doing what needs to be done, doing what is right, *despite* your fears or the danger before you."

She turned to the blackboard and wrote the word *cowardice.*

"What about the definition of this word?" she asked, facing her students again. This time, she didn't give anyone a chance to respond. "It means acting *without* courage. For instance, it takes no bravery to hurt or kill something smaller or weaker than you are." She looked directly at Mark. "It takes no courage to sneak around and do things in hiding. A brave man does the things he believes in—things he is proud of and feels are right—out in the open, where others can see. A courageous man doesn't try to frighten or intimidate others. Those who operate in deception or try to rule others by cruelty are cowards . . . or fools. Perhaps both."

Mark's face turned red. His eyes were full of resentment as he glared at her.

She let her gaze sweep the rest of the class one final time. She could feel the tension in the air. Most of the children looked confused, and she guessed it was as much because of her stern tone of voice as by the lesson. Those who had known about Mark's trick understood all too well what the meaning of the lesson was.

Finally she set down the piece of chalk and said, "I believe it's time for a recess." Then she stepped down from the riser and led the way to the back of the building.

Fifteen minutes later, when she returned to her desk, she found the mice gone from the drawer. She didn't know who'd removed them, but much to her disappointment, she was certain it hadn't been Mark. She only hoped he'd learned something from the incident.

Doris McLeod hung the "Closed" sign on the door of the Homestead Post Office, then turned to her left and walked toward home. The September sun was pleasantly warm, and she drew in a deep breath, enjoying the lingering Indian summer days. The older she got, the more she dreaded the coming of winter. The cold seemed to seep into her bones and stay there until she thought she'd never be warm again.

Instead of the silence that usually greeted her when she entered the house, she heard familiar chatter coming from the kitchen. A broad smile appeared on her lips.

"Where's my Sarah?" she called.

Doris's two-year-old granddaughter came running into the parlor, giggling, her pudgy arms held out toward her. Doris picked the girl up and gave her a hearty hug.

"How's Grandma's angel?" she asked.

"Helpin' Mama."

"Are you?" She kissed one rosy cheek. "What are you helping your mother with?"

"San'iches!"

Doris carried the toddler into the kitchen. Her daughter-in-law was there, carving meat and placing it between thick slices of fresh bread.

Maria glanced up and smiled, a smile very much like Sarah's. "Hello, Mother McLeod. I thought I'd surprise you and have lunch ready when you came home. You're early."

"I know." Doris sat down on one of the chairs at the table, still holding Sarah on her lap. "There's never much work to be done on Mondays. Last week's mail's all been picked up, and everyone knows the stage won't come again 'til Wednesday, so there's no rush to post letters today." She pushed her bonnet back from her hair, leaving it hanging against her back.

"Will Father McLeod be home for lunch, too?"

Doris raised her eyebrows. Maria knew as well as she did that Hank always came home to eat, unless he had a prisoner—which was almost never. On those rare occasions, Doris packed up meals for her husband—and whoever was behind bars—and took the food to the jailhouse. "He'll be here," she replied.

When Maria turned around again, Doris noticed the pink flush on her daughter-in-law's otherwise pale complexion. Maria's blue eyes looked feverish, and she kept darting a glance toward the back door, almost nervously.

Doris knew Maria had no cause to be nervous about Hank's presence. Hank loved Maria the same as he loved his own daughter, and Doris loved her, too. She couldn't have chosen a better, more perfect wife for her son. But something was causing Maria's agitation. What was it?

Just as she was about to ask, the back door opened, and Tom walked in, followed by his father. Doris felt a sting of alarm. Her son never came here for lunch. He either ate at the mill or went to his own home. What was going on? she wondered as her eyes met Hank's. He shrugged, as if he'd heard the question.

"Hello, Mother." Tom walked over and dropped a kiss on her cheek, then rounded the table to put his arm around Maria's shoulders.

Her tension only increased as she watched her son's face. He was grinning from ear to ear, but she recognized the strain just beneath the surface.

"Sit down, Father," Tom said, then waited while Hank did so. "Maria and I have some good news for you. We wanted to tell you sooner, but we had to wait until we were sure nothing would go wrong."

Doris's gaze shot instantly to Maria. Her heart skipped a beat. Of course! She should have guessed it sooner. The signs had been there—Maria's finicky appetite and fatigue, the thickening of her waistline.

"You're going to have another baby," she said, sounding breathless. Her eyes darted to Hank, then back to Maria.

Maria nodded, her face wreathed in smiles.

Doris subdued the chill of misgiving. She rose from her chair and hurried over to hug the young woman. "Oh, Maria, Tom. I'm happy for you both." Her hands gripped Maria just below her shoulders. She forced her voice to sound calm. "What does the doctor say?"

"He says I should be able to carry this one to full term, just as I did Sarah. He says everything looks fine, and there's no reason to be afraid I'll miscarry again."

"When? When is it due?"

Tom answered, "Mid-December, Doc says."

Doris hugged her son. "We'll pray for a strong, healthy boy."

She saw a flash of fear and sorrow in his slate-colored eyes. She understood. She and Hank had suffered along with Tom and Maria when the other babies, all of them boys, were lost. The first three, about a year apart, had been born prematurely, much too early to survive, no matter how hard Doc Varney had tried to save them. The next one had been full term but stillborn. When Sarah was born, everyone in the family had thought her a miracle.

The doctor had suggested then that Maria give her body a rest, that she should avoid getting pregnant again for at least two years. But before Sarah's first birthday, Maria had miscarried another baby when she was only three months along. The doctor had warned she might never have another child. Maria had been heartbroken. She wanted to give her husband a son. Doris knew Tom had told his wife it didn't matter, that Sarah was all he needed, but Maria had always insisted she wanted more children.

The memories flashed through Doris's mind as she hugged Tom a second time. *Please, God,* she silently prayed, *keep Maria safe and strong.*

Addie checked the watch pinned to her bodice. It was nearly four o'clock. For the moment, the morning's unpleasantness with the dead mice was completely forgotten. There was another reason for her stomach to be filled with butterflies. Today she was to begin her riding lessons with Will.

She rose from her desk, drawing the expectant attention of her students. "Class is dismissed. Don't forget your assignments for tomorrow."

As usual, their departure was somewhat less than orderly. At normal school, she'd been instructed that children should rise from their desks and stand quietly until they could depart in single-file. Addie supposed her instructors had been right, but she just couldn't bring herself to demand it from her students. Secretly, she rather enjoyed the sudden burst of energy that occurred when school let out.

Lark remained behind and helped Addie clean the blackboards. Then, together, they went outside and started the long walk out to the Rocking R Ranch. Will had already taken Addie's mare back to his place. He'd told her he would keep the horse there until either the new buggy was ready or Addie felt capable of riding alone, whichever came first.

For the first mile, neither Addie nor Lark spoke, but it was a companionable silence. More than once, Addie had wondered about the instant connection she'd felt with the girl and the way Lark had responded to her in return. Of course, Addie had always liked children, but Lark was special somehow. Addie needed to be very cautious in the schoolroom not to let that translate into preference. Lark had enough strikes against her without being labeled the teacher's pet.

She glanced down at the girl. Her skin tone was slightly darker than most, but other than that, there was nothing about her that bespoke her Indian heritage. Even if something about her looks did set her apart, Addie didn't understand why it should earn Lark the animosity of others. She was an adorable girl, and she promised to be a great beauty when she was grown. But when all was said and done, she was just like any other child, needing love and acceptance and understanding.

Lark looked up, saw Addie watching her, and said, "Miss Sherwood?"

"Yes."

"Do you like Mr. Turner? The blacksmith?"

The question was totally unexpected. "Well, yes. He seems like a pleasant man. Why do you ask? Don't you like him?"

Lark turned her eyes onto the road again. "I guess so. I was just wonderin'. I saw you talkin' to him after church yesterday, and Rose said he's sparkin' you."

"Sparking me?" Addie felt herself blush—and silently cursed her tendency to do so. She hoped Lark wouldn't glance up again until the color faded from her cheeks.

"Is that true?" Lark wondered. "*Is* he sparkin' you?"

Addie was about to deny it, but the words seemed to stick in her throat. Could it be true?

She thought back to yesterday. Chad had greeted her after Sunday service, and she had paused to return the greeting. He'd told her the buggy she'd ordered was progressing nicely. It would be done by Saturday, and he would bring it out to her place. She'd thanked him and started to turn away when he'd mentioned the harvest dance the town was planning. He'd told her it would be held in Doc Varney's barn. He'd named the musicians and told her what the other ladies were bringing for refreshments. He hadn't actually asked her to the dance, but . . .

Addie's eyes widened. *Could* Chad Turner be courting her?

"Miss Sherwood?"

"Hmmm," she replied absently, still wondering about Chad.

"Uncle Will likes you, too."

Addie felt a knot form in her stomach. It took a great deal of control to make her voice sound normal. "Your uncle's a fine man, Lark. I'm sure we're going to be good friends."

Chapter Fourteen

Will tightened the cinch around the sorrel's belly, slipping the strap through the dee ring and knotting it securely. "It's always a good idea to wait a minute or two, then check it again. Most horses will relax, let out the extra air, and you'll need to tighten the cinch up a bit. You don't want the saddle to slip while you're ridin'."

He turned his head to look at Addie. She was leaning forward, her shoulder nearly touching his, her eyes studying every movement of his hands. She was concentrating so hard, he could almost see the way her mind was analyzing and memorizing each step. He didn't doubt she'd be able to fasten the cinch perfectly when he asked her to.

He'd been wrong, he thought suddenly. She wasn't truly plain. Her features were . . . intriguing.

Her nose was long and straight. Noble looking. Aristocratic. Of course, the sprinkling of freckles that danced across the bridge of her nose and onto her cheeks dispelled the notion of nobility.

He decided he liked the freckles.

Her mouth was full, her lips a soft rose color. He particularly liked them at the moment, when they were curved up at the corners, ever so slightly. It wasn't really a smile, but it wasn't *not* a smile either. Whatever it was, it made him feel good inside.

It was actually quite a kissable mouth.

As if she felt his gaze upon her, she lifted her eyes to meet his. Beautiful, unusual, enticing, enchanting, mysterious eyes.

He felt something hot moving through him, tightening his vitals and making his mouth go dry.

Damned if he didn't want to kiss her!

Addie straightened and stepped backward abruptly. He saw her stumble. She grabbed for her straw bonnet as it slipped forward but only succeeded in dislodging it completely. The mare, startled by the flying hat, shied, jerking back with her head, her front hooves leaving the ground. Will reached for Addie just as the horse broke her lead and spun around.

He wasn't quite certain what happened after that, only it felt like he'd been hit by a steam engine. The next thing he knew, he was lying on his back with shards of pain shooting through his body. The world was spinning wildly. He kept his eyes closed, hoping it would stop.

"Mr. Rider! Oh, no! What have I done? Mr. Rider!" Addie knelt beside him on the ground and cradled his head on her thighs. "Mr. Rider, please look at me."

Will cracked open one eye. Despite the pain in his side, he couldn't help noticing how pale her skin looked against the fiery color of her hair. Actually, she looked as she if she might pass out. "I'm not dead," he said through clenched teeth.

A relieved sigh rushed out of her. "Oh, thank God!" she whispered.

He tried to sit up, then clutched his side as he quickly sank back onto her lap. "You're going to have to help get me into the house. I think your little filly broke some of my ribs."

"Oh no. Your ribs? Broken? I'm so sorry. It's all my fault. It's all my fault."

"Miss Sherwood . . ." He squeezed his eyes closed and gritted his teeth against a sudden jab of pain.

She was damn well right it was her fault. That was what he got for trying to teach a woman to saddle her own horse and ride.

No, that wasn't fair. It was what he got for thinking about kissing a woman. Kissing this particular woman. That was what had laid him out flat in the middle of the corral.

He looked at her again. "It was an accident. It's not the first time I've had a horse bust somethin' of mine." He tried to drag in some air, then held it when the pain worsened. "I imagine it won't be the last," he added in a breathless voice.

"Uncle Will!"

He turned his head sideways and watched Lark come running across the yard from the house.

"Uncle Will, what happened?" She slipped through the corral rails. If possible, her face was even paler than Addie's.

He took hold of her hand and forced himself to smile. He tried to sound reassuring when he said, "Seems Miss Sherwood's mare took a sudden dislike to me and let me know it with the business end of her hind legs." He pressed his other hand against his side. "Now, why don't you two ladies get me on my feet and into the house before one of the men sees me lyin' out here on my back. I won't ever live it down if they do."

"Perhaps we should get one of them to carry you inside," Addie suggested.

He shot her a scowl but said nothing.

"Come on, Lark. Help me get your uncle up. We'll get him inside, and then I'll send someone for the doctor."

It was well after dark by the time Doc Varney came out of Will's bedroom. Addie and Lark both rose from their chairs and looked at him expectantly.

"It's nothing too serious. He's got a couple of cracked ribs, just like he thought. He'll be mighty sore for a while, but as long as he doesn't go trying to do anything too soon, he'll heal up okay. I told him to stay in bed for the rest of the week, just take it easy." He set his gaze on Lark. "Do you think you can see that he obeys me?"

The girl nodded.

"Good. I'll come by tomorrow and look in on him." He glanced at Addie. "Let me give you a lift home, Miss Sherwood."

Addie was reluctant to leave. She could see how frightened Lark still was, no matter how much the doctor might reassure her, but she also knew she couldn't stay. It wouldn't look right to folks in town. Besides, Lark wasn't alone. Frosty, the Rocking R cook, lived in a room at the back of the house, and Griff Simpson, the ranch foreman, was only a shout away, sleeping in the bunkhouse.

She leaned low and put her hands on Lark's shoulders. "You don't worry about anything. You stay home the rest of the week and take care of your uncle. I'll come over after school and give you your lessons so you won't fall behind." She offered an encouraging smile. "All right?"

Lark nodded.

"You're not scared anymore?"

Lark shook her head, bravely denying her true feelings.

"If you need me, you just send one of the men for me. Okay?"

The little girl nodded one more time.

Addie hugged her, then straightened, picked up her books and the bonnet that had caused the entire incident, and turned toward the doctor. "I'm ready."

She didn't feel much like talking during the drive from the Rocking R to her cabin beside Pony Creek, and the doctor seemed to understand her mood. She was grateful he didn't ask what she'd been doing at the ranch. Perhaps he didn't have to ask. Most likely Will had told him how the accident had happened. Tomorrow the entire town would probably know she'd asked the handsome rancher to give her riding lessons and then had nearly gotten him killed.

She replayed the moment in her mind, seeing again the mare's hooves landing so hard against his chest, the way they'd lifted him off the ground and tossed him backward. When he'd fallen to the ground, he'd lain so still she'd been certain he was dead. And it had been all her fault. If only she hadn't moved so suddenly. If only she hadn't stumbled and knocked her bonnet from her head. If only . . .

Her mind skipped back to the instant she'd turned and caught him watching her. He'd had the strangest look in his eyes, one that had made her go all soft and warm inside. The look had started a strange ache in the pit of her stomach—no, the ache had been lower and, somehow, very intimate. She'd felt an indescribable, almost inescapable urge to move into his arms, to press her body close to his, to offer him her lips, to . . .

She wasn't merely blushing on her cheeks now. The images her mind had conjured up made her entire body feel as if it were aflame. She was grateful for the darkness that concealed her from the doctor. Surely, if he could see her, he would guess the lustful, wanton turn of her thoughts.

Her little cabin was a welcome sight. The moment the buggy stopped, she thanked the doctor and stepped down without waiting for his help.

"Don't you worry about Will, Miss Sherwood. It takes more than a cantankerous horse to stop a man like him."

"I'm sure you're right, Dr. Varney. Thank you again for bringing me home." With those words, she turned and fled inside.

By the light of the moon which spilled through the opening in the curtains, Addie lit the lamp, then sank down onto a corner of her bed. With heart pounding and thoughts racing, she faced a frightening truth.

She was falling in love with Will Rider.

Why him? Why did it have to be Will?

Her thoughts flew back to the day he'd proposed to her outside this cabin. It had been clear he'd felt no real attraction to her. He'd found her acceptable as a mother to his niece, but he'd wanted no part of her as a woman. He'd offered her a home and a room of her own. She would have been little more than a housekeeper for him and a governess for his niece. He'd given her no reason to love him. None at all.

I wish I'd said yes. I should have accepted his offer of marriage.

The pain in her chest hurt so badly she wanted to keen and wail. She wanted to strike out at something, anything. It was so unfair. Why was she losing her heart to this man? Hadn't she learned her lesson? If she must love, why someone like Will? Why a man who could only see her as a spinster schoolmarm?

Why not Chad?

She thought of the blacksmith. He must care for her, at least a little. Not in a decade—not since Robert had first come calling when she was seventeen—had a man shown her the same kind of attention as Chad had. Rose and Lark were right. Chad Turner *was* courting her. She could *learn* to love him, couldn't she? He was handsome, likeable, pleasant.

But even as she contemplated loving another man, thoughts of Will returned, forcing out any other.

Addie lay back on her bed and closed her eyes against the burning tears. She'd been so careful for so many years. She'd known she wasn't the sort of woman with whom men fell in love. She'd realized she wasn't destined to marry and have a family. She'd resigned herself to a solitary future. Why had she been so foolish as to forget how carefully she'd guarded her heart against just this sort of pain?

Images of Will flitted through her mind—the first day they'd met, when he'd tried to deny her use of the cabin; the time he'd come to check the roof; the expression he wore whenever he looked at his niece; the beauty of him—sun glinting off his tawny hair, muscles bulging in his arms—as he'd shown his horses to her; the moment when he'd asked her to teach him to read. It seemed she'd gathered many memories of him in a very short period of time.

Addie forced herself to draw several deep breaths and let them out slowly, waiting until she felt more in control of her emotions before she opened her eyes to stare up at the ceiling overhead.

She reminded herself of the strict code to which a teacher was expected to adhere. If anyone were to guess what she was feeling for Will, especially when her feelings weren't reciprocated, she might very well find herself denounced, censured, rebuked. The townsfolk might suspect her of improper behavior. She could lose her teaching position. And then what would she do?

I wouldn't care what they said, if only he could love me, too.

But he didn't love her, would never love her. Men like Will Rider didn't love women like Adelaide Louise Sherwood. She had to acknowledge the truth again. Men didn't fall in love with women who were too tall, too straight and thin, women with wild, red hair and cat-like eyes and plain faces. She had spent her adult life facing that same painful truth. It had been imprudent of her to forget it, even for a moment.

She sat up on the bed, took another deep breath, then blew it out through pursed lips. Finally, she leveled her shoulders and lifted her chin.

She would forget her feelings for Will. She would put them behind her as she'd put so many other hopes and dreams behind her. She had no other choice.

She wished she did.

Chapter Fifteen

By the end of the first week of his convalescence, Will was feeling restless. Lark was a dedicated, though somewhat anxious nurse, but he was forced to walk a fine line between reassuring her he wasn't going to die and making her feel better by allowing her to fuss over him. He found it more exhausting than twelve hours in the saddle riding herd.

There was one bright spot in his day, however. It was the time when Addie arrived, books in arms. He liked listening to her as she sat beside Lark at the kitchen table, explaining the girl's lessons to her. Addie had a lovely voice, gentle yet firm, and in some way almost melodic.

He would have liked it if she visited a little with him, but she never did. She only spoke to him when he asked her a question. He couldn't help wondering if she was angry with him for some reason, the way she avoided looking him directly in the eyes. Addie was always faultlessly polite—reserved, perhaps a bit stiff and prim—but he'd seen that in her before. He suspected that her constrained behavior was a facade to hide behind when she was feeling uncertain.

Reserved or not, by the week's end, she seemed to have a change of heart. She addressed him in that gentle yet firm tone of hers, informing him that it was time for his own lessons to begin.

"You have to stay quiet until your ribs are healed, Mr. Rider," she said as she handed him a reader. "You might as well put the time to good use."

And so she began to teach him to read, starting by finding out how much he already knew. It was difficult for Will at first, talking about his lack of schooling. He'd always hated admitting a weakness. He knew full well that many people couldn't read. Some folks couldn't even write their names or do a little ciphering. At least he could manage that. Still, the knowledge that others shared his weakness didn't make it any easier on him. He was still ashamed.

As the days passed, Addie imparted her quiet confidence to him, and before long, he wasn't embarrassed about it anymore. Even once he was up and moving around and Lark had returned to school, Will was glad for the days Addie accompanied his niece back from Homestead—Lark seated on Dark Feather, Addie driving her new buggy, her mare prancing smartly in harness—glad for his private lessons, glad he was learning to read, glad for Addie's quiet companionship.

It was the last that surprised him most of all.

For Addie, the hours spent with Will were filled with bittersweet moments. Sometimes when she looked at him, his head bent over the reader, lamplight reflecting off his golden hair, she thought of the things that might have been, if only they could love each other. She pondered what it might be like to see him seated at that same table every day, to hear his rich voice speaking to her, saying her name.

She cherished the way he smiled when understanding dawned as he tackled a more difficult lesson. Satisfaction would shine in his sky-blue eyes and, for a breathless heartbeat, Addie would feel she was a part of something wonderful.

Every now and then, Will would give her a glimpse of his past, mentioning a word or two about his family. She had a thousand questions she would have liked to ask him, but she never asked. She couldn't. It was too personal. Such questions were asked by lovers, by wives. She was neither of these to Will Rider. She never would be.

Will finished reading the short passage, then closed the book and glanced up. He caught just a glimpse of what had been a smile on Addie's lips. It vanished as her back straightened. It was almost as if she had a steel rod running up her spine.

"You've a quick mind, Mr. Rider. You won't need my help for long." She pushed back from the table and rose from her chair. "I'd best be on my way. It's getting dark much earlier these days."

"Why don't you let me see you home?"

Her eyes widened. "I wouldn't think of it," she replied hastily. "You . . . you're not fit yet for riding. Lark told me what Doc Varney said. You're not to overdo too soon."

"Then at least stay long enough to have supper with Lark and me. You shouldn't have to go home and cook for yourself this late in the day." His chair grated against the floor as he, too, got to his feet. "It's only fair. After all, you're not getting your part of the bargain yet."

She glanced away from him. "I really cannot." Her voice was soft, little more than a whisper.

Will was surprised by the disappointment he felt at her refusal.

He walked around the table and paused in front of her, forcing her to glance up at him. "I hope this isn't . . ." he began, then stopped and tried to find the right words. "I hope you're not . . ."

Her eyebrows arched slightly.

He started to inhale deeply but stopped when a sudden shard of pain ripped through him.

Unconsciously, he held one hand against his rib cage, then tried again to say what was on his mind. "What I'm trying to say is . . . well, I hope you've forgiven me for . . . proposin' to you the way I did. You can see how good Lark and I are gettin' along. You were right to refuse me. It wasn't the right thing for me to do, and I'm glad you were smart enough to see it wouldn't work."

Up went her chin in that now-familiar way she had. "It's quite forgotten, Mr. Rider."

"I just hope you understand. I didn't mean any disrespect." He shrugged, wishing he'd never started this train of conversation. "I'm just not the marryin' kind, Miss Sherwood. I don't hold much faith in the institution. I guess it suits some folks, but it's not for me."

"I understand." She reached for her books on the table. "I really must go."

"Wait." He placed a hand on her shoulder, stopping her. "What I'd like to say is . . . I appreciate all you've done for Lark. And for me, too. I'm glad to have you for a friend."

She turned her gaze up to meet his. He knew in that instant that he'd failed to say what he really meant. He knew his words had been all wrong, that what he was beginning to feel for her was more than friendship.

The strength and suddenness of his desire caught him totally off guard. The urge to kiss her was overwhelming. He didn't even try to resist it.

She was staring at his mouth as he slowly lowered his head toward hers. The look in her eyes reminded him a little of a cornered animal, yet she didn't try to escape. She simply awaited her fate.

Their lips touched lightly, like the brush of a feather, but his reaction to the kiss was anything but light. He wanted to pull her into his arms and sample her mouth more thoroughly. He moved to do just that, but the sudden movement caused another shot of pain to sear through him, stealing his breath. He froze in place, waiting for the sharp torture to stop.

The moment of inaction broke the spell. Addie stepped abruptly away from him. Her face had lost all its color. Even her freckles seemed to have disappeared.

"I must go," she whispered hoarsely. She grabbed for her books, then almost ran for the front door, not bothering to say good-bye to Lark—who had gone up to her room minutes before—as she normally did.

Will sank down onto the nearest chair, his gaze locked on the closed door. His breathing was irregular, and pain still lingered in his torso.

What on earth had possessed him to kiss her? That mare must have done more than just break his ribs with her well-placed kick. She'd knocked good sense clean out of his head at the same time.

* * *

Addie didn't remember a single moment of the drive back to her place. She scarcely recalled racing out of Will's home. She knew she must have climbed into the buggy and guided the mare along the country road, for suddenly the cabin was before her.

Moving by rote, she unhitched the horse, led her into the corral, tossed some feed into the trough, then closed the gate and hurried into the house. Her movements were as agitated as her thoughts as she bustled about the cabin, preparing herself a light supper. When it was ready, she ate the food without tasting it.

He'd kissed her. Why had he kissed her?

I'm just not the marryin' kind, Miss Sherwood.

"I know that, Mr. Rider," she whispered.

But he'd kissed her. Why?

Were her feelings so obvious? Had he seen how she felt about him, despite how carefully she'd tried to hide it? Had he been afraid she would throw herself at him?

An even worse thought occurred to her. *Had* she thrown herself at him? Was the kiss her own fault? Had she unknowingly enticed him, led him to believe she was offering herself to him?

She pushed her supper plate across the table, then laid her head against her hands. What a muddle she was making of everything! Why hadn't she stayed away from the Rocking R? She could have. She could have forgotten all about their bargain. She hadn't needed to go by his ranch this week. She hadn't been needed, not once Lark was back in school. Oh, if only she'd stayed away . . .

The knock on her door caused her to jump up from the table, a squeal lodged in her throat, her heart hammering in her ears. What if he'd followed her home? What could he want? What would she say to him?

"Addie, are you in there?" Chad's strong voice penetrated the door.

She let out a long breath of air, only then realizing she'd been holding it. "Just a moment," she called. She ran the palms of her hands over her hair, then smoothed the fabric of her skirt before walking to the door and lifting the latch. "Hello, Chad. This is a surprise." Amazingly, she sounded normal.

"I was doin' some shoein' out west of here. Just thought I'd stop by to say hello on my way back to town." He glanced over her shoulder, as if he expected to see someone else in the room. "You got a minute?"

"I . . . I'm sorry, Chad." She opened the door wider. "Won't you come inside? There's coffee on the stove if you'd like some."

"No, thanks. Can't stay long. It's already gettin' late." He turned the hat he held in his hands, sliding his fingers around the brim. "I just thought I'd best get around to askin' you before someone else did. Nobody's asked you, have they?"

"Asked me what?"

"To the harvest dance. It's next Saturday."

It seemed she could still feel Will's lips upon hers.

I'm just not the marryin' kind. . . . I'm glad to have you for a friend. . . .

"No," she answered softly, "no one has asked me."

"Well, it'd make me proud if you'd see fit to go with me. I'm not much of a dancer." He shrugged. "Ma always said my feet were too big for dancin'. But I'll do my best not to step on your toes."

She thought what it would be like to walk into the dance holding on to Will's arm. She thought what it would be like to step into his embrace and dance with him.

You were right to refuse me. . . . I'm glad you were smart enough to see it wouldn't work. . . .

Will didn't love her, would never love her. He wasn't interested in marriage, not with Addie, apparently not with any woman. She couldn't allow herself to want what would never be hers.

"What about it, Addie? Will you go with me?"

She liked Chad Turner. He had always shown her the utmost respect and courtesy. Ever since they'd first met, he'd gone out of his way to be of help to her, looking at horses with her and mending her corral fence and lean-to. And now he'd asked her to the dance.

She stared up into his brown eyes. Chad was, indeed, courting her. Perhaps it was only because single females were at a premium in the valley, but she thought he must find her at least somewhat attractive. Why couldn't she feel for him what she was feeling for Will?

Perhaps she could love Chad if she tried hard enough, she decided. She would *make* herself fall in love with him.

"I would be happy to go to the dance with you, Chad. Thank you for asking me."

The blacksmith grinned as he placed his hat back over his dark hair. "Guess I'd better be gettin' back to town. See you in church on Sunday."

"Yes. Church on Sunday. Good evening, Chad."

She closed the door without waiting to watch him ride away, feeling as if she were closing the door to her heart.

Glen guided the team of horses toward the mill just as dusk was settling over Homestead. He was tired but satisfied. He'd made a tidy profit from today's trip. It still amazed him how simple it was to stash away a few boards out of every order until he had enough to sell to settlers on the other side of Tin Horn Pass. Tom McLeod sure wasn't any the wiser.

Glen patted the pocket of his jacket, enjoying the sound of coins jingling. First thing he was going to do after unhitching the team was buy himself a bottle of whiskey. Then he was going to settle back and relax for the night.

Hell, what else was there to do in this do-nothing town? What Homestead needed was a saloon, some place where a man could go and enjoy himself for an evening, maybe find himself a game of cards. Maybe he should open one up himself.

The idea intrigued him. Why shouldn't he open a saloon? He'd sure like that a whole lot more than working for McLeod. But where was he going to get the kind of money it would take to get started?

His good mood vanished as he considered his limited funds. It didn't matter how hard he worked at the sawmill or even how much extra he managed to make on the side, selling the pilfered lumber—he didn't ever seem to be able to get ahead. If he didn't have a wife and kids hanging like millstones around his neck, things would be different. Without them, he probably would have been a man of consequence in this town. Naw, not this town. He wouldn't choose to live in this godforsaken backwater if he were on his own.

It was Virginia's fault. If it weren't for her, he wouldn't be stuck working in that mill, spending his money on her and those two good-for-nothing kids.

He never should have made Mark return to school after the teacher had sent him home for fighting. He should have made him get a job. The boy was fourteen. He should be helping Glen. But Virginia had just kept harping on the boy having an education. Fool woman. He hadn't thought he'd ever get her to shut up about it.

His hand clenched into a fist. He needed that whiskey. And his wife damn well better not give him any grief over it either. He wasn't in the mood for any of her naggin'.

Chapter Sixteen

Addie was surprised to hear the soft knock on her door on Sunday morning. She pushed aside the window curtains and peeked outside. Dark Feather stood in the clearing, his reins dragging on the ground.

Quickly, Addie moved to lift the latch and open the door. Her gaze dropped to the child standing just beyond the threshold. "Lark, is something wrong? Your uncle . . ."

"He's okay," the girl answered. "But he still isn't feeling up to going to church, and I promised Rose I'd be there today. It's her birthday. So I came over to ride in with you, if that's all right. Uncle Will said I could."

Relief flooded Addie's chest. "Of course it's all right. Come inside. I'm almost ready."

Lark pulled out a chair from the table and sat down while Addie returned to the mirror she'd hung on the wall near the foot of the bed. She picked up the brush and began the task of trying to tame the curly tresses.

"Why don't you leave your hair down?" Lark asked. "I like it that way. It's real pretty."

Addie glanced at the girl's reflection in the mirror. "A woman my age doesn't wear her hair down."

"Mama did. That's how my pa liked it. He always said it looked like sunshine, all yellow and soft." Her eyes took on a faraway look.

Addie tried to think of something comforting to say, then decided it was best to say nothing at all.

The girl's gaze cleared, and she looked once more at her teacher. "I bet Uncle Will would like your hair down, too."

Addie subdued the spark of expectation she felt at the sound of Will's name. She wasn't going to feel such things, she reminded herself. At least not about Will Rider. Not ever again about Will.

"You didn't come over to help Uncle Will with his reading yesterday," Lark continued, unmindful of Addie's silent quandary.

"I had other things to do, Lark. I can't come out to the Rocking R every day. Besides, your uncle is doing quite well on his own now."

"He was real disappointed when you didn't come."

Addie concentrated on twisting her hair into a tight roll at the nape. She was certain Lark was wrong about her uncle's disappointment. Mr. Rider was most likely relieved when the schoolmarm didn't show up to make a fool of herself over him.

She raised her chin in a show of determination. She absolutely would not allow herself to behave like a fool again.

Finished with her hair, she placed her gray satin bonnet on her head. She smoothed one of the ostrich plumes, dyed gray to match the hat, then tied the ribbon beneath her chin, making certain the bow was perfectly shaped. Finally, she turned from the mirror, picked up her gray satin pocketbook from the dresser, and headed for the door.

"Come along, Lark," she said briskly. "We don't want to be late for services."

Rose came alone to church that morning.

Her pa never attended Sunday services, of course, for which Rose was mighty glad. School and church were the two places where she knew she could get away from him.

Mark had declared this morning that he was old enough to decide what he wanted to do, and he didn't want to go to church no more. If Pa didn't have to go, why should he? Rose didn't miss her brother either.

But her ma's absence bothered Rose plenty. Ma couldn't come because of the black-and-purple shiner she had around her right eye.

Pa had given it to her two nights before after he'd come home with a bottle of whiskey and set to finishing every last drop of it. He'd sat in the parlor, throwing back glass after glass, muttering about how Virginia and her brats had held him back, complaining about the way life had treated him. Everyone had known what he was working up to. Virginia had tried to escape by first sending the children to bed and then retiring to her own bedroom. It hadn't helped. Glen had just gone after her there.

Rose set her mouth. Church wasn't a very good place to be thinking how much she hated her pa. Her ma always said Pa couldn't help himself, and that it was her fault 'cause she did things to provoke him. But Rose knew better. Rose knew her pa was just mean, plain and simple. He just liked to hit folks who were smaller and weaker than he was. He especially liked to hit Ma.

She shook her head, as if to clear it. She didn't want to think about such things. Not today. Today was her birthday, and she wanted to think about happy things. Lark's birthday present was going to be the best she'd ever gotten—a ride on Lark's pony. Rose could hardly wait for church to be over.

She glanced at her friend, sitting beside her on the bench. She was glad Lark had come to live in Homestead. She was the best friend Rose had ever had. She didn't care what Mark or their pa said about Lark being part Indian and not fit company for white folk.

Rose's gaze shifted to the woman beside her friend. Miss Sherwood sat with back straight, her eyes turned upon the reverend at the front of the room. Rose thought Miss Sherwood was about the nicest grown-up she'd ever known.

And the teacher was brave, too. She'd stood up to Mark and then marched over to Rose's house and told their ma what she expected of Mark before he could come back to school. Their pa had been in a real fury that night after he'd heard about it. Nobody had been more surprised—or sorry—than she when Pa said Mark had to go back to school the next day.

The congregation rose from the benches to sing the closing hymn, the reverend said a final prayer, and then the church service was over. Rose grabbed Lark's hand, and the two girls dashed outside together.

Addie smiled to herself as she stared after the children. To be young and carefree . . .

"Addie?"

She turned her head to find Emma and Stanley standing in the aisle beside her.

"You haven't been into the store for over a week, and you rushed out of here so quick last Sunday, I didn't even have a chance to say hello. I wanted to ask you how things are going with the school."

Addie rose from the bench. "Quite well, I think. The children are all settling in. Most seem to enjoy their studies."

"I heard you had some trouble with the Townsend boy."

"Some, but I think we've worked things out between us." Addie realized she was being overly optimistic. Mark despised her. She didn't doubt that he was just waiting for another opportunity to play a prank on her. "Your children are all doing well," she said to Emma, intentionally turning her thoughts away from Mark. "Albert has a fine mind for mathematics, and Rachel is very creative with words. She could be a writer one day if she cares to pursue it."

Emma's expression was filled with pleasure and pride. "I'm real glad to hear it." She glanced at her husband, then back at Addie. "Would you care to stay in town, take Sunday supper with us? We'd love to have you."

"Thank you, Emma, but I really mustn't. I have so much to do at home before another school week begins."

The older woman frowned as she gently scolded, "But it's the Lord's day. You should be resting and enjoying yourself."

Addie didn't say anything. She merely shook her head as she stepped into the aisle and walked out of the church, Emma beside her, Stanley bringing up the rear.

It wasn't that she wouldn't have enjoyed spending the afternoon with the Barbers, but she really did have too many things to do. Keeping up with her own washing and ironing and mending, along with cleaning her house and preparing her lessons, took all of her weekend hours, and her evenings as well. She'd fallen behind on everything over the past two weeks. She'd spent far too many hours at the Rocking R Ranch.

In her mind, she saw Will standing before her. In her heart, she felt the warmth of his kiss. The memory came and was gone in a flash, but it left her shaken to the core.

When they reached the landing outside the front door, Addie's gaze swept the churchyard until she found Lark. The girl was standing beside Dark Feather, holding the reins, while Rose scrambled up onto the saddle. She couldn't hear the instructions Lark was giving Rose, but she knew the girl must sound very much like her uncle.

Her heart squeezed again.

"Sure am glad to see how well she's gettin' along," Emma said, her gaze following Addie's. "Can't believe how much Lark's changed, come into her own, since she came here. Will, too. Done him a world of good, havin' someone to take care of and love. He's a mighty lonely man, though he's too thick-headed to see it. Shame he seems so set against marryin'. Don't know why. He's never talked much about himself, though he's always been friendly enough."

No! Addie's mind objected. *Don't talk about Will. Please don't.*

Emma started down the stairs. "What about that horse he sold you? Is it giving you any more trouble?"

Addie looked blankly at the other woman as they descended the steps side by side, her thoughts centered on Will, not her horse.

Emma didn't seem to notice her friend's hesitation. "We heard all about the accident," she continued. "Doc said Will was showin' you a horse and it kicked him." Emma shook her head. "I'm surprised you went and bought the animal after that. What if it decides to kick you when you're all alone at your place? You wouldn't have anyone to send for help."

Addie managed to subdue the blush, grateful Will hadn't told the doctor the entire, unvarnished truth. "The mare is really quite gentle."

Emma made a sound of disbelief.

"Honestly. It was my fault she shied and kicked Mr. Rider. I'm the one who spooked her."

"All the same, he shouldn't have sold you a flighty animal. We don't need our schoolteacher getting hurt by some green-broke horse. And I mean to tell him so next time I see him."

"Oh, please don't do that, Emma," she protested quickly.

From the corner of her eye, she saw someone walking toward them. She turned her head to see who it was, relieved for an excuse—*any* excuse—to change the subject.

Chad removed his hat and offered everyone a friendly smile. "Nice day, isn't it?" he said by way of greeting.

A few minutes later, after exchanging more comments about the weather and some other pleasantries, the Barbers said good-bye and headed off to their home at the other end of town, leaving Chad and Addie standing together in the almost deserted churchyard.

"Nice folks, the Barbers," Chad said.

"Yes, they are."

"Emma worked real hard to get the school started and a teacher hired. Never saw a woman so set on anything in my life as she was on Homestead havin' a school."

Addie looked up at Chad. "It's important to a community."

He grinned. "It's important to me, too."

"To you?"

"It brought you to Homestead."

Addie tried to listen to what he was saying, tried to summon the proper response, but all she could think about was what it would be like if Will were there in his place, if only it were Will who was sweet-talking her.

She looked away from Chad, ashamed of herself. Her gaze returned to Lark and Rose, who were riding double on the bay, using them as an excuse to escape hearing what she wasn't ready to hear.

She'd waited a decade for a man to show an interest in her. She'd convinced herself it never would happen. But it was happening. She should have been glad. She should have been filled with joy. Only she wasn't. She wasn't because he was the wrong man.

I can learn to love Chad Turner.

Could she?

I don't really love Will Rider.

Didn't she?

Her head began to pound, and her stomach felt as if it were twisted in a vice. "I must be getting home," she said, her voice sounding strained in her ears. "Lark!"

The girl stopped her horse.

"It's time to go. We can ride together as far as my place."

She watched the disappointed exchange of looks between the two girls, then saw Rose slide her right leg over Dark Feather's rump and slip to the ground.

Chad placed his hand lightly in the small of Addie's back as she started toward her buggy. Then he took hold of her hand and assisted her up onto the seat. As she picked up the reins, he said, "I'll call for you at six o'clock on Saturday."

"I'll be ready," she replied softly. She made herself look at him.

He wore a tender smile, and his dark eyes held a gentle warmth as they watched her. It was what she'd longed for all these years. He was a good man, too. He was a hard worker, and he would be a good provider. If she were to marry him—and she was certain he meant to ask her—he would be kind to her. She sensed that about him.

Then, yet again, thoughts of Will intruded. She felt the storm of emotions start up inside, felt the fire of passion his lone kiss had ignited within her.

She wanted to feel that fiery passion again. Heaven help her, she *needed* to feel it.

"Until Saturday," she whispered, then slapped the reins against the mare's back and turned the buggy toward home.

Chapter Seventeen

Will kept a tight rein on Pal, not allowing the powerful horse to go beyond a sedate walk. Still, he felt tormented by every step the horse took.

He was beginning to think this idea wasn't a very good one and was more than a little relieved when the old cabin came into view, even though it presented him with the problem of dismounting. Once he stopped the buckskin, he took in a few shallow gulps of air, held his breath, and swung his leg over the saddle, lowering himself to the ground with great care.

He cradled his side with his right arm, trying to still the throb of pain his movements had started. With his left hand, he reached into the saddlebag and withdrew the reader.

If the teacher won't come to the student . . . The thought made him irritable.

He walked up to the door and rapped on it with his fist. It was a few moments before it opened.

Addie's face looked pale. "Will . . ." Her voice had a breathless quality. She glanced behind him, then met his gaze again. "You rode over here on horseback?"

He held out the reader. "I finished it." He didn't immediately release his grip after Addie took hold of the book. "Lark told me you've been too busy to come out to the ranch this week."

Her eyes dropped to the item held between them. "Yes."

"You're not giving up on me, are you?" He released his hold, his earlier irritation forgotten. He couldn't even remember what had made him feel angry.

"No. It's just . . ."

"I'm real sorry about . . . about what happened last week," Will said—and immediately knew it wasn't true. He wasn't sorry he'd kissed her. He'd like nothing more than to kiss her again.

She turned away from him, clutching the book against her breast. "It's not important, Mr. Rider. I . . . it's forgotten."

He could see the rigid set of her shoulders. He was tempted to reach out and lay his hand on one of them but refrained.

"You're wrong," he said. "It *is* important if it keeps you from coming to the ranch." He took a step closer, then lowered his voice.

"I'm counting on you to teach me to read and write."

Fiery wisps of hair curled along her nape like upside-down question marks. The skin on the back of her neck was creamy-white and appeared very soft. He found himself wanting to kiss the curve of her neck, to push the red tendrils aside and taste the creamy softness of her skin.

Addie turned and found him standing close behind her. Her eyes widened. Her tongue moistened her lips, and he could see the rapid rise and fall of her breasts.

"Perhaps I'm not the right person to be teaching you, Mr. Rider."

"I liked it better when you called me Will."

"I never . . ."

He nodded. "Yes, you did."

Her gaze dropped from his, lingered a moment on his lips, then fell to the floor. "I really think you should go, Mr. Rider."

"I thought we were friends, Addie."

He wasn't being fair. He knew it, but he didn't care. Something was happening between them. Something he didn't understand. Something he'd never felt before. He wanted to be with this woman. He wanted to hold her, kiss her, make love to her.

"We *are* friends," she replied, not looking up.

He tipped her chin with his index finger, forcing her to lift her gaze to meet his. She had the most amazing eyes. Right from the very first, he'd felt mesmerized by them.

"Then you'll come back to the ranch?" he asked. "You'll continue the lessons?"

He saw her indecision, her confusion, as it flickered across her face. He felt the slight tremor of her body through the finger he still held beneath her chin. He knew it would be simple to lean down and kiss her. He sensed that she wouldn't pull away from him.

What was this strange allure that drew them together? She felt it, too. He knew she did.

"Will you?" he asked again.

"I'll come," she whispered. "But not until next week."

Lord, he wanted to kiss her. He wanted to hold her body against his, feel the beat of her heart against his chest. He wanted to possess her as he'd never wanted to possess a woman before. It went beyond feeling a woman's naked body beneath his, although he wanted that, too. This desire was foreign to him. He knew instinctively that it wouldn't be satisfied by a mere physical joining.

Addie stepped back from him, stopping when she was pressed against the table. "I . . . I'm behind on my lesson planning. I'll come out to your ranch on Monday after school." There was a pleading look in her eyes. "I promise."

He could understand why she looked half-frightened. He was half-frightened himself. He'd never felt anything this intense in his life.

He nodded. "I'll see you then."

She moistened her lips with the tip of her tongue again, unknowingly causing the flame of desire to flare even hotter inside him. He knew he had to get out of there before he did something that would truly frighten her. If he'd thought he could stop with a mere kiss, he might have tried to steal one from her, but something told him he wouldn't be able to stop once he started.

"See you Monday," he said again, then hurried toward the waiting buckskin, ignoring the pain in his ribs as he stepped up into the saddle and turned the horse toward home.

"Tom? What's troubling you?" Maria walked up behind her husband and laid a hand on his shoulder. She kissed the top of his head, then stared down at the papers strewn across the table.

He placed his hand over hers as he looked up. "Nothing really. Just going over some accounts from the mill."

"I've seen that look before, Tom McLeod. You're worried about something."

Tom pushed the chair back from the table, then pulled his wife onto his lap. "The only thing that worries me is having you *worrying* that something's worrying me."

"Oh, you." She popped him playfully on the head. "Be serious."

"I am serious. Doc Varney said you're not to do anything but rest and take care of yourself for the next three months. I'm going to make sure you do just that." He nuzzled her neck.

Maria sighed. "It's going to be a very boring three months if I'm not allowed to even think for myself." She gave him one of her most determined looks. "Now tell me what's troubling you. If you don't, I'll only worry more."

Her husband acknowledged defeat with a wry smile. "All right. It just seems we're not getting the amount of lumber I think we should be getting from the trees we're cutting."

"Are we in financial trouble?"

Tom shook his head. "No. No, it's not as serious as all that. It's just . . . I don't know. I thought our profits would be higher this year, what with all the new building going on, all the new families moving into the area. Maybe I just estimated our income too high for the year, but I don't think that's it. I don't know. Maybe it's nothing."

Maria kissed his brow. "You've a good head for business. You'll figure it out. Just don't . . ." She stopped abruptly. She grabbed Tom's hand and moved it onto her abdomen.

"What is it?" he asked, his tone alarmed.

She smiled. "Wait." She smiled softly. "There. Did you feel it?" The movement in her womb brought tears of joy to her eyes.

Tom glanced up at her, his gaze filled with warmth and love. "I feel it."

"Our son," Maria whispered as she laid her head on her husband's shoulder. "Sarah's little brother."

"I love you, Maria," Tom replied softly, the accounts from the mill completely forgotten.

Addie lay on her side beneath the warm quilts, staring toward the hearth. Try as she might, she hadn't been able to go to sleep. She felt as if her body were filled with coals as hot as those in the fireplace, and she knew only Will could extinguish the hot agony she suffered.

There had been a moment when he'd looked at her earlier today, and she'd thought he wanted her as badly as she wanted him. It seemed an impossible notion, but now she wondered. Did he feel the same thing she was feeling?

And what if he did? She wasn't a complete fool. She knew passion could be a temporary, fleeting thing. It wasn't the same as love and devotion and commitment. While he might want to use her body, she knew he wasn't offering any of those things her heart truly desired.

You're twenty-seven years old. Wouldn't it be better to have one night than nothing?

She rolled onto her other side and covered her head with the blanket, trying to shut out her indecent thoughts. She wished her father had never told her about the coupling of men and women. She wished he hadn't explained the special union that brought pleasure as well as providing for procreation. She wished she were as ignorant of such things as most unmarried girls and women.

But her father had never failed to answer any question she'd ever asked, not even about the sexual union. She understood too much, at least on an intellectual level, and now her imagination had begun to run wild with what knowledge it had. She was visualizing all sorts of things, and they made her body ache with a growing frustration.

Chad . . . Think of Chad.

She closed her eyes and tried to see the blacksmith. She saw his broad shoulders and his massive chest and his dark hair and his brown eyes. Yes, she could see Chad.

But as quickly as she conjured his image, it vanished, replaced by the ever-present memory of Will.

Fear mingled with physical frustration. She was afraid of what lay ahead of her, afraid her desire was so strong she would sacrifice everything—her honor, her self-respect, everything—for just one night in Will Rider's arms.

Will stepped outside onto the covered porch. He leaned against the support post as he rolled a cigarette and lit it. Overhead, the late September sky was spattered with countless stars, a sliver of moon rising in the east. A cool breeze rustled the turning leaves of nearby trees. A horse nickered, another snorted in reply. They were familiar sights, peaceful sounds.

But there was nothing peaceful about the way Will was feeling tonight.

"You're a poor excuse for a man, Phillip Rider."

His mother's words, spoken so many years before, pulled him back in time. It was as if he were standing there in the wretched apartment where they'd lived in the decade before his father's death, watching, listening, living it all over again.

"How could you do this to me?" Martha yelled at her husband as she stood in the small parlor of the run-down flat. "How could you bring me to a place like this?"

"I had no choice, Martha." Phillip's voice was weary. "Our money is gone. If we didn't sell the house, they would have taken it from us."

"If my father were alive, he never would have let you bring me to such a place."

"Well, your father isn't alive."

"If it weren't for this baby"—Her hand dropped to her rounded abdomen—"I would leave you. I would find a man who could take care of me properly." She sank onto a worn chair and laid her forehead against its back as she wept. "I was so beautiful. All the men wanted me. Look at me now. I look like a cow. If I could just be rid of it . . ."

Phillip moved toward her, laying his hand on her neck. "Martha, please . . ."

"I hate you, Phillip. I hate you for making me fat with your child. I hate you for bringing me to this place. I'll see you live to regret all the sorrow you've caused me. So help me, I will."

Will dropped the cigarette and crushed it with his boot. There were other memories—too many of them—all of them ugly, all of them painful to recall. He tried never to remember them, but lately they'd haunted his thoughts far too often.

"*. . . I'll see you live to regret all the sorrow you've caused me. So help me, I will.*"

His mother had kept her promise. She had made Phillip Rider regret just about everything in life, even his life itself. Eventually, she'd found other men who would care for her, who'd bought her pretty things, who'd told her over and over how beautiful she was.

"She wasn't always like this," Phillip had told him once, not long before he died.

His father's words, meant to comfort, had only made Will more determined to never get trapped in the marriage snare. He'd been convinced that no woman could be trusted. He'd believed that, beneath their carefully constructed facades, all women were like Martha Rider—greedy, manipulative, selfish, unfaithful. Certainly Justine hadn't disabused him of his beliefs. His beautiful one-time mistress had only served to solidify them.

But what if he was wrong? What if all women weren't like his mother and Justine? What if some of them were exactly as they appeared?

What about Addie?

Chapter Eighteen

By the time the folks of Homestead were finished, Doc Varney's barn was nearly as clean as his examination room. The hard-packed dirt floor had been swept free of any debris. The air smelled of fresh straw, mingled with a faint odor of vinegar. Long tables had been made from planks and sawhorses and disguised with white tablecloths, and these makeshift tables were quickly covered with all manner of food. Chinese lanterns hung from the rafters, shedding a golden light over everything below. A riser for the musicians stood at one end of the barn, exactly opposite the door. All was ready for the Homestead Harvest Dance.

Carrying a platter in her hands, Addie walked into the improvised dance hall beside Chad Turner. The building was already filled with people. Voices rose and fell in volume, depending upon the tune the fiddler and other musicians were playing.

She smiled as she looked about her, her heart already feeling lighter than it had in days. She was determined to have a wonderful time tonight. She'd sworn to herself that she wasn't going to lose another wink of sleep or waste another moment thinking about Will Rider. The harvest dance seemed a good place to begin.

Several women waved to her, motioning for her to join them at the food tables.

"I'd better take this cake over there," she said to Chad.

He nodded and smiled as she moved away from his side.

"You didn't tell me you were comin' with Chad," Emma said, glancing over Addie's shoulder toward the young man in question.

Addie shrugged. "I guess I forgot to mention it last time we talked."

Emma's expression was speculative.

"It's not what you think," Addie whispered to her.

The other woman grinned, clearly not believing what Addie said. "You remember Doris and Maria, of course." She motioned to the two women who were standing on the opposite side of the table, removing towels from the plates and platters of food.

"Doesn't the place look festive?" Maria asked. "I can't believe what they were able to do with Doc's barn."

Addie had to agree. It certainly didn't look like any barn she'd ever seen.

"We're lucky the weather hasn't turned cold on us yet." Doris folded a cloth and placed it into a wicker basket. "Mark me, we'll see our first snow in the next week or so. I feel it in my bones."

Emma laughed. "You and your bones, Doris. I swear, you weren't right once all last winter."

"You'll see that I'm right this time." Doris looked offended.

Maria patted her mother-in-law's back. "Don't you mind her, Mother McLeod. Emma's just trying to get under your skin." She looked at Addie again. "Come with me. There's some people here you haven't met yet. I'll introduce you to everyone."

Maria took hold of Addie's arm and drew her through the crowd and across the barn toward three men and two women. The older man had salt-and-pepper hair and bushy gray eyebrows. The woman beside him looked much the same, her face weathered by the sun and years. On closer look, she could see that the two younger men were barely more than boys, perhaps seventeen and eighteen years old. The young woman, a beauty if ever Addie had seen one, was obviously their older sister. She had the same ebony-colored hair and obsidian eyes as the young men. She also had porcelain-like skin and a sweet smile which could make the angels sing.

She was just the sort of woman who had always brought out all of Addie's insecurities. Tonight was no different. Addie couldn't help comparing herself to the dark-haired beauty and finding herself wanting.

"Addie, I'd like you to meet the Hendersons," Maria said, turning her first toward the older couple. "This is Bradley and Ida Henderson. Mr. and Mrs. Henderson, this is Addie Sherwood, our schoolteacher."

"How do you do?" the Hendersons said in unison.

"How do you do?" Addie returned.

Maria continued, "And these are their children. Fillmore . . ."

"Pleased to meet you, Miss Sherwood."

"And Norman . . ."

"A pleasure, Miss Sherwood."

"And their sister, Ophelia."

"Hello."

Addie returned each of the greetings in turn.

"The Hendersons live on the other side of Tin Horn Pass. They're originally from Massachusetts." Maria glanced back at Ida. "Addie moved here from Connecticut in August. She's doing a wonderful job teaching the children in the valley. We're thrilled to have her as part of the community." She touched the gentle swell of her abdomen in a maternal gesture as old as time itself. "It's comforting to know my children will receive a good education when they're old enough."

"Where are you from in Connecticut?" Ida Henderson asked Addie.

"Kingsbury."

"Really?" Bradley frowned in concentration. "I think I had an uncle from around Kingsbury."

"No, dear," Ida said. "It wasn't an uncle. It was a cousin on your mother's side."

Addie saw Ophelia roll her eyes. Then their gazes met. Ophelia looked embarrassed by her action, but Addie couldn't help smiling in response. In that moment, Addie decided she wasn't going to let Ophelia's beauty and her own lack of same keep them from becoming friends if Ophelia was willing.

"There you are." Chad's voice came from just behind her right shoulder.

Addie turned toward him—but not before she saw Ophelia's eyes widen hopefully.

"I thought I'd lost you," Chad said in a voice meant for Addie's ears only.

"Maria wanted to introduce me to the Hendersons. Do you know them?"

Chad answered in the affirmative, then gave a quick greeting to the family.

Addie was especially interested in watching Ophelia's reaction. The young woman was obviously infatuated with the handsome blacksmith, but—much to Addie's astonishment—Chad didn't seem to notice.

Chad shared a few polite words of conversation before pulling Addie away, leading her into the center of the barn where other couples were dancing to a lively tune.

He leaned forward, placing his mouth close to her ear. "I didn't come here to spend time talkin' on the sidelines when I could be spending time dancin' with you."

Addie flushed, unused to receiving compliments and ill-prepared on how to respond.

Will paused in the doorway. At his back, night had already fallen across the valley floor, only a first quarter moon keeping total darkness at bay. With the setting of the sun had come a crisp October chill, but here in Doc Varney's barn, one would never know it. The place was filled with warmth and laughter.

His gaze scanned the crowd, seeing all the familiar faces. He'd been through good times and bad with many of the people in this room. When he and Rick had come to this valley back in 'seventy-four, he never would have guessed he'd become part of a growing community. If he'd been asked, he would have said it would be just Rick, a few cowpokes, him, and the cows for a long time to come. He also would have said he'd prefer it that way. Now he wasn't so sure that was true.

Will didn't realize he'd been searching for Addie with his eyes until he found her dancing in Chad Turner's arms. She was almost as tall as the blacksmith, but the man's muscular chest and arms, honed by years at the forge, made her look tiny by comparison.

She was wearing a striped, yellow-silk gown, all bustled and draped and flounced—easily the prettiest dress in the room. A yellow-and-white satin fan hung from a cord wrapped around her right wrist. Her hair was gathered in a cluster of curls on the back of her head. She wore a garniture of artificial daisies and yellow ribbons rather than a bonnet. She looked quite young and fetching, he thought. Much too fetching, as far as he was concerned.

Addie's head was cocked slightly to one side, and she wore a smile as she listened to whatever Chad was saying. Will could tell by her expression that she was straining to hear her partner's words above the music and general commotion.

Will had a strong desire to put his fist right into the center of Chad's grin.

"Uncle Will?"

He glanced down at Lark. For a moment, he'd forgotten his niece was with him.

"Can I go over with Rose and Leslie?"

"Sure. Go on ahead."

He watched the little girl wend her way through the crowd until she reached the other children, some of them sitting on a stack of hay in the corner, others climbing up a ladder into the loft. Then his gaze swung back to the dancers just as the music stopped.

Chad placed his hand beneath Addie's elbow and steered her toward the punch bowl set up on one of the tables. Her cheeks had a rosy hue, and somehow he knew her green eyes were twinkling, even though he couldn't see them.

"Will! How are you?"

He turned his head as Hank stepped up beside him.

"Heard about your accident. Glad to see you're doin' better. I told Doris there wasn't a horse in the territory that could keep you down for long, but I didn't expect to see you here tonight."

Will shrugged as he pressed his arm against his ribs. The ache in his side had started up again, as if in response to the sheriff's words. "Couldn't very well miss this shindig, could I? Lark's been talking about it for the last two weeks."

"From the looks of the little gal, things are workin' out for the two of you?"

He nodded. "We're getting on all right."

The sheriff wore a satisfied grin, looking as if he were responsible for the outcome. "Never thought you wouldn't."

Will's attention wandered back toward the punch bowl, but Addie and Chad weren't there. This time he knew he was looking for them when his gaze swept the room. He found them back on the dance floor.

Wasn't Chad holding Addie just a little too close?

"Say, Will," Hank said, "I almost forgot. Brad Henderson was lookin' for you."

"Who?" He glanced at the sheriff.

"Bradley Henderson. He and his family bought Zeb Jensen's place over a year ago. Remember?"

"Oh, yeah. I remember."

Hank placed a hand on Will's shoulder blade. "Well, come with me. My guess is Brad's in the market for some good saddle horses."

From the corner of Will's eye, he caught a flash of yellow silk as it whirled by. Setting his jaw, he managed to go along with Hank without glancing toward the dance floor.

Addie's laugh bubbled up from inside her when the music stopped. The tune had been lively, and the musicians had all played their instruments with great gusto if not always with great expertise. She'd never been to a dance quite like this one before.

"More punch?" Chad asked.

She snapped open her fan and began stirring the air with it. "Yes," she gasped. "I'd love some."

Guiding her with his hand at her elbow, he steered her toward the refreshment table. Doris McLeod and Zoe Potter were manning the punch bowl.

"Having a good time?" Doris asked as she filled a cup and handed it to Addie.

"Oh, yes." She glanced at Zoe. "Your husband is quite talented, Mrs. Potter."

The woman smiled, clearly pleased. "I guess he should be. He plays that mouth organ almost every night. Helps him relax, he says."

Addie turned her head as the players struck up a new song. That was when she saw him—and her heart plummeted to the floor.

Will led Ophelia Henderson onto the dance floor, took hold of her right hand with his left, then placed his right hand near the small of her back. Addie didn't know if she'd ever seen such a perfect-looking couple in her entire life—Will with his golden hair in contrast to Ophelia's ebony tresses; Will so tall, lean and strong, Ophelia petite and delicate; Will all virile masculinity, Ophelia sweetly feminine.

She looked away, the sight of them too painful to bear.

"Is something wrong?" Chad asked solicitously.

Addie glanced up at her escort. "No," she lied, forcing an apologetic smile. "Except I'm feeling a bit tired. Might we sit down for a while?"

"Of course."

He immediately walked her over to one wall of the barn, where a row of chairs and benches had been set. Most of them were occupied by elder citizens of Long Bow Valley, but they managed to find one chair that was vacant. Addie sank onto it, realizing once she was sitting that her knees had felt as wobbly as a newborn colt's. It was a wonder she hadn't fallen down.

She returned the greetings from those seated nearby. She even managed to say a few intelligent words and appear to take part in the conversation. She thought she was doing admirably well and was proud of herself for resisting the urge to turn toward the dance floor.

What did I expect?

The world was full of beautiful women. Addie just wasn't one of them.

He said he was glad you're his friend. He never said he wanted anything more from you.

No man would want Ophelia just for a friend, just to care for his children. Men would simply want Ophelia.

"Evening, Chad."

Her head snapped up at the sound of his voice. Her heart rose into her throat.

"Evenin', Will."

Her gaze caressed his face, but he was looking at Chad.

"Mind if I ask Miss Sherwood for a dance?"

Chad shrugged. "Guess not, if she's willin'."

Will turned his eyes in her direction. "Addie?" He held out his hand.

She couldn't have stopped herself if she'd wanted to—which she didn't. She placed her fingers in his, felt his hand tighten around hers. Effortlessly, she rose from the chair as he led her toward the dance floor in the center of the barn.

Once, when she was seventeen, she'd gone with her father and Robert to a gala ball in New York City. The ballroom had been gigantic, the walls covered with gilded mirrors, crystal chandeliers hanging from a frescoed ceiling. The floor had been polished until it gleamed almost as brightly as the mirror. A stringed orchestra had played waltzes and quadrilles and reels until the wee hours. She'd felt like Cinderella from the fairy tale. It had been a magical night.

But it had been nothing compared to this.

Will didn't smile. He didn't speak. He simply held her in his arms and began to move in time to the music.

It was a waltz, and no orchestra had ever played a melody more beautifully than the odd assortment of musicians who were gathered on the riser in Doc Varney's barn that night. Addie's feet seemed to float on air.

For this brief moment in time, she felt as beautiful as Eliza Dearborn and Ophelia Henderson combined. For this brief moment, she could believe anything was possible. Anything.

Chapter Nineteen

Chad supposed there were thousands of men in this world who were a whole heck of a lot smarter than he was, but he figured he'd have to be an idiot—and deaf and blind to boot—not to guess what Addie Sherwood was feeling for Will Rider. But if luck was with him, Addie wouldn't have figured it out yet, and that would give him some time to make his move.

He hoped so. He'd already decided this was the night he was going to propose.

The moment he stopped the buggy in front of her cabin, he hopped down and hurried around the vehicle, then gave Addie his hand.

"I had a wonderful time tonight," she said softly as they walked toward the door.

"Me, too. Listen, Addie, do you think . . ." His mouth went dry. His mind went blank.

She paused as she reached for the latch. She glanced up at him expectantly.

He swallowed and tried again. "May I come in for just a moment? I won't stay long, I promise. It's just . . . well, I'd like a word with you."

Uncertainty wavered in her voice, as she said, "I suppose it will be all right." She opened the door and led the way inside.

While Addie removed her cloak, Chad walked over to the fireplace and stirred up the coals. He added several logs and some kindling, and before long, there was a hardy blaze taking the chill from the room.

When he straightened and turned, he found her standing with her hands resting on the back of one of the chairs. She was watching him; her eyes were filled with a terrible sadness. He figured she was wishing he was Will. At the moment, so did he. Then maybe she'd smile.

She'd make a man a fine wife, he thought. She had a good heart. She cared about people's feelings. She'd know how to love a man. Maybe she might still learn to care for him.

"Addie?" He stepped toward her.

She watched him approach, never moving, not even blinking.

He placed his hands lightly on her upper arms. "Addie, I guess you know I've taken a likin' to you from the moment we met."

"Chad . . ." She shook her head.

"No. Let me finish. This is hard enough as it is."

He thought he saw a look of resignation in her eyes before she lowered her gaze. He ignored it and rushed on.

"A man reaches a point in his life when he knows he doesn't want to go on livin' all by himself. He knows he's missing something, feels like half a person. That's how I was feelin' when you walked into the livery a month ago."

"Oh, Chad . . ." She didn't look up.

His fingers tightened on her arms. "It occurred to me that you and I might do well together, Addie Sherwood. I'd do my best to make you happy. I think you're one of the finest women I've ever met."

He pulled her toward him, lowered his head, and found her lips with his. The kiss was short but sweet.

He continued softly, "What I'm askin' is if you'd consent to be my wife?"

"Oh, Chad," she whispered again.

He steeled himself for her reply, already certain he knew what it was going to be.

"I can't marry you, Chad. It's not that I don't think you're a fine man, and I'm very flattered you asked me. It's . . . it's just that I want to go on teaching. The school board might not allow that if we were to marry. The children mean so much to me, I couldn't bear to risk losing my job." She stepped back from him, but he kept his hands on her arms.

He felt a spark of sorrow but no surprise. He'd suspected all along she would turn him down. He'd suspected it the moment he'd seen her in

Will Rider's arms at the dance tonight.

"So you're turning me down 'cause you'd rather teach than be a wife, is that it?" He released her arms.

"Yes."

He raised his hand and caught a tear with his index finger as it slipped from her eye onto her cheek. Even though he was fairly certain it wasn't him she was crying for, he offered a patient smile. "Are you just lyin' to me or to yourself, too?"

Her chin lifted. She sniffed. "I don't know what you mean."

"Don't you?"

"No."

Chad took hold of one of her hands and pressed it between both of his. Then he leaned forward and placed a tender kiss on her cheek. "I think maybe you do," he said softly. "You just don't want to admit it." He released her hand and stepped back, taking one last long look at her. "Well, who knows. You just might change your mind, given a bit of time. Stranger things have happened. You think on it. Maybe I'll grow on you."

Looking at Chad, Addie wished she did love him. She knew Chad would have tried his best to make her happy.

"We can be friends, Chad," she replied softly.

"Probably." He offered a half-hearted smile. "Well, I'll be on my way. Good night, Addie."

She followed him to the door. "Good night, Chad. Thanks again for a wonderful evening."

"You're more'n welcome."

Despite the night chill, she watched until the buggy had disappeared into the darkness. Then she closed the door, dropped the bolt into place, and leaned against it.

He'd been right, of course. The reason she'd given for refusing his proposal wasn't the truth.

She thought of Chad's kiss. It had been sweet, tender—but that was all. Memories of the passions stirred by Will's kisses caused a flurry in the pit of her stomach. If only . . .

She closed her eyes as she pressed her hands against her abdomen. She drew in several deep breaths and let them out slowly. Finally she opened her eyes and made her way across the room to the foot of the bed. She faced the looking glass and stared at her shadowed reflection.

How odd, she thought as she began removing her hairpins. She wondered how many other tall, plain women her age could expect to receive three proposals of marriage in a matter of five months. And if those other tall, plain women *were* to receive such proposals, would any other but she turn them all down?

She picked up her brush from the bureau and began pulling it through her hair.

You wouldn't believe what has happened to me, Papa.

Chad hadn't said he loved her, of course, but she believed he cared for her. Perhaps a year ago, perhaps even three months ago, she might have accepted his offer of marriage. It had certainly been more heartfelt than the others she'd received.

Why couldn't she accept Chad's offer now?

She knew the answer. Because she loved another man. Because she loved Will Rider so much it hurt. No, she hadn't been lying to herself, only to Chad, when she'd said why she wouldn't marry him. She would have given up teaching if it had been Will who'd asked for her hand a second time.

She unbuttoned the yellow silk and hung it on a peg. Then she removed her undergarments and pulled her nightgown over her head. She was just folding back the blankets on her bed when she heard the sound of hoofbeats outside.

She grew still, listening. Was she mistaken? Was it only her own mare moving about in the corral?

No, there it was again. Someone was coming. But who could it be at this time of night?

Slipping into her wrapper, she walked over to the window and opened the curtain a crack— just as Will dismounted from his buckskin.

Her heart seemed to stop beating entirely. Why was he here?

Will didn't know why he'd come to her place. It was late. She was probably already asleep. She wouldn't want to see him now.

But he wanted to see her. He wanted another chance to hold her in his arms. He didn't know what it was about Addie. He just knew he couldn't go to sleep, thinking about another man dancing with her, thinking about another man taking her home, thinking about another man kissing her.

He'd turned back several times on the ride over, only to change his mind again and again. Now that he'd arrived, he didn't know what he planned to do. At first, he simply stared at her door. Then, in the spare light of the moon, he saw the curtain in the window move.

She was awake. She'd seen him. She knew he was there.

Will strode toward the door and knocked. He heard the bolt slide out of its slot, saw the latch lift, waited as the door creaked open. She stared at him without speaking, one hand still braced against the edge of the door, the other clutching her wrapper closed over her breasts.

Wordlessly, he pressed his palm against the door, inching it open wider. She stepped backward. He followed her inside.

Firelight danced in her hair, making the red tresses sparkle, as if sprinkled with rubies. He liked the way it looked, tumbling over her shoulders and down her back. Such glorious hair.

She was watching him, waiting. The air around them seemed to pulse with expectancy.

Staring down at her, Will wondered how he could ever have thought her looks plain. At this moment, he realized that she was beautiful. Not beautiful in an ordinary, easily recognized fashion. No, hers was a beauty that was not so readily seen, but it was beauty nonetheless.

He pushed the door closed. "Addie . . ."

For a moment, her hand tightened on the wrapper. Then she released the fabric. Her hands fell to her sides.

The desire he'd been trying to deny for days flared to life. He shrugged off his jacket, dropping it on the floor as he stepped forward and gathered her into his arms.

Addie responded by instinct. Her arms curved beneath his, her elbows pressed against his sides, until her fingers gripped his shoulders. She tilted her head to offer him easier access to her mouth. The instant their lips met, her body was filled with a storm of wanting more violent than any she'd known before.

A flicker of common sense tried to intrude, warning her that what she was about to do would alter her life forever. She didn't care. Only a few days ago she'd wondered if one night of passion would be enough. She didn't want to wonder any longer. She wanted to know. She closed the door on the part of her mind that cried its dire warnings and, instead of heeding them, gave herself over to the burning desires raging through her.

She could feel the rapid beat of his heart against hers. Her lips parted at the urging of his tongue. The intimate sensation as their tongues met sent another jolt through her body, weakening her knees. She clung to him lest she should fall.

How long they stood there, unmoving except for their hungry kisses, she didn't know. It seemed forever. It seemed only a moment in time.

And then his hands began to stroke her back, first in small circles, then gliding over the silky fabric of her wrapper until his fingers paused at the small of her back. Finally, they slid down to cup her buttocks. He drew her toward him, pressing her body even more closely against his until she could feel the hardness of his desire.

Even in her innocence, her body reacted. A groan tore from her throat.

Will lifted his head. She looked up at him. His eyes had darkened with emotions, emotions that seemed to swirl in stormy blue pools. She knew her own gaze mirrored his.

His hands moved up to her shoulders. Once there, he gently pushed the wrapper away. It slid from her body, ending in a satiny pool at her feet. Gooseflesh rose on her arms, but it wasn't because she felt cold. It was anticipation that caused her body to shiver.

With nimble fingers, Will released the buttons closing the front of her nightgown. Then he paused, his gaze once again boring into hers, waiting. She understood his hesitation. It was a chance for her to stop what would be an irreversible act.

"Will," she whispered—and reached to remove his cravat.

Chapter Twenty

The blazing fire on the hearth had burned low, and it shed little illumination upon the couple who stood in the middle of the room.

Now, as Will began to remove Addie's night-clothes, she was grateful for the lack of light. She knew she was too thin and lacked the abundant curves she thought men preferred. She was certain Will would find her deficient. She would rather not see the discovery in his eyes when he looked upon her naked figure and found her wanting.

A shiver of apprehension ran through her as her nightgown joined the wrapper on the floor. She felt the urge to grab something with which to cover herself. She ignored it. She was a grown woman. She understood the risk she was taking. Would she rather go to her grave without knowing what it was like to love a man? To love *this* man?

No.

Taking hold of Will's hand, she stepped backward, drawing him with her to the far side of the room. When the back of her legs touched the edge of the mattress, she rose on tiptoe to kiss him again, then sank onto the bed. She slid to the opposite side, making room for him beside her, and waited.

For one terrible moment, she feared he would change his mind. Though the deep shadows of the cabin hid his face from view, she knew he was staring down at her, considering his actions, wondering if what they were about to do was a mistake.

"Addie?"

"Don't talk, Will," she replied in a whisper. "Just join me."

Her words seemed to make his decision for him. Quickly, he removed his shirt, then shed his boots and trousers. Moments later, he lay down beside her, his body as naked as hers except for the bandage around his torso.

He drew her into his embrace, his mouth claiming hers again. Her senses reeled as he pulled her close—skin against skin, her bare breasts crushed against his chest, his erection pressed against her pelvis. It was frightening. It was exhilarating.

His body was so different from her own. His was all hard muscles beneath the sun-bronzed skin. His chest was covered with a light matting of hair. Though she'd been glad for the lack of light to hide her own flaws, she wished she could see him. All of him.

Will's mouth released hers, and he spread kisses across her cheek to her ear, then dropped to her throat. One hand slipped from her back to cup her right breast. She sucked in a surprised breath as he began kneading the sensitive flesh. Her body jerked involuntarily. He responded by pressing his tumescence closer still.

When he gently pushed her onto her back and trailed kisses down to her left breast, a moan escaped her throat. His tongue teased her nipple until it was taut and erect as his thumb stroked the same response from her other breast.

Tension continued to build in her until it became an urgent pulsing, crying for release. Intellectually, she knew what was to happen between them, but nothing her father had ever told her had prepared her for what she was feeling now. She felt swept away by sensations foreign and new. She'd lost all control of her responses. She moved without thought, guided solely by instinct.

His lips returned to hers. This time, she opened her mouth for his kisses without prompting, as eager to taste him as he was to taste her. She sucked his tongue into her mouth, then released it.

And all the while, his hands were roaming over her bare flesh. Everywhere he touched, her skin felt electrified. She reveled in the sensation.

Nothing that had gone before had prepared her, however, for the moment when his hand sought the tender flesh at the apex of her thighs. When his fingers began to probe and stroke, her heart seemed to stop beating, then began to race. Her head dropped back as her hips thrust upward. While his hand worked its mastery, his lips took advantage of her exposed throat, finding the tender flesh where her pulse pounded.

She began to writhe, part of her wishing to pull away from his touch before her body shattered into a thousand pieces, another part wanting to press ever closer for fear she *wouldn't* shatter.

"Will . . . Will?" she whispered, not certain what she was asking of him, not certain what she wanted, but knowing he could help her find it.

Suddenly, she felt something explode inside her. She arched against his hand, her breath caught in her throat. A kaleidoscope of colors burst against her closed eyelids. She felt as if she were soaring, spinning, whirling. Then, ever so slowly, she drifted back to earth.

For a moment, neither of them moved. Addie thought it was over, her father's explanations forgotten in the afterglow. Her body felt drained. She felt certain she couldn't have moved if her life depended upon it.

And then Will's hand began to stroke her once again. Her body responded instantly. When he moved above her, she opened herself to him without hesitation. Even so, the feeling of his erection entering her was a shock. She felt a flash of fear. Her eyes flew open, and her body stilled, tensed. He paused as he met the resistance of her virgin body.

The earth itself seemed to be holding its breath, waiting.

Then her own desires overcame her trepidation. Her hands pressed against his buttocks, forcing him deeper inside her. There was pain, but she paid it no heed. Slowly, he began to move. The glorious tension returned.

Instinctively, she joined him in the intimate dance, a dance as old as time itself.

He moved—and she moved with him.

His heart raced—and so did hers.

He carried her to places as yet unknown to her, and she clung to him, reveling in each discovery.

When he cried her name, she whispered his in return.

The universe trembled, and they found shelter in each other's embrace.

Will listened to Addie's even breathing and knew she slept. He smiled, enjoying the feel of her head on his shoulder, her body still pressed close to his, her thick hair spread across his chest. He ignored the pain in his side which their lovemaking had set afire.

Now he knew. Now he knew what it was supposed to be like. This was what made a man cleave to one woman, promising to be faithful to her until death. It wasn't simply the act of love. He'd lain with his share of women, and he'd enjoyed them as much as they'd enjoyed him. But this was something else, something more.

He turned his head and kissed Addie's temple. She murmured something in her sleep, a contented sound, then snuggled closer against him.

His smile broadened. Who'd have thought the rigid and upright Miss Sherwood was capable of such passion? And who'd have thought Addie would be the one to stir to life such unfamiliar feelings within Will Rider, the man who didn't believe in marriage or families—or love?

She stirred again. He felt her tense and knew she'd awakened and was surprised to find him holding her.

She pulled away from his embrace. Cool air slithered along his skin where moments before they had been touching. He felt her draw the blankets up tight beneath her chin. If her face were visible to him, he knew he would see confusion and timidity where earlier there had been confidence, even boldness.

"You needn't become prudish now, Miss Sherwood," he said, his tone teasing. "I believe we've gone past that point."

He wished he'd risen earlier and stoked the fire. He wanted to see her face. He knew she must be blushing. Addie blushed so easily.

"I imagine this means we'll have to marry," he continued. "I know the last time I proposed you said you preferred not to wed, but I think you'll agree that what happened between us tonight has changed matters. I don't believe you have any other choice but to agree to be my wife."

Addie felt her body turn to ice as she listened to him. The joy she'd known beneath his tender and erotic touch was dashed by his cold assessment of their new circumstances. For a brief time, while their passions had run wild, she'd dared to believe he might care for her. Truly care for her.

She'd been sorely mistaken.

She sat up, taking the top blanket with her. She wrapped it around her body as she rose from the bed. "No one need ever know what happened here tonight. Certainly you should not feel obligated to marry me." She rounded the bed, searched for and found her nightgown and wrapper on the floor, and picked them up, clutching them in her hands before her. "I certainly feel under no obligation to marry you," she finished.

"Addie, you don't seem to understand." He got up and followed her to the center of the room. Placing his hands on her shoulders, he turned her to face him.

She tilted her chin proudly. "I'm a grown woman, Will Rider. I know my own mind." Her heart was breaking. The pain ran so deep, it was almost unbearable. "I will not be forced into marriage."

"But I thought . . ." He brushed her hair back from her face with his fingertips.

"You thought wrong, Mr. Rider," she whispered. She wished he would leave before she fell apart. "I told you before I didn't wish to marry. Not to raise your niece and certainly not to warm your bed."

"That's not why!"

"Isn't it? Then please explain to me why."

"You have to ask after what happened here tonight?"

Her silence was her stubborn reply to his question.

"Good Lord, woman. This isn't the time to behave as if you haven't a brain in your head. Think! I know you were a virgin, but surely you must realize that you could be with child after what we've just done."

"So you want to marry me to protect me from scandal?"

"Of course! What kind of son of a bitch do you think I am?"

She pulled away from him. "I assure you, Mr. Rider, I don't think you're a . . . anything of the kind." She turned her back to him. "You'd better go."

He sounded angry. "I'll go, but I'll be back. We haven't finished this discussion."

Addie turned and crossed to the fireplace. She stared down into the glowing embers beneath black ashes, proof that a fire had once burned hot. It was rather like what she felt now. She remembered the heat of desire, but all that remained were the cold, black ashes of despair and disappointment.

She listened to the sounds of Will dressing, heard him walk across the room to stand behind her. She didn't move. She prayed he wouldn't touch her. If he touched her, she would be lost.

"I'll be back tomorrow. We'll finish this conversation then."

He crossed to the door. It slammed behind him. She was alone again. More alone than ever before in her life.

Wearily, she reached for some wood to rekindle the fire on the hearth. She didn't think it would help. She was certain she would never feel warm again.

She watched as the wood caught fire. Images of Will splitting the logs fluttered through the recesses of her mind, and with them came another jab of pain.

If only he'd said he loved her . . . or even that he cared a little. . . .

She pulled a chair close to the fireplace and sat down, still wrapped in the blanket. She stared into the flickering firelight and faced the brutal truth.

She'd known he didn't love her. She'd known his desire was purely a physical need. She'd made the decision to have one night rather than nothing at all. She was getting just what she'd expected.

Or was she?

She hadn't expected him to offer to marry her, the soiled spinster. Once, not very many days ago, she'd wished she'd accepted his offer of marriage when it was nothing more than a platonic business offer, a convenient arrangement to provide a mother for his niece. He'd given her a second chance, and she'd turned him down again. She'd actually turned him down again.

Of course, she never would have guessed it could hurt even more this time than it had before. But it did. It hurt a hundred times more, for now she loved him.

She closed her eyes and felt again the way his hands had played upon her body, extracting from it a poignant melody of unbelievable beauty. While he'd done so, she'd been filled with a sense of hope, a sense of wonder. Now there was nothing. Nothing but pain and the dream of what might have been.

Suddenly, she laughed, a sharp, bitter sound in the silence of the night. This made *four* proposals of marriage in a matter of five months that she'd rejected. Four proposals for the tall, plain spinster from Connecticut and none of them for the reason of love.

Addie covered her face with her hands and wept.

Chapter Twenty-One

Reverend Pendroy always arrived at the church early on Sunday mornings, especially now that it was being used during the week as the school. The first thing he did on this particular Sunday was stoke the wood stove to take the chill from the air. Then he set about pulling the benches into place and setting hymn books on the end of each pew for the parishioners to share.

"Bringing in the sheaves," he sang, his rich baritone filling the room. "Bringing in the sheaves. We shall come rejoicing, bringing in the . . ."

"Reverend?"

The words of the hymn died abruptly as he turned in response to the child's voice. "Why, Rose, good morning. You're here early."

"I wanted to ask you a question, sir." Her hands were clenched into fists at her side, and her face was filled with tension. She shifted her weight nervously from one foot to the other.

"Of course," the reverend replied, his tone now serious. "Come sit down, and we'll talk." He motioned to one of the benches.

Rose sat as she was told and placed her hands in her lap. She immediately began twisting the folds of her worn calico dress.

Watching her, the reverend couldn't help wondering how a pair like Glen and Virginia Townsend had ever produced a child like Rose. She was not only pretty and sweet-natured, but she was bright and intuitive far beyond her years. She was also a brave little thing. She had to be with a father like hers. No one in town, least of all the reverend, was blind to what went on inside the Townsend house, especially when Glen was drinking—which was most of the time.

When Rose continued to stare at her hands in her lap, Reverend Pendroy cleared his throat, then said, "You seem troubled, Rose. What can I do to help?"

"I . . . I was just wonderin' something." She tilted her head to one side, looking at him from beneath long lashes. "If you knew of someone who was . . . who was . . . ah, doin' something dishonest—at least, you *thought* he was—what would be the right thing to do?"

He considered her question carefully before answering. "The first thing I would do is talk to him, try to explain the error of his ways and give him an opportunity to make amends on his own. The Good Book says, 'If thy brother shall trespass against thee, go and tell him his fault between thee and him alone.' Christ commands His people to restore a brother caught in sin in a spirit of gentleness, Rose. I would hope I could do so."

The girl pursed her lips thoughtfully, then shook her head. "What if that didn't work?"

"Well, then I suppose I would have no choice but to speak to his parents."

She sighed. "What if he wasn't a child? What if he was a grown-up?"

Reverend Pendroy could see Rose was very serious about finding the right answer to her dilemma. He wondered about the nature of the dishonesty and how she had come to know about it. *Lord,* he prayed silently, *give me wisdom.*

"Would you go to the sheriff?" she asked softly, a quiver in her voice.

He frowned. "Is it as serious as that, Rose?"

She nodded.

"Perhaps you should tell me the exact nature of this dishonesty."

This time she shook her head. "I can't," she whispered as she dropped her gaze to the folds of her skirt.

"I would keep your confidence, child."

"I know, sir." She slid forward on the bench until her feet touched the floor, then stood.

She kept her eyes pointed toward the ground. "I better go."

Reverend Pendroy rose, too, and watched as she hurried out of the church. He let out a lengthy sigh, feeling a great heaviness settling on his heart. He wondered what Glen Townsend—and he didn't doubt for a moment they'd been talking about Rose's father—might be doing to cause the girl such distress.

Addie couldn't go to church. The pain was still too raw to hide. She was afraid everyone would be able see the truth written in her eyes, and she would forever be scorned and rejected by the good and decent citizens of Homestead.

Yet she couldn't stay home either. Will had said he would be back to talk to her today. She didn't want to be there when he came. She didn't want to listen to him offering to take her for his wife out of pity for her fallen status.

She dressed warmly against the October morning chill, then harnessed her mare to the buggy and set off for a drive. She had no particular direction in mind. Wherever the horse took her would be fine.

The paintbrush of autumn had been busy in recent days, tinting the valley and surrounding mountains with shades of yellow and orange and red. At another time, Addie might have enjoyed the beauty of the landscape, but this morning, her thoughts were turned inward.

There was no order to her private musings. So many scenes from different moments of her life swirled about in her head. There were snatches from her childhood, memories of young womanhood and of Robert, remembrances of the years when she and her father had lived alone in the house on Bayview Lane, the years when she had watched Matthew Sherwood grow old and then die. She recalled the fears and the triumphs, the uncertainties and the moments of decision. There had been times of great joy and times of great sorrow. There had been times when the future had seemed bright and hopeful and times when there'd seemed to be no future at all. She pondered all the strange turnings of her life that had somehow brought her to Homestead, and she wondered if it hadn't been fate that had brought her to this place.

And then, despite herself, she thought of Will. From the very first moment she'd seen him, he had made her feel more alive than she'd ever felt in her life. It was more than simply his handsome face, much more than the glorious strength of his body. There was something in his spirit which had touched her heart, her very soul, and caused her to love him as she had never loved before—and would never love again.

She drew in the reins, bringing the horse and buggy to a stop near the aspen-covered skirt of the mountains.

Never before had she loved this way. . . .

And never again would she.

This might be her last chance at happiness. Did she mean to let her pride get in the way? Wouldn't it be better to marry Will, loving him as she did, and hope he would grow to love her in time? It could happen. People often married first and love came later.

Again she thought of the twists of fate that had brought her to Homestead. She might have married Robert. She might have married Mr. Bainbridge. Her father might never have sold the house or he might have saved money enough for her to stay on in Kingsbury. She might have answered another advertisement for a teacher. So many things might have kept her away, but they hadn't. Surely it was fate that she should meet Will Rider. Surely it was preordained that she should love him.

The mare pawed the ground restlessly, then shook her head, rattling the harness.

Running and hiding, Addie thought. She'd spent her life running away and hiding. She didn't want to do either of them anymore.

"Let's go back, girl," she said softly, slapping the animal's back lightly with the reins. "Let's go back."

Rose wished she could tell her mother what she knew about Pa. It would be a real relief to let someone else decide what to do. But one look at Ma—sitting beside her on the church pew—and she knew she couldn't add another burden to her mother's already heavy lot. Virginia Townsend always looked tired, but today she looked old as well.

Besides, her ma wouldn't do anything about it anyway. She'd just tell Rose not to worry about such things. It wasn't a woman's place to question what her husband did, and it certainly wasn't a child's place to question her father's actions. Children were to be obedient and respectful and quiet. For that matter, so were women. At least, that's what her pa expected of his wife and daughter.

Rose squirmed on the hard bench and tried to make herself concentrate on the reverend's sermon, but she couldn't. She kept seeing her pa, lounging drunkenly in the stuffed chair near the fireplace late one night last week. She kept hearing his voice as he'd talked to himself.

"Takes too long, doin' it this way. . . . Takes too damn long. . . . Always the mill safe . . . Full o' money end of month . . . There's ways . . . Never know was me . . . Could do it . . . Buy me that saloon . . ."

Rose had backed out of the parlor without being seen. She'd returned to her room and tried to pretend she hadn't heard and didn't understand.

But she *had* heard and she *did* understand—at least enough to know Pa meant to take money from the mill. He meant to steal money that didn't belong to him.

Rose glanced over her shoulder. She saw Lark sitting beside her uncle. Sometimes she wished she was sitting in her best friend's place. She wished she was Mr. Rider's niece. She'd never seen him drunk or heard him raise his voice. She'd bet he was good to Lark all the time. Her friend didn't ever have to be afraid to go home after school. Lark didn't have to hope Mr. Rider would stay away from the house until everybody was in bed and asleep.

Her gaze moved on, not stopping until she found Sheriff McLeod. When she was younger, she'd been afraid of the burly lawman with the guns strapped to his thighs, but she wasn't afraid anymore. He was nice and friendly with all the children of Homestead. He treated her the same way he treated all the others, even though he had to arrest Glen Townsend more often than anybody else in these parts.

Would the sheriff believe her if she told him what she'd heard? Would he be able to stop Pa before he stole from Tom McLeod?

As Rose turned her eyes toward the front of the church again, she suddenly imagined what her pa would do if he ever found out she'd told anyone what she'd heard, and her blood ran like ice through her veins.

Reverend Pendroy seemed especially long-winded today, Will thought as he crossed his right ankle over his left knee and leaned against the back wall of the church. He would blame his restlessness on the dull ache in his ribs, but in all honesty, he knew it had more to do with Addie's absence in church than anything else.

All the way into town he'd practiced what he was going to say when he saw her. When she hadn't arrived, he'd wished he hadn't come either. He wanted to get things sorted out, and they weren't going to get things settled between them if she tried to avoid him.

And her scarcity this morning was proof that she *was* avoiding him. It was the only Sunday service she'd missed since coming to Homestead. Will wasn't fooled. He knew *he* was the reason she wasn't there now.

He didn't understand Addie's reluctance to accept his proposal, let alone the sudden anger she'd shown last night. What had he said that was so terrible? After all, he'd merely done the right and honorable thing, offering to marry her after what had happened between them. He was willing to admit that maybe he shouldn't have let things get so carried away. He shouldn't have made love to her until after they were married.

But a person would've thought he'd offered to set her up as his mistress or have her scourged in public, the way she'd reacted. If she only knew what a momentous step this was for him, maybe she wouldn't be acting so gall-darn crazy.

Women! This was just why he'd spent his life avoiding any kind of personal involvement with them. They were impossible for a man to understand. If he'd had any sense, he wouldn't have gone to Addie's last night—and he certainly wouldn't have offered to marry her.

As quickly as that thought came to him, he knew it wasn't true. The truth was, he wasn't sorry he'd asked her to marry him. The truth was, he was looking forward to having Addie for his wife.

It had taken him a long time to work through the feelings he'd had about women and marriage and families, but he'd finally realized he couldn't judge all women by his mother or Justine, nor could he judge all marriages by his parents' failed union or all families by his own miserable experiences. He felt something special toward Addie. He sensed they would be right together. And besides, she would be a good mother to Lark.

The congregation rose for the closing anthem, interrupting Will's thoughts. He stood with the others, glad the service was over. He wanted to take Lark back to the ranch, then head over to Addie's and finish this matter between them, once and for all.

And he had no intention of taking no for an answer.

Addie heard the approaching rider but didn't rise from the chair. She simply waited, feeling a strange sense of calm now that she'd reached her decision.

Will's knock on the door was firm. She waited a breathless moment, then called, "Come in."

The door opened, letting in a gust of cool autumn air. Will stood in the doorway, his legs braced like a captain at the helm of a storm-tossed ship. A frown creased his forehead, and his blue eyes peered at her with resolve.

"We've got to talk," he said as he closed the door behind him.

"Yes," she replied simply. She motioned to the other chair on the opposite side of the table. "Won't you sit down? Would you care for some coffee? It's hot."

His expression altered slightly. His gaze became somewhat suspicious. "No, thanks." He stepped forward. "Listen, Addie, I guess I didn't say things right last night, and I'm real sorry I made you mad. I never pretended I was good with words. I'm not, and there's no changin' that. But I do know what I think is right, and I think the right thing for us to do is get married."

Addie remained silent as she continued to watch him. He was so remarkably handsome. No one back in Kingsbury would ever believe Addie Sherwood could receive *one* proposal from such a man, let alone three. Even she found it hard to believe.

"I know I've gone about this all wrong, askin' you to marry me before we had a chance to hardly know each other, just so Lark would have a mother. Things are better between the girl and me now. You were right that she and I needed to get to know each other, to get close. I guess you were right to turn me down then."

Addie inclined her head slightly. They weren't exactly the kind of proposals all girls dreamed of receiving. Every young woman hoped for declarations of undying love and devotion. Every girl wanted flowers and poetry and promises of a bright future. Will hadn't offered any of these things, but it didn't seem to matter quite as much now.

"But you weren't right about last night," he continued, his voice rising slightly. "You know as well as I do that the right thing for us to do is get married and get married soon."

"Yes."

"I don't claim I'll be the best husband around, but I'll . . ." He stopped talking. His eyebrows lifted. "What'd you say?"

"I said yes."

"Yes what?"

"Yes, I'll marry you." Her heart was hammering so hard in her chest, she would have sworn it could be heard all the way into Homestead.

"You will?"

She laughed softly at his bemused expression. "Isn't that what you wanted me to say, Will?"

"Well, yes, but I . . ." His confusion cleared. He stepped around the table, reached for her hand, and drew her to her feet. "You won't be sorry," he promised in a solemn tone. "I'll take good care of you. You won't want for anything."

It would have been nice if he loved her, she thought as she looked up into his eyes, but perhaps, if she were lucky, that might come later. She would be content for now with what he offered. She would simply have to love enough for two. The way her heart felt now, she thought she already did.

When he pulled her toward him and lowered his mouth toward hers, she tilted her head slightly and waited for the jolt of sensations she knew would shoot through her at his touch. She wasn't disappointed. It was as if no time at all had passed since they'd lain in bed together. She felt the fury of desire spring instantly to life.

He raised his head. She glanced up at him, wondering if he felt the same storm of emotions.

Will's voice sounded husky. "I guess I'd better go home and tell Lark the news."

"I'll speak to Emma after school tomorrow." She stepped back from him, trying to restore a sense of calm by speaking of everyday things. "I would like to finish out the school term if they'll let me."

"I see no reason they shouldn't, but you don't have to. It's not like the pay is all that much, and we won't need the money. The ranch is doing well, and . . ."

"I know. But it won't be easy for them to find a replacement this time of year. I don't want to leave the children without a teacher so soon. They're all doing so well with their studies."

"If that's what you want, it's okay with me." He nodded, then bent forward and kissed her cheek. "I'll be going then." He turned and walked to the door.

She wished she could call after him, tell him she loved him. There were so many emotions roiling inside her. She wanted to share them with him, but she knew she couldn't. Not now. Not just yet. Perhaps someday . . .

Will glanced back as he opened the door. "I think the wedding should be soon. Two . . . three weeks. No point putting it off that I can see."

"If that's what you wish."

Even two weeks seemed an eternity to Addie.

Chapter Twenty-Two

"You promise not to tell?" Lark asked as she leaned toward her friend. "I'm not supposed to say anything yet."

It was recess, and the two girls had walked back into the grove of aspens near the school and were sitting amidst the fallen leaves and underbrush, their heads close together, their voices hushed.

"I promise," Rose replied impatiently. "What *is* it?"

"Uncle Will asked Miss Sherwood to marry him."

Rose felt a stab of envy. "Miss Sherwood's gonna be your ma?" She was immediately ashamed of herself. She loved her own mother. It was just . . . well, it would be nice to live with someone like Miss Sherwood. "She's really gonna be your ma?"

Lark nodded and her eyes sparkled with excitement. "That's what Uncle Will says."

Miss Sherwood for a mother and Mr. Rider for a father. Rose thought Lark Whitetail must be about the luckiest girl in Homestead. "When?" she asked. "When are they gonna get married?"

"In a few weeks. And then she'll come live at the ranch with us. I like having her there. When Uncle Will got hurt, she came over to give me my lessons after school."

"Is that right?"

Both girls started in surprise as Mark stepped into view.

"What kind of lessons was she givin' your uncle?"

Rose didn't know what her brother meant, but she could tell from the sneer he was wearing that it wasn't anything good.

"Go away," she told him. "We were here first."

He ignored her. His gaze was fastened on Lark. The younger girl drew back from him, her expression fearful.

Mark's grin was malicious. "You think Miss Sherwood's gonna want you livin' with her once she nabs herself a husband? You're not just a *breed*. You're a *stupid* breed."

"You shut up, Mark Townsend!" Rose shouted as she jumped to her feet.

"She's not gonna want you around," he continued unabated. "She'll be sendin' you back to that orphanage so fast your head's gonna spin."

"Shut up, Mark." Rose clenched her hands into fists. She glanced down at her friend.

Lark was staring at the ground. Her face was white and her mouth quivered.

Mark laughed. "A woman don't want someone else's brat around the house. You'll see. She'll send you packin'."

Rose picked up a dried branch and threw it at her brother. "Go away."

Mark easily dodged the projectile, then darted forward and grabbed his sister by the arm. He jerked her toward him, pulling her up until only the tips of her toes touched the ground. His fingers bit into the flesh on her arm. "Mind your ways, Rose. We're not at school all the time. Miss Sherwood can't protect you at home, can she?" He shoved her away from him.

Rose stumbled backward until she slammed against a tree trunk. She watched her brother disappear through the aspen grove. She swallowed the threatening tears. She wasn't going to let Mark make her blubber like a baby. She'd learned a long time ago that he liked to make her cry, and she wasn't about to give him that pleasure.

Then she looked at Lark again and forgot her brother's threats. She hurried across the leaf-strewn ground and knelt beside her friend, placing a hand on the other girl's shoulder as she said, "Don't you believe a word he said. He's just bein' mean like he always is."

"Maybe he's right." Lark sniffed as she raised luminous eyes toward Rose. "Maybe Miss Sherwood won't want me living in her house. What if she does send me away? What'll I do then?"

"She's *not* gonna send you away." Rose sounded sure of herself. She just hoped she was right. After all, she'd been wrong about grown-ups before.

Emma knew, the minute Stanley showed Addie into the kitchen about a half hour after school let out, that the schoolteacher had a lot on her mind. She exchanged a quick glance with Doris McLeod, who had come calling with Maria and Sarah, then invited Addie to sit down at the table with the others and have a cup of tea.

"Doris brought over some of her oatmeal cookies. You'd better have one. They're the best I've ever eaten."

Addie shook her head. "No, thank you. But I would like some of that tea."

Little Sarah squirmed in Maria's lap. "Down!" she demanded. "Down!"

Maria spoke softly into the toddler's ear, but the child didn't quiet.

Emma stepped through the doorway into the parlor, calling up the stairs, "Annalee!" As soon as her oldest daughter appeared, she said, "Come down here and mind Sarah while we women have a chat. Young Mrs. McLeod looks plum tuckered out from wrestlin' with that child."

Annalee grinned as she hurried down the stairs. Emma's oldest girl adored children. Ever since Addie had come to Homestead, she'd been talking about going to normal school and becoming a teacher "just like Miss Sherwood." Emma supposed the girl would be going away soon. After all, Annalee was fifteen now. A young lady. Before long, she'd be bringing some young man home for her pa to meet.

Emma shook off the thoughts and turned back into the kitchen just as Annalee carried Sarah from the room.

Maria looked up. "Thank you," she said with a deep sigh, adding a weary but grateful smile at the end.

Emma returned the smile as she sat down across from Addie. "No point havin' a house chock full of young'ns if you can't make use of 'em now and again." She set her gaze on the teacher. "How're things going at the school?"

"Very well." Addie smiled softly, then sipped her tea.

Emma wondered if Addie's news was private. Maybe she didn't want to talk about it in front of Doris and Maria. "My children all doin' their work as they should?"

"Yes." Addie set down her teacup and folded her hands on the table. She looked like she might say something more, then closed her mouth abruptly.

Doris glanced at her daughter-in-law, then at Addie. "You seem to have something important on your mind," she said, echoing Emma's thoughts. "Would you like to speak to Emma about it privately? Maria and I should probably be getting on anyway."

"No," Addie replied. "No, that isn't necessary." She took a deep breath of air. "I do have something to tell you, and everyone will hear about it soon enough." Again, her shoulders moved up and down as she drew in a breath and let it out. Then she smiled uncertainly. "Will Rider has proposed marriage, and I have accepted his offer."

"Land o' Goshen," Emma whispered, stunned almost speechless.

Will Rider and the schoolmarm? Not that Emma hadn't expected Addie Sherwood to find a husband. No, it was the rancher she was surprised to hear about. She'd thought Will was a sworn bachelor. He'd never paid much mind to any of the single women or widows in Long Bow Valley. Not that he'd acted as if he didn't like women—just as long as he didn't have to live with one.

Will Rider and the schoolmarm. She'd never have guessed it in a million years.

Maria was the first one to break the silence. "I think it's wonderful, Addie. When is the wedding?"

"We haven't decided." A blush rose from the collar of her blouse, coloring her entire face. Addie dropped her gaze to her teacup. "Will would like it to be soon. In a couple of weeks."

"Land o' Goshen," Emma whispered again,

this time smiling from ear to ear. "When we hired you to teach our young'ns, we sure never expected we'd be seein' Will Rider gettin' married because of it."

Doris laughed. "Especially when we thought A. L. Sherwood was a *man*."

Everyone laughed then, even Addie.

"Addie," Maria said when she'd caught her breath, "do you have a wedding gown? Because if you don't," she went on quickly, "I'd be pleased to let you wear mine."

Addie's laughter faded, but she still wore a smile. "Oh, Maria, that's very kind of you. But I'm taller than you. It wouldn't be long enough."

"We can let it out. It has a wide hem. I'm sure it would fit you with just a little work, and I'm very good with a needle. Just ask Mother McLeod." She placed a hand on her rounded abdomen beneath her apron. "I may not look like it now, but usually I'm quite slender. I'm sure the dress can be made to fit you." She reached over the corner of the table and touched Addie's arm. "It's a truly beautiful gown. I know you'd look lovely in it. Just try it on. Please say you'll at least look at it."

Addie's green eyes swam with tears. "I . . . I'd love to try it on. Thank you."

"Well, my goodness," Emma said, fighting a lump in her throat. "What are we doin', gettin' all wet-eyed about this? We should be celebratin', not cryin' in our tea."

"Emma's right," Doris chimed in. "We haven't

had a wedding in Homestead in almost three years. We didn't even have the church built yet. Remember, Emma?"

"I remember."

"Emma . . ." Addie straightened in her chair. "There's something we haven't talked about yet." Her voice was serious again.

She met the teacher's gaze. "What's that?"

"About my continuing teaching. Will the school board allow it? I'd like to fulfill my contract."

"Oh, my," Emma whispered.

"I don't want the children to be without a teacher before this term is even over," Addie went on quickly. "They've all come so far in so little time. It would be a shame to lose all that progress."

"Of course." Emma mentally ran through the members of the school board. She knew there would be some opposition, especially from those who hadn't wanted a woman teacher to begin with, but she thought most would be reasonable. "I'm certain the board will agree to keep you on, if that's what you want."

A look of relief flooded Addie's face. "I'm glad," she said softly. "You know, I've learned as much from the children as they have from me. I'll always remember these months with them."

Glen took a quick swig of whiskey, then slipped the flask back into his coat pocket as he stared through the office doorway at Tom

McLeod's back. The man's desk was strewn with ledgers and papers, and Tom was bent over them, intently studying the entries.

Glen turned and went back to loading the wagon with lumber. Tom wanted the load delivered first thing in the morning and had demanded it be ready to go before Glen left for the night.

Hell, it could have waited, Glen thought as he grabbed another length of wood, carried it to the wagon, and slid it into place. That was the trouble with working for Tom McLeod. He drove a man hard, never giving a moment's rest.

Glen stopped again and took another long swig from the whiskey flask. He knew it was dangerous to drink when Tom was around the mill. If he caught Glen drinking again while he was working, he was likely to fire him. He'd given him several warnings. But, hell, he didn't care what his boss thought. He could handle his liquor, and if he wanted a drink to help get him through this miserable job, then he was going to have one.

He set his jaw and moved more lumber onto the wagon, mentally grumbling to himself. This wasn't the sort of work he should be doing. He was meant to have his own business. The more and more he thought about it, the more he liked the idea of owning that saloon.

He glanced toward the office again. The safe wouldn't have much cash in it now. Tom always sent a deposit down to Boise City at the first of each month. But in another week or two . . .

His gaze swept the inside of the mill. Place like this would go up in flames fast. There wouldn't be any hope of saving it. And no one would ever know what was missing. Not as long as Tom McLeod wasn't around to tell anyone.

"Pa?"

Guiltily, Glen whirled toward his son's voice. "What are you doin', sneakin' around like that?" He took a step toward the boy, his arm raised to strike.

"I wasn't sneakin'. I came t'tell you somethin' I thought you'd want to know. About the teacher."

He stopped still and raised an eyebrow. "What?"

"She and Mr. Rider are gettin' married."

Glen cursed. "What do I care about that?" He turned and reached for another length of lumber.

"Miss Sherwood was goin' over to his ranch and takin' care of him while he was laid up. I heard that little breed of his tellin' Rose."

"Takin' care of him?" He glanced over his shoulder at his son.

It was easy to see what Mark was thinking. The boy's mind worked a lot like his own. He knew what kind of takin' care of he'd want if he was livin' out on that ranch without a woman.

"That's what she said. And now they're gettin' married." Mark grinned. "Maybe they don't got no choice."

"Yeah, maybe they don't," he said in a low voice, mulling over the notion. Wouldn't that just go to prove to the rest of this town that he'd been right about hiring a schoolteacher—especially a *female* teacher. They should have sent her packing the day she'd arrived.

Trouble was all she was. Coming by his house to complain about his boy, saying she wouldn't have Mark whippin' his sister. Everyone knew it wasn't her place to interfere like that. If Rose needed to be brought into line, then Mark had every right as her brother to do it.

He felt his anger growing in his chest. Automatically, he reached for the flask inside his coat and took several quick drinks.

He'd show that teacher not to meddle in his affairs. Damn right, he was going to show her.

Will leaned against the corral railing, staring with unseeing eyes at the horses enclosed within.

Married . . . I'm getting married.

His stomach felt like a cinch yanked up beneath a horse's belly and knotted through the dee ring.

The doubts hadn't started up until this afternoon. All day yesterday, he'd felt pretty good about his decision. Lark had accepted the news with a smile and twinkling eyes, making him feel confident he was doing the right thing.

He wasn't sure why he'd begun to doubt his decision now. Maybe it was Lark's moodiness. She'd seemed so withdrawn, so dejected, ever since she'd come home from school this afternoon. She'd resembled the unhappy, timid child who'd arrived by stage in August. Will had thought that unhappy little girl was gone for good. Apparently he'd been wrong about that.

Maybe he was wrong about marrying Addie, too.

He closed his eyes against the pounding in his head and rubbed his temples with his fingertips. He saw her then in his mind—his mother. The sights and sounds of Chicago filled his head as he pictured Martha Rider, walking on the arm of another man. She hadn't seen her son—still a boy in the eyes of many, but old enough to understand what he was seeing. But she hadn't seen him because she was too busy staring up at the stranger with adoring eyes. He remembered her laughter floating back to him as the couple hurried up the steps leading to a mansion made of bricks and stately columns. They disappeared inside, oblivious to everything but each other.

He'd waited for hours, and when she'd come out, he'd known from the look of her what had gone on behind the closed doors of that house. He'd known, and he'd hated her for taking a lover, for deceiving his father, for betraying all of them.

Another memory came on the heels of the first, a memory even more painful, something he'd forced himself to forget many years before.

His father lay dying. . . .

Will entered the shabby apartment quietly, not wanting to disturb his father. Phillip had been ill for many days now, and Will knew the doctor held out no hope for the man's recovery.

As he silently closed the door behind him, he heard soft laughter coming from the bedroom. His mother's laughter.

What had she to laugh about?

Will moved stealthily toward his parents' bedroom, already fearing what he would see there.

First he saw his father's unconscious body lying still and motionless on the bed, his face a pasty, unhealthy white, his eyes sunken in dark circles. It was the face of a dying man.

Then he saw his mother . . . wrapped in the arms of a stranger. Again he heard her soft laughter as the man ran his hands up and down her back.

"Behave yourself, Geoffrey," she whispered.

"I can't wait another day for you. Come with me now."

"What would people say if I deserted my husband on his deathbed? Think, Geoffrey. Phillip can't hang on much longer, and then we shall be together. I promise."

Will wanted to kill her.

Martha turned suddenly, her gaze meeting her son's. "Will . . ."

Will drew a deep breath and drove the memory from his mind and from his heart as he had done years ago. He wouldn't let it torment him. He would not think of her, clad in that fancy pink dress her lover had paid for. He would not think of his mother embracing that same lover at the foot of her dying husband's bed.

How I hated her.

Phillip had died the next day without regaining consciousness. Will hadn't had a chance to say good-bye to his father—and he'd refused to say good-bye to his mother. He'd gone to the funeral and then left Chicago without speaking to Martha Rider again.

I still hate her, he thought as he rubbed his fingers across his eyes. *Even after all these years.*

He opened his eyes and stared once again at the horses within the corral, this time seeing them. He was looking at some of the best animals in the territory. The Rocking R Ranch's mares had produced a fine addition of healthy colts this spring, and this year's calf crop was their best ever.

He'd come a long way from that run-down flat in Chicago. He'd come even farther from the woman who'd given him life but nothing after that. He'd worked through all these emotions and memories before. He'd realized all women weren't like his mother. Why was he letting it come up again? Why was he letting her interfere with his life now?

His thoughts turned to Addie, and suddenly, he felt calm again. Addie was nothing like Martha Rider. Addie was different from his mother, different from Justine, different from any woman he'd ever known.

Addie would never betray him. Never.

Chapter Twenty-Three

"Monday for wealth, Tuesday for health, Wednesday the best day of all." Maria repeated the well-known rhyme as she bent over the cedar chest. "Thursday for losses, Friday for crosses, and Saturday no luck at all." Lovingly, she drew the wedding gown from the trunk and turned toward Addie. "Tom and I were married on a Wednesday. I'm glad you've decided to do the same. We've been so happy. I just know you and Mr. Rider will be, too."

Addie's heart fluttered with excitement as she stared at the bridal gown. She hadn't imagined anything so lovely when Maria had offered her the use of the dress. Certainly she'd never thought she might wear such a beautiful gown. She reached out and tentatively touched the delicate fabric.

Made from finely woven, cream silk faille and lined with cotton sateen, the long-sleeved dress had a fitted bodice trimmed with Belgian lace. Yards and yards of fabric made up the full skirt. The balayeuse—a deep-pleated, lace-trimmed ruffle—finished the underside of the skirt and the lengthy train.

"Do you like it?"

"Oh, Maria . . ." was all Addie could reply.

"Here. Stand up and let's see how much work we have to do. You haven't given us much time, you know. Two weeks. We're going to be very busy."

Addie stood before the cheval glass, feeling more and more like a storybook princess. It was three days since Will's proposal, and it still seemed unreal. Even the time they'd shared in her bed seemed only part of a dream.

She dropped her gaze from the mirror as the memory of those hours spread heat into her cheeks.

Maria laughed softly. "You're thinking about him."

Addie's eyes widened, and a chill of alarm shot through her. What if someone guessed what had happened between her and Will? If Maria could read her so easily, so might others.

"You love him very much, don't you?" Maria squeezed Addie's arm. "You needn't answer. I can see it in your eyes. They're aglow with love."

"Yes," she whispered, wanting to say it aloud. "I love him." She looked at Maria. "I didn't know it was possible to feel this way about anyone. Sometimes I think how awful it would have been if I'd never come to Homestead. What if we'd never met? I'd have gone to my grave without ever knowing . . ." She stopped abruptly, embarrassed by the baring of her soul.

"I understand. Everything seems so intense right now. It was that way with me when I first fell in love with Tom. It still is, really." As she talked, Maria helped Addie out of her dress, then into the wedding gown. "Sometimes I look at him, and I think I could die for happiness. I wonder why God saw fit to bless me so much." She grew still and her eyes stared off into space. "I don't think I could live without him," she added softly.

Addie felt her heart tighten. She understood exactly what Maria was saying—and with that understanding came a sudden fear. She was afraid to love so deeply, so passionately. She was afraid of the all-consuming pain that might follow.

An hour later, Addie climbed into her buggy and turned the mare toward the west. She was surprised to find the sun resting just above the mountains. Already the blue of the sky was taking on the slate color of dusk. She hadn't realized she'd been inside the McLeod house so long.

She was just about to slap the reins against the horse's back when she saw Chad come out of the livery and walk toward her. She pulled back on the reins.

"Afternoon, Addie," he greeted her.

"Good afternoon, Chad."

He tipped his hat back on his head. "Just heard the news about you and Will."

A twinge of guilt nudged her conscience as she remembered Chad's proposal of marriage—and the hours in Will's arms that had followed her refusal. She felt her cheeks color again.

Chad leaned an arm on the rump of Addie's mare. "'Course, I think you'd've been better off marryin' me, but I guess there's no accountin' for taste."

"Chad, I . . ."

"There's still time for you to change your mind, Addie. I'd rather set my mind on marryin' you."

"I'm sorry, Chad. I'm not going to change my mind."

He wore a hangdog expression. "I didn't figure you would, but I thought it'd do no harm to try."

"No, it didn't do any harm." She offered a friendly smile, then quickly sobered as a flash of inspiration came to her. "I would never be the right kind of wife for you anyway, Chad. The way Homestead and your business are growing, you need a wife who will devote herself to helping you in every way possible. How could I do that while I'm still teaching?"

"Well, I expect you'd . . ."

Addie rushed on. "I told you I wasn't going to quit teaching, not unless the school board forces me to." She shook her head. "No, you need a wife like . . ." She glanced up at the sky, as if considering all the possibilities. "Like Ophelia Henderson, for instance. What a lovely girl. I don't think I've ever seen anyone prettier than Ophelia."

"Ophelia? She's still a child," he protested.

"A *child?* Chad Turner, when was the last time you looked at her? I mean, *really* looked at her? Why, she's a beautiful young woman. And if you ask me, she's noticed what a fine man you are, too."

"She has?"

"Yes, she has." She smiled at him again. "How could you be so insightful about my feelings for Will and not see how that young lady feels about you?"

He seemed to give her question some serious thought. Finally, he returned her smile for the first time. "I guess you're admitting I was right about why you turned down my proposal. It's not 'cause you want to keep teaching."

She knew her cheeks were flushed again. "I told you, I do hope to keep teaching."

"Yeah, you did. Well, don't worry. The school board'd be crazy not to keep you on. You're the best thing that's happened to Homestead in a long time."

"Thank you, Chad." She felt warm and happy. "That's a very pleasant compliment."

"Just the truth, ma'am." He touched his hat brim and stepped back from her buggy. "And I do mean to give some thought to what you said. About Miss Henderson, I mean."

"I hope so." She wove the reins through her fingers and prepared to leave.

"Addie, I want you to know I meant my offer of marriage. I think you'd have made me a fine wife, despite the excuses you were givin' me. But the plain truth is, any fool could see you love Will. I'm glad he had the good sense to ask you to be his wife."

Her throat felt too tight to respond, so she simply nodded, slapped the reins against the mare's rump, and drove away.

The drive out to the cabin on Pony Creek wasn't a long one, but it gave Addie time to reflect on what Chad had said. She wondered if it were true. Could "any fool" see she loved Will? Could Will see it? Sadly, she didn't think so.

She closed her eyes against the ardent pain in her heart. No one had ever told her it could feel like this—this horrible, wonderful loving that welled up from somewhere deep inside. Even when she'd been in love with Robert—or had she merely thought herself in love?—no one had warned her there were more intense feelings to be experienced. Was it because she'd been little more than a child then and was a woman now? Or was it because now she loved Will? Was it because she had so much more to lose this time?

She felt the rig slowing and opened her eyes as the mare turned off the main road and followed the beaten track toward the cabin. She mentally reproached herself for growing melancholy. This was a time for joy. She was going to marry the man she loved, and she was going to be wearing the most beautiful wedding gown she'd ever seen. What had she to be fearful of?

But despite the silent scolding she'd just given herself, Addie heard a trill of alarm inside her head when she saw Will waiting for her outside her cabin.

He dismounted as she drove toward him. When the buggy stopped, he stepped forward and offered her a hand down. She felt her heart skip as his fingers closed around hers.

"I . . . I didn't expect to see you today, Will," she said, looking into his troubled eyes. "Is something wrong?"

"I'm not sure. I was hoping you could tell me."

She drew her hand from his and moved toward the door, her back straight and her head held high. If he was there to call off the wedding, she wasn't going to let him see her heartbreak. "Well, it's too cool to talk over things outside. Come in, and I'll make us some coffee."

"I'll take care of the horse for you first. You go on ahead."

Addie paused at the door and glanced over her shoulder. Will was already leading the mare toward the corral. It was such a domestic thing to do, taking care of the horse, then joining her inside for coffee as dusk gathered over the valley. She'd wanted to share many evenings in just such a way. She wished her dreams hadn't been so short-lived.

She hurried inside and busied herself with stoking the fire and putting a fresh pot of coffee on the stove. Then she removed her bonnet and tried to smooth her hair before Will joined her. As usual, it was absolutely hopeless. Tendrils of red curls framed her face and straggled against her nape.

The door opened without a warning knock. She turned from the mirror as Will stepped inside.

He took off his hat, then tapped it against his thigh as he looked at her. She tilted her chin a bit higher. She wouldn't break down in front of him. She wouldn't let him see all her insecurities, her vulnerabilities.

"What was it you wanted to see me about, Will?" she asked stoically, certain she already knew the answer to her question.

"It's Lark."

Her eyes widened. "Lark?"

Will nodded as he stepped forward. "I'm worried about her. I thought maybe you could help."

"Sit down, Will." She had trouble keeping her breathless relief from sounding in her voice. She was glad to sink onto a chair and escape the perilous support of her quaking knees. "Tell me what's wrong with Lark."

"I was hoping you might be able to tell me," he said as he sat down across from her. He set his hat in the center of the table. "Did something happen at school?"

She was being selfish, she realized. Will had come to her with a problem, and her only thoughts were for her own feelings. She pushed aside her earlier anxieties and focused her attention on the man opposite her. "Happen? I don't know what you mean."

"I'm not sure either. It's just . . . well, she seemed so happy up until a couple of days ago. We've been gettin' along fine. And now, all of a sudden, she's withdrawn again. Just like she was when she first came here from the orphanage. She acts . . . well, almost afraid."

Addie pondered his words. Belatedly, she realized that Lark had been acting differently at school for the past two days. She should have noticed, but she'd been all wrapped up in thoughts about Will and plans for her wedding.

What kind of teacher ignored the needs of her students?

"I thought maybe Mark Townsend had been giving her a bad time again," Will suggested.

She shook her head. "I don't think so. I'd know if something like that had happened." She met his gaze. Her voice lowered to just above a whisper. "You don't think it's because of me, do you? Do you suppose she doesn't want me to marry you?"

His face didn't reveal his private thoughts. She waited anxiously for him to respond. Finally, he shook his head. "I don't think that's it. She seemed real pleased when I told her you'd agreed to be my wife." He leaned forward. "Would you mind talking to her, see if you can find out what's bothering her? I've tried"—he shrugged—"but I don't know how to talk to little girls."

"Of course I wouldn't mind." A satisfied warmth flowed through her veins. She forgot her previous anxiety completely. She was awash with a sense of rightness. He had come to her. He valued her opinion. He must care for her beyond the passion that had drawn him to her bed. Perhaps he would yet learn to love her.

Will's expression eased, and he leaned against the back of the chair, his gaze still resting on Addie's face. The corners of his mouth curved. "You've got nice hair, Addie."

"My hair?" Self-consciously, she touched the chignon on the back of her head. "It's a sight."

"I like it all tousled-like." His voice lowered. "It looks real pretty in the firelight."

She felt completely tongue-tied.

"I think I like it best when it's down."

She blushed as she dropped her gaze to her hands.

Will rose to his feet and rounded the table. Addie stiffened when she felt his hand upon her head. Her breath caught in her throat. Slowly, he pulled her hairpins free. His fingers raked gently through the thick hair as it tumbled down around her shoulders.

"Addie . . ."

She felt her insides turning soft and warm.

He hesitated, then said, "Guess I don't know how to talk to women either. Wish I did."

I wish you did, too.

There was so much she wanted him to say to her, so much she wanted to hear. She tilted her head slightly, pressing it against the palm of his hand.

She wanted him to make love to her. She wanted him to kiss her and undress her and lie with her in her bed. She wanted . . .

Will cleared his throat as he stepped away. His voice, when he spoke, sounded thick. "It's time I was headin' back to the ranch." He reached for his hat and settled it over his tawny-gold hair. "You'll let me know if you learn anything? About Lark, I mean."

"Of course." It was a wonder she could speak. Her insides were still all aflutter from his hand upon her hair.

As he walked toward the door, Will said, "The school board's meeting on Saturday. I'll be tellin' them I've got no objection to you stayin' on as the teacher, just as long as you've a mind to." He looked back at her. "You sure that's what you want to do? You don't need to."

She wasn't at all sure about it at the moment. She wasn't sure of anything except her desire to have Will take her in his arms and cover her mouth with his and touch her body the way he had the other night. She wished he hadn't resisted the temptation to do just that. She knew he'd felt what she was feeling. She'd heard it in his voice. She knew he was trying to protect her from scandal. She wished he wasn't.

Their eyes met across the small, dimly lit room.

"I'm glad you came to Homestead, Addie Sherwood," Will said softly. "Real glad." Then, before she could respond, he opened the door and left.

Chapter Twenty-Four

Addie's gaze moved slowly around the schoolroom as her students bent over their desks, their pencils scratching on their papers as they worked out their arithmetic problems.

My students, she thought. *My children.*

A contented smile pulled at the corners of her mouth as she watched them. When the time came to quit teaching, as it surely would, she would miss them. She loved them all, she realized. They truly had become her children. They were each so different, so wonderfully unique. There were the Barber children, all six of them, lively and intelligent and full of laughter. There were the Potter girls, so well-mannered, not a hair out of place and their clothes never wrinkled. There was the Morris boy, awkward and shy as he approached young manhood. And so many others, all ages and shapes and sizes, each unique and special in his or her own way.

Even Mark had found a reluctant place in her heart. She wanted to help the boy before it was too late, before he became like his father. Perhaps it was already too late, but she wanted an opportunity to make a difference. She wished she were wiser. She wished she knew what to do for him, how to make him see life through different eyes.

Her gaze came to rest on Rose and Lark, the two girls seated side by side. They had become fast friends in the weeks since school began. Addie wasn't sure why. They seemed such opposites.

Lark was shy and always likely to withdraw into a shell of silence if confronted. Rose was feisty, as likely to use her fists as she was her voice. Lark had neither mother or father, but she had a home with someone who loved her and wanted to give her the very best. Rose had both her parents, yet seemed to have no one at all.

Addie's gaze focused on Lark alone. For two days, she had tried to get the girl to open up and tell her what was wrong, but Lark remained unwilling to confide in her. Addie didn't understand why. From the first day they'd met, there had been a special affinity between Addie and Lark. Something had happened to change all that, but she didn't know what.

She doesn't want me to marry her uncle. The niggling doubt just wouldn't go away.

Addie dropped her gaze to the papers on her desk. What was she to do if her suspicions were true? Should she marry Will, knowing Lark would be unhappy, or should she deny herself her own chance at happiness for Lark's sake?

She cradled her face with her hands, her elbows resting on the desk, her fingers pressed against the sides of her nose near the corners of her eyes.

Papa, I wish I could talk to you. You'd know what to do. You always knew what to do.

Will was depending upon her to find out what was troubling Lark. What if she failed him? Or worse, what if she found out she was right? What would he do then? What would he choose to do?

Her head began to ache behind her eyes.

"Miss Sherwood?"

She glanced up at Rachel Barber, standing beside her desk.

The girl held out her slate. "I don't understand this problem."

Neither do I, Addie thought, meaning something totally different. Then she motioned Rachel closer and explained the multiplication equation one more time.

Delicious odors filled the kitchen when Tom entered his house a little before noon. He saw the black kettle on the stove and lifted the lid to peer at the contents. Beef stew simmered inside. His stomach growled.

He lowered the lid again and walked toward the parlor, pausing in the doorway when his gaze fell upon his wife. Her head was bent forward as she carefully stitched on the wedding gown. Anemic sunlight, filtered through a haze of high clouds, drifted through the window at her back. He saw the tender smile on her lips and knew she was thinking about the day she'd worn the gown nearly nine years before.

It was often like that between them, reading the other's thoughts, knowing what was in the other's heart without being told.

She must have sensed him standing there. She looked up. Their gazes met.

"I thought you looked like an angel," he said, not needing to explain. "I'd never seen anything prettier in my life."

Her smile reached her eyes.

Tom stepped into the parlor. "You aren't taking on too much, are you? You look a little tired." He leaned forward and kissed her on the lips.

"I'm fine." Maria lowered the sewing into her lap. One hand lightly touched her abdomen. "Your son has been very active today. Here." She took hold of his hand and pressed it against her stomach. "Feel that?"

He did. A grin spread across his face. "Yes." He sat down beside her on the settee and placed his free arm around her shoulders.

Maria leaned her head against his chest. "Your mother came by for Sarah again this morning. She's spoiling me with all her fussing."

"You deserve a bit of fussing over. Besides, she loves you." He kissed the top of her head. "Me, too," he whispered.

She turned her face toward him. "Nothing's going to go wrong this time, Tom. I know it. I *feel* it. Your son is going to survive and grow up to be a man we can be proud of."

He hoped so. Every man wanted a son to carry on his name. But more important to Tom was Maria's health. The doctor had warned them about another pregnancy, especially so soon after the last miscarriage. He'd tried to be careful. He'd tried to make sure she didn't get pregnant again, but Maria could make it hard to remember his intentions when she wanted to. His demure Maria had a way about her in the privacy of their bedroom.

He reined in his more amorous thoughts. They wouldn't be sharing any nights like that for a while.

Maria pulled away from him, set her sewing aside, and rose awkwardly from the couch. "I'd better get you your lunch."

He followed her into the kitchen. She was as beautiful pregnant as she had been as a bride, he thought as he watched her move around the kitchen. She had a glow about her, a radiance that couldn't be hidden.

You're a lucky man, Tom McLeod.

* * *

"Lark!" Addie called before the girl could leave the schoolroom.

Lark stopped and looked back at the teacher. "I'd like to speak with you a moment."

The child nodded and returned to her desk. Her expression was guarded as she sat down. She placed her books on her desk, then folded her hands before her.

Addie drew in a deep breath and let it out slowly before crossing the room and sitting in the desk next to Lark. She stared at the girl for a long time, hoping Lark would glance up, but she didn't.

Stifling a sigh, Addie finally said, "I think it's time we had a talk, don't you?"

The girl didn't respond.

"What's troubling you, Lark?"

"Nothing."

"That isn't true. I know it, and your uncle knows it."

Lark's gaze darted briefly up, then down again.

Addie reached out and covered the child's hands with one of her own. "I thought we were friends. Why won't you talk to me?"

The girl shook her head slowly.

Addie wished again that she could talk to her father. He would know what was best for her to say or do. He'd always understood young people so well.

But she couldn't talk to him. She had to do this on her own.

"It's because of me, isn't it, Lark? You don't want me to marry your uncle."

Again Lark glanced at her quickly, then away.

Addie's heart plummeted. It was true. She'd so hoped she was wrong about it, but it seemed she wasn't.

"Won't you tell me why? I thought we were friends. When I was new here, you made me feel not so alone. What changed, Lark?"

Still no answer.

Addie pulled her hand away. She rose from the desk and walked over to the window, staring out at the autumn-dried leaves clinging to the aspens. The most brilliant of the season's colors had faded. Winter would be upon them soon, according to Emma.

She shivered, already feeling the winter cold in her heart.

"Your uncle wants you to be happy, Lark. So do I. We both know neither of us can replace the parents you lost. We wouldn't even try. But we would like to care for you and give you a good home and try to make you happy, just like your own mother and father did." She breathed deeply again. "We don't want our marriage to cause you unhappiness."

She didn't hear Lark rise from the desk and cross the room. Just suddenly the girl was there beside her, taking hold of Addie's hand.

Large brown eyes stared up at the teacher. "You won't send me back?"

"Back where?" Addie asked as she kneeled on the floor.

"Back to the orphanage?"

"Oh, Lark, why would I want to do that?"

"Because . . . because . . ." Tears swam in her eyes.

Addie pulled the child against her, suddenly understanding. "I wish you *were* my little girl, Lark. I wish I really were your mother. But even if I were your real mother, I couldn't love you any more than I do now." She stroked Lark's hair with one hand. "Your uncle loves you, too. He's probably never told you. I don't think he's any good at saying the words, but he does love you. He wouldn't ever send you away, no matter what anybody said, no matter what happened. Neither would I." She released her tight hold on the child and leaned back, sitting on her heels, so she could look into Lark's eyes. "Do you believe me?"

The girl didn't speak. She just sniffed and wiped her nose on the sleeve of her dress.

Watching her, Addie realized just how true everything she'd said was. She did love Lark as if she were her own. It was different from the affection she felt for her other students. It was special, just as the love she felt for Will was special.

"I need you to believe me, Lark. Can you?"

Lark sniffed again. "Mark said you wouldn't want me around after you married Uncle Will. He said you wouldn't want a breed in your house and you'd send me back to the orphanage. He said . . ."

"Mark said all that?" Addie glowered as anger filled her chest. "I should have known." If the boy was there now, she'd take a paddle to him. She didn't care if he was as tall as she was and weighed a good deal more. Pushing thoughts of Mark aside, she stared hard into Lark's eyes. "I thought I told you before not to pay any attention to what that boy said. He doesn't know what he's talking about most of the time. Especially not about this. Do you understand?"

Lark nodded.

"Good." She rose from the floor. "Now, you'd better get on home. Your uncle will be wondering what's kept you after school. We don't want to worry him unnecessarily."

Lark turned toward the door.

"Don't forget your homework," Addie reminded her.

Lark grabbed her school books off her desk before glancing back at Addie. "I love you, too, Miss Sherwood," she said hastily, then dashed for the door.

The words left Addie frozen in a stunned silence.

I love you, too, Miss Sherwood.

A ghost of a smile played across her mouth. Who would have thought it? she wondered. Who would have believed her life could change so much in a few short months? She not only was soon to have a husband, but she was going to have a daughter as well. A beautiful daughter who loved her.

Her smile disappeared, anger returning quickly. She would soon be responsible for her new daughter's welfare, and she wasn't about to let Mark get away with torturing Lark with lies. She was going to set that boy straight. Not as a schoolteacher, but as a mother.

She hurried to erase the blackboard, then put on her coat, picked up her books and handbag, and left the school.

The door to the kitchen banged against the wall as Glen entered the house. Virginia jumped and whirled around, her face turning a pasty white as she stared at him.

"When's supper?" he growled at her without preamble.

"You . . . you're early."

Lord, how he detested the sight of the woman. What in heaven had ever possessed him to make her his wife? She sure wasn't anything to look at anymore. And there were more willing women than she when it came to nighttime activities.

He glared at Virginia. He could have had a good life if it weren't for her. She'd held him back. She'd always held him back. No matter what he'd wanted to do, she'd kept him from it, like a ball and chain around his ankle. Her and her kids—and Tom McLeod, too. His boss had been watching him like a hawk lately, as if he suspected Glen of something. Well, he couldn't confirm anything. Tom would have a hard time proving Glen had been selling off lumber on the side.

The anger burned hotter in his chest as he stared at his wife. He took a step toward her, and she made a fearful sound in her throat.

"Glen, please . . ." she whimpered, her eyes wide as she watched his approach.

A sharp rap on the front door made him pause. Virginia used that moment to move out of his reach.

Glen grunted. "Hurry up with my supper, woman. I'm hungry." Then he headed toward the front door, yanking it open, anger and frustration still roiling in his chest. It didn't make him feel any better to see the schoolteacher standing on his porch.

"Mr. Townsend." She sounded surprised.

"Yeah, it's me. What do *you* want?"

She stiffened at his surly tone of voice. "I wish to see your son."

"Don't you see enough of him at school? The boy's got chores to do. Talk to him on Monday."

"Mr. Townsend," she said quickly, before he could slam the door, "Mark is continuing to be disruptive at school. He has done his best to cause me difficulties. He is surly with the younger children and continues to threaten his sister with violence. He also has not stopped taunting Lark Whitetail, despite my very explicit instructions to the contrary."

Some man needed to take this woman down a notch or two. He'd know how to do it if he were her husband. "You're the teacher. You deal with it."

"Mr. Townsend, either you tell your son to stop interfering with Lark, or I shall expel him. I've warned him before about his inappropriate behavior. I won't tolerate it."

Glen saw red. It was all he could do to keep from striking her where she stood. "What makes you think you'll have any right to expel anybody, come tomorrow? You think the school board's gonna let you keep teachin' when they know what I know?"

She stared at him, dumbfounded.

"Cat got your tongue, Miss Sherwood?" He grinned. "Well, it ain't got mine. I've got plenty to tell folks about you. Plenty. Now get off my porch." He slammed the door in her face and spun around to find Virginia watching him from the doorway. "What're you lookin' at?" he shouted. "Get my supper on the table."

He could hardly wait for the meeting of the school board tomorrow. He'd teach Miss Sherwood to keep her nose out of his business.

Chapter Twenty-Five

Addie couldn't believe all the work Maria had accomplished in just a few days. She looked at her reflection in the cheval glass, her eyes wide with amazement. She didn't look skinny and shapeless any longer. She actually saw curves in all the right places.

It must be true. All brides *were* beautiful. At least for a short time they were—especially when they were wearing a gown like this one.

"It's incredible, Maria. I can't believe you've made the dress fit so well." She met Maria's gaze in the mirror. "I'll never be able to thank you enough. You know that, don't you? You didn't have to lend me the use of your wedding gown."

"It wasn't doing anyone any good, just lying in that chest. I hope Sarah will want to wear it one day, but if she grows up to be as independent-minded as she is now, she's likely to want something uniquely her own." Maria smiled. "Besides, it's enough thanks to be able to share this time with a friend."

Addie felt warm inside. How long had it been since she'd had a friend? A close friend, someone she could tell secrets to, someone she could trust with all her most private thoughts. Not since before her mother died, she realized. After that, her father had been her only friend.

She turned around and met Maria's gaze directly. "Do you believe in fate?" she asked.

"I believe God has a plan for our lives, yes."

Addie took hold of Maria's hand. "When I think of all I might have missed if I hadn't come to Homestead . . ." She broke off suddenly, her throat feeling tight as so many faces flashed in her mind. Will, Lark, Emma, Stanley, Hank, Doris, Reverend Pendroy, Chad Turner, and so many others. The thought that she might never have met any of them was too horrible to contemplate.

Maria smiled. "But you *did* come, and now you're going to marry Will and settle down and have a family of your own." They both heard Sarah's squeal from her room upstairs. Maria lifted her shoulders in a weary gesture, although her smile showed true contentment. "I can promise you this. When the babies start arriving, you won't want to keep teaching. You'll have your hands full at home."

Babies . . . Will's babies . . .

A different kind of warmth settled in Addie's stomach. She wished her wedding day would hurry and arrive.

Emma rapped her knuckles on the surface of Addie's desk, which sat on the riser beside the pulpit. "Ladies, gentlemen, shall we get on with the business that brought us here today?"

The other people in the room fell silent.

She looked at all the familiar faces. The members of the school board sat in the first two rows of benches, already set in place for the next day's Sunday services. Those members of the community who had requested permission to speak to the issue sat in the rows behind them.

Emma didn't know why they had to go to all this trouble. It just seemed like a waste of time to her. It was only reasonable that Addie be allowed to keep teaching if that's what she wanted to do. It was obvious she was doing a wonderful job with her students.

"You all know why we've come here today," she said in her take-charge voice. "Our new teacher, Miss Sherwood, is getting married in a little more than a week, and she's requested permission to continue to teach our children for the remainder of her contract. Personally, I don't see what difference it makes if my brood is taught by a miss or a missus, but apparently some folks think there is one." She glanced toward the back of the room where Will Rider was leaning against the wall. "Will? You had something you wanted to say?"

He straightened. "Emma tells me some towns won't let a woman keep teachin' once she marries. That sounds like a mighty strange rule to me, but I figure Emma knows what she's talkin' about."

Emma inclined her head in acknowledgment.

"I know that Addie—Miss Sherwood—has been doin' a fine job here," Will continued. "I've told her she doesn't need to work once we're married, but she seems set on not leavin' the children without a teacher. If there's any who think I might not approve of my wife workin', I just wanted to set 'em straight. If she wants to, it's fine with me. That's all I came to say. I hope you'll let her stay on."

"Keepin' her on will sure guarantee that niece of yours good grades, won't it now?"

All eyes turned toward Glen Townsend.

"Everybody knows an Injun ain't got no place in a white school, but I reckon the little breed will think she's as good as anyone else, just 'cause of who the teacher is."

Emma felt the hairs on the back of her neck stand on end. She was glad Addie hadn't come to the meeting. She had a feeling things weren't going to go as smoothly as she'd thought.

Will kept his body deceptively relaxed, though his voice was full of steel. "Lark has nothing to do with this discussion, Townsend."

"Don't she?" Glen got to his feet. "It's clear you don't know what a special interest Miss

Sherwood's got in your niece." He glared at the others in the room. "None of you do, or you wouldn't be thinkin' of lettin' it go on."

"Mr. Townsend . . ." Emma began, trying to interrupt.

Glen acted as if he hadn't heard her as his gaze returned to Will. "Maybe that's how she got you to propose marriage to her." He revealed a nasty grin. "Or maybe it was her daily visits to your ranch that did it. Maybe folks would feel differently about her if they knew she was spending so much time at your place."

Will heard the murmurs of surprise from others in the room, but he ignored them.

"Maybe you got other reasons for marryin' the schoolmarm. She better t'look at in bed, Rider, than she is with her clothes on?"

A shocked gasp accompanied Will's movement across the room. His fist connected with Glen's jaw, knocking the man backward. Will followed after him, his left arm striking a blow to Glen's midriff.

With a roar of anger, Glen struck back. His punch caught Will in the solar plexus. Air whooshed from his lungs, and colored stars flashed before his eyes as pain from his mending ribs tore through him. He wasn't ready for the fist that landed at the corner of his mouth, but he blocked Glen's next jab, then threw one of his own, only to have it blocked as well.

Glen lunged forward, knocking them both to the floor. Benches were pushed hither and yon as the two men rolled, first in one direction, then another.

"Gentlemen, not in God's house!" the minister cried.

But Will was beyond heeding anyone's cry for peace. He meant to make Townsend rue his remarks before he was through.

Glen was a more heavily built man than Will, and he used his weight advantage to roll the slimmer man against the wall, slamming him against it with enough force to cause a groan of pain to escape Will's throat.

Will ignored the throbbing in his side as he broke free of the other man's grasp and jumped to his feet, guided more by instinct and fury than anything else. Glen was still on his knees when Will connected another blow to his jaw. Then he grabbed Glen by his shirt collar and dragged him up from the floor before hitting him again, this time in the eye. When Glen's head bobbed forward, Will hit him again and then again, his rage building with every punch.

Suddenly, Will was grabbed from behind. Glen was about to take advantage of the situation when two other men captured his arms and hauled him backward.

"Enough!" Hank shouted.

Breathing hard, Will turned his head to look at the sheriff, who now stood by his side. "I won't have him sayin' things like that about Addie." He glanced back at Glen. "You hear me, Townsend?"

"The truth's the truth."

Will pulled against the hands that held him. "There wasn't anything improper goin' on at my ranch, and I won't have you sayin' there was. Addie came out to bring Lark her school lessons after a horse busted my ribs and that's all. Just ask Doc. He was there."

Doc Varney cleared his throat as everyone's attention turned upon him. "It's true. I was present a time or two when Miss Sherwood brought the girl her schoolwork. Lark stayed home to nurse her uncle after his accident." He stepped over a toppled bench. "And he may very well need her assistance again after today's spectacle." He gently touched Will's side.

Will grimaced but didn't move, his glare still aimed at Glen. "I expect you to apologize for what you said, Townsend."

"You gonna lie to these folks, Rider?" Glen snarled back. "Was the doc there *every* time she was at your ranch? You gonna tell these folks that the schoolmarm's still as pure as they think?"

Will glanced around the room. He saw doubt written on some of the faces. He felt a pang of guilt, knowing what Glen had implied wasn't completely without truth. But at least he could say with all honesty that nothing had happened when Addie had visited his ranch. He didn't care for himself what folks said or thought, but he did care for her sake. He'd lie to protect her from scandal if he had to.

Doc Varney cleared his throat again. His gaze briefly met Will's, then he said, "I beg the pardon of the ladies present, but the truth is, Mr. Rider wouldn't have been capable of any—ah, strenuous activities at that time." He took hold of Will's arm, and the sheriff let go. "Now, I think you'd better come to my office and let me have a look at those ribs or you're not going to be in any shape to get married in ten days."

Will held his ground. "I'm not going anywhere until Townsend apologizes."

"I ain't apologizin' for nothin'." Glen swept the room with his gaze. "You're all a bunch of sanctimonious fools. You can't see what's goin' on right in front of your noses, any of you. Well, I know what I know, and to hell with the rest of you." With an angry jerk of his arm, he pulled free of the men who'd helped stop the fight, then stormed out of the church.

"Come on, Will," the doctor said softly, breaking the ensuing silence. "Let's get you over to my office."

Will didn't try to argue this time as Doc Varney guided him outside and along the street toward the opposite end of town.

The front door of Maria's house opened, allowing Doris McLeod entry. There were spots of color in the older woman's cheeks, and her eyes had a look of agitation about them. She stopped when she saw Addie sitting on the sofa. Her gaze darted quickly to her daughter-in-law.

Maria straightened in her chair. "Mother McLeod, what is it? What's wrong?"

Again Doris glanced at Addie. It was apparent that she hadn't expected the schoolteacher to be there.

Addie's stomach sank. They weren't going to let her go on teaching. She was surprised by the depth of her disappointment. She'd known she would miss the children, but she'd also known it was more common for a woman to be required to stop teaching once she married.

"It's all right, Mrs. McLeod," she said, setting her teacup on the table near her arm. "Emma will be telling me the school board's decision soon enough. You needn't try to hide it from me. I was prepared for them to decide I shouldn't keep teaching."

"What?" Doris blinked in confusion. When understanding dawned, she waved her hand in dismissal. "Oh, no. That's not it. In fact, the board decided to keep you on. You can keep teaching as long as you like. We're more than pleased with your performance."

Addie looked at her in surprise. "They did?"

"Then what's the matter?" Maria quizzed.

Doris clucked her tongue. "I've never seen the like. Rolling around on the floor like a couple of schoolboys. Fighting in church. If Hank hadn't stopped them . . ."

Addie rose to her feet. "There was a *fight?*"

"Right there in the middle of the church. The doctor's taken Mr. Rider over to his office. He seemed . . ."

Addie didn't wait for the woman to finish speaking. She darted past her, forgetting her coat, forgetting her hat, forgetting everything except the need to see Will and make sure he was all right.

Holding her skirts above her ankles, she ran down the center of the street, past the livery, past the post office, past the jail house. Panting for breath, she arrived at Doc Varney's office and burst inside.

"Doctor!" she called.

The curtain was drawn across the door to his examination room.

"Doc Varney!"

A moment later, his head appeared as the curtain parted.

"Will? Is he . . ."

"He's fine," Doc reassured her. "A bit bruised but fine, considering." He pushed the curtains aside. "Come in and see for yourself."

Will was sitting up, his legs hanging over one side of the doctor's examination table. As Addie entered the room, he was just finishing buttoning his shirt. His face looked pale beneath his tan, and one corner of his mouth had been bleeding, though it had stopped now.

"Excuse me," the doctor said. "I believe I'd better go attend my other patient—if he'll let me." He glanced at Will. "You'd best not let her stay too long. You understand me?"

Will nodded.

The door closed behind the doctor.

"How'd you hear about it?" Will asked as he met Addie's anxious gaze.

"Mrs. McLeod told me. Will, what happened? Are you all right? Your ribs, they're not . . ."

"Just a few bruises."

She moved a step closer. "Who were you fighting with?" Even before she asked, she was afraid she knew.

"Townsend."

She remembered Glen Townsend's threat. *I've got plenty to tell folks about you. Plenty. Now get off my porch.* She felt a tiny shiver.

"Why?" she asked in a whisper.

Will shook his head. "It doesn't matter."

"What did he say about me, Will?" She straightened her shoulders and raised her chin. "I have a right to know."

Will's eyes became icy cold as he said, "He insinuated you were doin' more than bringing Lark schoolwork when you came out to my ranch. I thought he owed you an apology."

Her shock was followed by a strange but quite pleasurable feeling. "You fought over my honor?" she asked, disbelieving.

He shrugged, as if admitting that's what he'd done but not wanting anything made of it.

Addie moved toward him. She picked up a cloth from the doctor's worktable, moistened it in the water basin, then dabbed it against the corner of Will's mouth. She tried to look stern. "You shouldn't have done that, you know."

"I know."

"Brawling in church," she scolded, staring hard at his split lip, afraid to look him straight in the eyes for fear he would see too much in hers. "You'll have everyone talking. What will they think?"

"They'll think I'm not about to let anyone say things like that about my wife."

She had a spinning sort of feeling in the pit of her stomach—not unpleasant, just unsettling.

At last, she lifted her gaze to meet his. "They're going to let me keep teaching," she said softly.

"I'm glad. You deserve to have what'll make you happy."

You make me happy, she wanted to say but couldn't.

At least, not yet.

Chapter Twenty-Six

As she worked, Doris was alert for sounds of the arriving stagecoach up from Boise City. She was running late this Wednesday, and Doris hated to be tardy, especially when it came to her official duties as Postmistress of Homestead. She'd never yet met the stage without the mail pouch being in her hand and ready to go. She wasn't about to let today be the first.

Wednesday was always her busiest day of the week. Plenty of folks stopped by on Wednesday mornings with their letters to post. Most all of them would stay a while to chat—men commenting on the weather or their crops, women talking about their husbands or their children—and usually Doris enjoyed their company. But this morning, her friends and neighbors had all seemed to want to talk longer than usual. And most of the talk was about the same subject—the fight between Will Rider and Glen Townsend. The gossip still hadn't died down, even after four days.

"Thank goodness I wasn't there," Zoe Potter said in a breathless voice as she watched Doris sorting the mail. "Disgraceful. Absolutely disgraceful."

Doris merely nodded. She knew Zoe would have given her eyeteeth to have seen the two men scrapping in the middle of the church. It was one of those rare moments of excitement that happened in this town, and Zoe felt deprived because she hadn't been present to see it firsthand.

Zoe leaned forward and lowered her voice. "Do you think there's any truth to what Mr. Townsend . . ."

"Zoe Potter!" Doris exclaimed as she slapped the letters down on the counter, cutting the woman off before she could finish her question. "I'm surprised at you. Asking me such a thing. It's nothing more than vicious gossip, and well you know it."

The other woman had the decency to look ashamed.

"After all," Doris grumbled, returning her attention to her sorting, "one only has to consider the source."

If Zoe had intended to say anything more, it was forgotten as the stage rolled noisily into town, pulling to a stop in front of the building that housed not only the Post Office but served as the stage office as well.

Doris stuffed the last of the letters into the mail pouch and carried it across the room. She set the pouch on a nearby slat-back chair, then lifted her coat off a hook and slipped into it before opening the door.

Rain was still falling from leaden skies. It had already turned the lone street of Homestead into a sea of mud and showed no sign of letting up soon.

"Afternoon, Miz McLeod," the driver called as he hopped down from his perch atop the stage.

"Good afternoon, Mr. Ridley," she returned.

Water streamed in a steady rivulet off Ridley's wide hat brim and onto his slicker. "The Lord shore musta pulled the cork. I ain't seen rain like this in a month o' Sundays." He shook his slicker as if to prove it to her, then reached for the stagecoach door. "Got us a passenger."

Doris's eyes widened. "A passenger?"

The man jumped from the stage to the boardwalk, avoiding the boggy earth in between. It was quickly clear to Doris, judging by the quality of his double-breasted coat with its fur collar, that this was a man of circumstance. Average in height, he had a sharp-featured, patrician-like face with deep-set brown eyes capped with expressive brows.

The stranger tipped his bowler in her direction. "Good day, madam. I take it this is

Homestead?" He looked at her with a gaze that demanded—and got—an immediate response.

"Yes."

"Thank God," he muttered beneath his breath. His eyes quickly raked the length of the town. Louder, he said, "I'm looking for Miss Adelaide Sherwood. Can you tell me where might I find her?"

"Addie?"

His piercing gaze met hers again.

"She . . . she's at the school." Doris pointed west. "The church there. That's where she's teaching."

"Very good. Is there a hotel in town? Some place for me to stay?"

"Townsend's Rooming House." Again Doris pointed.

The man turned toward the stage driver. "Would you see that my bags get over to the rooming house?" He handed over several coins. "I'd appreciate it."

"I'll do it, sir."

With a nod, the stranger set off toward the church, trying to avoid the worst of the muddy street, his short-brimmed derby useless against the drenching rain.

"Who *is* that, Mr. Ridley?" Doris asked.

"Name's Harris. Robert Harris. He's a lawyer from back East somewhere. Told me he's on his way to Oregon to set up practice. You ask me, he won't last long. He's so green he don't savvy cow 'less it's dished up in a stew."

* * *

While her students completed their geography assignments, Addie stared out the window. The gray skies and pouring rain might make others feel dismal, but not Addie. She hadn't seen rain like this since leaving home. She thought if she closed her eyes, she might be able to imagine the smell of the sea and the sounds of the surf crashing against a rocky shoreline. She had hoped she was over the poignant yearning for the sea and Kingsbury and her home, but today she felt the homesickness so strongly it nearly brought tears to her eyes.

"Miss Sherwood?"

She looked down at her side. "What is it, Rose?"

"I can't read this word." The girl held up her folio page geography.

Addie started to take the oversized book from Rose, then heard the door at the back of the church open and close. She glanced up, waiting to see who would step out of the tiny narthex where the children hung their coats each morning. She expected to see one of the parents.

The man stepped into view, then stopped. His hat and coat were drenched, and there was mud splattered on his trouser legs. She hadn't seen fancy clothes like his since leaving Connecticut, and she thought he looked very out of place in her rustic schoolroom. He removed his bowler and held it in one hand at his side.

It was a moment more before she recognized him. When she did, it was accompanied by a sense of unreality, as if she'd stepped through a doorway into the past, as if her homesickness had carried her back in time.

It had been raining then, too, the last time she'd seen Robert. He had stood in the entry hall of the house on Bayview Lane, clad in his coat and holding his hat in his hand. He'd smiled at her, their eyes almost level, and said, "I'll call for you on Friday at six."

He'd given her a proper kiss on the cheek—Robert had never once tried anything improper with her; it would have been unthinkable—then left Professor Sherwood's house on Bayview Lane. She'd never heard from him again, except through her father, who had told her of Robert's decision to break their engagement.

She blinked her eyes, trying to clear the old, painful images, but Robert remained standing at the back of the classroom. He was not some figment of her imagination. He was really and truly there.

Addie turned and walked to the front of the room, stepping up onto the raised platform, then faced her students. She stood ramrod straight, her hands folded in front of her waist. She didn't allow her sudden agitation to reveal itself in her voice. "Children, I'm going to let you go early today because of the weather. No homework tonight. I don't want your books getting ruined by the rain. It doesn't look like it's going to let up, so you must all promise me you'll go directly home and not linger about, catching your death of cold. Understood?" She paused, then said, "All right, you're dismissed."

The children's exit was as noisy and confusing as it always was. Laughter and chatter filled the building as they struggled into their outer garments and left the church. Most of them noticed the stranger standing at the back of the room, but he wasn't important enough to delay their bid for early freedom.

It was only a matter of minutes before the church house was quiet again. The patter of rain on the roof was the only sound breaking an otherwise complete and utter silence.

"Hello, Adelaide."

The pain in her chest surprised her. "Robert."

He came forward. "It's been a long time."

"Yes." She sat behind her desk.

"You look the same, Adelaide."

There was a salting of gray in his dark brown hair. He wore a neatly trimmed mustache where before he'd been clean-shaven. There were lines around his eyes and at the corners of his mouth.

"You don't," she replied honestly.

"No. I don't."

She drew in a deep breath. "What are you doing here, Robert?"

"I'm on my way to Oregon to start a new law practice. My widowed aunt lives there, and she's told me it's ripe with opportunity for men of vision. Besides, I've wanted to see a bit of this vast nation of ours. When I heard you were living in Idaho Territory, I thought, since it was on the route to Oregon . . ."

He made it sound as if he'd merely walked a block out of his way to pay an evening social call. That was just like Robert. Understated, unruffled, always business-like. He hadn't changed much after all.

Her pulse slowed to a more normal rate. The dizzy, other-worldly sensation began to clear from her head. "I never expected to see you again." She relaxed her folded hands slightly. "How is Eliza?"

A shadow crossed his face. "She died last winter."

"Oh . . . I'm sorry, Robert. I didn't know."

He stood on the opposite side of her desk. "I heard about your father. I'm sorry, too. I always admired Matthew."

"Thank you."

Robert looked around the room, turning slowly until their eyes met again. "So you finally became a teacher. I wondered if you would." His voice lowered. "I've thought about you often over the years."

His words caught her by surprise.

"I know it seems crazy, Adelaide, after so long, but I wanted to know why. I wanted you to tell me yourself. Why did you do it, Adelaide?"

"I don't know what you mean."

"Of course you do. I want to know why you so suddenly refused to see me again. What made you turn against me?" He shook his head. "What happened? What did I do that was so terrible? We never quarreled. You never let on that you had lost your affection for me. What happened?"

She stared at him, wondering if his grief over his wife's death had caused him to lose his mind.

"Mr. Bainbridge told me you never married."

"No. No, I never married."

"Then why did you break our engagement if you didn't intend to marry someone else? When your father wouldn't give me any reason, I was sure that was it. I was certain you'd fallen in love with another man."

Something inside Addie snapped. Anger boiled up and over. She rose quickly to her feet. "This is a very poor joke, Robert Harris, and certainly not worth a trip all the way to Idaho by stagecoach to play it."

He took a step backward, looking as if he thought she might hit him.

"Do you want to know what *I've* wondered through the years, Robert? I've wondered why you didn't have the decency to write me a letter, explaining your actions. That wasn't like you. Good manners have always demanded an engagement be broken in writing, and you were always such a stickler for following the rules." She turned her back on him. "You could have told me you'd fallen in love with Eliza. I wouldn't have tried to hold on to you."

She heard the creak of wood and knew Robert had sat down on one of the benches. She'd hoped he would simply leave after she made it clear she was ending the conversation.

"Adelaide." He spoke her name slowly, distinctly.

She sighed and turned around, holding her body stiffly.

"Adelaide, it wasn't I who broke our engagement."

She felt a niggle of dread in the back of her mind. "Robert, don't do this."

"I *didn't* break the engagement. Your father told me you'd decided you never wanted to see me again. And I did write to you. I wrote to you again and again, asking to see you, begging for another chance. All my letters were sent back unopened."

"Robert, don't say any more."

"I'm telling you the truth."

"It isn't possible."

He stared back at her, letting his eyes say what she forbade him to speak aloud.

The silent accusation hung between them. Addie tried to ignore it, tried to deny it, but it was there, all the same.

She shook her head. "My father wouldn't do such a thing. He wouldn't do it."

"I loved you, Adelaide."

"Go away, Robert." She felt cold. So very, very cold.

"Adelaide . . ."

"Please go away."

For a moment, he didn't move. He simply stared at her, his gaze thoughtful. Finally, in a voice just barely loud enough for her to hear, he said, "He wanted to keep you all to himself, didn't he? He was afraid to be left alone after your mother died, and so he made sure you would never leave him." He shook his head, as if trying to clear it. A little louder, he said, "Why didn't I see it? Why didn't I guess?"

"No. No, it isn't true."

"It *is* true, Adelaide." He placed his bowler back over his hair. "I'm staying at the rooming house for a few days. I'll be back to see you tomorrow. We have more to talk about." Then he turned and walked out of the building.

Addie sank back onto her chair. "Papa," she whispered, her heart in her throat, "how could you have done this to me?"

That night, alone in her tiny cabin, Addie stared into the fire, her heart aching, her body numb. Her whole life, everything she had ever believed in, had seemed to shatter in one harsh moment in the church that afternoon. Now she was trying desperately to put the pieces back together.

Again and again, she had asked herself, "Why?" But there was no definitive answer. Her father was dead, and he was the only one who could have answered that question with any certainty. She could only guess at the reasons.

I trusted you, Papa. Why? Why did you send him away?

Robert's parting words played through her mind once again. "He wanted to keep you all to himself, didn't he? He was afraid to be left alone after your mother died, and so he made sure you would never leave him."

Papa loved me.

But if her father had loved her, how could he have lied to her? How could he have watched her suffer the way she had?

And if she couldn't trust her father, how could she ever trust anyone again? He had forced her to be dependent upon him. He had told her lies and half-truths for years. He hadn't even told her when he'd sold their home. He'd paid no thought to what would happen to her after he was gone, gave her no chance to prepare. He hadn't wanted her to teach, hadn't wanted her to make friends, hadn't wanted her to have a life separate from his. And she hadn't known, she hadn't guessed.

"Oh, Papa."

She'd tried to tell herself that he'd done it for her sake. When she'd been so alone and afraid, with so little money and few friends, she'd told herself her father had acted in her best interests, thrusting her suddenly out into the world because he'd known she would stay hidden if possible. She'd tried to tell herself he'd done it to teach her independence, that she'd been the one who had clung so tightly to him.

But all the while, it had been her papa who'd been hanging on to her for dear life.

What was she to do now? If she could be so wrong about her own father, how could she be sure of anything?

How could she be sure she was supposed to be a teacher?

How could she be sure fate had brought her to Homestead?

How could she be so sure she should marry Will?

She wasn't sure. She wasn't sure of anything now.

Chapter Twenty-Seven

"Thank you for packing the food, Mrs. Townsend," Robert said as he picked up the basket. "I'll bring back the dishes as soon as the lunch recess is over."

He left the boarding house and made his way across the muddy street to the church just as children came pouring out the door. A bit of mud didn't seem to dampen their spirits, he thought as several of them sped by him on their way to the outhouse.

He entered the building, making certain the door was closed snugly behind him against the autumn chill, then stepped around the wall that divided the narthex from the main room. Several children had opted to eat their lunches indoors today. Addie was at her desk.

He paused a moment to study her unobserved.

He hadn't lied when he'd told Addie she hadn't changed. Her hair was still a wild, fiery red. Her eyes were still a surprising shade of green. She never had been a conventional beauty, but that hadn't mattered to Robert. He could see now that he'd been right. Addie had a quality which wore well with age. He would bet his last dollar that she would grow prettier with every passing year.

Addie glanced up and found him watching her. For a moment, her expression was tense; then she smiled, albeit somewhat sadly, and rose from her chair.

Robert held up the picnic basket. "I thought I could buy you lunch. It's not the Cambridge, but it's the best I could do in Homestead."

"How thoughtful."

He was mindful of all the children watching him as he walked toward the front of the schoolroom and set the basket on Addie's desk.

Speaking in a confidential voice, he said, "I'm sorry about what happened yesterday, Adelaide. If I'd known the truth, I wouldn't have been so blunt. I would have found some other way . . ."

She waved her hand in the air. "Don't, Robert. It doesn't matter. It's over now. We'll never know for sure why Papa did what he did. Perhaps it was for the best." She forced another smile. "Why don't you tell me about your life?

What's happened with you during the past nine years?"

While she spoke, she opened the basket and spread the tablecloth over her desk, then carefully unpacked the lunch of cold fried chicken, fresh bread spread with honey butter, and crisp apples.

After a few awkward starts, Robert found himself telling her about his marriage. It hadn't been a love match. He had married the exquisitely beautiful Eliza Dearborn to let Addie know he didn't care that she'd broken their engagement. He had wanted Addie to know he hadn't needed her. It wasn't the best reason to take a wife, and the union hadn't been particularly happy at first. But with time, he had grown to care for Eliza, and they'd found contentment together. They'd had a son, but the boy had died of diphtheria when he was two. There had never been any more children.

"And your law practice?" Addie asked a long while later. "You were successful?"

"Yes, I did very well. But after Eliza died, it just wasn't the same. When the opportunity came to go to Oregon, I decided I should take the chance, have a new adventure. There wasn't anything keeping me in New York." He met Addie's gaze. "Then I thought of you. I knew I couldn't leave the East until I had some answers. I went to Kingsbury to see you. Mr. Bainbridge told me where I could find you." He touched the back of her hand. "I'm sorry for . . . well . . ." He pressed her hand. "At least

I have the answers to my questions."

Addie glanced down at his hand on hers. Her mouth quivered slightly, and he suspected she was fighting tears.

"What about you, Addie? What has your life been like?"

"Nothing so impressive as yours. I stayed with Papa until he died. He sold our house when he became ill, and there was very little money left after the funeral. I had to earn a living. The only thing I could do was teach, and so I came here."

"It was a long way to come. Were there no openings for teachers in Connecticut?"

She lifted her gaze. Her eyes were still a bit glassy with unshed tears, but she managed a faint smile. "I guess I wanted an adventure, too."

"And did you find one?"

"Yes."

Robert had made a career out of reading people's faces—and learning as much by what they didn't say as by what they did—and Addie's face was very easily read. She was afraid and uncertain and . . . and something else he couldn't quite put his finger on.

"I've made many wonderful friends here, Robert. I'll never be sorry I came to Homestead."

He saw it then, that "something else" he'd failed to identify before.

Addie was in love.

* * *

Resting his forearms on his thighs, Will leaned forward on the wagon seat as the team trotted along the road toward Homestead. Overhead, the sky was still heavy with clouds, but for now, the rain had stopped.

He wasn't sure why he'd been so dead set on going into town for supplies. There wasn't anything on his list they couldn't have done without for another day or two, probably longer. He supposed, if he were honest with himself, it had something to do with seeing Addie.

Will hadn't talked to her since right after his fight with Glen. He still felt a trifle embarrassed about the way he'd lost his temper. He usually kept a tighter rein on his emotions than that. Public brawling wasn't anything he'd ever taken part in, and he was still surprised about the way he'd gone after Glen. Sure, Glen shouldn't have said what he did, but Will could have found another way to handle the situation.

Women. It was always women who made trouble for men.

Will shifted uneasily on the wagon seat as he remembered what Lark had told him at supper last night. She'd said some stranger—a man—had come to the school yesterday, and Miss Sherwood had released the students early.

"She acted real upset," Lark had said as she lifted another forkful of potatoes and gravy up to her mouth.

The man was probably just another newcomer to the valley, just another farmer finding out about schooling for his children. There wasn't any reason to think it was anything more than that.

"Giddup there," he called to the horses as he slapped the reins against their backsides, causing them to quicken their pace.

He guessed it wouldn't hurt to stop by the school after he'd picked up the supplies. School would be letting out soon. He could offer Lark a ride home in the wagon if she wanted it. If anything was on Addie's mind, she could tell him then.

When Will entered the Barber Mercantile a short while later, he discovered several women gathered in one corner of the store, their heads close together as they talked. They paid no heed to the ringing of the bell above the door.

"He went into the school," Ellen Pendroy said in a stage whisper, "just as bold as you please, carrying that lunch basket he had Mrs. Townsend pack for him. He *says* he's a friend of Miss Sherwood's. . . ."

The words set Will's teeth on edge.

Stanley came out of the stockroom at that moment. He stopped when he saw Will, then glanced toward the gaggle of gossiping women and back again. "Hello, Will," he called, a bit more loudly than necessary.

Four heads, all but Emma's covered with bonnets, turned in his direction. Miss Pendroy blushed a bright red.

"I really must get home," she said.

"Supper to fix," said Zoe Potter.

"Days just aren't long enough," Thelma Adamson muttered.

In a matter of minutes, the store was empty except for Will and the mercantile's proprietors.

Will walked over to the counter and handed Stanley his list of supplies. He kept the tension he was feeling out of his voice. "I get the feeling I interrupted something." His gaze swept to Emma.

She looked nearly as flustered as the reverend's sister had.

"We've had us a bit of excitement," Stanley replied. "A stranger came in by stage yesterday. He's stayin' at the Townsend's Rooming House. From what I just heard the ladies sayin', I guess he took over a picnic lunch to the school and shared it with Miss Sherwood." He cast a wry glance toward his wife. "It don't take much to get folks a-talkin' 'round here."

"What's his name?" Will asked with feigned nonchalance.

Emma didn't reply until Stanley gave her a pointed glance. "I believe it's Mr. Harris. He's a lawyer from New York City, but he's on his way to Oregon to open a new law practice there. Ellen Pendroy says he's a widower and that he grew up in the same town in Connecticut as Addie."

Stanley shook his head. "I don't know how she does it," he muttered softly. "I haven't even laid eyes on the man yet, and she already knows where he's from and where he's goin'."

"Hmmm." Will was too distracted to notice the exchange of glances that passed between Stanley and Emma. "Why don't you put those things together for me, Stanley? I have . . . something to do while I'm in town. I'll check back in a little while." He headed for the door.

"Sure thing, Will."

The stove in the back of the church kept the cold out and the teacher and students warm, but by the end of the day, the air in the room was insufferably stuffy and close. The combined odors of sweaty children and drying woolen clothing didn't help matters any.

Addie was more than ready for a breath of fresh air when she dismissed the children that afternoon. She hastened to clean the blackboard and be on her way. She felt both mentally and physically exhausted.

When she heard the door close again, she assumed one of the children had forgotten something. She looked up to find Will standing at the back of the room.

All her uncertainties, all her insecurities, bubbled to the surface. What if she was making a mistake by marrying him? Once she quit teaching, she would be completely dependent upon him, just as she'd been upon her father. What if she was wrong about Will, too? What if he wasn't the man she thought he was? She'd been wrong about her father. What if she was wrong about Will?

"Hi." He stood with his hands stuck in his back pockets. His expression was unreadable, yet she sensed an undercurrent of tension.

"Hello."

"I came into town for some supplies. Thought I'd have Lark ride home with me."

"Oh."

"She decided she didn't want to wait while I talked to you. She rode on ahead without me." He glanced around the room. "Heard you got a friend visitin' from back East." His gaze met hers again.

"Yes. Robert. Robert Harris. We knew each other in Kingsbury. We sort of grew up together."

"Hmmm." His blue gaze could be so unsettling. "Anything else I should know about him?"

"Well . . . I . . . I suppose you should know we were engaged once, many years ago."

"Who broke it off?" he asked in a quiet voice.

She felt a bit breathless. "He did." *At least, I thought he did.*

"Would you marry him now if you had the chance?"

"No," she whispered, then louder, "No, I wouldn't."

His sudden and swift movement was totally unexpected. It only took him a few quick strides to cross the room. In another second, he'd pulled her into his arms and was kissing her soundly on the mouth.

Addie was too shocked at first to do anything but just stand there and let him kiss her. And then, seemingly of their own volition, her arms found their way around his neck and she was holding on to him and returning his kiss. Heat flowed through her like a hot lava flow.

When he finally released her, she discovered that her knees felt rubbery and her stomach seemed to be filled with a hundred fluttering butterflies. She felt as if she'd been branded by his lips. It was not an unpleasant feeling.

He stared down at her with those startling blue eyes of his. "Why don't you invite Mr. Harris out for dinner at the Rocking R on Saturday? I think I'd like to meet him."

She nodded.

"Is he going to be here for our wedding?"

This was her chance. She could tell him she couldn't marry him. She wouldn't have to worry about whether she'd misread him. She wouldn't have to worry about being dependent upon him. She wouldn't ever have to see him again if she didn't want to. She could find a teaching job in another town and move away—hundreds, even thousands of miles away—if that was what she wanted. She could be independent, free, completely in charge of her own life, her own destiny.

That was when she knew. That was when she knew her love was greater than her fears. And she *was* afraid. She was afraid of the hurt that could be before her. But she was more terrified of never knowing what she might find as Will's wife. She had to take the risk.

"Is he?" Will prompted. "Coming to the wedding?"

"I don't know," she answered huskily.

"Well, tell him he's welcome if he wants to come."

"I'll tell him."

He kissed her again, gently this time, a kiss that lingered, that savored, that seemed to cherish every moment it lasted. Finally, he released her and stepped back. "See you Saturday," he said, then turned and promptly left the schoolroom.

A bemused smile curved the corners of Addie's mouth. She wasn't completely sure what had just happened. In fact, the past week had left her more surprised and hurt, content and confused than she'd ever been in her life.

This much, however, she knew. Her life had been very predictable back in Kingsbury, Connecticut. It was anything *but* predictable in Homestead, Idaho.

She wondered if it would ever be predictable again.

Chapter Twenty-Eight

Robert glanced at the pewter-gray canopy of sky. "Feels like it could snow."

"Do you think so?" Addie asked, following his gaze skyward.

He knew it was a rhetorical question. She didn't expect an answer, and he didn't give her one. Instead, while her eyes were engaged elsewhere, he took the opportunity to study the woman seated in the buggy beside him.

She was wearing a deep-gold bonnet trimmed with brown feathers and amber ribbons. Robert thought it a flattering combination of colors on Addie, bringing out the warmth of her skin tones. Beneath the rich brown cloak, she wore a costume made of gold cashmere with appliqué velvet leaves on the corsage, apron, and drapery bow. While the design was several years old—Robert hadn't lived with Eliza for eight years without learning something about fashion—and wouldn't have been considered in style in New York, he was certain Addie would have made whoever saw her in it think it was something new and chic.

She turned her head at that moment and caught him staring at her. Her cheeks pinkened. "What are you looking at?"

"Just you."

"Why?" She touched the tie of her bonnet, then smoothed the twist of hair at her nape with her fingertips as if searching for a stray wisp.

He shrugged. "I suppose I was trying to find the girl I was once engaged to." He paused, then said, "She isn't there."

Addie looked puzzled by his statement.

He wondered if he could find the words to explain what he meant. How did he tell her he came to Homestead expecting to find her unchanged from the girl he'd last seen nine years before? Instead, he'd found a woman. Oh, she looked much the same on the surface, but underneath she was very different.

He knew she'd been devastated by the discovery of what her father had done, and he knew it would take a long time for her to reconcile her feelings toward the man she'd loved and respected above all others. Matthew Sherwood's deception had been a cruel blow to his daughter. But she hadn't let it knock her down. Already he sensed a quiet acceptance. This Adelaide would never give in to the difficulties life tossed her way.

Robert hid a smile as he remembered his meeting yesterday with Emma Barber at the mercantile. It hadn't taken him more than five minutes to understand how she and the rest of the town felt about Addie. Mrs. Barber had made it clear—without saying it directly—that Robert had better not have come to Homestead to cause Addie any unhappiness.

And if that estimable woman hadn't made the townsfolk's feelings clear enough, the blacksmith certainly would have. When Robert went into the livery to hire this buggy for the day, Chad Turner had given Robert a subtle, but nonetheless thorough, questioning. Robert figured he must have checked out or he was sure Mr. Turner would never have rented him the buggy. More than likely, if he'd thought Robert meant to cause Addie trouble, the blacksmith would have used his beefy arms and mallet-like fists to convince Robert of the error of his ways—and then escorted him out of town.

Robert couldn't hide his smile any longer. "You know, Adelaide, I came to Homestead to settle something unfinished from my past. I wanted some answers to questions I couldn't seem to forget. But perhaps I was also halfway hoping to find I might still love you—and that you might love me, too."

Her eyes grew wide, reminding him of a wild animal, startled by the sudden appearance of a hunter.

"Don't worry," he said with a chuckle. "I discovered very quickly that I can't go back. Our time to be together, if there ever was such a time, was years ago. We're not that young couple I remember any longer. We've changed, both of us."

She seemed to relax slightly.

"But you've changed most of all. The Adelaide Sherwood I knew would never have had the courage to come West all by herself. The girl I remember was painfully shy and very insecure. I remember how surprised I was that she even had the courage to accept my proposal of marriage." He shook his head, still grinning. "And the girl I remember liked all the comforts of home. She would never have been content to live in a one-room cabin with hard dirt floors and only one window."

"I know it isn't much," Addie interjected quickly, "but it isn't so bad really. Everything's quiet and still in the mornings. Sometimes the deer come down to drink at the creek, and I can watch them through my window. The fireplace and the stove keep the place toasty, even when it's very cold outside. Actually, I think I'll miss it a little when I leave it." She stopped, looking embarrassed over her fervent defense of her rustic home.

Robert offered a tender smile. "I'm a bit sorry we don't still love each other, Adelaide. You're going to make a remarkable wife."

This time, she blushed all the way up to her hairline.

I hope Will Rider knows he's a lucky man, Robert added to himself, then turned his eyes back to the road.

Addie pondered the things Robert had said about her. She thought he was wrong. She hadn't changed so terribly much. She wasn't courageous. She'd come West because she'd had no other choice—unless she counted marrying Mr. Bainbridge a choice. She didn't.

She was definitely still the same, insecure person Robert remembered. She was belabored with unanswered questions, always uncertain if she was making the right choice. When she looked back over her life, it seemed she was forever making the same mistakes.

No, she hadn't changed so terribly much. Robert was wrong about her.

As the hired buggy approached the Rocking R ranch house, Addie saw the front door open and Will step outside onto the veranda. He was wearing a coat with a fur collar, denim trousers, and boots. As usual, his head was covered with a wide-brimmed hat, but she knew he was watching them with intent blue eyes. She felt her heartbeat quicken, as it always did when she looked at him.

Will stepped down off the porch as the buggy drew to a halt. He offered Addie a hand and assisted her to the ground before Robert could climb out the other side and walk around the rear of the buggy.

Will turned and the two men perused each other in silence. Addie felt a nervous tremble.

"Will, this is Robert Harris, my friend from Kingsbury, Connecticut. Robert, this is Will Rider."

Robert was the first to hold out his hand. "I'm pleased to make your acquaintance, Mr. Rider."

"Likewise, Mr. Harris."

They shook hands.

"So you're the man Adelaide is going to marry," Robert said.

"And you're the man she didn't."

Addie gasped. "Will!" she whispered, heat rushing to her cheeks.

Neither of the men bothered to look at her. Robert grinned, then so did Will. Robert's smile was friendly. Will's wasn't.

"Let's go inside," Will suggested. "It's too cold to stand out here jawin'." He took hold of Addie's arm and steered her toward the front door, leaving Robert to follow behind them.

Again, Addie felt a shiver of nerves and wondered what other surprises this day would bring.

Glen stood in the doorway to Tom McLeod's office, his gaze leveled on the safe. Tomorrow, McLeod should be getting payment for the new Henderson barn. Sometime this week, he should also collect for the big shipment of lumber that had gone up to the mining district. When he did, that safe would have plenty of money in it. Enough money for a man to start up his own business, if he had a mind to.

He glanced around him at the silent mill. Nobody was working today. Glen's boss had gone home to see to his wife, who was feeling poorly. He'd given the men the rest of the day off. Only Glen remained, his mind playing with thoughts of the money which would soon be his.

He wouldn't open his saloon here in Homestead. He'd pack up and go elsewhere, some place where there was a bit of life and excitement.

He thought of Virginia, and his lip curled. He didn't want to be saddled with a woman like her when he started up a new and better life somewhere else. Made more sense to simply just be on his way. The boy could take care of his ma and sister. Mark was fourteen. Darn near a man. Time he took on some responsibility. He sure as hell didn't need to be gettin' any more schooling.

Glen's jaw twitched. Schooling. That schoolmarm. Will Rider . . . Lord, he'd like to get even with those two before he left. That woman needed a man to put her in her place. As for the rancher . . .

His hands knotted into fists as a string of vile curses tumbled from his mouth.

The sheriff had made it plenty clear what would happen to Glen next time he took to fighting. He couldn't risk being thrown into jail. Not when his opportunity was here at last.

There was too much at stake. Too much that would be sitting right there in that safe in just a few days.

Glen turned abruptly and headed for the boarding house. He was hungry, and Virginia had darn well better have dinner on the table, or he'd know the reason why.

Addie felt as if she'd stepped through the looking glass with Alice. This had been the strangest afternoon of her life.

She looked at Will, standing near the fireplace, his right elbow resting on the mantel, his stance relaxed. He'd played the role of the welcoming host ever since she and Robert had arrived, yet she hadn't been able to relax for a moment, not since he'd made his remark about Robert being the man she *hadn't* married. And that hadn't been the last thing he'd said which had made her feel uneasy.

It wasn't that Will had been truly rude or uncordial. On the contrary, the two men had spent much of the afternoon talking like old friends. Still, Addie couldn't shake the tension that twisted her stomach. Her taut nerves had made it almost impossible for her to eat a single bite of the delicious dinner Frosty had prepared.

She glanced toward Robert. *He* certainly didn't look the least bit unsettled. In fact, he'd smiled and laughed often. He seemed to be enjoying himself immensely. For some reason, this irritated Addie no end.

Robert had been enjoying himself. The day had been a very enlightening one. Certainly his visit to Homestead, Idaho, had been nothing like what he'd expected.

Leaning back on the comfortable upholstered chair, he turned his head and caught Addie watching him. He smiled, but she didn't smile back. Instead, a frown brought a tiny vertical crease to her forehead between her eyebrows. Then she looked away.

He'd spoken the truth when he'd told Addie he was just a bit sorry the two of them weren't still in love. The more he'd watched her today, the more he'd admired the woman she'd become.

Then again, it was just as well he didn't love her, because nothing could have been plainer than the way these two people felt about each other. Addie's green eyes fairly glowed with love when she looked at Will, even when she was frowning as she was now. And only a man in love acted as jealous and possessive as Will had all afternoon.

Robert rather wished Homestead needed a good attorney. It might have been nice to settle in such a place and start off with a couple of friends like Will and Addie nearby. He would have enjoyed watching how much more Addie might blossom as a wife and a mother.

Robert rose from the chair. "I think I'd better be getting Addie back to her place before it grows any later. I don't want to get lost in the dark trying to find my way back to

Homestead." He moved toward Addie. "Shall we go, Adelaide?"

Will stepped into his path. "I wouldn't want you to risk getting lost," he said, his tone friendly, his eyes less so. "Why don't I see Addie home?"

Robert opened his mouth to insist that he didn't mind since it was on his way. Then he thought better of it. He wasn't sure just how far he wanted to push Will Rider.

"If that's what you want," he said. He glanced at Addie. "Guess I'll see you at church tomorrow." He turned once more toward Will. "Thanks again for the fine dinner."

"More'n welcome. Come any time."

Robert didn't believe a word of it.

Chapter Twenty-Nine

Will was silent during the drive to Addie's cabin. He'd spent the afternoon making certain Robert Harris understood that Addie belonged to him. He'd felt confident and sure of himself then. He'd known the attorney—from Connecticut by way of New York City—had understood his carefully expressed message.

But now he was alone with Addie, and he wondered if *she* understood what he'd been telling Robert. Did *she* know she belonged to him? Did *she* know she would always belong to him?

Dusk was gathering over the countryside as the wagon approached the cabin on Pony Creek. A cold wind whistled through the trees, and the night air had a bite of winter in it.

Will drew the team of horses to a halt, then stepped across the wagon in front of Addie and hopped to the ground. Turning, he raised his arms and took hold of her about the waist, then lifted her down.

He stared into her eyes for a moment before saying, "It's going to be a cold night. I'll bring in some extra wood for you." He didn't give her a chance to respond before escorting her indoors.

Will made several trips between the wood box inside the cabin and the wood stack under the lean-to. He brought in enough firewood to hold her for several days.

Until the wedding, he thought as he placed the last log in place near the stove. After that, he wouldn't have to worry about that Harris fellow coming 'round anymore.

He turned. Light from the blazing fire spilled over the room, capturing Addie in its golden glow. She'd removed her coat and was standing in the center of the room, watching him with a hesitant expression. She looked lovely. Too damned lovely.

When had this happened? When had she changed from being merely plain, perhaps even unattractive, into an enticing, desirable woman? He'd looked at her when she'd first come to Homestead. He'd seen the long, narrow nose, the wide mouth, the sloping eyes, and the flaming red hair, and as a whole, he'd seen nothing beyond ordinary. When had all these separate attributes fused together into a creature of irresistible loveliness?

A surge of wanting sent a rush of warmth through him, the heat pooling in his loins. Since the night they'd made love, he'd managed to keep his desire for her in check. Even when he'd kissed her in the schoolhouse two days ago, he'd been in control. But not any longer. Desire raged through him, demanding relief.

Four days, he reminded himself. Just four more days and she would be his. Four days and she would be in his bed, and he could roll onto his side and gather her into his arms whenever he wanted to. And from the way he felt now, he would always want to.

"Will? Is something wrong?" she asked softly.

"Damn right," he muttered as he stepped across the room and pulled her into his embrace.

This wasn't exactly what Addie had meant, but she didn't argue with him. She was happy enough to surrender to the white heat his kisses stirred in her blood.

"Addie Sherwood," he whispered, his lips hovering over hers, his hands cupping the sides of her face, "you could drive a man insane."

His words caused a flash of pleasure in her chest. She'd never been the type to inspire men to words of passion. She could scarcely believe she was hearing Will speaking them now.

What she *could* believe was the storm of feelings his touch ignited as his hands began to roam over her body, sliding up and down the length of her arms, then coming to rest on the sides of her breasts.

Addie turned her body slightly, pressing her right breast into his left palm. She felt her nipples harden, her entire body straining against the bonds of her clothing. She ached to feel the touch of his hands on her bare skin.

She drew closer to him. Through the thickness of her gown and petticoats, she could feel his erection pressing against the juncture of her legs. Instinctively, she wiggled closer, trying to assuage the growing need.

"Don't do that," Will whispered harshly.

"What?" she asked as her lips brushed against his cheek.

"Don't tempt me, Addie, or I won't be able to stop."

She opened her eyes and stared up at him. For two weeks she'd lain alone in that bed, wishing he were back in it with her. Would it be so terrible for them to make love again? The wedding was only four days away. They were nearly man and wife now. What harm could there be in letting him hold her, kiss her, caress her, make love to her?

A soft groan escaped her slightly parted lips. In response, Will made a tortured sound in his throat and reached for the fastenings on her gown.

Their undressing was not done leisurely but with fevered haste. Addie heard a tiny button pop loose from her bodice and roll across the floor, but it didn't matter now.

Nothing mattered but getting rid of her clothing, getting rid of his clothing. Nothing mattered but touching him and having him touch her.

Will lifted her from the puddle of clothing lying around her feet. She laid her head in the curve of his neck and shoulder and breathed deeply, drawing in the masculine scent of him until she felt as if her lungs were filled with his very essence. He carried her over to the bed, lowering her slowly, then lay down beside her.

His mouth covered hers again, his tongue teasing her lips until they parted for him. She tasted him as her hands encouraged him to draw closer. The bandage was gone from his torso, and his skin felt warm and wonderful beneath her exploring fingertips.

She wanted him. She wanted him completely. She wanted him now.

"Will . . ."

"You're mine, Addie," he whispered hoarsely as he rose above her. "Don't ever forget it. You're mine."

And then there was no room left for mere words.

Addie floated back to reality on a cloud of pure satisfaction. Her body still tingled with pleasure. She felt almost as if she could purr, then felt herself blush as she remembered the sounds she had made during their lovemaking.

You're mine, Addie. Don't ever forget it.

He'd wanted her. He'd laid claim to her. Surely that meant he loved her—at least a little. In time, he would tell her so. In time, she would tell him, too.

"Are you awake?" he asked, his voice sounding sleepy, sated.

"Mmmm."

"I should leave, get back to the ranch."

"Uh huh."

"They'll be wondering what's keeping me. Wouldn't do for someone to see my wagon outside with the cabin all dark."

Reluctantly, she opened her eyes. He was right. The cabin was dark. How had the fire burned low this quickly? Had it really been so long ago that he'd started to undress her? Impossible!

"I think I'll like it better when you don't have to leave the bed afterward to go home." Her cheeks grew hot with embarrassment. She couldn't believe she'd had the courage to say such a risqué thing.

She heard his low chuckle. "I'm going to like that better, too."

"Will?"

"Yes."

"I'll do my best to be a good wife to you and—and a good mother to Lark."

He was silent a painfully long time before he said, "I know you will."

Say it. Tell me you care.

"And you'll never want for anything, Addie. I give you my word."

That wasn't what she'd wanted him to say. That wasn't it at all.

"I'd better go," he said again. Only this time, he tossed back the blanket and lowered his legs over the side of the bed.

In the low flicker of firelight, she watched him pull on his clothes. He was little more than a shadow against the darkness, yet she still appreciated what little she could see. She thought she must truly be a wanton, the way she wanted to look at him, the way she longed to feast her eyes on him.

When he was finished dressing, he picked up his hat, raked his hair back with the fingers of one hand, then placed the Stetson on his head. Finally, he crossed the room to the door.

Before opening it, he said, "You have your things packed up Wednesday morning. I'll send a couple of the men over for your trunks first thing."

"Will . . ."

He turned. She could feel him staring at her through the darkness.

"Will, I . . ." *I love you.* "I . . ." *I love you more than I thought it was possible to love.*

"What is it, Addie?" His voice was gentle, encouraging.

But she couldn't say the words. Not yet. To speak them aloud was too great a risk. And so she said the first thing that popped into her head. "I hope you mean to keep our bargain."

"Our bargain?" He sounded confused.

Why on earth had she said that? Well, there was nothing to do now but bungle forward.

"Yes, our bargain. I . . . I taught you to read. You said you would . . . you would teach me to ride."

There was a long, silent pause. Then he chuckled. "There's plenty I mean to teach you, Miss Adelaide Sherwood. You've got my word on it."

Chapter Thirty

The remaining days leading up to the wedding seemed both to fly past and to drag by interminably. Addie found herself easily distracted, her thoughts frequently drifting to Will when she should have been concentrating on her lessons and her students. All too often she thought of the pleasures he'd taught her, and she longed for his kisses and caresses.

Robert called at the school during the lunch break each day, and Addie was surprised and pleased at the warm friendship that had sprung up between them. The pain and insecurities brought on by their broken romance nine years before had faded to nothing, and with them had gone Addie's last doubts about marrying Will. More and more, with each passing day, she was certain it was destiny that had brought her to

Homestead and to Will Rider.

Addie had her last fitting of the borrowed wedding gown on Tuesday after school. When she saw herself in the cheval glass, tears welled in her eyes, blurring her reflection.

Standing beside her, Maria placed an arm around Addie's back and squeezed. "I've never seen a more beautiful bride."

"It's the dress," Addie whispered through the thickness in her throat.

"Nonsense. It's you who make the dress beautiful." She gave another tiny squeeze, then stepped over to a stool in front of her dressing table. "Sit down, Addie, and let's see what we want to do with your hair."

Addie blinked away the remaining tears. "Help me out of this first. I don't want to wrinkle it."

"It won't matter. I have to do some final pressing anyway."

"It does matter," Addie replied, glancing at the other woman, noting—not for the first time—the circles under Maria's eyes. "And *I* mean to do the ironing. You're doing too much as it is. Tom must be angry with me for causing you all this work."

"I haven't done so much. Just sat in a chair and stitched. Mother McLeod has been helping with Sarah and the housework. She's making certain I get plenty of rest. Truly, I feel absolutely spoiled."

Addie stood her ground, waiting until Maria returned and began to loosen the fastenings along the back of the gown. Clad only in her chemise and petticoat, she then helped Maria carefully lay the wedding dress across the bed before she sat down on the stool as earlier instructed.

Maria pulled the hairpins and combs from Addie's hair and began to brush the thick mass of curls. "I knew a girl when I was little who had hair almost this color. I always wished I did, too."

"And I always wished for golden hair like yours." Memories of her childhood drifted through her mind—the tall, gawky, red-haired girl who'd never seemed to fit in. "Do you suppose we all wish we were someone else sometime in our lives?" she asked softly. "Or at least different from what we are?"

"Yes, I think we probably do."

Addie stared into the looking glass on the dresser. She thought of Will and the extraordinary way he touched her and the love she felt for him in her heart.

"I'm glad I'm me," she whispered.

Later that evening, Will stood in the doorway of Lark's bedroom and looked down at the sleeping child. She'd been so excited at supper, he'd wondered if she would ever be able to fall asleep. She'd chattered on and on about the wedding and Addie coming to live with them. Her uncle had watched and listened, and he'd wondered at the resilience of children. This hardly seemed the same girl who had gotten off the stage last summer, so sad and shy and afraid.

He thought of Addie, of the special way she had with Lark, and he wondered what would have become of his niece without Addie's unique understanding of the child. And then he wondered what would have become of him without her.

It was in that moment that he finally acknowledged the truth. He'd fallen in love with Addie Sherwood.

It wasn't just desire. It wasn't just lust. It wasn't just anything. It was love.

Will closed the door to Lark's room and went down the stairs. Without putting on his coat, he stepped outside.

Long Bow Valley had gotten a reprieve from the threat of snow and was enjoying one last glimpse of Indian summer. The night air was cold, but today had been warm and tomorrow promised to be the same. Tomorrow would be a lovely day for a wedding.

He loved her.

How had this happened? When had he lowered his guard and let Addie find her way into his heart? It was a dangerous thing for a man to do. He'd learned that lesson years ago. It should have been enough to hold Addie in high regard. It should have been enough for them to be content together, companionable, good friends. It should have been enough for them to share the mutual desire they'd found in bed.

But, instead, he'd let himself fall in love.

Standing on the front porch, looking up at the stars glittering in a clear night sky, Will hoped he was right about Addie being different. He didn't know if he could bear to be wrong this time around.

Maria leaned over and kissed Sarah on the forehead, then smoothed the sleeping youngster's pale hair back from her face.

Straightening, she laid her hand on her protruding abdomen and thanked God another day was done. She longed for December and the birth of this baby. It seemed she was weary all the time, even when she did nothing more than sit in a chair all day long.

"Dear Father," she prayed, "keep him healthy. No matter what happens to me, keep my son healthy and strong."

Tom's hand alighted on her shoulder, causing her to start. "Sarah asleep?" he asked.

"Yes." She turned to look at her husband, careful to smile, careful not to let him see the fatigue that dogged her day and night. She could only hope he hadn't heard her whispered prayer. He worried enough about her already. She could see the strain in his eyes.

He didn't seem to be fooled by her smile. "Are you sure you should go to the wedding tomorrow? Maybe you should stay home and rest."

"I can't miss Addie's wedding, Tom. She's become such a good friend to me." She laid her head against his shoulder.

"Besides, I want to see her walking down the aisle in my dress. It will remind me of our wedding."

His arm went around her back, and he drew her closer. "I don't need to see the dress on Addie to remember how you looked that day." His lips brushed her temple in a feather-light kiss. "Like an angel."

"You've made me so very happy, Tom."

He kissed her temple again, then said, "Let's go to bed. I feel like holding you in my arms."

"I'd like that," she replied softly as she turned and led the way to their bedroom.

Rose covered her ears with her hands, trying to block out the unmistakable sounds coming through her bedroom wall. She knew exactly what it sounded like when her pa's hand smacked against her ma's cheek, and she recognized the tiny mewling sounds her ma made, even when muffled behind closed doors.

Pa wasn't shouting tonight. He never did when they had a boarder. Not that she thought Pa cared what folks said about him or the way he treated his family. After all, he'd spoken his mind clear enough and often enough about a man's right to discipline his wife. He'd sure never seemed troubled to have folks see her sporting a black eye or a swollen lip.

Rose winced with the sound of shattering glass.

She had known the fight was coming all evening long. She'd watched her pa drinking, heard the surly insults he'd tossed at his wife, seen her ma trembling with fear. She didn't know what had set Pa off, but she'd known he was spoiling for a fight. She'd been thankful to escape to her bedroom without being the one to incur his wrath, but now she felt guilty for her selfishness. Maybe if she'd been with Ma, her pa wouldn't have started hitting her. Maybe he would have gone out and caused trouble elsewhere.

She pulled the pillow over her head. "Stop it, Pa," she whimpered. "Stop it."

But her soft pleading was in vain. Even if she'd shouted it, even if she'd been in the same room with him, she knew it would have been in vain. Once Pa got started, he didn't quit 'til he was damn good and ready. Usually that meant he passed out on the bed.

I hate you. I wish you'd go away. I wish you'd die.

She tried to hide from the awful noises by thinking of something nice. She tried to think about tomorrow. There wouldn't be any school tomorrow or for the rest of the week. Tomorrow was Miss Sherwood and Mr. Rider's wedding. The whole town would be at the church to watch Reverend Pendroy marry them.

Something crashed against the wall separating her bedroom from her parents' room.

Lucky Lark. Lucky, lucky Lark.

Emma liked to spend the evening sitting by the fireside after the children were all in bed.

It seemed like the only time of day when there was a minute's peace in the Barber household. Not that she minded. She counted each one of her children a blessing. But she had to admit there were times when she would have come close to selling her soul for just five minutes of uninterrupted solitude.

She glanced across the room at her husband. Stanley had a book open in his lap, but his head had dropped forward, his chin resting on his chest, and he was snoring softly.

Emma shook her head and smiled. Stanley couldn't ever read more than a couple of pages before falling asleep, whether he was lying in bed or sitting in his favorite chair. Of course, he would deny it if she accused him of it.

"Just resting my eyes," he would insist. "Just resting my eyes."

A woman learned a lot about a man after she married him. During the courtship, the rules of polite society dictated most of a couple's behavior. Even if a woman was one of the lucky ones who loved her bridegroom on her wedding day, she was destined for plenty of surprises after she started living with a man.

Emma wondered what sort of things Addie would be learning about Will in the months and years to come. Whatever things they were, she figured the two of them would weather the storms of marriage. Emma had always been a pretty fair judge of character, and she thought highly of both Addie Sherwood and Will Rider. The two of them would be good together. She'd lay odds on it, even though she wasn't a betting woman.

Emma's attention returned to the man across the room from her. She'd been one of those lucky women. She'd been in love with Stanley from the time she was eight years old. She never had wanted to marry anyone but Stanley. That hadn't changed after marriage, but her idealized image of what a husband was like had changed quickly enough. There were no gallant knights on white chargers, just men with feet of clay.

And Emma Barber happened to be very fond of Stanley's feet.

Addie lay in her bed, staring up at the ceiling. Her trunks were packed and waiting to be picked up and taken to the Rocking R Ranch. Her best dress was pressed and ready to wear into town first thing in the morning. The borrowed wedding gown was waiting for her in Maria's bedroom. Doris McLeod had baked the cake, and Emma Barber had made the punch which would be served after the wedding. All was in readiness.

Tomorrow is my wedding day.

It didn't seem at all real to Addie.

I wish you were here, Papa.

She felt a spark of bitterness but shoved it aside. It served no purpose to feel angry and resentful toward her father for what he'd done. The past couldn't be changed. And perhaps that was just as well. Her life with Matthew

Sherwood hadn't been a bad one. He'd been a good father to her, even if he'd done his best to keep her to himself. Could she hold it against him that he'd been afraid of being left alone with no one? Didn't she know that fear herself?

I wish you were here, Papa, she thought again, smiling this time. *I wish you could know Will. You would have liked him. He makes me so very happy, and I love him. I want him to love me, too. I hope someday he will.*

She closed her eyes and pretended her father was there, tucking her into bed as he'd done when she was a very little girl.

"He'll love you, Addie," she imagined him saying. *"He can't help but love you."*

She went to sleep, holding on to the promise of her father's words.

Chapter Thirty-One

Addie had looked at her reflection in this same cheval glass several times in the past two weeks, but this morning, she seemed to look different than before. Perhaps it was the careful arranging of her hair, caught back with ivory combs, then allowed to tumble down her back in a cascade of curls beneath the white netting of the veil. Or perhaps it was simply because today was the day she was truly a bride.

"Are you ready?" Maria asked softly.

Addie turned around. "I don't know. I'm not sure. I . . . I . . ."

The young mother smiled. "It's that way with all brides, no matter how much we love our bridegrooms." She held out her hand, squeezing Addie's fingers when she took hold of it. "You'll be fine soon enough."

The McLeod house was silent as the two women made their way down the stairs to the parlor. Addie commented on it when they paused near the front door.

"Mother McLeod has already taken Sarah over to the church. Tom had to go to the mill earlier this morning, but he'll be there for the wedding. He says he wouldn't . . . miss seeing Will Rider take a wife for anything."

Despite her own anxieties, Addie couldn't help noticing Maria's catch of breath in the midst of her reply. "Is something wrong?"

"No." Maria pressed her fingertips against the small of her back. "The baby is just restless today. It's all the excitement, I think. Don't worry. I'll be fine."

"Maybe I should go for Tom."

"Don't be silly. He'll be joining us at the church in just a few minutes. In fact, he may beat us there if we don't get going." She reached up and pulled the veil over Addie's face. "Ready?"

Her heart in her throat, Addie nodded.

With Addie's help, Maria gathered the lengthy train in her arms, holding the cream-colored silk fabric high and away from the dusty road they would follow to the church.

Neither woman spoke after leaving Maria's house. Addie felt as if she couldn't put together one full sentence to save her soul. Maria seemed to understand and respect her need for silence.

Much as it had been on Addie's first Sunday in Homestead, the church was surrounded by wagons and buggies. Only this time, folks hadn't come to meet the new schoolmarm but to see her wed. Just two months ago, they had all been strangers to her. Now many of them were her friends.

Two months. Just two months.

Addie felt her mouth grow dry. Two months wasn't a very long time. How could she be sure she loved Will? She'd known Robert most of her life, and yet the love she'd thought she felt for him hadn't lasted. What if this didn't last either? What if she were just a desperate old maid? Oh Lord, how was she to know if this was the right thing to do?

Tom glanced at his pocket watch. Dad blast it! He was going to be late. Maria would have his hide if he wasn't standing beside her when Will and Addie exchanged their vows.

He shut the ledger, then placed the money into the safe. He'd just closed his fingers over the safe handle when he heard a noise behind him. He started to turn, but saw nothing before he was blinded by a crashing pain in his head. There was a momentary flash of light behind his eyelids, followed by a spiral into total darkness.

Maria . . .

Will stood at the front of the church, trying not to look nervous. His starched collar seemed to be choking him. He longed to stick his finger between it and his throat and give the collar a yank to try to loosen it, but he didn't. However, he did stretch his neck a little, unmindful of how much the turtle-like movement said about the case of nerves he was trying so hard to hide.

Everyone in the church fell silent when they heard the door open and, a few seconds later, close again. A moment more and Maria came into view. Her gaze met Will's. She smiled, as if to encourage him, then moved quickly to stand beside Hank and Doris McLeod.

Will kept his gaze trained on the back of the church. He was having a hard time breathing. It was even worse than when Addie's horse had kicked him and broken his ribs.

And then she stepped through the opening, like a cloud of silk and lace and pearls. A gasp went up from those in the pews. Will knew exactly how they felt, only he felt doubly so.

He'd never seen anything more beautiful in his life.

Lord, how he loved her. And she was going to be his wife. He didn't know if a luckier man had ever lived.

Addie knew everyone in the church was staring at her, but she had eyes only for one—Will. She realized then that she'd been afraid he wouldn't show up, that he would change his mind and leave her standing at the altar.

But there he was, looking so incredibly handsome in his dark suit, his tawny hair slicked back on his head. The corners of his mouth curved upward as he watched her, and she thought she could see a glimmer of approval in his glorious blue eyes.

Ellen Pendroy struck up a melody on the church organ. At least, Addie thought she did. It could have been the joyous song of her heart she heard.

She started forward, moving toward Will. She'd been moving toward Will all of her life, she thought, and just hadn't known it.

When she reached him, he took hold of her right hand, then turned with her to face the minister.

Reverend Pendroy looked appropriately solemn. "Dearly beloved, we are gathered here today . . ."

Maria wondered what was keeping Tom. It wasn't like him to disappoint her. He'd promised that his paperwork at the mill would take no more than an hour. He'd promised to meet her at the church.

There had to be something wrong to keep him away. Maria tried to tell herself not to worry, tried to reassure herself that he'd merely lost track of time.

She felt a sudden sharp stab in her lower back and just barely managed to stifle a gasp. Of all the pains she'd felt that morning, this was the worst.

Doris glanced at her daughter-in-law. Maria's face looked pinched and pale, and her mouth seemed taut. A niggle of fear pricked Doris's chest.

Not again.

No, not again. It couldn't happen again. It was simply because Tom wasn't there. That was all that was bothering Maria.

And Doris was going to give her son a thorough tongue-lashing for making the girl worry this way.

Rose craned her neck to see past Mrs. Potter's store-bought hat with its broad brim, long feathers, and huge, colorful flowers. She grinned, feeling happier than she'd felt in a long, long time.

Pa was gone. When Rose had come downstairs this morning, her ma had told her Pa had packed up and left after their fight the night before. He'd said he wasn't coming back. Rose wasn't sure how her ma felt about it, but Rose couldn't be happier—unless her pa had taken Mark with him.

Now the only thing she wanted to do was watch Miss Sherwood marrying Mr. Rider.

Robert sat at the back of the church, his arms folded across his chest. Heaven knew, Will Rider was one lucky man. And unless he was sadly mistaken, Will knew it, too.

Robert wished he didn't have to leave on the afternoon stage. It seemed too soon. He felt just a bit proprietary toward Addie now that he'd seen her again. After all, they'd nearly been man and wife. If things had been just a little bit different . . .

Ah, but that didn't matter now. What mattered was Addie's happiness. He felt as sure as a man could ever feel that she would find happiness with Will.

Emma patted Stanley's knee as she fought back tears.

Land o' Goshen, she did wish her eyes weren't so prone to waterin'. There were few enough times in a body's life when she felt so overflowing with joy. Emma didn't want to witness Addie's moment of happiness through a blur of tears. After all, Emma was the one who'd fought to bring the schoolteacher to Homestead. If it weren't for her, Will and Addie never would have met.

She thought she had a right to take just a bit of credit for the happy event taking place this morning in the Homestead Community Church.

"Do you, Will, take Adelaide . . ."

This moment would forever be etched in Will's mind and heart. It wasn't just because he was taking Addie for his wife. It was also because he was doing it without a shred of lingering doubt. They were all gone. The doubts, the anger, the bitterness, the hate. Nothing his mother or Justine or any other woman had or might have done in the past counted for a hill of beans.

Only Addie. Only Addie mattered now.

"I do."

"Do you, Adelaide, take Will . . ."

Her heart was racing so hard she could scarcely hear the minister. This was like being in a dream. And as with any wonderful dream, she was afraid she would wake up before the ending. She was afraid she would wake up and discover herself all alone in her bed. She wished Reverend Pendroy would speak faster. She wished he would get to the part where he pronounced them man and wife.

It seemed she'd been waiting for that part all of her life.

"I do."

" . . . And so, by the power vested in me, I now pronounce you man and wife. What God has joined together, let no man put asunder." Reverend Pendroy smiled at the couple before him. "Will, you may kiss your bride."

Will didn't need any urging. He turned toward Addie and slowly lifted her veil. Gently cupping her face with his hands, he stared down into her wonderfully expressive green eyes, willing her to see what he felt but didn't know how to put into words. Then he lowered his mouth to hers in a tender kiss.

When he raised his head, she looked up at him with wonder. Everyone in the church seemed to be holding their breath, including Will.

Then she smiled.

Immediately, everyone rose to their feet. Someone shouted a word of congratulations.

Someone else pounded Will on the back. Before he knew what was happening, folks were crowding in around them, separating him from Addie. He tried to keep hold of her hand, but even that tie was broken as Addie was enveloped in hugs by the many weeping women of Homestead.

"Never thought I'd see the day," Chad said as he gave Will a hearty slap on the back. "Glad you had the good sense to make her your wife."

Will grinned. "Me, too."

Chad leaned forward and whispered, "At least I don't have to worry about you going after Miss Henderson." Chad's gaze darted across the church to Ophelia. The pretty dark-haired girl gave him a shy smile before looking away.

Before Will could respond, other men demanded his attention, shaking his hand and patting his back with enthusiasm. He grinned and thanked them, wishing all the while that he still had Addie in his arms.

Above the heads of the crowd, he caught her eye. Their gazes held, and for a moment, they were no longer separated by others. It was as if they stood face-to-face instead of being segregated at opposite sides of the room.

Enough is enough, Will thought. He started to force his way through the crowd.

The door at the back of the church slammed open.

"Fire!" Albert Barber burst into view. "The mill's on fire!"

Chapter Thirty-Two

Rabid flames shot through a cloud of dense black smoke, the sawmill completely obscured from view. Amid shouted commands, the men raced toward the burning building, followed by women and children.

Addie would have followed, too, but she was stayed by Maria's scream. She turned, prepared to reassure her friend that Tom was all right, then saw that she was mistaken about the reason for the woman's outcry.

Maria was doubled over, her mother-in-law standing behind her, steadying her with her hands.

"It's the baby," Doris told Addie. "Help me get her back to the house." She glanced toward Emma. "Sarah."

Emma understood. "I'll have Annalee watch Sarah. You go on. I'll get the doctor."

Addie grasped one of Maria's arms, then gathered up the cumbersome train as best she could and started toward Maria and Tom McLeod's home, Doris holding on to Maria's other arm. She tried not to look at the furious conflagration that was so quickly consuming the Richmond sawmill. She tried not to think about why Tom McLeod hadn't shown up for her wedding.

Glancing at Maria, she saw the beads of sweat on the young woman's forehead, saw the terror in her eyes as she stared at the fire.

"We'd best take her to my house," Doris said. "If the wind comes up, Tom's house could be in danger, too."

Addie hadn't thought of that. She hadn't thought about the rest of the town being in danger.

Maria stopped abruptly, bending forward, a groan torn from her lips. Seconds later, still gasping for breath, she whispered, "Something's wrong, Mother McLeod. Something's terribly wrong."

"Don't say it, Maria," her mother-in-law responded. "Don't even think it. Everything is going to be fine."

Between them, Doris and Addie managed to get Maria to the elder McLeod family's home and into the bedroom.

As soon as Maria was lying on the bed, Doris turned to Addie. "You go get changed out of that dress. We could have a long day ahead of us, and you can't be trying to work around that blasted gown."

"I'll hurry," Addie promised before racing out of the house.

The sight that greeted her eyes was terrifying. The air was filled with black smoke and soot, making her eyes sting and her throat burn. The crackle of the hungry fire was as loud as thunder and never ceasing.

And Will was there, fighting it. Will was standing somewhere close to those flames, trying to douse them with water.

She wanted to go look for him, but she couldn't. Maria needed her now.

"God, keep him safe," she whispered as she ran, her skirts held up to her knees, across the road and toward the Tom McLeod house.

Rose stood back, horrified, and watched the mill burn. And all the while, a voice whispered inside her head, *Pa did this. Pa set the fire.*

She knew it was true. Pa had taken money from the mill safe. She'd heard him talking to himself about it when he was in a drunken stupor. He'd taken the money and then he'd set the fire.

She should tell someone. She should tell the sheriff.

But if she did, they would go after her pa. They would go after him and bring him back to Homestead, and if he didn't go to jail, he would be home living with them again. Rose didn't want that. She couldn't bear it. Not now when she had some future to hope for.

So Rose kept quiet and watched the sawmill burn.

"He's in there!" Hank shouted above the inferno. "Tom's got to be in there!"

The sheriff held his arm in front of his face and started through the blazing doorway. Will grabbed him and pulled him back, both men coughing and choking from the smoke.

"It's no use, Hank. You can't go in that way. Stay here. I'll try around at the back."

He left the older man and raced around to the rear of the sawmill, grabbing a water-soaked blanket from one of the other men on his way. The fire wasn't as hot here. At least, not yet. There was a chance he could make it inside, have a quick look for Tom. There was a slight chance he might find the man and bring him out alive.

Holding the wet blanket over his head, he rushed toward the fire-engulfed building, bursting through the doorway into a world of smoke and ash.

Will had known moments of fear in his life, but he'd never felt anything like this. Terror turned his blood to ice in his veins as he plunged forward, shouting Tom's name.

"Tom, are you in here? Tom, it's Will. Can you hear me?"

Only the roar of the fire answered him.

Nothing could survive in here. Nothing.

Something tumbled and crashed off to his left. He turned to his right, feeling suddenly disoriented, unsure which way he'd come in. He seemed surrounded by orange and red flames. The intense heat forced its way through the blanket. It felt as if it would melt the skin from his bones.

He didn't discover Tom's body so much as stumble across it. Even before he bent over to check, he was convinced the man was dead, and he was right. He'd arrived too late to be of any help. But he couldn't just leave him there. He grabbed Tom beneath the arms and started to drag him in what he hoped was the direction of safety.

He heard something overhead creak, heard the trembling of the timbers, felt the ground shaking beneath his feet. He tightened his grip on Tom's arms and tried to lever the body up to carry on his back. Thick smoke barreled all around him. The heat was intense, unbearable. Time was growing short.

He had to hurry. He had to get back to Addie.

There was another loud cracking sound, so close he felt deafened by it. Then something hard and heavy hit him from behind. He lost his grip on Tom's arms and pitched forward into darkness—alone.

"Push, Maria," Doc Varney shouted. "I can see the baby's head. It's almost over. Push."

Maria's hand squeezed Addie's fingers, but the pressure was weak. Addie returned the squeeze, trying to transmit encouragement and strength through her hand.

Addie had never seen a woman in childbirth before, but she sensed this one was not going as it should. It was all happening faster than she'd expected—not more than twenty minutes had passed—yet neither the doctor nor Doris seemed pleased. She could see the worry etched in Doc Varney's face. She saw the dread written in Doris McLeod's eyes. Addie thought she could even smell fear in the room.

A groan tore from Maria's throat, a groan that would have been a scream if she'd had the energy.

Addie leaned forward. "Help us, Maria. Your son is almost here. Just a little longer."

Again, Maria's fingers tightened around Addie's. Again she groaned.

Addie mopped the sweat from Maria's brow with a cool cloth. *God, help her,* she prayed. *And help Will. Wherever he is, help Will.*

"I've got him!" the doctor shouted. "He's coming. Push just once more, Maria. Just once more!"

Maria's face screwed up as she lifted her head off the pillow, straining with every ounce of remaining strength to rid her body of the life it had nurtured for over seven months.

"It's a boy," Doc Varney announced as he pulled the infant free of the birth canal. A moment later, a baby's cry filled the room.

"Let me see him," Maria whispered. "Let me see him." Weakly, she lifted her arms in supplication, then let them fall once more at her side.

Addie stepped aside as Doris took the infant from the doctor and carried the tiny bundle of life to his mother. The baby stopped crying the moment Maria's arm closed around him.

"Will he live, Doctor?" the new mother asked.

"He came early, Maria, but he looks and sounds healthy. He's got a chance. He's got a good chance. We'll do all we can for him."

Addie watched it all with awe and a sort of reverence for what had just transpired. It was such a wonderful miracle, this new life. She wasn't mindful of the tears of joy streaking her cheeks. She backhanded them away but couldn't seem to stem the tide.

"Doris!" Doc Varney's voice was low but harsh. "I need you." Lower still, he added, "She's hemorrhaging."

The tears dried on Addie's cheeks as the sense of dread returned. She moved back to the bedside, placing a hand on Maria's shoulder, trying to ignore the desperate activity at the foot of the bed, trying to transmit some of her own strength to Maria through her touch.

The woman on the bed looked up. Her eyes seemed to look at Addie from a great distance. "Tom's gone," she whispered.

"No. No, I'm sure you're wrong, Maria. He'll be here any moment." Frightened, Addie glanced toward the doctor just in time to see him shake his head sadly, his shoulders slumped in despair.

White-faced, Doris returned to the side of the bed. Addie moved back to make room for her. Doris knelt on the floor and covered Maria's hand where it lay on top of the newborn.

Maria turned her head on the pillow. "Mother McLeod?" Her voice was growing softer. "Name him Tom, after his father. Tell him to wear the name with pride as his father did."

"Of course." Doris brushed the hair back from Maria's forehead. "Tom's going to be mighty delighted with his son. Just wait until he sees him. He's going to be so proud."

"Tell him . . . tell little Tom his mother loved him. Tell Sarah, too."

Addie didn't know she was crying again until she tasted the salty tears on her lips.

"Love Sarah and little Tom enough . . . enough for both . . . of us," Maria whispered.

Then the room was totally still.

Robert figured he had to be crazy to go running into the burning mill, but he couldn't let Addie lose her husband on her wedding day. At least he wasn't the only madman in Homestead. Someone else had followed him inside. It was a good thing, too, because Robert couldn't have pulled Will from beneath the fallen timber all by himself.

Coughing on the smoke, he recognized the blacksmith standing opposite him. "Lift when I say go," he shouted.

Chad nodded.

"Go!"

As the blacksmith strained against the timber, Robert pulled on Will's arms until he'd dragged him free. He knelt beside the bridegroom and laid his hand on Will's chest. He felt a heartbeat.

"He's alive," he called to the other man.

Chad nodded. "You get him out. I'll get Tom."

Robert stood and yanked Will up from the ground, managing to keep him upright long enough to get a shoulder beneath him. As soon as he released him, Will's upper body dropped forward over Robert's back, then Robert straightened and headed for the rear door, followed closely by the blacksmith.

When they were in the clear, Robert stopped and lowered Will back onto the ground. He glanced toward Chad as he did the same with his burden. For a moment, the two men's gazes met. Chad shook his head in answer to Robert's silent question.

Someone came running toward them. Robert didn't bother to try to see who it was. "Get the doctor," he shouted. "We've got some injured men here."

Behind him, more timbers crashed inside the mill, sending a shower of sparks high into the air. He flinched as he glanced over his shoulder. He hoped the wind wouldn't come up before the fire was finished feeding on the sawmill. If it did, the whole town could be wiped out by nightfall.

* * *

Addie was still staring at Maria's lifeless body when she heard the front door of Doris's home burst open.

"Doc! Doc, come quick!"

Doc Varney grabbed his black bag and turned toward the bedroom door. "What is it?" he asked as he stepped out into the parlor.

"Some men were trapped in the fire. They just pulled 'em out."

Doris looked up, her gaze meeting Addie's. *Who?* they both were wondering. *Who was trapped in the fire?*

Addie felt the answer in her heart. *Will!*

"I've got to go," she whispered frantically.

Doris nodded silently.

Addie followed hard on the doctor's heels, a terrible rushing sound in her ears, an awful pain in her chest. Fear was like a physical presence, running beside her.

As she ran around to the back of the sawmill, she saw the townsfolk gathered in a circle. That was when she knew for certain. If Will had been all right, he would have seen her, he would have come to her.

"Let me through!" she cried as she shouldered her way amongst them.

The last of the onlookers parted, revealing the two men lying on the ground. Before she could drop to her knees at Will's side, Robert grabbed her by the upper arms, keeping her on her feet.

"Let the doctor see to him, Adelaide," he said sternly.

She tried to wriggle free of his grasp.

"Adelaide!" Robert gave her a tiny shake. "Look at me."

She pulled her gaze free of Will's utterly still form.

"He's alive, Adelaide. Let the doctor take care of him."

"He's alive?" She was afraid to believe him, afraid not to believe him.

He nodded.

She dragged in a deep breath, fighting the shivers of relief that shook her body. "And Tom?"

He hesitated, then shook his head.

Addie took another deep breath and turned to gaze down at her husband.

I've waited all my life for you, Will Rider. You can't leave me now. You can't leave me when I'm just learning what it really means to love. You promised I'd never want for anything if I married you. Well, you're all I want. Without you, I have nothing. Please, Will. Please don't leave me now.

Chapter Thirty-Three

Will remained unconscious. The doctor cleansed the baseball-sized lump on the back of his head where the timber had struck him and put salve on the burns on his back and one shoulder.

"The burns will be painful for quite some time," Doc Varney told Addie. "It's actually a blessing he's unconscious for now. When he starts to come around, we'll give him morphine to stop the pain and help him rest. His body must work hard to fight any infection."

After one night in the doctor's office, Addie at Will's side the entire time, Doc allowed Will to be taken home to the Rocking R Ranch.

Addie remained by Will's bed for hours on end, holding his hand and talking to him. Hour after hour, she tended to her husband's needs, spooning sips of water into his mouth and, when he thrashed about in pain, giving him the morphine the doctor had left with her. Weariness dragged at her, but she couldn't be persuaded to leave his side, no matter how exhausted she might be. She ignored the cot the ranch foreman set up in Will's bedroom.

The truth was, she was afraid to sleep, afraid Will would slip away from her while she wasn't watching, and she knew she couldn't bear it if she lost him. She had to keep watch. She had to be there if he needed her.

Please, God, don't let me lose him now.

He saw her standing on the horizon, her arms outstretched, beckoning for him to come to her. Sometimes he thought he heard her voice calling to him from a great distance.

All around him was darkness, a great, vast darkness. He wanted to go to her, but his legs and arms wouldn't move. He was suspended in space, in time, just him and the nothingness that surrounded him.

Addie . . .

He felt a bright light piercing the darkness behind him. He knew he could turn. He knew he could walk toward the light. There wouldn't be any more fear or pain or hurt if he chose to go in that direction.

Addie . . .

Her image seemed to be growing dimmer against the horizon.

Addie . . . I want to stay with Addie . . .

With great effort, he moved a leg one step forward, and then took another step and another step, each one as difficult as the last. But he wasn't going to give up. Each step was taking him one step closer to Addie.

"It snowed last night," Addie said softly as she pulled the blanket snug across Will's chest. "Not much. Only an inch or two. But the valley looks lovely, all white and clean." She lifted his head with her left hand and dribbled water from a spoon into his mouth. "The sun's shining now, and everything is sparkling. The trees look like they've been sprinkled with diamonds. You should open your eyes and look at it, Will, before it all melts away."

Wake up, Will. Wake up and look at the snow before it's too late.

"Lark is being very brave. You know how upset she was when my horse kicked you. But she's being so brave this time. And she's a great help to me. I was going to leave her with Emma, but she wanted to be here. I'm glad I let her stay. We're good for each other."

But we need you, Will. We both love you too much to go on without you. You make us a family. I love Lark as if she were my very own child, and that won't ever change, but it's you who make us a family.

"Griff told me my mare is going to have a foal come spring. Isn't that something? I thought she was just getting fat." She chuckled softly, then shook her head. "I'm afraid Lark was very disappointed in me when she discovered I'd never gotten around to naming my horse. She decided she wasn't going to wait for me to do it any longer."

Addie leaned forward and brushed her fingertips through Will's tawny-gold hair, pushing it back from his face. He looked so peaceful, so very handsome, even with several days growth of stubble on his chin. His facial hair was much darker than the hair on his head. It was a rich, sable brown with reddish highlights. She imagined he would be quite striking with a beard.

I know you wouldn't ever want me to say so, Will, but I think you're beautiful. Everything about you is beautiful. The way you walk, your smile, your eyes. If I were an artist, I would paint your portrait and hang it up for all to see.

"Lark named the mare Rapunzel because of her long mane and tail." Tears pooled in Addie's eyes. Her voice became a hoarse whisper in a thickened throat. "She told me you read the fairy tale to her."

She could see him in her mind, the tall man seated on the child's bed, reading from the storybook. She could almost hear his voice, deep and rich, perhaps a bit halting. She could imagine Lark sitting beside him, her head leaning against his shoulder as she listened.

I want you to read a fairy tale to me someday. I want you to live and read fairy tales to me and to Lark and to all our children yet to be born.

She clutched his hand and pressed the back of it to her cheek. "You must live," she whispered. "I love you, Will. I love you more than I knew it was possible to love. And I need you. Come back to me. Please come back."

He began to flail in the air, then he tried to tear the gauze covering from his burns.

"Frosty! Frosty, help me!"

As soon as the cook raced into the room, Addie reached for the bottle of morphine and filled a spoon, forcing it into Will's mouth and down his throat.

Oh, God in heaven, please don't take him from me.

Will wanted to open his eyes. He tried, but it was as if they were leaded shut. He tried to speak, but he had no voice.

Addie.

The world seemed to reel and whirl. He felt dizzy. And he hurt. Lord, he hurt as he'd never hurt before.

Addie.

Where was she? Why wasn't she with him? He'd worked so hard to get there. Where was she now?

Addie.

"Miz Rider?"

She lowered Will's hand back to the bed and turned toward the door. Griff stood in the hallway.

"Mr. Harris is here to see you, ma'am. If'n you'd like, I can set a spell with the boss."

Addie shook her head. "No. I want to stay. Send Robert up here, if you would, please."

"Shore thing."

Addie returned her attention to the still form on the bed. "Robert's come to see you, Will. If it weren't for him, I would have lost you. Chad told me Robert led the way into the mill to rescue you. He found you there under that beam. If he hadn't . . ." Hot tears returned, choking off her words.

She heard footsteps behind her but didn't turn around.

"Adelaide?"

"Hello, Robert," she whispered.

"How is Will?"

"There's no change."

He laid his hand on her shoulder. His voice was gentle. "And how are you?"

Not good. She mouthed the words because, for the moment, she couldn't speak.

"Come here." Robert's hands closed over her arms, then he drew her up from her chair and turned her toward him. Carefully, tenderly, he took her into his embrace. He stroked her hair with one hand as he crooned words of comfort. "It'll be all right, Adelaide. It's going to be all right."

Will didn't know where he was, didn't know how he'd come to this place. It seemed he'd been walking for ages, seeking something. He wasn't sure what.

The rooms looked oddly familiar, but they didn't feel like home. He was standing in a hallway, a long hallway. He'd been here before, but when?

He felt a shiver of trepidation. He shouldn't go down the hallway. There was something dark and dangerous waiting for him there. He shouldn't go.

But he did.

She stood in the center of Will's bedroom—encircled by Robert's arms, her face pressed against his chest—and wept copious tears. There was nothing dainty or ladylike about her crying. The sobs were torn from the depths of her soul, filled with fear and despair.

She cried until she didn't think she could have any tears left—and then she cried some more. She hadn't meant to do this, hadn't wanted to do this. She'd meant to remain steadfast and strong. For her own sake and for Lark's sake. She hadn't meant to admit she was afraid Will wasn't going to wake up. She didn't want to consider that even a possibility.

Robert didn't say a word. He simply held her and let her cry it out. Occasionally he patted her back. Sometimes he stroked her hair. Otherwise, he was silent and let her do the crying.

Finally, her tears slowed, the sobbing stopped. The only sound in the room was an occasional hiccup as she regained her breath.

Robert handed her a handkerchief. "Here."

"Thank you," she whispered, taking it and drying her eyes.

"Better?" He framed her face with his hands, forcing her to look up and meet his gaze. "It's okay to be afraid, you know. Will's hurt and you're scared. It's okay to admit it."

"Oh, Robert, I love him so much. I couldn't bear it if . . ." She couldn't finish the sentence.

"It's okay. I understand."

"But you don't. He doesn't know I love him. I've never told him. I . . . I was afraid to tell him. Afraid if he . . . if he didn't love me too . . ."

"He does love you," Robert said.

"He's never . . ."

"Take my word for it. Will Rider loves you."

Addie felt a lightness in her chest. "Do you really think so?"

Robert nodded. "I do." He leaned forward and kissed Addie's forehead. "Trust me on this one."

He heard Addie crying. No. No, it wasn't crying. It was laughter. But what had Addie to laugh about?

He moved along the hallway toward the bedroom. When he looked inside, he saw someone lying on the bed. He thought he should know who it was. If he could only see his face . . .

He moved toward the figure on the bed, and when he looked down, he discovered he was looking at himself. But how could that be? How could he see himself? It wasn't possible. This wasn't happening. It couldn't be happening.

A force outside of himself seemed to be pulling him down onto the bed. He resisted, knowing something wasn't right, but finally, he could resist no longer. He gave in and lay down on the bed beside himself.

And then he wasn't separate from his body any longer. He was there, lying on the bed, and his eyes were open.

That's when he saw Addie—in that fancy pink dress he'd hated all his life—wrapped in the arms of another man. Again he heard her soft laughter as the man ran his hands up and down her back.

"Behave yourself, Robert," she whispered.

"I can't wait another day for you. Come with me now."

"What would people say if I deserted my husband on his deathbed? Think, Robert. Will can't hang on much longer, and then we shall be together. I promise."

He must have made some noise, for she turned suddenly, and her gaze met his.

"Will . . ."

"Will!" Addie called breathlessly as his eyelids closed. She hurried back to the side of the bed. "Will, open your eyes. Look at me. Will!"

He moaned, but he didn't obey her command.

"Robert, send for the doctor. Tell him Will's coming around."

"Adelaide, are you sure you didn't just imagine . . ."

"No!" She whirled on him. "I didn't imagine it. His eyes were open. He saw me. He recognized me. I know he did. Now go. Get the doctor. Please."

"I'm on my way."

Addie sank onto the chair and grabbed hold of Will's hand. "Come back, Will. I saw you. You were here for a moment. Come back."

Addie and Robert . . .

It had been a long struggle out of the darkness. Time and again, Will had heard her voice, urging him on, urging him forward. It had been difficult, so very difficult, but he'd come because she'd called him.

Addie and Robert . . .

The light had hurt his eyes, but what had hurt more was seeing Robert holding and kissing Addie. He wanted to deny what he'd seen, but he couldn't. It was real. He'd seen it with his own eyes.

God, let me die.

He'd fought his way back. He could have let go. He could have found a place without pain and struggle, but he'd thought he'd heard her calling to him and so he'd fought his way back. He'd fought his way back only to discover he'd made the wrong choice.

Addie and Robert . . .

He sought to escape into the pit of blackness again, but he couldn't. It was gone. He was alive—and wished he weren't.

Addie and Robert . . .

Addie remained beside Will's bed, her anxious heart filled with hope. She knew she wasn't mistaken. She had seen Will's eyes. For just a moment, he'd been conscious.

Watching him, she knew he slept now. But it was just that—sleep—and nothing more. Next time he awakened, he wouldn't slip away again so quickly. Next time, she would be there. She would take hold of his hand and let him know how much she loved him.

Next time . . .

Chapter Thirty-Four

Dressed in a warm, sheepskin-lined jacket, Hank McLeod stood looking down at the graves of his son and daughter-in-law. The rounded piles of freshly turned dirt were covered with snow, as if nature were trying to disguise them. But Hank wasn't fooled. He knew what lay beneath the pure white blanket.

From the direction of the church, he heard the voices of the congregation raised in a song of praise. Hank couldn't find any reason in his heart to praise God today. He was too filled with anger and countless unanswered questions.

Why? he wondered bitterly. Why had God taken both Tom and Maria? Why had He left those two babies without a mother or a father?

He thought of his wife. Doris was at home this morning, caring for Sarah and little Tom.

The coming years weren't going to be easy ones for her, trying to raise their grandchildren. She wasn't a young woman any longer, and he wasn't a young man. Would either of them live long enough to see the children grown?

Hank's heart ached as he pictured his tiny grandson. He'd arrived in the world so early. He was going to have to fight hard to survive the coming weeks and months. They'd found a woman willing to wet-nurse, and the doctor had told them there was a good chance little Tom would survive. A chance . . . Only a good chance. Hank didn't know if *he* could survive if the baby didn't.

And Sarah, her grandpa's little angel. She should have had her mother with her as she grew up. She needed Maria to braid her hair and kiss her skinned elbows and tell her about boys and watch her get married.

Why, God? Why did you take them?

He felt the cold dampness as tears streaked his cheeks. He backhanded them away, glad no one was around to see him crying.

"Hank?" Doris's hand alighted on his arm.

He glanced at her as she stepped up beside him. Her face was pinched with concern and heartache.

"I knew I'd find you here," she said softly. Her gaze fell to the graves.

Hank put his arm around his wife's shoulders. "I'm angry, Doris. I'm so damned angry."

"I know."

"Do you suppose I tempted fate by sayin' this wouldn't happen?"

Doris looked up at him. "What do you mean?"

The pain in Hank's chest was nearly unbearable. "Remember the day Addie Sherwood came to Homestead? We were in the kitchen and you wondered what would become of Sarah if Tom and Maria were to die, like Lark's parents did, and I said we'd raise her like we did our own two and not to fret about it 'cause it wasn't about to happen anyway."

"Oh, Hank . . ." Doris wrapped her arms around his barrel-like chest and pressed her face against his coat. She held on to him for a long time before glancing up and saying, "This isn't your fault, you foolish man. God didn't take our son and Maria because of anything you said. God didn't take them at all. Doc warned Maria against having another baby. He told her it could be dangerous. She knew she could die. She knew a baby might not survive. And Tom . . . Tom's death was an accident. Just a terrible, tragic accident. Don't go blaming yourself *or* God for what happened." She pressed her face against his coat again.

Hank's eyes swam with tears. This time he didn't try to stop them or wipe them away as they streaked down his cheeks. He guessed a man had a right to cry over the death of his only son.

* * *

Addie carried a tray into Will's bedroom. As she set it on the stand beside the bed, Will opened his eyes and looked at her. An icy chill shot along her spine as she met the blank, emotionless stare.

She forced a smile onto her lips. "Good morning, Will. I've brought you something to eat."

Without a reply, he closed his eyes and turned his face toward the wall.

Addie sank onto the nearby chair. She felt awash with helplessness. She didn't know how to reach out and help him. He'd been like a stranger since he'd awakened yesterday. He hadn't said a word to her. Not one. He'd simply looked at her with those cold, emotionless eyes. It was as if he could see right through her, as if she didn't even exist.

She remembered the way he'd looked at her on their wedding day. There had been such warmth, such caring in his gaze. She was certain she hadn't imagined it. Why was it gone now?

She drew in a shaky breath and leaned forward. "Will, you must eat something. Doc says you need to eat to get your strength back."

He didn't move.

She touched him, and he flinched as if she'd shocked him. "Please, Will. You must try." She removed her hand from his arm.

"Aunt Addie? May I come in?"

She glanced toward the doorway. "Of course, Lark. Your uncle is awake. Perhaps he'll talk to you."

"Uncle Will?" Lark hurried over to the bed, stopping beside Addie's chair. "Uncle Will, it's Lark."

This time when Will turned his head on the pillow, there was a spark of life in his blue eyes as they settled on Lark. Then his gaze moved to Addie again, and the blue of his eyes had never seemed colder.

He hates me . . . But why?

Pain and panic hit Addie square in the chest. She rose abruptly from her chair. "See if you can get your uncle to eat something," she said tightly, then left the room, her head held high, her hands clenched into fists at her sides.

Will recognized the proud stiffness of Addie's departure. He'd seen her like this before, when she was trying to put a brave face on her emotions. She was confused, he knew. She didn't know why he refused to speak, why he refused to eat. She didn't know he'd seen her with Robert. She didn't know he'd seen her perfidy.

Well, he didn't care what she was feeling or what she was thinking. He didn't give a damn about anything about Addie Sherwood. No, not Addie Sherwood. Her name was Addie Rider now. She was his wife. She was the wife who had already betrayed him, betrayed him before they'd been married even four full days.

Come to think of it, he wasn't really surprised. He'd been half-expecting this sort of betrayal from the moment he'd asked her to marry him. Wasn't it what women did, betray their men? Wasn't that why he'd avoided marriage all these years, because he'd known this would happen?

But Addie was supposed to be different. I love her.

He saw them again, embracing, Addie in her pink dress.

His head hurt. His burns hurt. He needed something for the pain. He needed something to make him sleep, to make him forget. Where was the morphine?

That pink dress.

"Uncle Will?"

That damned pink dress.

"Uncle Will?"

He heard the uncertain tremble in Lark's voice and returned his gaze to his niece. He saw the fear in her dark eyes and felt a sting in his heart. Lark had found a fragile happiness with Will. He couldn't fail her now.

"Will you try to eat somethin'? Frosty made this broth up special for you." She grabbed another pillow and reached for his head. "Put this behind you, and it'll make it easier to sit up and eat."

He did what he could to help her brace his back. He was exhausted before she'd brought the first spoonful of broth to his mouth, but he somehow found the strength to remain sitting up. Obediently, he opened his mouth and allowed her to feed him.

"Just about everybody's been out to see how you're doin'," Lark said as she scooped more broth into the spoon. "Mrs. Barber's likely to be out after church today."

He tried to concentrate on what Lark was saying, but it was hard. His mind seemed to drift off on its own. The morphine, Doc had told him, could have strange effects. He'd warned Will about taking it more than necessary. But Will thought the side effects worth it if the drug could make him forget what he'd seen.

Addie and Robert . . . If only he could forget.

"Mrs. Barber's tried to spell Aunt Addie whenever she can, but Aunt Addie hasn't left your room for hardly a minute since you were hurt."

Aunt Addie . . . How easily she'd won the child's affections. How easily she'd won his affections, too . . . only to betray them.

Will shook his head when Lark tried to give him another mouthful of broth. Then he slid down on the pillows and closed his eyes, shutting out the world. He tried to shut out the memories too. It didn't work.

I thought you were different, Addie. I really thought you were different.

And once again they were there, Addie and Robert, standing at the foot of his bed. God, how he hated that damned pink dress.

* * *

Coming out of the church, Rose saw the sheriff and his wife standing in the little graveyard. A tremor of guilt flashed through her.

Pa killed Mr. McLeod.

She should tell Sheriff McLeod. She should have told him long ago what she'd heard her pa saying about the mill safe.

Then she thought of her ma. The swelling on Virginia's face had gone down enough so she could go to church this morning with Rose. She'd even managed to hide the last evidence of her bruised cheek with the help of a bit of cosmetics from the jars she kept hidden in her chest of drawers. Virginia Townsend had actually smiled at Rose this morning as they'd left the house for Sunday services. It had been a long time since Rose had seen her mother look truly happy.

What, she wondered, would Pa do to her ma if the law was to bring him back? He'd kill her, that's what. One day he was going to hit her too hard, and he was going to kill her.

No, she couldn't tell the sheriff. Besides, she didn't know for *sure* Pa had set the fire. Maybe he really had left Homestead the night before the fire, just like Ma'd said. Maybe . . . just maybe.

Night fell over the valley, bringing with it a chill wind that moaned in the branches of the leaf-bare trees and screamed around the corners of the ranch house.

Addie stood at the bedroom window, staring up at the moonless sky. Stars glittered across the expanse of heaven, but she saw no beauty in them. They seemed remote and cold and lifeless.

Rather like Will, she thought as she hugged herself.

She felt his gaze upon her and turned her head to meet it. She caught a glimpse of what she suspected was pain. Then an invisible shield seemed to drop between them, closing him off from her. He closed his eyes and feigned sleep.

What happened, Will? Why won't you talk to me?

"Head wounds can have strange effects on people," Doc Varney had told her earlier in the day when she'd mentioned Will's odd behavior. "So can the morphine. Give him time. He'll be himself before long."

Addie wasn't so sure. She couldn't rid herself of the notion that Will hated her, truly hated her.

Drawing in a deep breath and straightening her shoulders, she walked over to the side of the bed. "Do you need anything before you go to sleep, Will? I can bring you up something from the kitchen."

He ignored her as if she hadn't made a sound.

She reached out, stopping just short of touching his shoulder. She swallowed the lump in her throat as she slowly drew her hand back to her side. She blinked rapidly to clear her eyes of the threatening tears.

"If you need anything in the night," she said in a choked voice, "I'll be right here. I'm a light sleeper. Just call and I'll wake right up."

Nothing he did confirmed he'd heard her. He was absolutely motionless.

Wearily, Addie leaned down and snuffed the lamp. She disrobed in the dark, then pulled her nightgown over her head and crawled beneath the covers on her cot. She lay on her side, staring toward the four-poster.

This should have been their honeymoon. They should have been joyously sharing the intimacy of their marriage bed.

She closed her eyes, memories of Will's love-making drifting through her head, making her skin warm. How she ached to feel his hands upon her flesh. How she yearned for his passionate kisses. How she longed for his desire, longed to feel him grow hard and demand entrance into her own willing body.

She stifled a cry from her breaking heart and rolled onto her other side.

It wasn't just his lovemaking she wanted. It was Will. It was all of him—his hopes, his dreams, his smile, his laughter, his arms holding her tightly against him, the sound of his voice when he whispered her name.

For a short time before the wedding, she'd caught a glimpse of those promises, and now they were gone.

She was afraid. She was more afraid than

she'd ever been in her life. She had found what she'd wanted, and now, before she could savor it, it was slipping away from her. She didn't know why. She just knew she was losing it.

Will, come back to me. Please . . .

Will's recovery went surprisingly well over the course of the next week. His appetite returned, and soon he was up and walking around. The lump on his head had nearly disappeared, and his burns became less painful. He talked daily with Griff Simpson, the ranch foreman, and he welcomed the folks from town when they came out to see him.

Only Addie seemed to know all was not right. Only Addie saw Will was different from the man she'd married.

She waited, hoping that one day he would look at her and the iciness would be gone from his eyes. She listened for him to speak her name, to tell her what was troubling him, but he never did. They simply continued as they were, sharing the same house like a couple of strangers.

And while Will became stronger with each passing day, Addie felt herself slipping into an abyss of sorrow from which she feared there would be no escape.

By the end of the second week, the Rider household had settled into a pattern of politeness. Will began speaking to Addie, but only when Lark or someone else was with them. When they were alone, which was only at night, he rolled onto his side, turning his back on Addie's cot—he'd made it clear she wasn't wanted in his bed—and feigned instant sleep.

By the end of the third week, Will was out tending cattle again, looking as if he'd never suffered a life-threatening injury. But Addie believed their marriage had suffered a fatal blow. It would never recover if something didn't change soon.

"Will, we have to talk." Addie closed the bedroom door and leaned her back against it, barring his only way of escape.

She watched as he slipped the last button on his shirt through the buttonhole before glancing up at her. He didn't speak.

"We can't go on like this, Will. What's wrong? You must tell me."

He stepped forward, but she stood her ground, pressing herself even harder against the door.

"Get out of my way," he said in a low voice.

"No." She tilted her chin defiantly. "Not until we talk this out. If you'll only tell me, maybe I can help."

His eyes narrowed. "You can't help, Addie."

"Why not?" She raised her hand in a pleading gesture. "We'll never know unless you let me try." Her voice dropped to a near whisper. "I'm your wife, Will. Let me help you if I can."

He stared at her, long and hard, his eyes growing colder and more remote with each passing heartbeat. Finally, one corner of his mouth twisted up in what could have been a wry grin. "You can't help, Addie, because you being my wife *is* the problem."

She gasped. "Will . . ."

"We shouldn't have married. I knew it all along, but somehow you made me think you were different. But you're not different. You're like all women. You want security and money and status. Well, you're secure now. We've got enough money for you to spend on the things you want. The folks of Homestead look up to you, think you're a fine lady. What more do you want? We needn't pretend to feel things we don't."

"Will, I don't understand. What have I . . ."

"Get out of my way."

Frightened by the intense loathing she saw in his eyes, she stepped aside.

Will yanked open the door, then glanced over at her. "We'll keep up the pretense for Lark's sake. She's grown to love you. I don't want her hurt. Do you understand me, Addie? She's not to be hurt." He stormed out of the room, leaving her in confused silence.

Minutes later, Will shrugged his shoulders against the cold as he rode Pal across the snow-covered ground. His angry words replayed in his mind, and he kept recalling the shocked look on Addie's face as she'd listened.

He hated her.

No . . . he *wished* he hated her.

He was angry because he *didn't* hate her. He was angry because he still loved her. Despite her duplicity, he still loved her.

And it was the loving her that was killing him inside.

Chapter Thirty-Five

A warming wind blew in from the west, melting the snow that had turned the valley and mountains a pristine white. Now the world outside Addie's window was drab and brown, a sea of mud stretching between the ranch house and the barn. The landscape seemed fitting for Addie's mood.

She lay her forehead against the cool windowpane and closed her eyes. Taking a slow breath into her lungs, she tried to steady her frayed nerves, but it didn't help. She doubted anything could.

She hadn't seen Will since returning from school this afternoon. She knew he wouldn't come to the house until suppertime. He was avoiding her, and he would continue to avoid her.

He hates me, she thought again. *But why?*

It was the same question that had been plaguing her ever since he'd regained consciousness. Why should he hate her? What had she done to have earned such enmity?

She opened her eyes and was preparing to turn from the window when she caught sight of the horse and buggy approaching the house. She recognized Robert sitting beneath the fringed top of the light carriage.

Stepping into the entry hall, she grabbed a shawl from the coat tree and threw it over her shoulders. Then she went outside, awaiting his arrival.

She hadn't seen much of Robert in the past two weeks, not since just after Will had awakened. Robert had been such a stalwart friend during the week of crisis when she'd feared her husband might die. She knew she never would have made it through that time without his help.

Robert stopped the buggy close to the porch and stepped down into the sloppy brown earth. He didn't seem to notice the mud that clung to his expensive leather boots as he climbed onto the porch.

"Hello, Robert," Addie said softly.

His eyes carefully perused her. "Hello, Adelaide." He reached forward and clasped her hands in his. "How are you?"

She forced a smile. "I'm all right."

"You look tired. You shouldn't have resumed teaching so soon."

"It was time." She shrugged. "Will is much better. He didn't need me here any longer."

Robert's brows drew together in a frown. "Adelaide . . ."

"It's far too cool to stand out here," she interrupted. "Come inside. Frosty always has a pot of coffee on the stove. I'll get you some."

She led the way inside. Pausing just long enough to motion Robert into the parlor, she went quickly to the kitchen and poured two cups full of the strong brew the men of the Rocking R preferred. When she returned to the parlor, Robert was seated on the edge of the sofa, his forearms resting near his knees, his hands clasped together between them.

"Here," she said, setting the cup on a nearby table. "This will warm you up."

Robert ignored the coffee. Instead, he continued to stare at Addie as she took her seat across from him. "I've come to say good-bye," he said at last.

"Good-bye?"

"I've stayed much longer than I'd planned. I need to get down out of these mountains before I'm snowed in for the winter."

She nodded.

"I'd have left sooner, but I wanted to be certain Will was going to get well and you would be all right." He raised an eyebrow. "You *are* all right, aren't you, Adelaide?"

She clenched her hands in her lap and stiffened her spine. "I'm fine. Will is doing much better. In fact, I can't get him to stay in bed long enough to get a proper rest. If it weren't for his burns, you'd never know he'd been so severely injured. It really is amazing."

"Adelaide . . ."

She glanced toward the window. "Honestly, Robert, things couldn't be better. I was so frightened when I thought Will might die, but now that he's well . . ." She swallowed, unable to go on.

"Adelaide . . ." His voice was soft and encouraging.

Unwillingly, her gaze was dragged from the window and back to his.

"Tell me what's wrong. This is your friend. Robert. Remember?"

She fought back the tears. She wanted to tell him. She wanted more than anything to tell him the way Will was behaving. Perhaps he could help her if she explained how things were. But she couldn't. She sensed she would be betraying Will if she were to talk about it to anyone else. No, this was something she had to work out on her own.

The silence stretched out between them.

Finally, Robert sighed and reached for his cup. He took a few swallows of the coffee, then looked at Addie again. His expression was serious, matching his tone when he spoke. "I've got a big house in Oregon. My new associate had it built to my specifications, and my aunt is already living there. If you ever need anywhere to go, for any reason, you're more than welcome to stay with us."

She didn't mean to do it. She'd thought she was controlling her wretched tears quite well. Only suddenly, they were streaking down her cheeks and Robert was coming over to stand beside her chair, his hand on her shoulder.

"Won't you tell me what's wrong?" he asked in a whisper.

She shook her head.

"I doubt my wife will have reason to visit you in Oregon. Her place is here with her family."

Addie gasped at the harsh sound of Will's voice, her gaze flying toward the doorway. She would have jumped to her feet, except that Robert's hand on her shoulder held her down.

"Afternoon, Will," he said smoothly.

Will nodded in reply.

"I just came to say good-bye to Adelaide. And to you, too. I'm leaving for Oregon on tomorrow's stage."

"Really?" Will's expression could only be described as skeptical. "So soon?" His tone could only be described as sarcastic. "Well, don't let us keep you. You must have plenty to do before you leave town tomorrow."

"Will," Addie whispered plaintively.

Robert's fingers squeezed her shoulder. "You're quite right. There is much I need to do." His hand slipped to her upper arm, and he guided her to her feet. Then he turned her toward him. "Don't forget what I said."

She shook her head.

Robert walked across the parlor. He paused before Will, and the two men stared solemnly at each other for a long time. Finally, Robert glanced over his shoulder, nodded at Addie, then picked up his hat and left the house.

Addie felt the tension crackling in the air. Her hands clenched before her as her gaze locked on Will. He was staring at the door, his body rigid.

She took a step toward him.

He looked her way. "When did you plan to join him?"

"What?"

"Robert. When did you plan to join him in Oregon? Next week? Next month? Next year?"

"I don't know what you're talking about. I don't plan . . ."

"Don't lie to me anymore, Addie. I know the truth. I saw you with him."

Addie felt as if the earth were shifting beneath her feet. She grabbed for the back of the chair to steady herself. "Will, you're not making any sense. Ever since you came out of your coma, you've been . . . different. You've treated me differently. You won't tell me what's wrong. You refuse to talk to me." Her fingers tightened on the chair back. She lifted her chin and met his gaze with a direct look of her own. "Don't shut me out this way. Let me help you. Doc Varney said . . ."

His voice rose sharply. "You're wasting your theatrics on me, Addie. Don't bother."

"Don't bother!" Her anger flared to match his. "I have a right to know why you hate me."

"Did you think I didn't have eyes, that I wouldn't see? Did you think I wouldn't care that you brought him here, into my own house? How long did you wait to take him for your lover? A day after we married? Two days? Or was he sharing your bed before we married?"

It felt as if he'd struck her. The blood rushed from her face, all her anger draining with it.

Will strode toward her, stopping just an arm's length away. His voice was low, his words clipped, when he continued, "I'll never forget the look of you in that pink dress. The way you let him put his hands on you. The way you let him kiss you. Never."

She tried to find some compassion, some sign that he was willing to listen to reason, but there was nothing but cold disdain in his eyes. "You don't know what you're saying," she whispered.

"You deny it? Even now, you deny it?"

"There's nothing to deny, Will." She held herself a little straighter, but her voice was filled with futility. "I don't even own a pink dress."

Will stepped back. Contempt dripped from each word as he said, "You're just like her after all."

And then he was gone, the door slamming behind him, the sound echoing through the house—and through her heart.

"Just like who?" she asked, but there was no one left to answer her question.

Addie waited up past midnight for Will to return. Finally, exhausted both in body and in spirit, she retired to the bedroom.

She glanced at the cot. It was where she'd slept ever since coming to live in this house as Will's wife. First, it had been because he was ill. Later, it had been because she'd known he didn't want her in his bed. But tonight she couldn't bear to sleep there. Tonight she needed to feel close to Will.

Swallowing hot tears, she shed her clothes as quickly as possible, slipped on her nightgown, and crawled beneath the sheets of Will's bed. She buried her face in his pillow as she hugged it against her. She breathed deeply, catching the faint but familiar scent of him. With her eyes closed, she could almost imagine she was holding him.

She would have to leave. She had no choice but to leave this house, to leave Homestead. Will had made up his mind, and nothing she said was going to make any difference.

Addie rolled onto her back, still clutching the pillow against her chest. She recalled Lark's sad expression at supper earlier in the evening. Addie had tried to pretend everything was fine, that Will would return soon, but Lark hadn't been fooled.

I'll never forget the look of you in that pink dress. . . . You're just like her after all.

She didn't understand any of it—except that Will was accusing her of taking Robert for a lover.

"I love you," she whispered. "Why can't you see that I love you?"

Will tossed restlessly on the bed of hay he'd made in the barn. He pulled the coarse blanket more closely around his shoulders, but it did little to warm him.

You don't know what you're saying. . . . I don't even own a pink dress.

But he'd seen her. If he closed his eyes, he could still see her, enfolded in Robert's arms, letting him kiss her, letting him run his hands over her back. The image was clear in his mind. So very clear.

Only, when he did close his eyes, there was something different about the memory. He didn't know what it was, but something was different. Something very important.

Chapter Thirty-Six

Dear Will,

It is clear I shall never be able to give you the happiness you deserve, and so I must leave. I will send for my things as soon as I find a new teaching position. Wherever I go, you and Lark will be with me always in my heart.

Your wife,
Addie Rider

Carrying only a small satchel, Addie slipped from the house at dawn. The mountain air was cold, but not as cold as the emptiness of her heart.

She paused at the end of the yard and gazed back at the house. She'd wanted so very much to find a home here. But it wasn't to be. Perhaps she would never feel at home anywhere again.

She turned and began walking.

The muddy ground had hardened during the night, and she stumbled often over the ruts in the road. Twice, she nearly fell. But she didn't slow her pace. She walked briskly, head held high, back straight, and shoulders stiff. She had done her crying during the night. She was determined not to cry anymore.

When she reached Homestead, she stopped and let her eyes sweep over the small town. She saw the beginnings of the new schoolhouse. It would be finished before spring. She looked at the church and thought of her students and the hours they'd all spent within those walls. She saw the ruins of the sawmill and felt anew the tragedy that had befallen the town that day.

That day . . . Her wedding day . . .

She blinked frantically at the threatening tears. She *wasn't* going to cry, she reminded herself.

Her gaze moved on, touching briefly on each building, thinking about the people inside them, thinking about her many friends in the little town of Homestead.

This wasn't how it was supposed to end.

Lifting her chin a little higher, she headed in the direction of Townsend's Rooming House.

Will felt a terrible emptiness in his chest as he read the note. She'd left him.

Hadn't he known she would?

He wrinkled the paper in his hand into a small wad and hardened his heart against the pain. Was he going to believe the lies? Always love him . . . She'd never loved him.

He closed his eyes and tried to recall the image of Addie in Robert's arms. The memory came to him, but not as clear as it had been in the past. The couple was there, at the foot of the bed, but he couldn't see their faces, couldn't hear their voices. It was them, but it wasn't. It was this room, but it wasn't. Confusion wrestled with his sense of betrayal. Why didn't he feel the same righteous anger?

Go after her.

No! No, he wouldn't go after her. She'd lied to him. She'd been unfaithful to him. She'd betrayed him just as every other woman in his life had betrayed him.

He tossed the note into the fireplace and watched it burn.

Robert rose from the breakfast table as Addie was shown into the dining room. Her face was pale, her expression strained.

"Good morning, Robert," she said softly.

"Adelaide, what's wrong?"

She shook her head. Her chin quivered, but she didn't speak.

Robert moved quickly to pull out a chair for her. As she sank onto it, he glanced at Virginia Townsend. The woman nodded with understanding and quickly left the room, closing the door behind her.

"What is it, Adelaide?"

She looked up at him with a tortured gaze. "I . . . I'm leaving Homestead. I thought you might want company on the stage down to Boise City."

Robert sat on the closest chair to Addie, then reached out and took hold of her hands. "Tell me everything. No pretending, Adelaide. I want the whole truth."

He could see she was fighting tears.

Softening his voice, he said, "You've got to tell someone. Tell me."

Though the November morning was still cool, the sun had thawed the ground, turning it once again into a brown slime that oozed and sucked at a man's boots. Will cursed the mud, just as he'd cursed everything else about the day.

Three times this morning, he'd started to saddle his buckskin, intending to ride into Homestead and retrieve his wife. Three times, he'd damned his own stupidity and stopped himself from doing it.

He stepped out of the muddy corral and closed the gate behind him, swearing he wouldn't change his mind again. If Addie wanted to run away with Robert, it was her business. Will was better off without her. He didn't care what she did. He didn't love her. He'd been a fool to ever trust a woman. He'd known better.

Go after her.

He cursed again as he rammed his hands into the pockets of his coat and headed toward the house. It was the sound of a galloping horse that caused him to stop and turn. His eyes widened in surprise when he realized that the horseman was none other than Robert Harris.

Clods of mud flew up from the horse's hooves as the hard-breathing animal slid to a stop. Robert stared down at Will for a moment.

"What do you want here?" Will asked abruptly. "Addie's already gone. There's nothing left here for you to take."

Robert dismounted. A few quick strides carried him toward Will. His eyes narrowed. "You're a damn fool, Rider," he snapped.

Before Will knew what was coming, Robert's fist hit him square on the jaw. He stumbled backward but caught his balance before falling to the ground.

"Damn you for hurting her this way," Robert shouted. "She deserves better than you."

Will rubbed his jaw. Fighting to control his anger, he said, "And you're better, I suppose. Why don't the two of you just leave town? There's no reason for this. You've got what you want."

"What sort of blind idiot are you? Adelaide never left your bedside the whole time you were unconscious. She doesn't want to leave now. She loves you, a whole hell of a lot more than you deserve, I might add."

"That's just the problem. I'm *not* blind. I saw the two of you. I heard you."

"You saw *what?*" Robert demanded, taking a step forward.

Fury exploded inside Will. "I saw the two of you. You thought I was still unconscious, but I saw you together. I heard you say you couldn't wait another day for her and ask her to go away with you. And I heard her say I couldn't hang on much longer. Well, I guess I messed up your plans, didn't I? Addie won't get to play the grieving widow before she marries you."

Will wasn't expecting Robert's second punch any more than he had the first. The lawyer's fist caught him in the abdomen, knocking the air from his lungs.

With a cry of rage, Will threw himself forward, ramming his shoulder into the other man's rib cage. The two of them locked arms around each other as they fell to the ground. They rolled first to the right, then to the left, both of them fighting for a grip on the other's throat. When they rolled beneath the horse, the animal shied and whinnied in fright, then trotted away.

The two men broke apart and scrambled to their feet, then went after each other again with arms swinging. Will managed to land a couple of solid punches before Robert did the same.

From the corner of his eye, he saw the Rocking R cowboys running out of the bunkhouse, Griff Simpson leading the way.

"Stay out of this!" he shouted when Griff moved to stop the fight.

Before the words were out of his mouth, Robert's fist smashed into his eye, and he went down into the mud for a second time.

"Addie?" Emma stepped into the parlor of the rooming house. "What are you doing here? The children came home and said there'd be no school until a new teacher was found. Annalee said you're leavin' Homestead. Is it true?"

"Yes," Addie answered softly. "I'm leaving."

"But why?"

Addie shook her head. "I must, that's all."

"But . . ."

"Emma, you've been a true friend to me ever since I came to Homestead. You stood up for me when so many others thought the teacher should be a man. You supported me when I wanted to live in my own place. You fought for me to be able to keep teaching after I was married." Addie glanced down at her half-filled coffee cup. "I wish I could stay, but I can't. Things just haven't worked out as they should."

"But your husband . . ."

Addie's eyes flooded with tears. "Will doesn't want me, Emma. I have to go. Please don't ask me why."

Robert threw his entire body into his right jab. "You stubborn son of a bitch!" he shouted as his fist connected with Will's cheekbone.

The rancher staggered backward but managed to keep his balance this time.

Both men were winded from a fight that had already gone on far too long. Each punch they threw was slower than the one before. But neither seemed ready to give up.

Especially not Will. Not yet. Not until he'd gotten even with Robert Harris for stealing Addie.

He plunged forward, landing two solid jabs before wrapping his arms around Robert's torso and knocking them both to the ground again. Mud slopped into his eyes, blinding him momentarily.

Robert seized the opportunity to break free of Will's grasp. In unison, they scrambled to their feet, both of them swiping mud from their eyes and face.

"Listen, Rider . . ." Robert began.

Will took another swing at him, but missed this time.

The lawyer swore loudly as he hooked his fist upward, clashing with surprising intensity with Will's jaw.

Will saw stars as he toppled backward. Mud and blood mingled on his tongue. He spat, trying to rid the taste from his mouth as he prepared to rise.

Robert's boot on his chest stopped him.

"I've faced a lot of ignorant men in the courtroom, but none of them held a candle to you, Rider." Robert gasped for air and flung off the mud that clung to his fingers. "Do you think I'd be out here, fighting with you, if Adelaide wanted to be with me? I'd take her away in a minute if I thought it'd make her happy." He gave a little push with his foot, then stepped back. "That timber must've knocked every lick of sense out of that thick skull of yours. Adelaide loves you. She loves you more than she should, if you ask me."

"I saw you . . ."

"You didn't *see* anything. There wasn't anything *to* see. What you should be seeing is that you love her as much as she loves you, and if you had any sense left, you'd get on that horse of yours and go tell her so." Robert raised his hands in a gesture of futility. "God keep me from idiots." He turned and strode across the yard to his horse. When he was mounted again, he glanced over his shoulder and said, "The stage'll be in soon. This may be your last chance."

Will watched him ride away, not bothering to get up out of the mud.

Could he be wrong about what he'd seen?

No, it had been so clear. He'd seen them together.

I don't even own a pink dress.

He closed his eyes and replayed the scene in his mind. He saw the couple standing at the foot of the bed. He saw the man's hand sliding over her back. He saw the sunlight filtering through the window.

And as he watched the scene play itself out, the room began to change. The wall coverings were old and faded. The window was set in a different wall than the window in his bedroom.

With his mind's eye, he looked at the bed and saw the dying man. The *old* dying man . . . His father.

And Addie's hair . . . It wasn't the glorious, fiery red he loved. It was yellow, like the sun. Like his mother's . . .

"Boss, you all right?" Griff's hand closed around Will's arm and hauled him up out of the mud.

Will stared at his foreman as if he'd never seen him before.

How could it have become so confused in his head? How had he placed Addie in that old and hated memory? Was it the concussion? Was it the morphine? Or was he simply mad?

But then, it didn't matter how it had happened. It only mattered that he'd been mistaken. He'd blamed Addie for something she hadn't done, and if he didn't act quickly, he could lose her. He might already be too late.

"Boss?"

"Bring me my saddle," he ordered sharply. "I'm going into town."

Chapter Thirty-Seven

Addie picked her way across the street, trying to find the least muddy place to walk. Not that it did any good. The hem of her dress was already stained brown.

She felt Robert's absence. She had expected him to be with her. She couldn't imagine what business had taken him away so suddenly. It seemed that one moment he'd been telling her he was her friend, and the next he was gone.

She knew it was silly, but she felt as if he'd deserted her, too.

Perhaps it was just as well he'd given her time alone, she thought now. After Emma had left the rooming house, Addie had had plenty of time to sort through her thoughts and get them in order. She'd also faced some hard facts.

She had left Connecticut and come West

because she hadn't been willing to settle for a loveless marriage. And yet, that was just what she'd done with Will. Despite the two nights of passion they'd shared, he'd never said he loved her, had never pretended love was the reason he'd proposed marriage to her. But because she loved him, she'd taken the gamble for happiness.

It hadn't paid off.

Hearing the murmur of voices, she raised her eyes to see a small crowd waiting beneath the awning in front of the stage office. Hank and Doris McLeod were there. Stanley and Emma Barber and their children were there. Chad Turner and Doc Varney and Reverend Pendroy and his sister, Ellen, were there, too. Even Rose Townsend was there.

Addie felt a tightening in her chest. She wished they hadn't come to see her off. It was going to be difficult enough to climb on the stage when it arrived.

As if in answer to her thoughts, she heard a shout and the rattle of harness. She glanced to her left as the stage rumbled into town and drew to a halt in front of the office.

Addie finished crossing the street and stepped onto the boardwalk. She drew in a deep breath as she turned to face the townsfolk. The memory of the day she'd arrived in Homestead flashed through her mind. It seemed a lifetime ago.

Emma stepped forward. "Addie, we couldn't let you leave without us comin' to say good-bye. We're going to miss you."

"Thank you, Emma." She swept the small crowd with her gaze. "Thank you all."

At that moment, she caught sight of Robert, standing behind the others. When he leaned to one side, she couldn't help but notice the purple bruise that stained the swelling around his eyes—or the dried mud that covered him from head to toe.

"Robert?"

He stepped forward, wearing a sheepish grin.

"Robert, what happened?"

His gaze flicked to a spot behind her, then met her eyes again. "Why don't you ask him?" He gestured with his head.

She turned around and saw Will riding toward them. Even before he came any closer, she could see that his clothes were caked with mud, too.

Will stopped his buckskin in front of the stagecoach, then dismounted and stepped up onto the boardwalk. She felt the townsfolk move back as he focused his attention on her.

She swallowed a quick gasp of air. Beneath the grime, Will's face was even more bruised than Robert's.

"Will, what happened?" she asked, forgetting to feel angry or hurt.

"Somebody tried to knock some sense back into my head," he replied in a grim tone.

She looked behind her at Robert, then returned her gaze to Will. She felt a sudden pain in her heart. He'd come because Robert had made him come.

"He did a good job, Addie." Will took a step closer, forcing her to look up at him. "We need to talk. Come back to the ranch with me."

She shook her head. "No."

"I'm sorry, Addie. I was wrong. I was wrong about a lot of things."

She wanted to go back. She wanted to go home with Will more than anything she'd ever wanted in her life. But if she did it, she would be settling for less again. She didn't want to settle for less. Not again. Not this time. She didn't want to live with a man who'd been beaten into keeping her for his wife.

"Addie, please . . ."

She stiffened her back. "Why should I, Will? Why do you want me to go back with you?"

"Because I was wrong. If you'll give me a chance to explain . . ." He looked behind her at the crowd of curious onlookers. "Let's go somewhere where we can talk in private."

Again she shook her head. "Not until you tell me why," she said stubbornly.

He seemed to consider for an interminably long time before he said, "It was all mixed up in my head, Addie. I blamed you for things others had done. Maybe it was because of the blow on the head or maybe it was just 'cause I'm a damned fool like Robert told me I am. Anyway, I know you didn't do what I said you did. I know you stood right by me. I was wrong, and if you'll give me a chance, I'll never doubt you again. I swear it."

She saw the suffering in his blue eyes. She was tempted to reach out and tenderly touch the swollen bruises that marred his handsome face. She wanted to move into his arms and promise she would never even think of leaving again.

But she didn't. She couldn't. He still hadn't said the words that would make her stay.

The stage driver cleared his throat. "We need to get goin', folks. Any of you travelin' with me?"

"I am," Robert said as he stepped forward.

Addie continued to stare into Will's eyes.

"Don't go, Addie," he said softly.

"Why? Tell me why I shouldn't go. Tell me why you want me to stay."

"I told you."

"No, you didn't."

Again, he looked at those standing behind her.

She felt certain he never would say the words that would keep her in Homestead. He couldn't because he didn't feel them. And if he didn't feel them . . .

Desperation swept over Will. Suddenly, he didn't care who was watching, who was listening. Nothing mattered except keeping Addie with him.

He pulled her into his embrace, lowered his mouth, and claimed hers in a searing kiss. He could feel her heart racing against his chest.

Moments later, when he lifted his head and stared down into her eyes, he said, "Don't go."

"Why?" she whispered once again, her voice quavering. "Please tell me *why*."

"Because I don't want to face a life without you, Addie. I was a damned fool not to tell you before now, not to believe everything you told me. I want you to stay because Lark wants you for her mother and I want you for my wife. I want you to stay because you've made me feel things I never thought I'd feel. I want you to stay because you're beautiful, and I want to wake up every morning and see you smiling at me." He brushed his lips against hers again. "I want you to stay because I love you, Addie Rider."

Addie's full mouth curved up at the corners, and her apple-green eyes glittered with tears. "Say it again, Will."

"You're beautiful."

"Not that. The other."

"I love you, Addie. Stay."

In answer, she raised her arms and pressed her palms against his chest. "I love you, too, Will," she said softly. "I'll never leave you. Never."

With those few words, Addie unknowingly lifted a heavy weight from Will's heart, a weight he'd been carrying with him all of his life.

She moved one hand from his chest, caressing his bruised cheek.

He took hold of her hand and brought it to his lips. He kissed her knuckles, then whispered, "It's time we started back for the ranch."

She smiled, her heart in her eyes. "Yes, Will. It's time to take me home."

Epilogue

That night, as a cold, November wind whistled around the corner of the house, Addie drew closer to her husband. Will muttered something in his sleep as his arm circled her waist, pulling her more tightly against him. Addie smiled to herself, happiness flowing through her veins, warming her further.

Not for the first time that night, she marveled at the joy she'd found. It still seemed a little unreal, as if she were living in a beautiful dream.

But it wasn't a dream. It was real, and she was lying in Will's arms and nothing could ever take this happiness away from her.

Her thoughts drifted back to that fateful day in May when she'd stood in Mr. Bainbridge's office and learned the house she'd lived in since birth was no longer hers. She remembered the dreadful desperation she'd felt when she realized she had no home and no place to go.

If only she'd known . . .

"Why are you still awake?" Will whispered in her ear, his voice gruff with sleep.

"I was just thinking."

"Thinking what?"

"How glad I am I found my way home."

He kissed her forehead, then trailed tiny kisses downward until he found her mouth. "I didn't know you were lost," he said a few moments later.

Yes, she'd been lost. She'd been lost and homeless—even when she hadn't known it—until the day she'd given her heart to Will.

"I'm just glad to be home," she said softly, snuggling closer into his embrace.

"Home . . ." he murmured. "Isn't that where the heart is?"

"Yes." She sighed contentedly. "Yes, it is."

And, as Addie knew, her heart would always be with Will.

Romantic Times' Storyteller of the Year!

Diego—Although he travels to California to honor his father's pledge to an old friend, he doesn't intend to make good on a marriage contract written before his birth. But then, he doesn't expect to find violet-eyed Leona awaiting him—or to find himself desiring a mysterious masked bandolera.
La Rosa—Into a valley torn asunder by greed, she rides with a small band of trusted men to bring justice to her people. To protect them all, she has sworn never to reveal her identity, not even to Diego, the man who has stolen her heart.
_3347-X $4.99 US/$5.99 CAN

orchester Publishing Co., Inc.
.O. Box 6640
Vayne, PA 19087-8640

lease add $1.75 for shipping and handling for the first book and .50 for each book thereafter. NY, NYC, and PA residents, lease add appropriate sales tax. No cash, stamps, or C.O.D.s. All rders shipped within 6 weeks via postal service book rate.
anadian orders require $2.00 extra postage and must be paid in .S. dollars through a U.S. banking facility.

ame____
ddress____
ity__________________________State________Zip__________
have enclosed $__________ in payment for the checked book(s).
ayment <u>must</u> accompany all orders. ❑ Please send a free catalog.

Winner of the *Romantic Times* Storyteller of the Year Award!

Cool as a cucumber, and totally dedicated to her career as a newspaper woman, Maggie Afton is just the kind of challenge brash Chase McGarrett enjoys. But he is exactly the kind of man she despises. Cold and hot, reserved and brazen, Maggie and Chase are a study in opposites. But when they join forces during the Klondike gold rush, the fiery sparks of their searing desire burn brighter than the northern lights.

___4193-6 $5.99 US/$6.99 CAN

Dorchester Publishing Co., Inc.
P.O. Box 6640
Wayne, PA 19087-8640

Please add $1.75 for shipping and handling for the first book an $.50 for each book thereafter. NY, NYC, and PA residents please add appropriate sales tax. No cash, stamps, or C.O.D.s. A orders shipped within 6 weeks via postal service book rate. Canadian orders require $2.00 extra postage and must be paid in U.S. dollars through a U.S. banking facility.

Name____
Address____
City_________________________State_______Zip__________
I have enclosed $__________ in payment for the checked book(s)
Payment must accompany all orders. ❑ Please send a free catalo

Winner Of The *Romantic Times* Storyteller Of The Year Award!

With a two-year-old son and no husband in sight, sultry Angelica is an object of scorn to the townspeople of her frontier home—and the target of Devlin Branigan's unabashed ardor. But Angelica needs more than a one-time lover. She needs a man who can give her respectability once she reaches her new homestead in Washington State. And after one earth-shattering kiss, Devlin is ready to prove he is all the man she'll ever desire.

_3907-9 $5.99 US/$7.99 CAN

Dorchester Publishing Co., Inc.
P.O. Box 6640
Wayne, PA 19087-8640

Please add $1.75 for shipping and handling for the first book and $.50 for each book thereafter. NY, NYC, and PA residents, please add appropriate sales tax. No cash, stamps, or C.O.D.s. All orders shipped within 6 weeks via postal service book rate. Canadian orders require $2.00 extra postage and must be paid in U.S. dollars through a U.S. banking facility.

Name____
Address____
City_____________________________State________Zip___________
I have enclosed $__________ in payment for the checked book(s).
Payment must accompany all orders. ❑ Please send a free catalog.

DIA HUNTER

THE BEHOLDING

Tess Harper should hate Luke Reeves. He enters her life with the news that her husband is dead—and he is the one who killed him. But despite the bounty hunter's cold expression and scarred face, despite his quick draw that makes men fear him, the young widow hopes against all hope that he will lead her out of her lonely life and make her forget her checkered past.

___4321-1 $4.99 US/$5.99 CAN

Dorchester Publishing Co., Inc.
P.O. Box 6640
Wayne, PA 19087-8640

Please add $1.75 for shipping and handling for the first book and $.50 for each book thereafter. NY, NYC, and PA residents, please add appropriate sales tax. No cash, stamps, or C.O.D.s. All orders shipped within 6 weeks via postal service book rate.
Canadian orders require $2.00 extra postage and must be paid in U.S. dollars through a U.S. banking facility.

Name____
Address____
City_________________________State________Zip__________
I have enclosed $__________ in payment for the checked book(s).
Payment must accompany all orders. ☐ Please send a free catalog.